THANK YOU

Thank you for supporting this Special Edition version of Fate Calls the Elf Queen.

Thank you!

JMK

FATE CALLS THE ELF QUEEN: SPECIAL EDITION

THE ELF QUEEN SERIES BOOK 3

J.M. KEARL

Fate Calls the Elf Queen

By J.M. Kearl
Copyright J.M. Kearl 2023
All rights reserved

Cover design by: Janie Hannan Kearl
Character art by: chrissabug

First Edition

This book is dedicated to all the queens reading my books. Keep your heads held high.

CONTENTS

CONTENT NOTICE

Please note this book includes content that may not be suitable for all audiences. Content includes violence, death, a villainous love interest, steamy content, and profanity.

NAME PRONUNCIATION GUIDE

Layala- Lay- all-uh

Valeen- Vuh-leen

Evalyn- Ev-uh-lynn

Athayel- Ath-ā-el

Fennan- Fen-en

Mathekis- Math-eh-kiss

Atarah- Uh-tar-uh

Zaurahel- Zar-uh-hel

Ronan- Ro-nan

Orlandia- Or-land-ee-uh

Tifapine- Tif-uh-pine

Balneir- Bal-neer

Katana- Kuh-t-on-uh.

Servante- Serv-on-tay

Presco- Press-co

Palenor- Pal-eh-nor

Calladira- Cal-uh-deer-uh

Svenarum- Sven-are-um

Vessache- Vess-ach

Ryvengaard- Riven-gard

Adalon- Ad-uh-lon

Murlian- Mer-lee-an

Zythara– Z-ith-ar-uh: the name of Valeen's goddess blade

Realms

Runevale

Ryvengaard

Adalon

Underrealm

Serenity

The 7 primordials - the 7 original gods of Runevale

Valeen, goddess of night

Katana, goddess of day

Elora, goddess of wisdom

Creed, god of nature

Atlanta, god of waters

Synick, god of elements

Era, god of time

Drivaar & Primevar—two opposing sides of the gods. Drivaar worship the All Mother as the highest deity. The Primevar worship the Maker. They believe in the existence of both.

BOOK 1 RECAP

Layala trained in hiding her entire life to kill the elf king, Tenebris, and his son, Prince Thane, for executing her parents and the raids in search of her, the last mage. Thane, her magic-bound mate from the time they were children, waited for the day to reunite with Layala but he couldn't do that until his evil father was gone. After Thane thought he killed King Tenebris, he went after Layala in her hometown of Briar Hollow where she lived among the humans. The time limit on their mate spell waned and he had to bring her to his home so she could take her place as Queen of Palenor beside him.

She had other plans, and after trying to take his life, they reached an agreement: if she could break their mate bond spell, they could part. She had eight weeks.

During those weeks she learned the enemy wanted to use her to raise the Black Mage, the creator of the pale ones. The twisted, cursed elves were drawn to her magic and sought to take her captive.

She also found that Thane wasn't the wicked king she believed him to be and with time and much back and forth they began to fall in love.

In the end she found a way to break the bond between them and chose not to.

Instead, she chose Thane.

They planned to marry and finish the mate spell before they would be cursed to turn into pale ones, but Thane's father returned from the "dead" and his lackey, the dragon shifter Varlett, broke the mate bond and abandoned Thane to die in the cursed forest.

After, Layala was taken captive and with a broken heart, left wondering: was Thane alive and if so, could he save her?

BOOK 2 RECAP

Layala was held for weeks by the evil King Tenebris and his minions, Mathekis, and the dragon shifter Varlett. Thane spent weeks recovering from nearly being killed by Varlett with the old mage Vesstan and Tifapine.

After Layala tried to escape, King Tenebris placed her in a prison cart and they moved toward the Void to use her to bring back the Black Mage, the long-gone creator of the Void and the pale one curse. She was always said to be his destroyer or his salvation. All the while, she was being haunted by the Black Mage's voice, calling to her, asking her to go to him.

Thane and the Ravens rescued her before she could be forced into the dangerous Void, and the group went on the run to find a way to destroy the Void and the Black Mage along with it.

But Layala's dreams of the wicked Black Mage grew with intensity and vividness, only pushing her more to find the answers they needed: why she was connected to him and how to stop him. They fought pale ones, sirens, lost a friend, and killed the Lord of Calladira for the All Seeing Stone and then went to the dragon kingdom to find the Scepter of Knowing.

There they meet Prince Ronan and the Royal Drakonan dragons, and Layala and Thane fought and bested the dragon prince Yoren to get the Scepter of Knowing.

Once the two pieces were put together, they accessed the goddess of wisdom, and she told them the key to ending the curse of the pale ones was the Black Mage's heart, and to get to him, Layala must wake him.

They go to battle at the Void, the Ravens versus King Tenebris and his army. Layala nearly killed Thane's sister Talon to save her Aunt Evalyn and the battle began. In an epic fight, Layala had her chance to end Tenebris but was dragged into the Void by Varlett.

Thane fought him and ended his father's life.

Layala was brought to the tower holding the Black Mage's body. When she saw him, she was surprised at how much he resembled Thane and how striking he was. With the intent to kill him and end the curse, she performed the magic to wake him, giving her blood and breath. But her blade broke on his chest, and he came to. His magic took hold of her, rendering her immobile, and with a wicked smile he announced that she was his wife, Valeen, the goddess of night reborn, and he was the god of mischief and magic, and Thane was his cousin, the god of war.

He wants revenge and his wife back.

CHAPTER 1

HEL

H el stared into the face of the goddess he once loved more than all of creation. Stunning wide blue eyes, the color of the celestial waters in Runevale, pierced him with fury. But not the anger of a scorned wife or the kind of loathing only a love once as deep as the darkest part of the night sky could harness. No, not that.

Every part of this beautiful being from his past beckoned to his soul. The waves of midnight hair he longed to grasp, the seductive curve of her waist to hips, and a face to bring even gods to their knees. Her very presence tempted and enchanted his senses, called upon memories long since buried. She smelled of jasmine and battlefields and... ruin.

How he hated her.

"Well, as lovely as it's been seeing you both again, I have things to do." He shoved Valeen into the waiting arms of her lover. Neither of them moved to attack as he stalked past them. "Keep her safe for me, cousin. I'll be seeing you both. Soon."

Taking hold of his general Mathekis's arm, they disappeared through darkness, time and space tugging at them, then they appeared on solid ground at the old mage's tower in Doonafel. It looked much the same as it did four hundred years before, craggy gray rock, overgrown with untamed vegetation creeping up the walls and at its base. As the pair walked the path, Hel thought back to the day he first met Valeen all those centuries ago when they were gods, untouchable, and of the belief that nothing could ever destroy them. How wrong they'd been.

The Past

Bright stars winked in the dark sky. Of the three moons of Runevale, Nuna with her golden rings, Luna with shades of soft pink and a crimson center, and Fennor silver and bright, only the two sisters were visible. Fennor hid behind the clouds. The darkness of night enticed with mysteries. In the veil of shadow, the treachery, the secrets, the wicked was expected. It was the day, in the sunlight, bright and beautiful, that fooled even the wisest. It harbored a false sense of security that those hiding in the shadows waited to seize on.

The wind rustled in the treetops and brought with it the scent of the wild lavender growing along the stone wall surrounding the palace, and the smell of an intruder. The hair on the back of Hel's neck prickled when the sizzling of the torches vanished, and the smoke from doused fire drifted his way. He didn't have to turn to recognize the light gait moving down the path.

With his forearms resting on the stone railing of the bridge, he watched a fish breach the surface of the pond below, swallowing a water skipper whole. Hel flicked the ash off the end of the finely rolled burning herbs between his fingers, and the fish jumped up to eat that too.

Without looking away from the moons' reflections off the shimmering blue water below, he said, "Why are you bothering me, War?" He brought the civar to his lips and took a pull. He closed his eyes for a moment, embracing the buzz of energy, even if it only lasted seconds. The sweet smoke filled his lungs, and he blew a cloud into the dark atmosphere.

His cousin slid next to him, leaning his backside against the railing of the bridge. He folded his thick, muscular arms, and with narrowed bright green eyes, he scowled. "Is that any way to greet your favorite god?"

Hel smirked and stood straight, tugging at the hem of his sleeve, careful to avoid singeing his clothing. "I could name several others I'd put on the list above you."

"I know a lie when I hear one."

"Only because I schooled you in how to detect them." He brought the civar to his lips again.

War shrugged and dropped his hands to his sides. "Why do you smoke civars? They're for mortals."

He looked at the orange embers at the end. It made him feel something even if for a fleeting moment. "Why not? It's not as if it will kill me."

"The party started an hour ago."

"I'm deliberating with the stars on which of the guests invited will take advantage of our family's graciousness and try to steal the rather rare and coveted Soulender on display tonight."

War's dark brows shot up and he glanced back at the looming white castle. Of its many peaks, the center rose highest though not by much. It was uniform and perfect the way most things the gods touched were. Lush greenery and bright blooms grew off the balconies, silver keeper owls and his uncle's spying ravens watched

15

from their perches, and lovers caressed in the shadows, whispering promises they didn't intend to keep.

"And that's why my mother insisted I leave Ryvengaard to attend tonight." War cocked his head to the side. "What are you planning?"

Hel smiled, dropped the civar onto the stone, and stamped it out with his heavy black boot. He placed his hands behind his back and turned to face the palace. Left here as a baby by a young mother who couldn't raise him on her own, this home held a piece of his heart while also reminding him of all that he never had. An uncle instead of a father, a caring aunt in place of a loving mother. "Who do you think it will be?"

"You."

Hel laughed. "War, you know if I were going to steal the Soulender, I'd have done it before now."

"But you do have something planned, don't you?"

"You thrive in battle. I flourish in mischief. We are what we are." And what fun would it be if he gave away his plans for the evening?

The two of them, more like brothers than cousins, walked side by side toward the party. Music whisked on the humid air, delicate strings and deep, slow drums, a melody that invited seduction and terrible decisions. With a flick of his fingers a goblet of wine appeared in hand. He smiled as he took a sip, terrible decisions indeed.

War raked his fingers through his long, dark brown hair. Sweat shined on his brow and his heart beat faster than it normally did. Hel clicked his tongue. "There are only two things that make you react this way. Battle and bad news. Actually, make that three, a divine set of tits. So, which is it? I hope the latter. I think I've seen about every pair in Runevale, covered or not, and although they are delicious, nothing has roused you this much since Lorna flashed you at the summer gods' festival."

16

War chuckled again and licked his lower lip, but he declined to answer.

"So, it is a maiden. Color me intrigued." Hel took another drink of his red berry wine. It was bitter and strong. Not much affected him but it dulled the inner desire to ruin lives. Immortality could be a bore, and although Hel was quite young amongst the gods, he was far superior at their games.

The stairs to the back entrance of the palace were made of pearl-colored stone that shined like crushed diamonds at night. Their boots hit the first step, and a snowy white owl hooted from its wooden perch at the palace's base. Its big yellow eyes followed him with suspicion. Hel smiled and winked at it. The bird ruffled its feathers in return and hissed.

"Fighting with the birds again?" War drawled. "How mature."

"I have no quarrel with them. They, however, seem to take issue with me."

To show off his fellowship with the birds, War stroked the top of the owl's head and it cooed. Hel rolled his eyes and quickened his pace up the sparkling stairs. Once he reached the apex, he downed his wine and tossed it into the night air where it promptly vanished into the aether. Mortal guards dressed in white and gold trimmed uniforms pulled the tall arched doors open to allow them entry. Both dropped their gazes to the ground as he approached and stayed firmly there.

Hel smiled to himself and strutted inside, where his boots clacked quietly on the glossy floor. That music he'd heard before changed to an even slower, more melancholy tune. His gaze shifted to the bright orbs floating above, giving off too much light for the setting. It wasn't but a moment later they dimmed. Better. As was customary for parties at Alefor, the combined territory of his aunt and uncle, the attendees wore black and white. The gowns on the maidens varied in shades of pearl to snow. Thank the Maker for the perpetually warm weather to make certain the scant fabric to display luscious feminine skin he so enjoyed. The bodies of goddesses were unlike any other. Curvy in all the right places. Hel looked the goddess of fury over from bare feet, up long bronzed legs, and to her half-exposed breasts.

Hel slid behind her and grazed her back with his fingertips. "You can take your fury out on me later, Eliza."

"Drop dead, Hel." Her bright orange eyes burned with her namesake. Her husband, the god of serenity of all things, touched her shoulder and the fire in her eyes dimmed.

"Midnight then," he said with a smirk and moved along the left side of the room toward the study where the only weapon left in all the realms that could truly kill a god waited, guarded by wards, hundreds of guards on the property, and magic that would melt even a god's hand off if they tried to touch it. The only one who had true access to it was his aunt, the goddess of love, the only one trusted not to use it.

He stopped beside the entry, where two sentries waited off to the sides. They moved away upon seeing him. To his utter disappointment no one had tried to steal it. What fun it would be to see the guard take out a thief. At least then something interesting would happen. Although the room had passing admirers filing in and out and the night was young. But Hel had something else in mind.

War appeared next to him, took an obvious look inside the study, and turned back. "I haven't seen it since I was a child."

"Me either," Hel lied. "Looks rather plain, doesn't it? You'd think one of the only weapons that can kill a god would be more impressive."

Hel stopped to scan the crowd. Gods and dragon shifters and even a few elves were in attendance. The elves were a favored race of many gods. They were ageless, attractive; many possessed their own magic, and unless provoked held an innate, boring, peaceful nature. A handful of human mortal servants carried trays of wine through the crowd. Amongst the most beautiful beings in the realms, the unsightly humans may as well have been invisible, an important defense mechanism. The last thing a fragile mortal wanted was the attention of a god. It never ended well, and it always ended.

"She's never been seen outside before," whispered Lord Vennal, a bureaucratic dragon shifter that Hel particularly despised, to the male next to him. A big-nosed, slight-chinned servant who was never far from his master. The servant whose name Hel never cared to remember, rubbed his yellowed nails over his weak jaw and pretended to care. Hel wanted to punch him just for the way he looked. A sniveling little rat. But much more interesting than the two of them was the topic of discussion.

On the other side of the room a female stepped in through the tall glass balcony doorway. A stranger in a red dress among a sea of white. Long black tresses cascaded down her back to the apex of her round hips. Her golden skin glowed with a hue only a goddess had. "Well, I'll be damned," Hel said. "It worked."

"What?" War asked following Hel's gaze across the room.

The goddess of night turned as if she knew they ogled her. Hel had never seen bluer eyes or a face so divine it made something deep inside him ache. She gave a coy smile, one that held secrets and mysteries he wanted to unfold, then she turned back to the golden-haired male beside her.

War's throat bobbed and that heart of his pounded. The god of war was as enamored as he. "What did you do?"

"Well, the illustrious goddess of night has declined invitations from every single House in Runevale and allows no one in her land. No one knows why so I had to do something. I convinced your mother to display Soulender tonight as a gift to allow everyone to see it, though I'd call it more of a snare."

"Why would she want Soulender?"

"She's Drivaar, War. I gambled that the weapon might be the only thing to draw her out and well, I was correct."

Many millennia ago, the gods split into two, the Drivaar who praise the All Mother as the highest deity and Primevar, who worship the Maker. Hel didn't worship anyone; the sides were more symbolic but one both would die for.

"There are a hundred other Drivaar here tonight." A peace agreement between the two sides of gods had lasted a millennium but there was always someone itching to start the conflict up again.

Hel leaned back against the wall wondering what she might smell like. He didn't care what enemy she'd want to use the dagger on. He'd let her have it and help her use it if that's what she desired. He wanted to know what her lips tasted like. "She's the ultimate conquest."

War smiled and shook his head. "I think she'd be the one to bring you to your knees, not the other way around."

"I don't fall in love, War. Love is for fools. I want bragging rights."

War rolled his eyes. "You're such an ass sometimes."

Their Uncle Synick, not related by blood but belonging to the same house as War and Hel's mentor, slid up behind them and placed a firm hand on each of their shoulders. "Stay away from that one, boys. She's not stable."

Hel glanced back. "What do you know about her?" If any of the gods knew, it would be Synick. He was a primordial god, one of the seven original gods of Runevale like her.

"She's a shut-in. And won't allow her people out of that prison. She's paranoid—and powerful. That's why."

"What happened?" War asked. No one talked to her, and it was rare for the history books to mention her; she'd hidden away since long before Hel was born.

From the sounds of it, she'd turned Synick down ages before and now he held a grudge against her. She was the only primordial who did not have children. The others had hundreds.

"After her sister died, she lost her mind." He shrugged. From across the room, she leveled Synick with a stare and didn't look away until he did. He licked his lips and turned on his heel. "Remember what I said. Stay away from her." He disappeared into the crowd.

Synick's warning only made him keener to be as close to her as he could.

Black shadow seeped out from the study and Hel shoved off the wall. She was no longer standing across the room. In a blink, he appeared at the back of the study where the golden dagger still waited on the desk. She looked at it for a moment as if bored and then stepped out through the double doors onto the terrace. Unable to help himself, Hel followed to find her alone under the cool night sky. He admired her hourglass shape and strode to the railing where she stood overlooking the grounds.

A light touch on his lower back and his hand flashed out, but too late. Wearing a mischievous grin, Valeen, oh yes, he knew her name, stood with the golden dagger in her hand. The true Soulender, he'd hidden it in his waist. Clever.

She inspected the sharp edge, gliding her fingers along it. "It is said Soulender was created from the heart of Luna and why she bleeds. Forged by the All Mother's hand herself." She slid her hand along the length of it and it disappeared. "Naturally, it belongs to me."

Hel slowly walked around her, inspecting her further. "I agree. That is why I retrieved it for you. Think of it as a gift."

She looked him up and down, a predator assessing another. There was no fear, no wariness, or trepidation that many had in his presence. Either she didn't know about his reputation, or she didn't care. Both intrigued him. "What do you want?" she asked.

"Nothing."

She smiled. "Don't lie to me. I hate liars. They belong in the underrealm with the thieves and traitors."

"You."

Her dark brow lifted, and the very corner of her red lip curved in the slightest way.

"To meet you," he added.

She smiled demurely. "And was it worth the trouble?"

"I don't know yet." He took a step closer and whispered, "But it is said the goddess of night was formed from a fallen star and the most beautiful blooms in all the realms, only to be seen again if she allows it." He slid his finger along the back of her arm and the hairs raised. "I'll show you mine, if you show me yours." Flames danced at the center of his palm.

She pulled her stare away from his first and then scanned his neck, his wrists, any exposed skin. "Rune marks on your skin. Dark hair. Eyes blue-green like oceans." She stepped back and trailed her gaze down his form inspecting him. "Hel, I presume."

"Yes."

"And I'm War. It's a pleasure, goddess." War joined them and leaned his shoulder against the dark wood door frame. Valeen's eyes lit with curiosity. "And it was most definitely worth his trouble to see you in the flesh."

CHAPTER 2

LAYALA

The normally beautiful elven forest smelled of death. Ebony clouds brought the kind of darkness that could be felt almost like a coating in the air. Tree bark bit into Layala's back and she took in a deep breath, steadying the sword in her hand. Not Lightbringer. Her father's sword still lay broken in pieces in the Black Mage's tower, where two months before she'd awakened him with every intention to end the curse. He'd taken complete control of the situation, claimed she was his long-lost wife, and then disappeared with the promise to return.

Seeing a dark lump on the forest floor, Layala studied it. Not a downed tree but... she held up her hand signaling Piper, her personal bodyguard and friend, and Leif, the flirtatious red-haired Raven warrior, to stop. With slow, careful steps she moved and crouched. She could just make out hair and the outline of a body. The pit in her stomach grew as she drew closer.

Leif crept to her side, silent as birds at night. "Don't touch it," he murmured in his rolling accent. As if he had to tell her. The female's mutilated body was missing an arm, bits of entrail hung out of her torso, face covered in gouges and copious amounts of blood; whoever she was would never be recognizable.

Layala couldn't help but wonder who might be missing her. Was she a mother? She wished she could find her family and at least let them bury her, but jewelry or anything personal other than bloodied, soiled clothes was gone. *Maker, please carry this poor soul safely home where she might find peace.*

"I don't think a pale one did this," Piper said, crouching down on the other side of the dead maiden. "They're brutal but they don't usually tear people apart unless they intend to eat them—she's not eaten."

The sound of a predator sniffing the air made Layala still and turn her head. She and the others rubbed pine oil on their wrists and hair to cover their scent, blend in with the forest.

"Think I smell she-elf," a gravelly voice hissed.

"Probably the dead one over there," another grumbled.

Leif huffed. "Not pale ones, eh Piper?"

She scowled at him.

Layala rubbed her fingertip over a sharp point of the five-tipped throwing star in her hand and peeked out from the side of the tree trunk. The source of the rotten scent in the air sat in a circle around a dying fire. How they could smell anything beyond themselves was incredible. White stringy hair hung down six different armored chests. Their black eyes were shocking against a face of snow-colored skin.

"We're close to the village," another said, picking his pointed teeth with a thin, bloody bone. "Maybe we can get one of the little ones."

Vile creatures. Layala's teeth clenched together until they began to ache.

"We're not even supposed to be killing the big ones."

"It wasn't me," the other one said in a slow deep voice. "Found her like that."

Perhaps Piper was correct after all. What could cause that sort of mutilation? A bear? They only roamed the deep forests. The creatures in the unnamed forest she'd battled previously couldn't escape its boundaries and they weren't near there...

"Master is awake now. We need to build our army for his plans."

Leif met Layala's gaze, and Piper shifted.

The hairs on the back of Layala's neck rose. *Yes, reveal his plans,* Layala thought. She wasn't waiting around, twiddling her thumbs for the Black Mage to find them. If she could bring his location to Thane, then they could plan an assault and take the offensive. In the past weeks she'd read everything she could about the Black Mage which only affirmed what she already knew. He was the deadliest, most powerful mage to ever exist in Adalon. Their only chance of beating him was a surprise attack. The goddess of knowledge within the scepter and stone spoke of the key to ending the curse and defeating him, and that was his heart. All they needed was to get a weapon through his heart, an arrow most likely.

A branch snapped somewhere among the dark wood to the south. The largest pale one stood and sniffed again, pulling out his jagged-edged sword. "Someone is here."

Layala groaned internally. What clumsy imbecile was out here about to get themselves killed? Everyone knew it wasn't safe to be out in the woods anymore, day or night. Layala nodded, Piper tugged her sword free, and Leif stood, pulling an arrow from his quiver. She stepped out from behind the tree, and the throwing star in her left hand whistled through the air, embedding between the big one's eyes.

"Assassins!" the teeth-picker shrieked. Leif's arrow speared through his neck and dropped the beast. Piper's sword slashed across the third pale one's throat, spewing black blood in an arc. Layala moved swiftly for another; she ducked under a heavy, starred mace that whooshed through the air. With a quick thrust, the tip of her blade shoved into her attacker's chest. She pushed harder, through armor and bones until she twisted her blade. She wanted him to *feel* his death. He squealed a horrible high-pitched sound until she kicked him free of her sword and he hit the ground with a heavy thud. Four down.

Block, sidestep, hack. Five down. She swiped the back of her sleeve across her cheek to clear away the splatters of warm blood.

The last pale one squared up with her, showing his pointed teeth in a grimace mixed between fear and rage. "You," he growled and slowly backed away. "Dark mage."

Layala and her little crew were growing a reputation among the enemy now. "Oh, it's most certainly me." She threw out her magical ebony vine until it wrapped around his neck. His boots dug into the soft dirt and foliage as she slowly dragged him closer. "Where is he? Where is the Black Mage?"

The pale one clawed at the vine, squealed and bucked like a wild mustang, trying to pull free of a rope.

"Answer me."

"Don't know," he wailed, falling to the ground, and writhing like a worm. "Don't know. Don't know."

That was what they all said. But someone knew. Someone must have seen the Black Mage. The pale ones wandered in packs throughout all of Palenor now, no longer drawn to the

Void as they had been before. Rumors were they roamed in the human lands and in Calladira unchecked. Even if Thane and the soldiers killed any they saw, small numbers of pale ones seemed to be everywhere. The enemy didn't gather in masses trying to take entire cities as they once did. They attacked here and there. Barging into homes in the middle of the night, stealing elves. The Ravens could take down a legion on a battle-field but when the pale ones hid, when they separated, they became weeds; kill one group and two more appeared some-where else. It was a kind of warfare Thane admitted to Layala he'd never dealt with before. So far, the Black Mage and his forces were getting the best of them.

"If you don't know then you're useless to me."

"Wait," Piper said. "You said you're building an army; for what?"

"For my master," he said through gurgled speech.

"It's no use." Leif slid his bow over his head and across his chest. "They're not smart enough to answer. Just like big, stupid trolls. We're wasting our time out here."

The pale one hissed, baring blacked bloodstained teeth.

"Where is your master?" Layala demanded.

"*He* will find *you*," the pale one said with a creepy smile. "When he's ready for his queen."

Heat crept up Layala's neck and she gritted her teeth. The vine snapped his neck, turning his head at an odd angle, and disappeared. Leif and Piper averted their eyes as soon as she looked at them. With a heavy sigh, she looked up. A part in the heavy clouds revealed a glimpse of the stars. They twinkled brightly in the gap. It didn't make her feel any different. The darkness that blanketed the land didn't infuse her with power or make her feel like the goddess that supposedly lived in her.

Her mind flashed back to what happened in that tower.

The Black Mage held her at his mercy, his grip on her throat relentless. Even now she shivered in disgust thinking about his tongue grazing her ear and the way he called her his wife. And his final words, the most haunting of all, "I'll be seeing you. Soon." He shoved her between the shoulder blades, sending her stumbling into Thane's arms, and vanished, along with Mathekis into nothing. And for two months, not a whisper. No dreams of him haunting her, not his voice in her head. They tried to keep his awakening quiet among the people, but rumors abounded. The elves could feel the shift in the air.

Layala dropped into a squat beside the largest pale one and pulled her throwing star out of his skull. The wet, sticky sound it elicited when it dislodged made her stomach turn.

"Where did a pretty elf like you learn to do that?"

A chill ran down Layala's spine at that voice, those words. He'd said that once before. She bit down on her lower lip to keep herself from smiling. She wiped the black blood off on the moss of a fallen log before she turned around. Thane, her beautiful Elf King, stood casually against the tree she'd previously hidden behind, arms folded, ankles crossed as if he didn't have a care in the world. He hadn't cut his hair in the last few months, and it now grew down past his chest to his upper rib cage. He kept it tied back tonight and wore plain clothes, not appearing as the king he was.

"Thane," Leif said, startled and nearly tripped over his own feet, dropping into a bow.

"What are you doing out here?" Piper shoved her sword back into the sheath on her back and pushed stray red hair off her fair-skinned, freckled face. "It's dangerous for the High King."

"It's dangerous for all of you. Why are you three going

28

behind my back, sneaking out at night? You think I wouldn't notice?"

Layala stood, stepping in front of her companions, shielding them from his wrath. She figured this day would come sooner or later. They'd been out here looking for pale ones for six weeks at least. She was sure he noticed prior to this night but why he came now instead of another day made her nervous. "I told them to come with me. Don't be angry with them."

"Of that I'm certain." He was quiet for a moment, bright emerald eyes searching the trees above as if they held the answers he needed. He finally leveled her with a hard stare. "You can't keep doing this. If any of you are bitten—"

"We won't be. How is this any different than fighting in battles near the Void?" This was the only thing that gave her purpose at the moment. The more she heard reports on death counts and burning homes, the more it drove her.

"It's not different," he snapped. "Which is exactly why I don't want you out here. Especially in the dark. All it takes is one single mistake. You're not invincible, Layala, and you're putting their lives at risk."

"So, what if it's dangerous? Everywhere in Palenor is dangerous now." She didn't even trust more than half the people in the castle walls.

He pushed off the tree and sauntered toward her. Leif and Piper shrunk back under his intimidating presence, but Layala stood her ground even if her heart beat faster. Thane had rarely been truly angry with her and tonight that fire in him flared. "Your *obsession* with finding him has to stop. When the Black Mage wants to make demands, he will."

"If we can find out where he is we can plan a sneak attack. Take the upper hand."

He glanced down at the black blood pooling near his boot. "They aren't going to tell you where he is. I wouldn't be surprised if magic kept them silent, making them unable to speak of his whereabouts. And the dead don't talk, Layala."

"Neither do the living. That's why they're dead."

Thane blew out a heavy breath and his nostrils flared. He shot a glare at Piper and Leif that would make lesser soldiers wither. "Get back to the castle."

They moved like fire licked at their heels.

Layala and Thane hadn't talked about the shift between them since the day Tenebris died and she'd nearly killed Talon. The very same day the claim about them being gods reincarnated put a chasm of uncertainty between them. He looked at her differently now, like she was someone else. Like she wasn't the elf maiden he fell in love with but someone he was uncertain of.

His unease wasn't simply that he held a grudge against her for the selfish move she made to save her aunt. The throwing star that nearly killed his sister seemed to still be lodged figuratively, even if he claimed he'd forgiven her. Talon still wouldn't look at her.

"Don't be angry with them," Layala whispered.

"I'm angry with you."

It took effort to meet his brilliant green eyes. "Be angry with me then but leave them out of it."

A moment later, he turned and yelled over his shoulder. "Come back!"

"Thane, don't punish Piper and Leif." Layala grabbed his hand and gave a gentle squeeze. She didn't want to use her feminine wiles to charm him, but she smiled and batted her eyes. His scowl only deepened.

"Who else have you dragged into your nightly crusades?"

"Just them. They want to fight, to make a difference."

"They have other jobs to do." He lowered his voice, and said, "I have spies all over Adalon looking for him and no one has seen him. He doesn't want to be found. And even if we did, I don't know if we're strong enough to take him out right now. I fear the day he shows himself, and so should you."

Layala blinked and opened her mouth to speak but couldn't find the words. Thane hadn't admitted he was afraid of the Black Mage ever before. She didn't think he feared anyone. "You don't understand, I must do something, Thane. I can't just wait around doing nothing."

He pulled his hand out of her grasp. "There are a thousand other things you could do other than trudging through the dark woods looking for trouble." His voice was sharp, edgy but not frightening. "You could practice your magic. Hell, you could even collect plants with your aunt again as long as you stay close to the Valley and in the daylight." He paused. "You could research the old gods—something to spark your memory."

"I don't want to remember. That life has *long* passed," she snapped.

He shook his head, and a small smile cracked his anger. "You're as stubborn as a mule. Worse even."

"You don't even remember—do you?" He wouldn't talk to her about it. She looked at his softening expression and wondered if maybe he did and he hadn't told her. This claim of them being gods from another realm was strange. Did his memory have something to do with not wanting to find the Black Mage? He mentioned Thane and him being related. Were they close once? "Do you?" she prodded.

Piper and Leif approached tentatively. Thane spared them a quick glance. "You three will join me for drinks."

"Drinks?" Leif questioned and grinned. "I thought I'd get a swift kick in the ass, not a pint of ale."

"The ass kicking is coming, trust me," Thane said with a sort of satisfaction that made Layala nervous for them. "But for now, we could all use a little downtime. And since I've chased you three half the night, I'm starving."

The group started walking back toward the city. "How did you find us anyway?" Layala asked.

"You know I'm good at just about everything I do, including tracking."

Piper and Layala looked at each other and rolled their eyes. "Your arrogance is a bit off-putting, you know," Layala drawled.

"You seem to like it."

Leif laughed. "If I looked like him, and fought like him, ruled like him, and had a gorgeous maiden who might actually be a goddess at my side, I'd be a cocky bastard too." He smirked and winked at Layala. "But if you get tired of him, my bedroom door's always open, Fightbringer."

Thane growled. "Your ass kicking just got a little more intense, Leif."

Leif laughed even harder.

"You think Thane's arrogant, you'd be much, much worse," Piper said, shoving Leif's shoulder. "Just becoming a Raven alone made you almost unbearable to be around. You wouldn't shut up about it for a month."

He slipped his arm around her shoulder and gave her a squeeze. "Pipe, if I had you at my side, I'd *never* shut up about it."

"Careful, Leif," Layala teased. "Dragon's fire is hot and their talon's sharp." The dragon prince who fancied Piper had been gone for the last two months but they still wrote letters regularly.

"And so is Fennan's blade," Thane added. Fennan, Thane's best friend and another admirer of Piper.

Piper shoved him off and smirked at all three of them. "Last one to the pub has to drink a shot of troll piss liquor."

All four of them took off in a sprint.

"DRINK IT," Piper called, pushing the short glass of yellow liquid closer to Leif. The pub was nearly empty at this hour. A pair of soldiers probably getting off from their night patrol sat in the corner booth and the barman cleaned glasses behind the bar top. Layala was surprised it was even open at four in the morning. Although when the High King knocked, doors opened.

Leif scrunched his face, wrinkling up his soft brown skin and pressed his lips together. "But it's so bad."

"You lost," Thane said. "Drink it."

He pointed a finger at Thane over the round wooden table. "You tripped me. You cheated."

"No one set any rules. And I didn't trip you. My boot simply got in your way," Thane said, leaning back in his chair with a smirk. It creaked under his muscular frame.

Leif blew out a breath, picked up the shot between two fingers and tossed it back. He grimaced and swallowed it down. "I hate you all," he said with watery blue eyes.

All three of them laughed at poor Leif. Layala picked up her mug of ale and took a sip. It wasn't the worst but not the best.

Thane leaned forward on the table. In this plain dark blue tunic and hair loosely tied back, and a light smudge of dirt on his cheek, he was as beautiful as when he wore fine High King's attire and styled his hair in braids. "So, while you have directly disobeyed me, did you find anything worthwhile?"

Leif, Piper, and Layala went quiet. Layala stared at the foam in her metal mug. They hadn't learned anything new. No news of the Black Mage. They might have saved people by killing pale ones when they could find them.

"Actually, yes," Piper said. "We found an elf with a very gruesome death. It wasn't by a pale one. We don't know what it was. And she wasn't the first."

"It *might* have been the pack of pale ones we killed," Leif said.

"She wasn't eaten, just torn apart. And they even admitted it wasn't them."

Thane tapped his fingers on the tabletop. "I've had reports of soldiers saying something similar. Only a few but enough it's not an isolated incident."

"What could it be?" Layala asked, remembering the she-elf's mutilated body. It made the ale suddenly sour.

"It could be a diseased animal. I hope it is so we can take care of the problem easily."

Layala watched Thane, trying to decipher his thoughts. If only she could feel his emotions like she once had. "But you don't think so?"

"I don't know. But my gut tells me something terrible is coming. You must stay close to the castle." His eyes seemed to darken as if he lied. Layala didn't question him further, but she had a feeling he knew more than he let on, and not just about this but about the Black Mage.

CHAPTER 3

LAYALA

A quick knock on Layala's bedchamber door startled her from sleep. If it were Thane he'd knock then enter. Anyone else would wait for her. Sunlight shined brightly through the windows, practically blinding. With one eye open she waited. The elf king didn't barge in, so it was indeed someone else. An annoyed groan bubbled in her throat. She got up and patted down her mess of black hair, took a breath and opened the door.

Two notes fluttered to the floor as if they'd been shoved in the crack. *Not again.* She sighed and swallowed to wet her dry throat. Both were folded in half but with different colors of paper. One was off-white and the other more yellow. She must enjoy torture because she pulled the first open to read it.

No one wants you here. The writing was masculine and a little sloppy. She crumpled it up and threw it back inside her room where it landed in the dark corner along with a pile of others.

With a shaky hand she opened the second. *Too bad High King Tenebris didn't kill you the day he killed your parents. We know what you've done.*

A pang hit her chest and instead of crumpling that one, she stepped over to the candle on the dresser top and set the edge of it in the flames. She watched the edges curling and blackening as the fire licked up.

Thane could only hold off the suspicion that the Black Mage was alive for so long. Rumors spread, and they started from soldiers who fought on the field and saw Layala go into the Void. Whispers of *his* name spread in the gossip parlors and in the pubs. The Black Mage hadn't been seen by anyone outside that tower, but the people talked. They suspected Layala had brought him back.

"Oh, dear me." Two little brown boots with holes poked out from the perch inside the green vine canopy above the bed. "Oh, dear plump pixie berries."

Layala slammed the door and whirled around. The little gnome in her ancient-looking floral print dress with mismatched patches held the *Palenor Scroll* in her hands, and Layala's heart clenched. "What?"

"Nothing. Just uh, nothing at all but good news." Tifapine scooted further into the dark hole of her hiding spot.

Layala stomped over to her and held out her hand. Was there another story about the attacks? Reports on who'd been stolen right out of their homes? "Let me see it."

Tif stuck the news scroll out and Layala snatched it. The first thing she saw in huge bold letters was, **Is Layala Lightbringer's True Mate the Black Mage?**

This wasn't just some gossip in the ladies' lounge. It was the front page of the *Palenor Scroll*.

· · ·

36

AN ANONYMOUS BUT *trusted source informed me last evening that High King Thane's betrothed Layala Lightbringer is mate bonded to the Black Mage and was able to bring him back to life. Yes, I gasped in horror as well. Just last week one of the soldiers present at the battle for the High King spoke of how he saw Layala Lightbringer taken into the Void by a dragon. Ever since that day the pale ones roam freely, no longer pulled to the Void, and they seem to have a greater purpose than to simply kill and maim.*

Is there proof the Black Mage is alive? Not yet, but is there proof they are mates? Many have long wondered about the lily's mark on Lightbringer's flesh the day she was born. The very midwife present at her birth attests she suspected immediately the child was cursed. Many of us there on the day of her testing knew she was destined for disaster in Adalon. We all saw the dark display of magic. You may be wondering if it's a mark of destiny for the Black Mage—a mate bond, why wouldn't the lily look like a common mate rune? Well, because it isn't. We don't understand it entirely but another source alive during the last war confirmed the Black Mage has that exact mark as well, among the many runes on his skin.

If he is awake and she is his mate, one can only imagine what lies in store for us when he steps into the light to claim her, a powerful mage in her own right. Where is he, you may ask? Perhaps he is not strong enough yet. Or he's gathering armies to take control of Palenor, or to recapture Lightbringer. Some say he's hunting down those who opposed him before and taking their heads. Many in Palenor deny his return but us believers know the truth will prevail.

Lastly, I want to give our condolences to the High King of Palenor, Thane Athayel. He must be heartbroken over this bitter and shocking news. He may be the only hope left for Palenor and all of Adalon but is our Warrior King strong enough to best the most powerful mage in history? Only time will tell. For now, stay safe.

Lock your doors. Don't go outside after dark, and whatever you do, don't try to fight a pale one. Hide.
　　—Telvian Botsberry, Chief Editor at the Palenor Scroll

WITH HER CHEEKS BURNING, Layala dropped the paper to her side. This was bad. Horrific might be a better word. Who was this anonymous source? Only her trusted friends, the Black Mage himself, Mathekis, and Varlett knew what happened in that tower. But which would tell? Obviously the Black Mage couldn't be the source—and no elf would trust Mathekis or Varlett would they? Had someone else seen? Did Fennan or Leif slip the truth while lying in some maiden's arms half drunk? Had Prince Ronan said something to someone?

"Has Thane seen this?" Layala asked, wishing she could find every one of these and burn them, but no doubt there were several nailed to poles and doors all over the city and being passed out in the pubs and down the main street of shops.

Tif pressed her lips together and twirled a brown curl around her finger. "I found it on his bed so..."

Layala tore the paper until it was in a pile of shreds on the ground. These people turned on her like vipers after she endured months of starvation and torture by Tenebris, lost friends, fought sirens and a bloody dragon to figure out how to save them all. Let that disgusting Lord Brunard put his lips and hands on her. She went into the Void, a place none of them would dare go to end the curse, and now she was going to be called a disaster for Adalon? She wanted to scream, to show them all what a nightmare she could truly be.

"Ehem. I should have kept my mouth shut." She slipped down the green vines draping over the bed acting as a canopy. Tifapine still wore the same red hat every day although Layala wondered if she had several of the same one stashed some-where. "I think we started our day off on a bad note reading that newspaper so let's start over." She hopped onto the bed and pulled a cupcake from behind her back. The base of it was larger than her palm with a dollop of chocolate frosting. "I made you a treat earlier and should have started with this. It's a special gnome recipe from what I'll one day call Tifapine's Bakery. I guarantee it's the best one you've ever had."

Layala took hold of it between two fingers, careful not to crush the gnome-sized cupcake in her grip. The chocolate frosting was whipped to a tall center and the white cupcake smelled like vanilla. The gnome's big brown eyes widened as she eagerly awaited Layala to taste.

"Thanks, Tif." She tried to keep the edge out of her voice but after reading that article, she was on the verge of tears. After peeling off the protective wrapper, she popped the cupcake into her mouth and the sweetness was perfect, the cake thick and warm. It was heavenly. "This is wonderful. It's definitely the best cupcake I've ever had."

"Why, thank you. Now, it's a fine day, isn't it? The sun is shining, and no sign of the creepy Black Mage to come steal you away. Although I will say that something feels a bit odd. The birds are squawking about shadows and a cloaked figure. But did the cupcake make you feel better?"

Layala nearly choked. "The birds are saying what?"

"You don't think... I mean, it's probably nothing." She chewed on her fingernail and with furrowed brows looked toward the window.

"The Black Mage won't be stealing me or anyone here," she reassured, not wanting Tif to go into a panic over bird gossip, but this was the first real clue she'd heard in months.

"I sure hope not. You don't think he'd want *me*, do you? I'm afraid if he heard my yodeling, he'd want me as some sort of court jester to entertain him while he's having people tortured and maimed. And I simply cannot yodel while such things are happening. If you see him, make sure to tell him I'm not useful at all and dreadfully annoying. Both of which are obvious lies but he don't need to know that." She smiled and patted her rosy cheeks.

Her yodeling would be almost worse than the sound of people being tortured. "I don't think that's anything you have to worry about. Did the birds mention where this cloaked figure might be?"

Layala got up and stood at the wide windows with her arms crossed. The guards patrolled as usual, the sun shined bright, and not even a cloud marred the blue sky. The lack of songbirds was a little disturbing but then an owl caught her eye. It was camouflaged in the shadows of Luminor's star-shaped leaves and thick branches. Big amber eyes blinked as it watched her with unnerving awareness.

"Whew! That's a relief," Tif said. "Anyway, what's on the schedule today? Oh, can we watch the new recruits train? It's hilarious watching Piper smack the boys in the back of the head. I peek sometimes."

"Tif, where did the birds say the cloaked figure was?"

She tapped her chubby fingers together nervously. "Oh, umm, they didn't say. Just that a cloaked figure was seen in the woods somewhere and it was dark there even in the day."

Her gaze swept across the land one more time. The waterfall roared white, flowing with more water than ever with the spring rains; horses trotted in the field near the stables with servants leading others, and the vast green landscape that stretched into the golden city was as bright and beautiful as ever.

"Dark even in the day" could mean the unnamed forest which wasn't even half a day's ride from there. The information wasn't much to go on, but she needed to inform Thane. Although they did just have an argument about her looking for the Black Mage. He wanted her to stop. To leave it be.

Maybe she was better off not bringing him up.

Layala crawled back into bed, buzzing with anxiousness even though her body craved rest after so many sleepless nights. She rolled onto her side and pulled up her lavender silk blanket. "Wake me up if you hear anything else."

"Are you in a melancholy? Mama says when people sleep during the day, they're in a melancholy, and you've been sleeping during the day for a long time. Months. I could yodel to make you happy."

"I'm fine, Tif. Just tired." She closed her eyes and even if it took hours, with a little hand patting her shoulder, she fell asleep.

WAKE UP.

Wake up. You're in danger.

Layala's eyes fluttered.

Get up now, Valeen. Get up, the deep voice urged. Layala's eyes flew open, and she shot upright in bed.

The sound of a door closing prickled the hairs on the back of her neck. Blinking away the blurriness in her vision, she turned to see who entered her room. But there wasn't anyone there. Slowly, she pushed herself upright and swept her gaze around the room. The fertility fern that hung on the shelf looked dull, and brown leaves settled on the floor below it. The two miniature statues, one of Layala, the other of Thane reaching toward one another needed polishing. Clothes hung out of her dresser drawers, and she noted the pile of dirty laundry had gotten rather tall. Pearl had taken two weeks off and Layala hadn't chosen another lady's maid. She didn't trust anyone else to come into her rooms for any reason. And she couldn't talk herself into cleaning. It was in desperate need of it, but it was easy to ignore when the effort was more than she could muster.

She dragged her fingers across her scalp and through her tangled black hair. Had she dreamed the voice warning her?

Or was it... No.

She hadn't heard his voice since before he woke up. Maker above, she hated always being on edge and feeling nervous and jumpy in her own home.

"Tif?" Layala called. Perhaps it was her who'd gone out of the room. No answer. "Piper?"

Did she forget to lock the door? One leg slipped out from under the blanket, then the other and bare feet hit the cold, stone floor. She reached under her pillow, pulled out a dagger and slid it from its sheath. The coiling in her gut grew tighter as she stepped silently toward the bathroom. She barely let her breath loose.

With her dagger poised to strike, she paused outside the doorway and listened. Afternoon birds sang merrily outside the windows and the sound of water dripping into the tub, *plop...* *plop... plop*, came from inside. In one leap she hopped inside and glanced around to find it empty.

I'm losing it.

She turned around, saw a tall, muscular figure, and jumped with a scream, plunging the dagger through the air before she could register who it was. Thane snatched her wrist before the blade impaled him. "Woah. It's me. Relax."

Her heart beat wildly in her chest and her hands trembled from the rush. "Do you think it's funny sneaking up on me like that?"

"I wasn't trying to. I just walked in." Completely unphased by how close she'd come to driving a dagger into his chest, Thane put a finger to her lips. "And keep your voice down or the guard will be in here."

Layala slapped his hand away from her mouth and shoved him in the chest. "Ugh! I could have stabbed you!" She pushed him again; her body still had the surge of energy from her fight reaction. "You could be dead right now. Give me some warning next time."

He almost looked offended when he said, "It would take more than that to kill me."

"I'm not in the mood for your... antics." She stalked past him and snatched the dagger sheath off her bed, shoved her dagger inside, and placed them both under her pillow. "You know I'm on edge as it is. What if *he* comes here?"

Here they were arguing about him again. The asshole called to her, haunted her dreams for too long, then popped up for one brief moment, hadn't been around for months, and he still drove a wedge between them.

Thane's eyes darkened at the mention of *him*. "I'm not going to let him take you from me. I don't care what he says about who you used to be."

"You don't?" Layala gritted her teeth and balled her hands into fists. This fight was long overdue. They'd both avoided it while avoiding each other. "Because it feels like you do. You haven't touched me in weeks. You won't even sleep in the same bed as me, which is how I could so easily sneak out. You look at me like I'm someone else entirely."

"Because you are."

Layala's jaw dropped. "It's still me! I'm still Layala. Even if you used to know me as someone else too, I'm still the elf you met in Briar Hollow."

"And you're still mine."

"Don't pull the possessive male horseshit if you're not going to step up and do something about it."

The look in his green eyes was practically feral. He grabbed her by the back of the thighs, lifted her, and pinned her against the wall. If all it took for him to stop being estranged was a little goading, then so be it. She squeezed her thighs against his hips and twirled a piece of his long hair around her finger. Too much time had passed since he even kissed her let alone took her to his bed.

"You don't understand," he practically growled.

"Then make me understand."

Whistling and small footfalls made Layala groan and Thane pull back. Tif came through her miniature door with an envelope in her hand, oblivious. Her polka dot sock-covered toes protruded from her boots and Layala contemplated insisting she get a new pair. How could that even be comfortable?

"There you two are. I've been looking everywhere..." her brows raised, taking in Layala and Thane's position against the wall. "Oh, my, did I interrupt something?" Her brows bounced up and down with a small mischievous smile.

"Yes," Thane snapped and backed up, running a hand through his hair.

At least she'd gotten him flustered. Maybe tonight he'd seek her out rather than avoid the bedroom altogether.

Tif lifted a shoulder. "Anyway, I came all the way from the kitchens with this. You know how long it takes me and my little legs to get around this castle? And the stairs, oye, I could lose my extra fluff, and I can't have that. I'll need extra dessert tonight." She patted her round belly, stopped beside Layala, and raised the envelope. "I was wandering around thinking about what I'd like for a snack, but sticking to the shadows to avoid the jumbos, you know, like I do, and I smelled delicious cinnamon rolls. But Mage Vesstan snuck up on me just as I was about to take one off the plate and tapped my shoulder and told me to give this to you. He said that if I got it sticky or lost it, he'd turn me into a toad so thought I better wait on the rolls. Anyway, can he really do that?"

Layala took the envelope and shrugged. She wasn't sure what Vesstan was capable of, though from his feeble appearance, not much. He'd stayed at the castle for the last few weeks. Thane didn't want him at the cottage alone with the number of pale ones running rampant.

"He most certainly can," Thane said with a sly smile. "I should have had him turn you into one at his cottage when you ignored my rules."

Her big brown eyes widened and then she stamped her foot. "I listened plenty good. You were just a grumpy ol' turd."

"You do realize I'm the High Elf King."

"I'm not a dumb dumb."

Thane looked at Layala and raised his eyebrows. "Will you get your *lady's maid* under control before I toss her out a window?" He glared down at her. "From the top floor."

Tif gasped and slapped her stubby little hand against her chest. "How could you use my worst fear against me? I knew there was something rotten about you."

"Oh, did you?" Thane asked mockingly. He lifted his foot a few inches off the ground. "I could just crush you under my boot but then I'd get it dirty."

She twirled around, turned her back to him, and folded her arms with a big pouty lip. "I'm not speaking to you anymore, and I certainly will *not* be yodeling at the ball as entertainment."

"Thank the Maker," Thane said, kissing the inside of his fingers and raising them up as a sign of praise. "There's one good thing about this day."

She turned back to glare at him, and even hissed like a cat. That was new.

"Stop it. Both of you," Layala said, shaking her head and trying not to laugh. Even in the worst of times that gnome could brighten her day. Layala smiled and pulled the note out of the envelope and it read:

Meet me at the stone circle for mage training just before sunset. I'll be waiting.

~Vesstan

"Since when does he want to train me?"

"Since I asked him to. It's time you learn to control your magic, rather than hide it," Thane said. "This will be good for you, Laya. I think you're capable of much more than we've seen."

"You think or you know?"

He smiled. "I know. Meet me in the Hall of Kings when you're ready. The new Lord of Calladira is hoping for an alliance. Bringing the elves together might finally happen."

Layala set the note on the dresser and walked over to the window. She had a feeling the new Lord of Calladira wouldn't be the only person making an appearance soon.

CHAPTER 4

THANE

Thane closed the door gently behind him and then leaned against it, slamming his eyes shut and heaving a breath. It was torture resisting her when he wanted nothing more than to give into those blue eyes begging him to touch her—to love her. Seeing her half-dressed, all that exposed skin and Maker above, he wanted to grab her and show her how much he loved her still. The thought of it set his pulse racing. But he wasn't the same elf he'd been months ago, and neither was she.

His vivid dreams kept him tossing and turning half the night since that day in the tower. Maybe it was Hel's awakening that triggered the memories, maybe something else. Awake, asleep, *Hel* kept flashing in his mind, of times of them together as children fighting against each other in a small dirt floor arena; someone he couldn't quite see clearly forced them to spar. Many nights of running through woods laughing, catching critters, or sitting on a mountain top counting the stars, a different sky than the one he looked at nowadays, surmising if they'd ever fall in love. Hel said he wouldn't. He hoped he would.

There was something broken about that young Hel, something that made him a little more ruthless, jaded. It prompted War to want to protect him, to make sure no one hurt him.

But it made Thane wary. He remembered how ruthless he could be to someone who stood against him, and they weren't on the same side anymore.

Then there was Valeen's infectious presence, her sheer power—a primordial goddess. She was like Layala in appearance but so sure of herself, so strong.

Unbreakable.

Flashes of him fighting beside her in a place with dragons where he was someone the shifters looked up to. It wasn't the same architecture or landscape he'd been to up north in Adalon, so he couldn't say it was just him dreaming of Prince Ronan's dragon kingdom. It was another realm with a landscape vastly different, a sky with two moons, rolling fields of amber and sparse trees. And although he knew he had feelings for her in these dreams, she wasn't his lover there.

Other times she was with Hel, he saw her in excruciating detail dancing with him, his hands all over her near a bonfire and half-shifted dragons partying around them. It made him insanely jealous, and he woke up from that dream covered in sweat.

But the absolute worst memory was the one that kept him awake at night. The one that made him pull away. The one that made him question everything. A week after they'd arrived home to Castle Dredwhich from the Void his mind slipped into a vision while he was still awake...

It was midnight and neither he nor Layala were able to sleep.

She'd paced the room, her feet quietly clapping on the stone floor. Her anxiousness put him on edge too. "Let's go for a walk, Laya, it will help you relax." She'd been like a penned-up wildcat since they returned home. Anxious to escape but to where?

They made their way outside, along the prim path around the side of the castle. "It's a warm night," Layala said conversationally. They'd done their arguing and fighting over what happened with Talon; she'd cried about it and asked for forgiveness for what she did to hurt him, and he gave it. They were passed it but their problems with the Black Mage—Hel had only begun.

Thane didn't respond to her comment on the weather. He was thinking about what Hel had said. "She's my wife. My mate. Queen of Villhara." He couldn't remember exactly what Villhara was yet.

Layala pointed to a bushel of jasmine, "Do you like the smell of jasmine? Aunt Evalyn always said it's too strong, but I love it. It's my favorite." It was Valeen's favorite too...

His gaze fell to the white blossoms. Their scent infiltrated his senses and the wedding flashed across his mind as vividly as if he'd stood in that garden of jasmine at midnight surrounded only by a few friends. Soft music played, strings and chimes from an invisible source.

She was radiant in a deep purple dress with stars and moons on the bodice, and a smile that wouldn't fade. They held hands, cut their skin, bound their union by blood. He'd promised her eternity, and she him. It wasn't coercion or forced or even arranged. There was no denying they loved each other. Hel never took his eyes off her. She kissed him hard on the mouth, pulled him in like she couldn't get close enough.

It gutted him to know their happiness, to have witnessed it. And to be so in love with her himself at that very moment... and to feel guilty for it. He even felt the guilt now in this life. He couldn't make sense of it. Why should he feel guilty? Why should he care about something so long ago? Another life that felt like him but not.

"Thane, what's wrong?" Layala had asked.

"Nothing. But I think I'm with Evalyn on this one... jasmine is too strong."

IT WAS THEN he backed off her. Then he decided he couldn't touch her even if every part of him wanted to, not until they both knew more.

There was a war inside him, between what he knew about how evil the Black Mage was and the fact that as High King he should do something about it, and the other side of him that wanted to call him Hel, call him cousin because of memories that danced at the dark edges of his mind.

He was certain Hel would show up sooner or later. Layala didn't need to go looking for him. The thought of her out in the woods searching for him bothered him for more reasons than he'd ever admit. Her safety certainly, but Hel claimed to be her husband still—her eternally bound mate and she was *looking* for him. To find his location for an attack, but what if it was more than that? What if she was drawn to him for another reason?

What if *Valeen* wanted her husband back?

He finally stilled to read the notes he'd taken from Layala's room in hand: *You're starting to look fat. You should stop eating.* With brows tugging down he turned it over. The other side was blank. He opened another and read: *My mother and sister are dead because of you. Do Palenor a favor and drive a dagger through your heart.*

Thane's stomach dropped and anger flushed his cheeks. Why hadn't she told him she was receiving threats and torment like this? How long had it been going on? There was a pile of at least fifty of these in that room. When he spotted it, he assumed she'd been writing things down and tossing them aside. He looked at the first one again. It was without a doubt Talon's handwriting, but he guessed the other to be a male's scribble. This wasn't just Talon being petty and mean. This was beyond that.

Gritting his teeth, he grabbed the nearest guard by the sleeve and jerked him close, but he spoke to all four of them standing around. The guard stiffened and his eyes blew wide. He waved the threatening note in all four of their faces. "If I find out that any of you have anything to do with this, I'll cut off your heads myself." He shoved his finger toward her room up the steps. "I want a guard watching her door at all times, so I know who's leaving these."

He crumpled the notes in his palm and started off on a jog toward Talon's usual spot.

The golden archway to the tearoom sparkled in the sunlight. The thick velvet tapestries were pulled across the entry. Giggling and snide remarks gave them away before he even stepped inside. He shoved aside the tapestries and found his sister Talon, with her golden-brown hair perfectly styled and painted pink lips to match her gown, and three of her friends with teacups in their hands. Well, her friends had teacups, Talon had a long-stemmed glass full of white wine. Of course.

Thane threw the note, and it nailed her right in the forehead before it fell onto her lap.

"Ugh, what was that for?" She set her glass on the table beside her and picked up the note. Then she glanced down at the paper and her skin paled. "I can explain."

"I don't think you can. You will be confined to your rooms

and not allowed to see any of your friends for two weeks. And no wine."

He glared at the others knowing they were in on it too. Vyra set her white teacup on the center table and brushed her hands over the folds of her yellow dress. "May I be excused, sire?"

"Not until I'm finished. You, Vyra, are not allowed on castle grounds any longer. I've put up with your shit long enough."

Talon stood, dropping the note to the floor, then she kicked it aside, sending it rolling under the sofa as if that would make him forget about it. "You can't do that!"

"Bet me on it."

"Mother won't allow it. You're not my father."

"Get out," he snarled at the others. They scrambled out into the hall like their lives depended on it. He strutted into the room, shoving one of the high-backed chairs aside and towered over Talon. She stiffened but didn't dare retreat. "I am the High King and what I say goes. You will be confined to your rooms for two weeks, and no friends for a month now. If I see you outside, you will be sent to clean in the kitchens rather than sit in your rooms."

Talon frowned but stared up at him defiantly. "The notes don't mean anything. We were just having a little fun."

"Do you see me laughing?"

"Thane, she nearly *killed* me, and you're treating me worse than you ever have treated her. Did you even consider leaving her for what she did? You had to *kill* our father for her! She threw a metal star into my neck! Did you confine her to her room, threaten kitchen duty? Did you even *lecture* her?"

He'd been lenient on her because what else could he do? She wasn't someone he could control. She was *Layala*. Even so her actions still left a bad taste in his mouth. Talon was a brat, but she didn't deserve what happened that day. He almost lost his little sister because of Layala's selfish move. "I've dealt with the issue. She won't ever touch you again."

"And Vyra is the one who wrote that no one wanted her here. It wasn't even me."

"Hence why she was banished."

"Thane," Talon whined. "She's my best friend."

He turned and headed out of the room. "Get new friends." As if he didn't have enough to deal with, he had to handle petty drama within his home.

ALONE IN THE Hall of Kings, leaning back on his throne, Thane closed his eyes and rubbed between his eyebrows. A pit grew heavier in his stomach, a feeling of impending darkness he couldn't shake. It had plagued him for weeks now, starting with the mutilated bodies his scouts found. He saw them himself and couldn't get the images out of his mind. There was more to it all, but he couldn't put his finger on it.

It was a beautiful day. The sun shone brightly through the tall windows, the smells of lavender and incense drifted through the open doors. Somewhere a flute played a soft melody that should soothe his nerves. Even this morning's reports told of no attacks, and yet he felt sick to his stomach.

The alone time and silence gave him time to ponder, and with his fingers drumming on the armrest, something flashed in his mind.

Drums beat, and battle cries went up all over a vast field where thousands of soldiers stood opposite of each other. Not elves but dragon shifters, hundreds soared above, the great whooshing of wings beat the air. Thane glanced over and... Hel stood beside him. "You love this, don't you?" Hel said. He looked different than he had

*in the tower, lighter, younger, even though the male he'd encoun-
tered in the Void didn't look a day over thirty.* "The anticipation of
the fight. It's going to be a bloodbath. You should join in. Stop it
before it starts."

"I'm here to oversee the battle, not pick a side. That's my role
here. Thanks for coming today by the way."

"You're my brother. I'll always come when you ask. But you
promised fun, War, and I'm craving a good fight."

"If the battle gets close, we'll have to defend ourselves, and it will
get close."

"You know she's mine, right?" *Hel smirked at the change in
subject.* "I'm going to have her, so don't get in my way."

"If you truly care for her, I won't."

Muffled chatter brought him out of the memory. It felt real,
as if he stood beside him now. His eyes flashed wide then the
doors clicked and opened. Thane rubbed his chest at the ache
beginning there. How was he supposed to fight someone who
called him brother? Someone he felt a bond with at this very
moment? More than even with Fennan.

Piper and Leif walked in, side by side, filthy. Leif grinned
with delight and Piper looked like she wanted to kill him for it.

"Sire," Leif boomed, strutting like a gnome who'd just
found a stash of his favorite treats. "Guess whose team won the
day?"

"How could I ever guess?"

Piper rolled her eyes and stroked the long red braid
bouncing against the front of her shoulder. She was in full
Raven armor although her winged helmet was tucked under
her arm. The metal clanked quietly off the high domed ceiling
with each step. "Barely."

"You know the winning factor, Red?" Leif said, looking over
at her as they stopped at the bottom of the steps that led up to

Thane's throne. The dirt on his cheek, in his hair, and all over his armor made Thane question if Piper had tackled him for winning. She was almost as disheveled and filthy as he. "It's morale. You're too mean. I'm fun."

Piper tapped her boot on the ground. "Considering my team won the last three days, I won't be changing my methods. My team's morale is plenty high. You're also a male and they see you as a leader without any effort. I have to earn it. I don't have the luxury of being their friend."

That heaviness in Thane's gut lifted some. His friends were a much-needed distraction.

"And where is Fennan? How did his team do?"

"My team crushed them," Leif said. "Easy. And he's making his team train extra because of it. He's a better loser than Piper though."

"Shut up or I'll throw you into the mud pit again."

"I liked it. It's not a threat, Red. Especially the part where you fell on top of me."

Thane slowly shook his head but smiled. "All of them need to be ready by next week. Will they be?" These boys were seventeen and eighteen. The typical minimum age was nineteen and he hated that he even needed to bring them into this so young, but desperate times. They'd lost many soldiers in the civil war against his father and through the attacks the past several months. Thankfully a common enemy brought the Ravens and general Palenor soldiers back together and brought more volunteers than ever.

Piper frowned. "I won't feel comfortable sending them out by next week."

"We have a new batch of recruits coming and cities need protection. They need to be ready. You have three days to get them there." Thane glanced at the double entry doors. He expected the new Lord of Calladira to show up at any moment. He was informed the lord and his group were close to the city. He hadn't heard the name of the new ruler yet. It felt like they were deliberately keeping it secret, and Thane had too many other things to deal with to worry about it sooner, but Thane's spies said they were struggling with the attacks just the same. Perhaps a common enemy would bring the woodland and high elves together or it would give Thane one more adversary to worry about.

The doors were opened by the guards and Layala strode through. The snug bodice of her strapless midnight blue dress shimmered like stars and the bunches of her silk skirt flowed around her ankles. Her hair was half pulled back with sprays of tiny white flowers tucked in, and her lips painted a soft berry. His heart beat faster, the way it often did in her presence, and then it sank. She'd been dealing with constant harassment, and he didn't even know it. Not just from the public eye, which he thought she was sheltered from within these walls.

He hated that things were different between them and that she didn't feel comfortable telling him everything, but ever since the tower he had a difficult time adjusting to the elf maiden he fell in love with and the mystery that hid somewhere deep down inside her.

He'd seen glimpses of the Valeen in his memories and the present like in the arena against the dragon prince, on the battlefield when she threw a throwing star at Talon. That was something Valeen would do. Then when she demanded he stay his hand rather than save his sister. When he thought back on it, there were other times too, when she was drawn to Hel's chair in the mage's tower, when she tore apart the woodland elves to save him from the cage.

One day the goddess would break free of the webs of darkness clouding her memory, and he didn't know what to expect. Would she still love him? Were the gossips correct and she would go with Hel? Was that where her heart would belong? He couldn't love her the way he wanted until she remembered —until they both did.

"Well, if it isn't Fightbringer, gracing us with her presence in the light of day," Leif said, folding his arms. "Where have you been? We're coming up on the final days of training and you've missed most of it."

She put on a smile, waved a dismissive hand, and quickened her pace across the glossy gray stone. "I've had things to do. Where are Fennan and Siegfried?" The way the sunlight shone down on her through the high windows made her golden skin glow in a way that made him shift slightly. In public they pretended everything was fine between them, though he knew they weren't fooling his friends.

"Fen is training still," Piper answered. "And Siegfried is in the south with his family. He was worried about their safety with his father's injury."

Leif tugged a small stick out of his unruly fire-orange hair. "Fightbringer, tell me you'll at least be at the ceremony and the ball afterward. It's a masked ball this time, celestial themed. Queen Orlandia and Princess Talon wanted to change things up a bit."

"I wouldn't miss it," Layala said. "Is it still this weekend?"

"You *have* been keeping track," Leif said. "Do you have time to come for a sparring lesson tomorrow? They'd be thrilled to see Lady Fightbringer."

"I might."

She strode up the steps, sat on the armrest next to Thane, and crossed her legs. He noticed her hands folded neatly on her lap, and the way she was slightly turned away from him.

Without thinking, he lifted his arm to touch her back but then he caught sight of the lily mark on her shoulder and reached up to tuck his hair behind his ear instead. Maker, it killed him. He'd forgiven her for Talon, for everything she ever did, but he couldn't shake the feeling that their union was doomed. That he could be her end. That fate destroyed them once and it would do it again.

"Can you give Layala and me a moment, please?"

Piper and Leif gave each other a quick glance and left without protest.

"I want to continue our conversation from earlier."

She turned to face him with an eager smile. "Alright."

"I have memories flooding in my head with you and him... it's driving me mad."

"But that isn't now. You need to realize that."

"I feel like I'm going insane as flashes of another place, of people I can't really remember hit me like a punch. It knocks the wind out of me sometimes."

He slipped his hand into hers and rubbed his thumb across the knuckles. When he looked at those bright blue eyes, the sea of dark hair, he couldn't stop himself from wanting to call her Valeen, to want to associate her with Hel and Runevale. In his mind, she wasn't the young elf maiden he'd met nearly a year ago, driven to end their mate bond then giving all of herself to him. She was someone he'd known for years, most of which were spent in another male's arms while he watched longingly from afar.

"I haven't been sleeping with you because I can't sleep, and when I do it's full of dreams that make no sense to me." Or worse, nightmares of Hel and Valeen together.

"You can talk to me, Thane."

He lifted his head. "But you don't want to hear it. You clam up and try to change the subject every time I bring up the past."

"Because it doesn't matter."

"Yes it does." He shoved up off his throne, fisting his hands at his sides. "Don't you remember anything? I think you're keeping things from me."

Layala stood, narrowing her eyes at him. "No, and you know why? I don't want to remember being his wife, alright? I don't want to feel conflicted like you. I don't want to think I ever cared for the Black Mage. I only want you. I'm more than happy to listen and hear about the places you remember but not him."

"So, the real reason you're off looking for the Black Mage every night isn't because Valeen wants to find him because she misses him? Because *you* want him?"

Layala's face shifted from understanding to pure venom. "How dare you say that to me."

With a boom, the doors flung open, and crashed into the wall. A cool wind swept inside, pushing Thane's loose dark locks away from his face. The hairs on the back of his neck stood and instinctually, his magic flared up, pulsing under his skin with an intense heat. The two guards dropped to the ground, sprawled out unconscious. On the floor, a shadow appeared in the doorway, followed by footsteps. Thane's body tingled and tensed, sensing a powerful magic and the threat of it shot his heart rate up. No power, not even the force Layala conjured against the dragon prince in the north rivaled this.

With his arms swaying at his sides, and not a weapon in sight on the fine-tailored black suit with red whirls down his chest, a cloak flowing out behind him, Hel stepped into the entryway with a smirk. Thane gulped and the memory of his standing beside him in battle flashed across his mind's eye again— *"You're my brother. I'll always come when you ask...she's mine so stay out of my way."* A small part of him wanted to walk forward and grip his hand and jerk him into a hug but the more dominant emotion made his hand twitch to reach for his sword.

This was not his brother, not anymore. This was the male who wanted to take Layala from him. The Black Mage who created the curse on the elves, destroying countless lives, and the reason Thane had to kill his own father.

As if oblivious of them, Hel looked around, first at the high stone arches above, then the stained-glass windows filtering warm light. He inspected the navy-blue tapestries and the red carpet that ran to Thane's throne. Then his gaze fell directly on Layala. "Hello, love. I heard you've been searching for me."

CHAPTER 5

LAYALA

"Oh, did I intrude on a lover's quarrel? You wouldn't be fighting about me, would you?" the Black Mage smiled as if it brought him great pleasure, and Layala was certain he'd heard every word of the argument she and Thane just had. About him.

Maker above.

She swallowed hard, watching him move with the grace and lethality of a cougar. In the cover of darkness, under the guise that she might be able to find his location and they'd make a plan with the advantage of a surprise, she felt confident, but there was no catching him off guard now. She felt like a rabbit locked in a cage and the hunter came to collect. The time in the tower came flooding back. He'd taken full control over her, and she couldn't even move unless he allowed it.

It was like the air was pulled from the room, making it hard to breathe, to think until the Black Mage set his garnet eyes on her, inspecting every inch, from her loose ebony curls to the

61

glittering slippers on her feet, and then their stares met and it felt like her heart stopped and started all over again. For a moment she wasn't afraid. It was like seeing the sunrise after only witnessing the dark, or the nostalgia of coming home after years of being away. He smiled at her as if he too might be feeling the same thing.

Her body temperature warmed, creeping up her neck and spilling into her cheeks. He was the kind of beautiful one didn't see every day, not even in Palenor amongst the elves, and the way he inspected her made her feel stripped bare. And his power, like a weight pressed against every inch of her flesh.

Thane stared as if he saw a ghost.

Casually, he sauntered down the red carpet and stopped in the center of the Hall of Kings folding his hands behind his back. "You know, it's been a long time, Val. Maybe you should let your obsession with me go. Although, I know I'm difficult to get over. There is no one quite like me."

Any sort of friendliness she felt vanished. Her own magic's cool sensation ran down her arms at his threatening presence, but it would be foolish to make a move now.

That must be why Thane sat back on his throne, one foot rested over his knee. He leaned on the left armrest as if the intruder bored him. As if the Black Mage, the most feared mage ever to exist, didn't just walk into their castle, into this very room.

Layala felt as if her throat closed up, like she couldn't speak. She wanted to fire back with a witty retort, at least a denial of his words, but it was like an invisible hand reached inside her chest and she couldn't breathe. Clenching her jaw, she slid her hand behind her back where a throwing star was hidden in the folds of her dress.

"I can say with certainty, she's over you," Thane said.

The Black Mage smiled at that, bringing out the single dimple on his cheek. "It's Thane now, correct? You've done well for yourself as an elf. The title of High King, a beautiful castle, armies at your behest." He gestured toward Layala, "My wife." He smirked as if there was a joke only he knew of. "You always seem to be dealt the best cards in every life."

What cards had Hel been dealt? Who was the elf before he was the Black Mage?

"You keep calling her that as if it is supposed to matter. *If she was ever your wife, it was another life. And even if she's bound to you in any way, she's free to do what she wishes.*"

Layala wanted that to be true more than anything, but there was a time when she and Thane had no choice, when magic compelled them, and the consequences were dire. But the lily mark on her arm that matched the Black Mage's chest mark, didn't resemble a mate rune.

The Black Mage looked at Layala and said, "You're awfully quiet today Miss Lightbringer. Are you going to tell him why you were looking for me or should I? Although I think he already figured it out." His voice whispered in her mind, *Because you missed me. You're drawn to me even if everything in you wants to fight it. You can't help it. So don't fret, love, I'm here now.*

Layala clenched her hands into fists, digging her nails into her palms. *The audacity of this arrogant male. Missed him! Missed him!* "I know what you're implying and it's pathetic that you still call me wife, when it's certainly not you in my bed."

I hear he's not in your bed either.

Layala quietly growled. How could he know that? "I want to end the chaos and hurt and fear you've caused everyone, by any means necessary." *And to get back to the way things were with Thane.* It was the person standing opposite them that caused

63

all the problems she had in her life right now. Every single one of them.

He let out a deep midnight laugh. "Any means necessary? We could get creative with that. Sounds like a good time to me."

Her heart quickened but she kept going as if compelled, "Have you seen what you've done? Have you seen what your creatures do? You're destroying this world." Some small part of him had to care... He wasn't a pale one or cursed to lose his conscience. She knew better than most that judging someone based on rumors could be a mistake. But then again, if he was the one to create the pale ones, he might be as much beast as they. These rumors about the Black Mage were well documented and told by people who knew him, not from humans and their prejudiced suspicions as it was in Thane's case.

The Black Mage held out his arms, an open invitation. "Then kill me. I'm standing right here. Give it your best."

Was this a test? There wasn't an ounce of fear in his strong posture, in the arrogant set to his jaw. Without waiting further, her throwing star flew from her fingertips, whistling through the hall. It stopped inches from between his eyes.

He plucked it out of the air and toyed with it between his fingers. "That wasn't your best shot. Not even close, *goddess*. I know what you're capable of." *In more ways than one, love,* he taunted in her mind.

Stay out of my head! she silently shouted.

Thane stood and tilted his head from side to side, cracking his neck. "That's enough. Get out of my castle."

"At the risk of sounding childish, make me."

"I don't want to fight you, so if you have demands, make them or leave."

"Always with the negotiations, but I want to see your

temper. We all know it's a doozy. He's one of those we called berserkers in Runevale. Those who lose themselves in battle and only see red." He placed his hands behind his back. "Is it truly you, War? You look like War, sound like War, but I don't know if I believe it."

Before this came to blows that might leave Thane dead, Layala grabbed his hand and gripped it tight. He turned to look down at her. The fury building on his face was evident, the clouds of battle darkening his eyes. She'd seen that look before; this was the edge of giving into the god whose namesake he might very well be.

"If you've come for me, rest assured, I won't be going anywhere. If this is about you or him, then I choose him."

"You heard her," Thane said. "Now leave."

"Is that so?" His scarred brow raised. "I think you'll be singing a different tune soon enough, wife. *Mate.* Unlike the bond you shared with him, ours is real, not artificially bound by magic. You know what that means, don't you?"

"Nothing to me anymore."

"Don't be like that. I am your destiny, love. He was a stand-in." His glare cut to Thane. "A want-to-be me."

"Thane, wait!" Layala reached to grab him, but her fingertips only brushed his top and he was gone. With his sword in hand, he flew at the Black Mage, the coat of his magic leaving a tang in the air. Layala's heart lurched; Thane's sword sliced through the air, the light glinted off the blade as it came down at the Black Mage and moments before he was about to strike, Thane was flung back, like an invisible wave smashed into him and sent him flying through the air onto his back.

"And here I thought you were the god of war," the Black Mage said and tsked his tongue.

A second later he was up, charging again. The Black Mage

moved to the side, dodged left, right, ducked under his blade. Thane roared and swung harder, his movements a blur.

"I trained with you your entire life," the Black Mage threw out his hand, another wave of power knocking Thane backward, "I know every move you're going to make. You certainly haven't learned anything new." His fist cracked into Thane's jaw and his head snapped to the side.

He snarled, taking the punch like it didn't hurt and jabbed his blade straight at the intruder's gut. The Black Mage vanished and appeared behind him. He was toying with Thane. With a snap of his fingers Thane froze, sweat glistened on his brow, slid down the side of his face. His entire body was stiff, unmovable.

She knew what he was going through all too well.

"Let's play a game," the Black Mage said. "If you don't get out of that in ten seconds, I snap your neck. If you do, I still snap your neck."

Layala tensed, mind reeling. If she didn't do something, Thane was going to get hurt, possibly killed. It was nearly impossible to get out of the Black Mage's hold once he had it.

With her pulse pounding, her magic soaring, she strode ahead. Darkness traveled with her, trailing in her wake. She knew it would take an immense amount of his power to hold Thane in place and she must take advantage of that.

"Here we go." The Black Mage eagerly awaited her.

Her vine shot out and hammered into the Black Mage's chest, pushing him back several feet, wrapping around him like a vice. He smiled and with a wave of his hand, her vines snapped and popped, broke and twisted away, until the Black Mage stood free. He adjusted his cloak, plucking a thorn from it and flicked it away. "You can do better. Where are your shadows, your moon power? Where is the goddess who captured legions by their hearts and brought even me to my knees?"

"She's not here."

"But I want her," he teased. "Bring her out."

"Don't you hurt her!" Thane barked, still struggling to break free.

"Why would I hurt my wife? Especially one with such a beautiful face. I wouldn't want to mess with it."

"She's mine now. Leave her alone."

"You two are acting like children, but I am not a toy to be fought over. I am not something to be possessed. So back off." She faced Thane. "Enough of this."

The two males glared at one another while she stood between them. She readied for the Black Mage to strike. Her magic fought to break free. "Why are you here?"

"I like it when you're bossy. Gives me the tingles."

It took everything to restrain herself from attacking him but that wouldn't get them anywhere. Deep down, she knew even she and Thane together weren't ready to take on the Black Mage. So, she met his stare and held it; even if it was false bravado, she wouldn't cower.

"Why are you here?" she repeated. "If you wanted to kill us you would, but instead you're playing games. So, what is it? Name your price."

A slow smile grew, and his eyes flicked down her form. "You have something I need. And no, I'm not talking about your ass. I've already had it."

Layala struck him across the face with her open palm and a bead of blood welled up at the corner of his mouth. A red welt developed on his smooth fair skin. That statement shouldn't have bothered her, but a beast deep down in her wanted to roar at his disrespect. "Prick."

"I suppose I deserved that." He licked the corner of his mouth. "But I do like it a bit rough, and the name calling, *oooo*." He shuddered like it was pleasurable.

Letting her anger get the best of her, Layala took advantage of surprise and kicked at his kneecap. He dodged. She plucked another throwing star and tried to jam it into his heart.

He sucked in a sharp breath and caught her wrist. Her arm shook with effort as she fought against him, but inch by inch he pushed her away. "This is foreplay for me, love. You're only making me want you more."

Shit, shit, shit. She pushed harder but it was like fighting against a gale-force wind.

You're not strong enough, he silently said. *But it is adorable you think you are.*

Layala spat in his face. His hand wrapped around her throat and squeezed, not hard enough to hurt but enough to hold her with magic. He forced her backward until he shoved her into the wall. "Ah there's my feisty girl." He shoved his knee between her thighs and leaned down to her ear. "Come with me, and I won't hurt him. Come with me, and I'll make you remember all the ways you craved me."

"Let go of me!" With a scream of rage, a blast of power radiated from her like a gust of wind and drove them apart several feet, but it wasn't far enough. She'd hoped to send him through the wall.

"That was the first interesting thing you've done since I woke up." By his straight posture and easy breathing her attack did nothing.

Thane broke free of the magical hold and dashed in front of her like a protective wall. "Touch her again and I will end you, family or not."

"Touch her and die, huh? Original. Too bad you couldn't even if every single life in this castle depended on it."

He flicked his fingers and one of the unconscious guards lifted into the air. The first one's head snapped to the side with a pop, and he fell to the ground. "Oops."

"Don't," Thane bit out as the second guard rose.

A dagger formed by magic appeared above his palm, bright blue, iridescent and the tip pointed at the second guard. "This is just to prove that I am a god, and you are still a pathetic mortal." The dagger flew at the guard and struck him right in the heart. His body convulsed for a moment then he plummeted to the floor. A pool of crimson grew wider with each passing moment.

Layala peeked out from behind Thane's wide frame and gripped his bicep, watching helplessly as the guard bled out. "I hate you," she said quietly.

He chuckled. "The feeling is mutual. Nevertheless, I think I'll stay for a while. It will be like old times with the three of us together again. Don't worry, I can find a room on my own." He winked and vanished in a puff of gray smoke.

CHAPTER 6

LAYALA

Layala hurried to the guard closest to her. Even if he stared up at the ceiling endlessly, she dropped to his side and leaned down over his mouth to listen for a breath. Maybe there was a bit of hope she could save him. No sound. She touched his neck to feel for a pulse, just in case. There was no familiar beating against her fingers. Damn it. The other was gone too. She didn't have to feel for a pulse to know.

Thane knelt beside her and wrapped his hand around her upper arm. "Are you alright?" he asked. "Did he hurt you?"

"No, I'm fine." Layala stood and stared at the spot the Black Mage disappeared from. The puff of cloud dissipated but his dark presence still lingered here. "What are we going to do? He said he's going to find a room?! A room. Here."

Looking like he was about to go on a murderous rampage, Thane marched into the corridor. Layala hurried to keep up with his long strides.

"I don't know yet."

"We're not going to allow this, are we? We can't."

"I'm trying to figure out a plan. I expected him to show up, but not to stay."

"Thane." Layala nibbled on her lower lip. "You called him *family*. That is not the Hel you grew up with. He's the Black Mage."

"How would you know?" Thane snapped. "I thought you didn't remember anything. Or are you trying to cover up how you truly feel about everything he said in there?"

Layala blinked in shock and halted. "Your pride is wounded, and I understand how you feel but—"

"But what? I mean it's true, isn't it? Our mate bond was placed by magic, but you and him..."

"Screw mate bonds, Thane. And if you keep walking away you'll ruin what we have."

Thane stopped and turned on his heel, shoving a hand into his hair. His jaw muscles twitched. "I'm sorry." His chest dropped with a heavy sigh. "We need to find him. Now. He could be doing anything, hurting anyone." He lowered his voice, "We need katagas serum to weaken him."

"Will that work?"

He shrugged. "I don't know. It's that or we don't go after him now but wait and get him to let his guard down."

"We can use me as bait. I'm what he's after."

Thane let out a low growl, the look in his eyes pure rage. "No, and it's not simply you or he would have taken you. As much as I hate to admit, he could have taken you two times, once in the tower and now in the throne room when he had you in his grip. But he didn't. I can't figure out why that is yet."

"I'll get the katagas serum while you try to find out what he wants. It's a game for him, and this is chess. He took out our pawns, but it's only just begun. We need to make a move."

"What did you mean to use you as bait?" he said slowly.

"I'll let him catch me alone and use the serum. You come in once he's vulnerable."

"Layala..." Thane shook his head.

"Remember I am Layala Lightbringer. I was always supposed to be the one to end him. Our mistake in that tower was not rendering his magic useless. I can do this."

"If you think I'll leave you to face him alone a second time, you don't know me at all. I should have been there in the tower." His brows shot up. "Piper, Leif," Thane said, in surprise, quieting Layala.

Piper looked back and forth between them suspiciously and then hooked her thumb over her shoulder. "I think I just saw," she shook her head. "No, never mind. It can't be. Are you two done having a word? Isn't the Lord of Calladira supposed to be here at any time?"

"Shit," Thane peeked back down the hallway. "Leif, grab Fennan and get the mess cleaned up in the throne room. You'll see it when you get there. Then stall the woodland elves. Piper, you go with Layala."

"I'm on it, but where are you going?" Leif said. "What am I supposed to tell Fennan?"

"I have a problem to take care of." Thane didn't stick around to explain and took off.

Layala silently counted *one, two, three...seven...ten.* Then she grabbed Piper's arm and dragged her along beside her.

"Thanks for just leaving me to clean up a mess alone," Leif called.

"What is happening?" Piper whispered.

Layala only pressed her finger to her lips. They needed to stay far enough back he wouldn't see or hear them following. But to let him face the Black Mage alone wasn't happening.

She'd grab the katagas serum after she found out what he wanted.

Peeking around the corner, she watched Thane disappear down a hall, and then another, and down a set of stairs. Over the last few months, she'd become quite familiar with this part of the castle. It was quiet, with paintings of old elven scholars lining the walls and tapestries of breathtaking landscapes. Often quills scratching over parchment and the flipping of pages were heard. The sign above the double entry doors read: "Knowledge is Power".

She didn't even want to know how Thane knew this was where the Black Mage would go. Maybe the library was somewhere they used to meet before.

They paused outside the double doors. "The library?" Piper hissed.

"Do not make a sound," Layala mouthed silently.

The librarian's desk sat empty with stacks of papers, books, and an open bottle of ink with a quill left in it. Thane must have sent her away. Poised in the double door entry, Layala listened for voices, footsteps, anything to figure out which way they went. The two of them swiftly and silently made their way down the rows of bone-white shelves under the cover of books. Until Layala heard voices and paused, holding up her hand to Piper. Peering between the cracks in the shelves the Black Mage sat at a round table and Thane's back was to them.

"Holy Maker," Piper breathed.

The intruder sat with his boots propped up on the table, crossed at the ankles and a lit cigarette between his lips. A black cloak lay across the wood surface leaving him in a raven-colored tunic with crimson whorls down the chest and the sleeves rolled up to his elbows. He took the cigarette between his fingers and blew out a cloud of sweet smoke. Something about the smell was familiar. It wasn't a typical cigarette or pipe tobacco with a harsh scent... *a civar,* she thought, though she didn't know how she knew that.

"Why are you here, Hel?" Thane asked.

The Black Mage smiled and flicked the ashes off the end of the smoke. "I mean, we were practically brothers and you're the proper age to remember. You should know why I'm here."

Layala's brows tugged down in confusion. *Practically brothers? There is a lot Thane hasn't told me.*

"You want Layala." Thane shook his head and ran his hand over his hair. "I think that ship sailed when she took me to her bed, over and over."

Hel chuckled and took another pull of smoke and said on his exhale, "You always had a mouth in you for great banter. You can have her for now, but I think we both know it won't be for long." He smiled in a taunting sort of way. "And as I said earlier, Valeen has something I need."

A warmth washed over Layala as the tang of Thane's magic sprang. "You're not going to use her."

Hel's eyebrow ticked up and he brought his civar to his lips. The wisps of smoke lifted in a stream that formed a hand holding up the middle finger before it slowly dissipated.

"Don't bother trying to attack me again. You'll only embarrass yourself. Or do. I enjoyed seeing the look of utter shock on your face. You're not the biggest and strongest in Adalon anymore and you're certainly not what you once were. It's a pity really."

Thane's anger rumbled through the room. Books all over the library fell to the ground with thuds, lit candles wobbled back and forth. Several books in front of Layala toppled, leaving her way too exposed. The Black Mage's garnet eyes swept directly to where she was. Heart caught in her throat, she

74

dropped into a crouch. *Shit, shit, did he see me?* From her crouch, she peered through the crack of books, but couldn't see his face from there. Thane stood in the way.

"You know, I keep asking myself why you two were reborn so much later than I was. Why it's so much different this time?"

This time? And he was so unbothered by Thane's power as if it were nothing but a passing breeze... Thane's boots shifted. "You know I can't allow you to stay here."

"You don't have a choice."

"This is *my* home. I think yours is a little further south. The black shit hole you created."

"It's not very brotherly of you to kick me out. I don't feel like I'm wanted."

"You're not."

Hel let out a dark chuckle. "It's amazing what one pair of tits can do to break a friendship bond like ours. I mean to think of how many times I had your back and you betrayed me over and over. Nonetheless, I'm not leaving until I get what I want. If you play nice, I'll play nice. I won't even expose you for allowing *the Black Mage* into your castle if you keep it under wraps. I'll just be a guest of the king. Your far more attractive and charming cousin."

"Hel, you're an asshole. You know the ladies always preferred my charm over yours."

"Except for one."

Thane let out a low growl. He was growing impatient, but far more patient than Layala would be. But he was trying to get answers, and Thane was tactical. "I'm assuming you want to be an immortal again."

He flicked his civar into the air and it vanished into nothing. "And they say you're the smart one."

"Not sure how we can help you there. Not a magic immortal potion in sight."

"That's for me to know and you to figure out," Hel said. "Do you remember how we were exiled?"

"No. And what does Layala have to do with this?"

"Layala doesn't. *Valeen* does. Does she know anything? She looked clueless to me."

"She remembers nothing."

"Interesting, well it looks like I'll be here awhile."

Her cheeks warmed and sweat dampened the back of her top. He was going to stay until she remembered her entire past? A past she wanted nothing to do with. Nausea churned in her gut, and she rocked back on her heels. Chair legs scraped against the stone floor, and he stood up. *Damn it.* Layala lightly pushed Piper toward the exit. Staying low, they quietly moved down the aisle toward the exit.

"I think you have company to deal with," the Black Mage said. "If my senses are correct, and they always are, your guests from Calladira have just arrived. Better go do your kingly duties. I'll wait here for you, catch up on a bit of light reading, smoke a few civars. I'll be a good boy all by myself, promise."

Layala and Piper dashed out of the library before either of them could find them eavesdropping.

When they got far enough away, Piper shoved Layala into a broom closet leaving the door cracked for light. "What the hell is going on? Holy Maker above, that was... *him*. And Thane was just talking to him? I'm beyond confused."

"Piper, we need katagas serum. I'll explain on the way."

LAYALA PATTED the leather pouch hooked on her weapons belt and felt the three barbs laced with katagas serum bounce around in there. There was a small stash in the storeroom left over from when Tenebris had his lackey use the serum on her every day for a month during her captivity.

"Thane said he'll be out here in a few minutes," Layala said more to herself than Piper. With her thumb, she rubbed the smooth steel on the hilt of her sword. Both of them were nervous to be out here with their arch nemesis on castle grounds.

"I heard, and he is going to drop a hint about where you are with the Black Mage in earshot," she said, reiterating the plan, and glanced over her shoulder. "It's too bad he has to tell Calladira the meeting is canceled."

"I know." Layala wanted to insist he take the meeting, but she knew he wouldn't now. Negotiations could be hours. He'd have to wine and dine them as was proper. "He's worked for months to arrange these meetings too. It's horrible timing."

Their boots tapped lightly over the cobblestone path leading to the stone circle where the scheduled training was to take place. The old elf Vesstan stared into a pond with green lily pads, toads croaking, and colorful fish swimming beneath the cool clear water. Forest green robes with off-white trim made the old mage look like part of the woods. His long white beard reached the top of his thighs and the staff in his hand matched its color. His shoulders were slightly hunched and the wrinkles and age spots on his skin were such a contrast to his elven ears.

Piper took a seat on the stone bench near the water with a good view of the castle and path. While Layala took up the spot next to Mage Vesstan. "I hope I'm not late."

With his eyes closed, he stayed silent.

After ten minutes of standing quietly with the old mage,

she looked at Piper for answers. Her friend shrugged and went back to keeping a watchful eye.

He hadn't so much as acknowledged her presence. The sun warmed her skin, but it wouldn't be long before it dipped behind the distant horizon. They had maybe an hour of daylight left, and they wasted it by standing here doing nothing. She could be inside planning while Thane dealt with the woodland elves, rather than wasting time.

"Should we get started?" she finally asked, glancing back at the castle. Vesstan made no acknowledgment but stood as still as the statue of an ancient elf queen at the center of the pond.

I guess not. Layala folded her hands in front of herself, then separated them and gripped the daggers on her hips. She tapped her foot and inspected the stone pillars forming a perfect circle off to the right of the pond. Elvish scrawl was etched into each one, symbols of elements. Fire, water, flora, lightning, wind, a crescent moon, a sun. They stood at the base of the rocky cliff on the far side of the castle grounds where nature ruled more than elf. No voices from guards or the neighing of horses existed in this part. It was quiet, almost eerily so.

"You typically conjure your magic out of rage or fear."

Layala startled and turned to face Vesstan. He leaned heavily on his white oak staff and stared into the water. Layala lightly bit down on her lower lip, wondering where he was going with this? Did it matter how her magic was conjured? "I only need it if I'm in danger."

"That is not true."

"It's destructive in nature. I can't use it for anything else."

"That is also not true."

She forced herself not to roll her eyes. As if he knew more

about her magic than she did? He'd never even seen her use it. "Enlighten me then."

"Yes, enlightenment is needed." He paused and closed his eyes. "What do you see? What do you hear?"

Layala dragged a hand over the back of her neck. "Um, water, trees, stone pillars—"

"Look in the water. What do you see?"

Clearing her throat, Layala leaned forward. A toad leapt from a lily pad and created tiny rippling waves. Once the water became placid, her reflection formed. "I see me."

"And who are you?"

"I'm Layala—"

"That is your name. Who *are* you?"

She stared at herself for a long time. She was reckless and full of anger and uncertainty. Powerful when she must be, but that confidence wavered, and at times was overshadowed by insecurity and harsh words. She touched her cheek. She didn't want the petty harassing notes, no doubt from Talon and her friends, to get to her but they were like tiny paper cuts, small, but they still stung. And she couldn't do anything about it because she promised Thane she'd never hurt or threaten Talon again.

Worse were those accusing her of being the reason their loved ones were gone forever.

"What do you hear?" he asked, interrupting her thoughts.

Layala stilled her breath and listened to nature around them for a moment. "I hear birds singing, ribbits from toads, the wind in the treetops. Your heartbeat and mine."

He touched her temple. "What do you hear in here?"

Tears suddenly burned her eyes and a wave of anger and sadness washed over her. She hadn't cried in months, but all the pent-up rage hit her. "I hear—" she didn't even want to voice her insecurities but as the frustrated tears slipped down her cheeks, she said, "Thane does not want me anymore. I never fit in anywhere I go. Everyone hates me because I woke the Black Mage." She swiped the angry tears spilling down her cheeks. "I was supposed to be their savior." She lifted her chin and blinked the last of her tears away. "But I am no savior at all."

She was the elf who could stop dragons and bring them to their knees, but she was also the elf who shattered the day she failed all of Adalon.

Vesstan placed a gentle, warm hand on her shoulder. "When I was your age, I thought I knew everything there was to know about magic. I was arrogant and foolish. I'd studied it since I was a child under the tutelage of Atarah, and she was a wonderful mentor. Until the day she took me onto a battlefield. The pale ones charged, slamming into our ranks, screeching and hollering, you know the sound. Weapons clashed, there was much blood, and the smell..." he brought his veiny, wrinkled hand to his nose and mouth as if the scent infiltrated him now. "I froze. Fear paralyzed me. See, Atarah taught me to find serenity, to feel nature and its calm and bring forth my power. At that moment I couldn't find it. I watched as a soldier twenty feet from me was torn into and murdered. I could have stopped it. I had the power, but I failed. I could have saved him. I could have been his savior, but I wasn't, and I cried too. But I learned from that failure. I learned I never wanted to feel that way again."

Layala nodded but he couldn't feel the enormous pressure she did.

"You have a fighting spirit, Layala, and you won't let this break you. Everyone fails, it's whether or not we get back up and fight again that matters more." He stroked his long white beard. "Thane told me you've been restless, jumpy, and paranoid."

Layala balked. "If he was in my situation he would be too."

"It's not a slight but we must forge peace and calm into you. You've never trained with your magic, and a restless soul and racing mind is detrimental to a warrior mage. You need a control that only someone with confidence in herself can have. A sense of knowing who you truly are."

"But what if I don't know who I am?"

He smiled, further wrinkling the skin around his eyes. "You will."

Thane must have told him about his suspicions of her being a goddess reborn. That's what he wanted to bring out. It was true she never trained her magic before. Only with weapons. Her power was reckless, and even if she was as stubborn as a mule as Thane so delicately put it, she knew on this she was a novice.

He hobbled over to a gray stone bench on the outside of the circle and sat beside Piper, resting the staff across his thighs. "Welcome."

His movements were stronger than the last time she'd seen him. As if he found a new source of energy.

"Now I want you to stand at the center, close your eyes, and find stillness."

With a sigh, Layala moved to where a smaller circle was carved into the stone and closed her eyes. All her fears and worries seemed to come crashing in. She worried about her upcoming confrontation with the Black Mage. She fought him once and failed. What if it happened a second time?

"I'm sensing anxiousness," Vesstan said in a soothing voice. "I can feel your energy."

Was that part of his magical power? "I don't know how to stop it."

"Clear your mind."

Because that's so easy? How do I stop my thoughts?

"You are in control of your mind; it doesn't control you. Silence it."

Layala forced herself to think of a black wall, of nothing, an eternal emptiness where nothing existed and that lasted for about three seconds before she began to worry if Vesstan could still feel her bad energy and she opened one eye.

"Layala," he murmured. "I want you to feel each of these statements as I say them and repeat them aloud but keep your eyes closed. Take a deep breath before each statement... I am powerful."

"I am powerful." *This is stupid,* she thought.

"I am worthy."

"I am worthy."

"I am light in a world of darkness."

"I am light in a world of darkness." That struck her core. She sat with those words, repeating them silently in her mind. *I am light in a world of darkness.* Could she be that? Her parents believed so. They named her *Lightbringer.* For a moment she felt hope. They had hope when they gave her that name.

Then a rogue thought came, *How can the goddess of night be a Lightbringer?* She furrowed her brows. *But maybe I am both.*

The sun disappeared from the sky, bringing about the cool evening air, and the crickets chirped in the tall grass before she opened her eyes again. Her tears were dry and sticky on her face and the deep breaths filling her lungs calmed her nerves. For a while she'd forgotten about her strained uncertain relationship with Thane, all the notes, and the *Palenor Scroll.*

Vesstan sat completely straight, shoulders pushed back,

and without opening his eyes he said, "You can go inside now. Come back at the same time tomorrow."

She was far from feeling at peace but there was hope. "May I walk you in?"

"I'll stay here a while longer. It's been years since I sat out under the stars at Castle Dredwich."

She glanced at the castle and a feeling of dread filled her gut. Far more than a few minutes had gone by since she and Piper saw Thane in the throne room. Why wasn't he here yet?

CHAPTER 7

THANE

Thane left Hel in the library smoking a civar. The sweet smell of it still lingered on his clothes and in his hair. Seeing him take Layala by the throat, press her into the wall, it made him lose it. He'd wanted to keep his cool, to be able to outwit Hel, but the bastard knew exactly what buttons to push. A bloody "stand-in" for his prick of a cousin huh? Oh, he was much more than that.

He paced back and forth, boots tapping lightly, anxiousness burning through him worrying about Layala and Piper headed out to train with Vesstan. Even armed with katagas serum, it felt like when she went into the Void alone. And this was the hard part, the part he almost didn't agree to.

He had to wait.

Leaving her alone even for a few minutes set his nerves on fire but he had to trust her. Thane had to give Hel a few minutes to do exactly what he knew he would do, follow Layala. He couldn't spot Thane there waiting. He had to catch her appearing vulnerable and then if she could get him with the serum, Thane would be ready. Layala's magic would hold him long enough to tie him up, and they would hold him in a prison cell in the dungeons.

How long would it take to break Hel and convince him to end the pale one curse? He needed to question him on why he did it in the first place, and the problem he mentioned. Something was coming... or someone.

Layala wanted him dead, but Thane couldn't do it. Even knowing every evil, horrible thing he was, knowing he wanted to take Layala, he couldn't imagine killing him. Once Layala remembered being Valeen, she wouldn't either.

The double doors flung open causing him to pause his pacing, and Leif and Fennan strutted in like a pair on a mission. "Tell me why we just cleaned up two dead bodies." Fennan said, in a fresh crisp dark blue tunic and clean black pants. He brushed a stray, short curl off his forehead.

Leif didn't bother changing and still had spots of blood on his clothes. Typical. "Who killed the guards? I knew one of them. He grew up next door to my nana's. And where are the Calladirans? We hurried to hide the bodies because they were supposed to be here early this afternoon."

"They could have been attacked on the road," Fennan added. "I'll send scouts to search for the party."

Hell, here we go. Thane lifted his chin and rested his hands on his hips. "He finally came, and he killed the guards."

Fennan looked appalled and at a loss for words. Leif was horrified. The fear in his features was palpable in the dying sunlight, filling the throne room. "The Black Mage. Here. N-now?" Leif stuttered. Ravens rarely showed fear, even in the face of demons like pale ones.

"Where is he?" Fennan went for his sword and jerked it

free. "Should I sound the alarm? We must evacuate your family and the servants at once."

"There's no need for all that," crooned Hel's mischievous, deep voice.

Thane whirled around and found him leaned up against the wall with a civar poised between his fingers. The sweet smoke curled around him like a caress. There was no way he'd been there long. He pushed off the wall and sauntered toward them, taking a puff of smoke. "You two certainly have your feathers all ruffled."

Fennan half stepped in front of Thane; Leif pulled a dagger from his hip and his sword from his back.

"Settle down, girls, I'm not going to hurt your king."

"Thane," Fennan prompted, tensing for an attack. They'd both be dead before they ever got close enough to strike.

"Stand down." Thane stepped around Fennan and put himself between his friends and Hel. Even if he knew Hel hated him for "stealing his wife", he wasn't here for revenge on him, or things would have gone much differently upon his arrival. He would, however, kill anyone Thane cared for without hesitation.

"It's rude not to introduce a guest, *High King*. I'm Hel, or better known around these parts as the Black Mage. War's cousin, *former* best friend." He stopped a few feet away and flicked his gaze over Fennan. "I suppose that's you now." He smirked at Leif. "And the reckless ginger." He took a deep inhale. "The quality of your company has certainly gone downhill, War."

"The quality of their hearts is better than yours in every way."

"I've heard about the Ravens. You're the best warriors Palenor has to offer. Want to put that to the test?"

"Not a chance," Thane said. "If you're going to fight anyone, it's me."

"I've put our past behind me for now, greater ambitions you see, so I won't snap your neck and pull out your heart for good measure, though it's what you deserve, *cousin*."

"Don't threaten my king," Fennan barked.

Thane threw up his fist, to silence him. "What is it going to take for you to remove the pale one curse, and go back to Runevale? You must back off the attacks on my people. Whatever friendship you and I once had is long past. We can negotiate what it is you need from Layala for something else."

He smirked and looked at Thane like he was a naive puppy. "You're thinking small, War. When's dinner? I'm starving."

Maker above, he was infuriating. "I have things to do. I don't have the patience for your games, certainly not dinner, and I don't have time to babysit you either. Your creatures need to stop, and you need to face the fact that Layala is with me now. Do you want gold? Silver? A magical relic?"

Hel let out a chuckle full of shadows and threats. "Even after it all, I did sort of miss this. But you're talking to me like that friendship is still intact." An invisible force suddenly clamped around Thane's throat, making it impossible to breathe. He stiffened, forcing his hands to stay at his sides, though he wanted to reach for his neck. His magic tingled and fought back but it was like pushing against a brick wall. "Like I won't destroy you and take pleasure in seeing you fall. I could take her away from you in a heartbeat, take your throne for mine, and leave you shattered with nothing. And I might do just that if you piss me off enough." He shoved the burning end of his civar into Thane's cheek. The smell of his cooking flesh overpowered the sweet smoke. "You were correct. We're not friends. I am not one of your subjects, and most definitely not your brother anymore. Don't make the mistake of speaking to me like I am any one of those again. Trust me when I say I can't be bought." He tossed the butt of the civar to the floor.

Thane couldn't focus on the burn when his body fought for air, but he didn't move, did not beg for mercy, or reach out. He pursed his lips, knowing Hel was correct about it all, but even if he couldn't breathe his fist cracked Hel in the jaw. His head snapped to the side, and he turned back with a growl.

"Do that again, I dare you." Hel shoved him in the chest and released his magic.

Thane sucked in air and fought against the urge to pull his weapons, to release his magic that fought to break free and tear apart this room, this castle, to prove who was the dominant male. It wouldn't end well, and his loyal friends would go down with him.

Fennan was furious, but smart enough to not move, and Leif's knuckles were white from gripping his weapons. "Sire," Leif's voice came out as almost a plea. He wanted the command to attack even if he was terrified.

"Tell them I'll be staying, and I better not find any guards following me around or they'll end up like the other two." He rammed his shoulder into Thane's and marched for the exit. When he reached it, he stopped and shoved his hands into his pockets. "Don't you find it strange your woodland elf friends haven't arrived yet?"

Then he was gone.

"Sire, what's the plan?" Leif was ready to charge after him.

Fennan sheathed his weapon. "Where are Layala and Piper?"

"Training with Vesstan." Thane marched for the double doors.

"You left them alone knowing he's here?"

"We have a plan. Let's move." Thane suddenly ran smack into what felt like a wall. "What in Maker's name..." He stood just inside the archway unable to pass. He placed his palm against an invisible force, and it slowly dawned on him. "Hel! There are no woodland elves coming, are there?" His fist crashed into the magical barrier. "HEL!"

His dark chuckle traveled down the corridor, echoing around him like a taunt.

LAYALA

LAYALA AND PIPER slowly traipsed over the cobblestone path back to the castle. She'd expected the Black Mage to come looking for her already and for Thane to be here.

"The lesson went well," Piper said conversationally. "Vesstan's methods are a little different but finding calm within is something you've needed for a long time."

"Thanks," Layala drawled.

Piper peeked over her shoulder. "But I feel like the Black Mage is going to pop up at any moment and yell, 'boo!'"

"When he does, we'll be ready."

"Maybe we shouldn't have left Vesstan out here alone."

"He's better off away from the castle and away from you-know-who."

"True."

"So, what's going on with you and Fennan? You haven't talked about him much on our nightly runs."

"It's... not going."

The bushy trees lining the path cast long shadows from the milky light of the moon. Layala's elf eyes saw well in the night but even she couldn't see what lurked in the edges of darkness. She suddenly wished she could conjure a light orb or fire, something to brighten the area to give her comfort. She glanced back and watched Vesstan grow smaller the further she moved away. Turning around the bend made him, and the stone circle disappear entirely but she still didn't feel like she and Piper were alone. Every sound seemed to grow louder. A rustle in the trees made the skin along her spine prickle. She slid one of her daggers from the holster on her hips, and her breath grew shallower.

"Why not? Are you still writing letters with Prince Ronan then?"

"Yes. He says he'll come visit soon, but the dragons are paranoid with the Black Mage back and the pale ones even more uncontrolled than before."

"I understand why you're upset with Fennan, but he does love you. And your parents would be thrilled with a match like him. He's captain of the Ravens."

"My mother is all about status as you know but it took another male going after me for him to recognize that. So, I don't think he truly does love me. It feels more like he doesn't want anyone else to have me."

Layala couldn't argue with her there even if she wanted to make excuses for Fennan because they were friends too.

Wings flapped and a brown owl burst from the tree to her right with a "hoo!" Layala's heart lurched, and she threw up her arms to shield her head as it swooped toward her then veered off. "Damn bird," she muttered, shaking her head as it flew into the night sky. "I don't know how Tif likes them so much. They're creepy."

Piper burst out laughing. "I thought you were going to jump out of your boots."

"Shut up. It scared you, too."

They were quiet for a moment. "Laya, I want you to know not everyone hates you. Thane, Evalyn, and your friends are here for you. Don't let the outside world get to your head."

The pathway forked ahead, and they stopped at its center. A torch cast orange-yellow light over the area, and it made the gnawing in her stomach settle some.

"As riveting as it was to watch you cry with the old mage, love, I'll be taking the lead on your training from here on."

Layala's heart crashed wildly in her chest, and she slowly looked over her shoulder. Piper jerked out her sword and stupidly half stepped in front of Layala.

The shadowy figure of the Black Mage stood in the center of the pathway just out of the light of the torch. Her eyes darted down the walkway to the left, it was at least three hundred yards to the castle and if she started running, she'd only feed into his predator-prey mentality. Because of one thing she was absolutely certain, he saw her as prey.

Swallowing down the nervous lump in her throat, she slowly turned and brought her hand up to the bag of katagas laced barbs in the leather pouch.

"You want to train *me*?"

How had neither she, Piper, or Vesstan noticed he was watching them from somewhere close by?

Her cheeks suddenly burned with shame. Maker, he'd seen her crying, knew how broken she was inside, even though she tried to hide it from everyone, and that was fuel for him.

He stepped into the orange firelight, and her heart beat even faster. Everything about him was power, from his prowl, to the curve of his strong jaw, the fierceness in his garnet eyes. His magic slithered out of him, whispering against her skin, making her want to run—and draw closer at once.

"Who better than the god of magic to teach you about magic? And start calling me Hel. If you call me the Black Mage one more time, I might seal both of your mouths shut." He gave Piper a once over. "The dragon prince is the obvious choice."

"Why do you want to train me?" she asked, getting his attention back on her. She didn't want him assessing Piper as a threat and doing something about it.

His tongue dragged over his lower lip, and he smirked. "It's complicated."

"I'm intelligent enough to keep up."

"I need Valeen. You're only a shell of her. You're weak and clueless, and that makes you a detriment to yourself and me."

Layala slowly tugged on the pouch strings, loosening the opening to the one thing that could weaken him. "In other words, you can't have someone kill me before you get what you want?"

"Precisely. Which leads me to my next question; why haven't you found the writer slandering you in the newspaper and snapped his neck yet? The writer for the *Palenor Scroll* is putting unnecessary targets on your back. Stirring up the hive."

"Excuse me?"

He took a step closer. "Why haven't you put that little bitch princess in her place? Are you going to sit back and allow *Thane* to do everything for you?"

Layala stepped away, wide-eyed. How could he know about Talon? Did he find the notes in her room?

"I heard about your adventure to the dragon court months back. They even built a statue of you. Well, a new one anyway." He looked her up and down. "It appears to be undeserved."

"You don't know the first thing about me," she snapped. "And killing someone because they write lies in a gossip paper is lunacy. I don't care what anyone says about me."

"You don't?" He chuckled. "After the waterworks back there," he hooked his thumb down the path behind him, "you certainly had me convinced you do. What I don't understand is why. The Valeen I know would never—"

"I'm not Valeen anymore. Get that through your head."

"I can see that. War said you can't remember anything. Is that true?"

Layala inspected his face, the thin white scar across his chin, the other line through the outer corner of his thick dark right brow, the near-black hair that brushed against his collar, curled slightly on his forehead and was long enough to just cover the pointed tips of his ears. It had grown since the tower.

He didn't wear braids or typical elven-styled hair. In fact, other than his inherent beauty he didn't look much like an elf at all. Black rune marks of various sizes peeked out from under the collar of his neck, the tops of his hands and even one longer swirling tattoo marked the length of his left ring finger. But no, there was nothing familiar about him, nothing to remember.

"Yes, that's true."

He rolled his eyes, and Layala scowled at him.

"Come then." He turned and started back toward the stone circle. "We have work to do."

Layala lifted her chin slightly and stood firm. "I'm not training with you." The very idea of it was absurd, but then again, this would give her a chance to get him with the serum. Piper jerked her head toward the training grounds as if she had the same idea.

"If you don't have that ass moving down the pathway in three seconds, I'll kill the old mage. Maybe I'll drown him in the pond you both stared so lovingly at, and you can watch as the last of the bubbles come up. Then the redhead is next."

"You can't do that!"

"Can't or won't? I assure you, I'm capable of both."

Seething, Layala stomped past him. She slipped her hand into the pouch and pulled out a barb, keeping it on the side opposite of him. Why would he train her so that she could become powerful enough to take him down even if it was so she could protect herself? It made absolutely no sense at all.

He knew she wanted him dead. But then it struck her like a slap to the face: on the chance they were truly mates, did that mean if he died... she died along with him? Her eyes snapped to his face and a wave of horror passed over her.

That couldn't be true. He was already dead once—although not technically *dead* she supposed, and wouldn't their bond have to be solidified in marriage? Ugh but he already called her wife. How did this make sense? And she'd slept with Thane, and he didn't die... then again as the gossip article said, it wasn't the same type of mate bond as the one she and Thane once shared.

Without another word passing between any of them, they made their way down the path to the stone circle. Piper trailed behind several feet; at least she stayed out of his vision.

Layala was aware of his every step, the two-foot distance between them, close enough she could whirl and jab the barb into him, but she needed the advantage of surprise first. She'd have to stick him, render his magic useless and then be able to deal a second strike. It would have to be the perfect opening.

Vesstan stood with both hands gripping his staff, facing them with tension etched over his wrinkled face. "Layala," he said in quiet worry, eyes flicking back and forth between them.

"I've never seen an elf suffer aging like this." Hel's dark gaze trailed over Vesstan.

"I used too many spells out of your book." He sounded tired

94

and weary as if the weight of those spells came crashing down on him.

Hel tsked and wagged a finger at him. "What you mean to say is you used too many spells that were beyond your natural capability to conjure. There is nothing about my spells that would cause you to grow weak and age if you have enough magic to use them. My magic isn't inherently evil or good. It's neutral. It's the user or the purpose of it that makes it one or the other."

Layala scoffed. "Except the pale one curse."

He turned his sharp glare on her, and the red in his eyes seemed to grow brighter. "It's the law of nature that there is a price and consequences for every action, good or bad. Even I am bound to those laws. If you want to blame anyone, blame yourselves or the All Mother who requires balance in all things." He waved a hand at Vesstan and sent him stumbling back onto the bench. "Sit. Take notes from the master."

When he turned back on Layala, a nervous sweat warmed her back. An invisible force moved her to the center of the stone circle and with his hands folded behind his back, he slowly circled her. "From what I hear, the power first to reveal itself was your vines. But as a full goddess formed by the All Mother, not a demi or a lesser god," he gave her a knowing look, "you are capable of much more. And the old mage was correct about one thing, you need to be able to conjure your power at will, with barely even a thought. You don't need to feel fear or anger or any emotion to use it. In fact, it's a hindrance. To be the best, you need assurance in your abilities, not fear."

There were diverse levels of gods in Runevale? "I don't need a lecture."

Suddenly a heavy weight pressed in on every inch of her flesh, an invisible force that crushed like an ocean squeezing in around her. It was only seconds before she had trouble dragging air into her lungs, and her ears began to ring. Every sound to her acute elven ears became muffled like she was underwater. She wanted to scream, to be able to move her body. This wasn't like the time in the tower when she simply couldn't move; right now, she felt like she was drowning. *I'm going to die. He's going to kill me!* Her magic roared in her chest, fighting to push through, but she was caged.

"If you weren't panicking, you could break free," he said as he continued to walk around her. "The key to break out of this is you being unafraid, calm. Relax."

Her shirt dampened with sweat, and black spots erupted across her vision. *Let me out, let me out!* But she couldn't find her voice.

Steady your heart, release your panic, his voice whispered in her mind.

But she couldn't. Inside she was screaming, clawing at the invisible force that trapped her, but she didn't move, and no sound came out.

"Control your breathing before you pass out," he snarled.

"*Layala.*" Piper sounded scared.

"Stay out of it, Red."

Her chest heaved as she wheezed. *Serenity, serenity,* she chanted taking in slow controlled breaths. She pictured a quiet field of wild colorful poppies in full bloom and imagined sitting among them with Thane, the sun shining on his beautiful face.

Or you could simply ask me to let you go, his voice came into her mind again, a mocking tone that made her anger flare. *Say, please Hel, I'm weak and I need you. Please Hel, the most wise and powerful god, I beg for your leniency.*

"Piss off," she wheezed and held her image of peace and the magic began to lift. Her heart slowed; the chains loosened.

Calming down worked and she was free. Fast as a cobra, she lunged and shoved the katagas barb into the first exposed skin she spotted, the top of his hand. The tip broke through. She almost couldn't believe it, and staggered back several steps, expecting quick retaliation.

His red eyes flicked down, and his brows furrowed. He pulled the black barb loose and inspected it. "Katagas serum."

Now! Layala regained her wits and a vine shot from her palm, the tip of it a spear aimed to wrap and coil around him. His hand came up and her vine hit an invisible wall and was forced upward and then melted to ash that blew away on the breeze.

Gulping, she took several more steps away. It didn't work. His magic should be unusable...

"Oh naive, Layala." He prowled toward her. "I took katagas serum every day for years until there was no effect on me anymore. I'm immune to it. There is nothing in this world that can render my magic useless." He stopped before her, reached up to touch her face and she noticed his hand trembling. And if she wasn't mistaken his skin was paler too. Although those weren't symptoms of katagas. Something was off. Hel's eyes flicked to his shaky hand and quickly tucked his hands behind his back.

Out of the corner of her eye, she saw Piper run and disappear into the dark. Thane. She was going to get Thane... but he should have already been here by now.

"Give me a detail about the past. One simple thing will do. I know you're hiding something."

"There's nothing to tell." If she couldn't beat him in a fight yet, she'd torture him with her *naiveness*.

"You shouldn't lie, Val, you hate liars and hypocrites."

"I may not remember anything about you but," her gaze

purposefully traveled slowly down and back up his form, "you've certainly got mother issues. I can just tell. And if even your mother didn't love you, well, who else could? You think the entire world is against you and you want to punish innocent people for your own shortcomings. You lack empathy, morals, and lean much too heavily on magic and it will be your downfall. Oh, and I'm guessing even though you have large feet it doesn't correlate to another area of your body."

His jaw muscles feathered, and his steely gaze narrowed. "I'm going to have a wonderful time torturing you in your training."

"I'll be ready for it." Her voice didn't come out as strong as she wished. Thane was right, if he wanted to truly hurt her, kill her, he'd have done it already. The best form of torture of her own was not giving him what he wanted, not remembering him.

"I can hear the quickening of your heart, like a little rabbit. You might talk boldly but you're a scared little girl deep down. Scared not just of me but scared that when you remember you will care for me." He twirled his finger and a black shadow like a serpent weaved its way around her torso and brushed against her neck, creating a cascade of chills down her body. "You're terrified that somewhere inside of you the people are right, and you have a darkness in your heart that you'd love to give into, and I'll bring it out."

"I could never care for someone like you." But sweat beaded on her brow and her heart raced at the thought.

"We'll see. Go to sleep, little rabbit, and dream of me." He snapped his fingers, and a deep chuckle was the last thing she heard before blackness enveloped her world.

CHAPTER 8

HEL

Hel flicked his wrist and a civar rolled in ashen white paper appeared in between his thumb and forefinger. The tremor in his hands had gotten worse since the confrontation in the throne room earlier. Though he'd never admit it, it took a considerable amount of magic to hold War. His body was slowly weakening over time, and he didn't know why. He knew it had something to do with the magic that put him in the long sleep and the spell to wake him. He had a gut feeling what the remedy would be.

Placing the civar between his lips, he inhaled and then looked down at Valeen, collapsed in the center of the summoning circle. It was strange to see her vulnerable and fragile, like a dried flower that could crumble into pieces at his touch. Once, she was a worthy opponent, worthy of being his queen, and then his greatest adversary. Now?

Hel faced the old mage. "Why is she so inexperienced?"

"She was taken away from us as an infant—"

"I know that," Hel said and pulled the civar from his mouth. Varlett and Mathekis filled him in on the details of the last four hundred years as well as this version of Valeen's life history as she knew it. Living amongst humans, training to kill War and his elven father. That part made him smile. Varlett didn't explicitly say she knew where Valeen had been while Mathekis searched for her, but he suspected. Varlett had reason to want her to be a lost little lamb, to be weak. "I mean why wouldn't she have used her magic on her own? It's natural to gravitate toward magic, not resist it."

The old mage blinked his round, sagging eyes several times before he said, "The use of her magic attracts the pale ones. She didn't like it."

He smirked and cocked his head slightly to the left. "A simple shielding rune would have stopped that."

"No one uses your rune magic anymore. It's not worth the risk."

He stepped over Valeen and sauntered closer to the mage to get a good look at him. Was he so brave he would lie right to Hel's face? No, that wasn't it. "Except mate runes, right?" He lifted a brow.

The old mage shifted slightly, gripping his staff tighter and his soft brown eyes darted to Valeen for a moment. "I did that under orders from my king. It's not something I would have chosen for either of them."

"You're lucky Varlett broke that spell before I woke, or I'd tear out your heart for spite." He ground his teeth thinking of her being mate bonded to War using his own spell, something they didn't even do before. They knew better. "On second thought..."

The old mage's eyes broadened but he lifted his chin and

stood slightly taller. He didn't shrink away at his impending death. Interesting. He wasn't afraid to die. He expected at least some begging and pleading. Maybe he could be more useful than Hel thought. A gentler hand for this weaker version of Valeen. "Be here tomorrow at the same time."

He turned on his heel and scooped Valeen into his arms, cradling her against his chest. At a casual pace, he moved down the path toward the castle. He kept his line of sight up, purposefully avoiding looking at Valeen. Every time he did, it brought up memories he didn't want to reminisce on. Made him *feel* things. She was the only one who ever made him feel warmth in his icy heart.

Up the steps of the castle he went, until he stood before the double doors. With a pause he glanced up at the silver moon. He listened to her steady breathing, to the quiet *thud thud thud* of her heart. Lifting her a little higher in his arms, and against his better judgment, he tilted his chin down and inspected her face. Her soft lips barely parted, and the breeze picked up stray black hair blowing across her golden skin...

The Past

"There's been an assassination."

Hel tucked his hands behind his back and scowled at his uncle. "You called me all the way here to tell me that?"

Sneering, his uncle Balneir rose up from his massive white stone seat. War nudged Hel with his elbow and gave the slightest shake of his head. A warning that his father was not in the mood for Hel's back talk.

"You didn't ask who. Which leads me to believe you already know, and that makes me think you did it."

Hel unclasped his hands and narrowed his eyes. "I haven't killed anyone in at least six months, since the last time I joined War in Ryvengaard." He'd killed some spy who'd wandered into his territory three months ago but still, this one wasn't him. "And I don't know or care who died. Some worthless lesser god? One of your human servants? Pity."

Balneir flew down the steps and drove his fist into Hel's chest. The blow took his breath away and sent him soaring several feet until his back met a stone pillar. The sounds of it cracking all the way to the high ceiling echoed through the great hall.

"You watch your tone with me." It was a move out of character for his usually serene uncle, a god of peace with an affinity for animals—birds in particular.

Chest and back throbbing, Hel slowly dropped forward onto one knee and thought about staying down for a moment but with a few deep breaths, he rose. Only a single piece of his uncle's black hair was out of place, dangling on his forehead. War stared at Hel, silently asking him to keep his mouth shut. War always was better at following orders, and he truly respected his father. The god who took Hel in and raised him when he was otherwise left unwanted.

"Synick is dead."

Hel clenched his hands at his sides and stood silently in shock. His uncle—though not by blood but that's what they called him—a god, one of the original seven, immortal, and the head of the council. "That's not possible."

"I assure you it is. I've seen his body myself. He was stabbed through the heart with an immortal weapon."

War and Hel met eyes. It couldn't be... why would she kill Synick? There was no reason for Valeen to have any qualms with him other than she was Drivaar, and he was Primevar.

"There are only two weapons capable, and we have both."

"Soulender is safe, but the Sword of Truth went missing. Synick was the last to possess it."

So, he believed that Soulender was still in the vault. Hel's replica was better than he thought. "That's unfortunate."

His uncle began to pace, heavy boots echoed in the chamber with each step. "It must be one of the Drivaar, an act of war."

"What if it was personal? Someone with a grudge against him," *War asked.* "It's not as if he doesn't have enemies. We shouldn't go to battle with the Drivaar until we know. We will lose thousands."

"I need you two to find out. Every god and goddess came to the party a fortnight ago." *He stopped and turned to face both of them. A spark of light lit within his blue-green eyes.* "Even the goddess of night. No one from her house has attended our parties for over a thousand years. And she left before I could speak to her. Go there and find out everything you can about why she came to our party. Tread carefully. From what I hear she's dangerous."

"None of the Primevar are allowed there," *War said, rubbing his smooth chin.* "She doesn't allow anyone from other houses in her territory."

"I'm well aware," *Balneir stated.* "Do what you must. One of the primordials is dead and we want to know why. And if the Sword of Truth is missing then the assassin may have it."

Hel and War hurried out of the great hall and down the back steps into the warm balmy air. Hel flicked his wrist and threw a silencing sphere around them. "Damn it all to the underrealm," *Hel cursed.*

War glared at him. "This is your fault. You gave it to her, and now the Sword of Truth is missing as well. If she has both weapons..."

"Fuck," *Hel cursed. Both weapons in the hands of the rival clan.* "You know, technically she stole Soulender from me."

Neither War nor Hel cared for Synick. He was a pompous ass who enslaved other races. They weren't paid for their work, often beaten and starved, and murdered. He believed every other race was below the gods and could be treated like animals—worse than animals. He treated his dogs better than those who worked in his territory. He was the god of elements, but Hel often called him the god of greed. And although Hel acknowledged the gods were superior, it made them beholden to be leaders, not to abuse the status they'd been given.

"We won't be able to teleport into the House of Night. There are wards there. Stronger than the ones Soulender had."

War chuckled. "You've tried before, haven't you?"

"My territory touches hers. Of course I have." He'd taken the land from one of the lesser gods four hundred years before. It now belonged to the House of Magic.

"So how are we going to get in?"

He smiled. "I've never tried simply walking across the border."

"That would be too easy," War said, and then they both vanished.

HEL TOUCHED *the veil that separated his land from Valeen's. It hummed with a current and was neither solid nor liquid. It reflected like a hazy mirror making it impossible to see inside. He watched his distorted reflection approach and with only a moment's hesitation, he pressed his hand against it, indenting the shield but not piercing through. Pulling his hand back made the magical ward bounce into place like a bubble.*

Gliding away, War dragged his hand along it, pressing here and there testing it for weaknesses. He pulled the ax from the holster on his back, taking it in both hands and turned to Hel with a sly smile.

"This should be good," Hel murmured.

War swung his ax and with blurred speed crushed the sharp edge into the ward. It sparked with the hit and sent him flying back fifty feet until he crashed into a large oak. The tree shuddered, drop-

ping leaves all around him, and new serrated leaves promptly grew in their place. Hel laughed and shook his head. "I could have told you that would happen."

War shook his head like a dog and strode back toward him, sliding his ax back into place. "My ax has broken through magical shields before."

"Imagine if the entire wall had come down. She'd think she was under attack and then where would we be?"

War rolled his eyes. "Well, you're the god of magic. Get us inside."

"Consider it done." Hel cleared his throat and approached the wall again. With his hand resting on the pliable magic, he let the hum of it enter his body, swirling around within him then he pushed his own power toward it silently saying, "I'm a friend."

"Primevar," it hissed back. "Primevar. Enemy. Unwelcome."

Hel smiled and shifted his energy to embody the night, the moons, darkness. "I am Drivaar. Friend. I am the night."

The solid wall gave way, and he stumbled inside. That was easy, he thought. Too easy. Why hadn't it worked when he tried it before? Lifting his chin, he peered up at the sky, dark as if no sun existed here at all but was instead lit with streaks of blue and green and purple lights that danced in shimmering waves. Rolling rocky black hills expanded across the land with great waterfalls and lush green-blue grass that glowed with its own dim light. It was unlike any land he'd ever seen. In the distance he made out a cluster of houses and lights shining from a city. Nearby under a poplar tree, a white chariot with two black-winged horses waited; someone was close.

"War, are you seeing this?" With a triumphant smile, he turned back to make sure War had gotten inside and then a cool blade slid across his throat.

"Trespassers are executed in my territory, Hel."

. . .

HEL MADE a deliberate turn and paused at the entry to the throne room. The little redheaded guard had run in and gotten herself trapped inside as well. The four of them stood near the center, no doubt plotting a way to get out. They wouldn't until he allowed it.

"What did you do to her!" Thane roared and charged. He looked unhinged, with his hair in disarray, his tunic off center, the panic in his eyes. What fun this was. He slammed into Hel's wall and punched it. "I swear, if you—"

"Oh, she's fine. More than fine," Hel drawled. "Having sweet dreams of me and her together. I'll go lay her down in bed and perhaps she and I can continue the fun when I wake her."

CHAPTER 9

THANE

After Hel disappeared, Thane's mother stepped around a hall corner in her cream nightdress and brown locks left to fall loosely. Thane almost screamed at her not to enter into this room and suddenly, his foot moved across the threshold. He went to shove against the wall and stumbled into the hallway. Whatever magic Hel placed there was gone.

She gave him a strange look. "Thane, dear, about Talon. Might you consider being less harsh on her? She's been through so much lately and she's still very young."

"Mother, you must go to the house in Brightheart. Leave tonight."

"What has gotten into you?" she peered around him into the throne room. "What's wrong?"

"Don't ask why, just go. Have your servants pack for a long stay. I need you to trust me. It's not safe here anymore. Take Talon with you."

Her hand pressed against her belly and fear took over her confusion. "Are the pale ones..."

"I don't have time to explain." He turned to his three friends. "Go with her and make sure she leaves. Stay away from my wing of the castle. Stay away from him."

"Thane," Fennan protested. "You can't go against him on your own."

"That is a direct order from your king, Fennan. I better not see any of you near there unless I say so, understood?"

Fennan sneered but grabbed Orlandia's arm and tugged her along with him. Leif gave him a long look before he silently followed, and yet Piper hung back. She was the only one who got away with being defiant, other than Layala.

"I'm not abandoning you."

Thane didn't stay for her argument, and his command didn't stop her from running to catch up to his pace.

"Thane, the katagas serum did nothing against him."

"It doesn't matter. I have to go to her."

"He's training her. He won't hurt her, but you, he will," Piper said. "And just so you know, Layala feels like you don't want her anymore." Her accusatory glare said she didn't blame her.

"Of course I do. And why would he want to train her?" Piper had said that before, but he hadn't taken it in until now. His mind raced at the possibilities. He couldn't remember enough to know why Hel would want to train her. He couldn't even remember why he was banished to this realm to begin with or who had the power to do that.

"He said her vulnerability is a detriment to him. I don't know what he wants from her but you're not going to find out by threatening him." Piper narrowed her eyes as they rounded the corner. "Where are all the guards?"

"I ordered them to go outside. I don't need anyone else dying."

They made it to Thane and Layala's wing and took the stairs two at a time until they reached the top, where Hel waited. Both of them froze in place until Piper shifted back half a step and moved slightly closer to him. Fury boiled and threatened to take control of him, but like Piper said, threats weren't getting him anywhere, so he balled his fists at his sides and stared Hel down. He wished he remembered more, knew him better to understand him at this game. Thane was unmatched in battle strategy, but mischief was Hel's arena.

"I bet you want to hurt me, don't you?" Hel said. "You can either attack me or go to her."

Thane didn't even hesitate and dashed to Layala's door and shoved through. The light filtering in from the hall illuminated her curled up on her side on top of the lavender down covers. "Laya."

Tifapine sat on the pillow behind her, stroking her hair. "She's fine, just asleep," Tif said and stood up. "Who was that elf who carried her in here? At first, I thought it was you but even in the dark I could tell it wasn't." She gulped and tugged at the ends of her curly brown hair.

Thane stepped across the room and touched Layala's shoulder. She still wore her battle leathers and weapons, and her hair was tied back in a single braid down her back. Soft breath escaped her, and she looked quite peaceful. "Did he say anything to you?"

"He just winked at me." She tapped a finger against her chin. "It was dark so I can't say for sure, but I feel like he's not too hard on the eyes."

"We need to find you a gnome boyfriend, so you stop pinning after dangerous elves."

She blushed and patted her ruddy cheeks. "So, he's dangerous? Who is he? And my, I don't know if I'm ready for a gnome boyfriend. Gnomes are so—not elves. Find me a gnome with a six-pack and buff arms and you got a deal."

With an eye roll, Thane turned and headed out the door, closing it gently. Piper paced alone with her arms crossed. "Is she alright?" Piper asked. Hel was nowhere in sight.

"She's asleep and doesn't appear to be injured. Where did he go?"

Piper sagged against the wall and pressed her hand to her forehead. "He said you owed him a bottle of wine and then disappeared. Literally vanished."

"Stay with Layala."

TOUCHING the sword on his back for reassurance and bringing the warmth of his magic to the surface, Thane pushed down on the door handle. It swung open and Hel waited behind a desk with his boots propped up on it. A rack of the finest wine in Palenor took up the entirety of one wall. The asshole had a glass of red in hand, from the most expensive and rare in Thane's collection. A bottle from the woodland elves from the time of the last war—the war Hel started.

"You look like a troll pissed in your morning tea." He picked up a crystal decanter of amber liquid, pulled the cork and brought the opening to his nose. "Smells interesting." He took a gulp and kept a straight face as if it didn't burn.

His maroon eyes flicked back to Thane, and he dropped his boots to the floor. Then with his swirling glass of wine he stood and walked toward Thane. They were about the same height and size although Hel was slightly leaner. He brought his glass of wine to his lips and sipped. "Did you have fun with your friends in the throne room?"

"If you hurt her..."

"I didn't."

"Then why is she unconscious?"

"She was annoying me, so I put her to sleep," he said. "She's arrogant, uncontrolled, much weaker than she should be, and it puts her in danger. What in the realms have you been doing with her this entire time? Walking through the gardens and picking wildflowers?"

Far, far from it. Their entire time together was spent in tension and battle. "*I* could explain in great detail some of the things we've done that involved her repeating my name, but I wouldn't want to hurt your precious feelings."

"That might sting more if you were still doing those things with her."

"And who is she in danger from, if not you?" The pale ones were his own creatures, and if he didn't want them to touch her, he could command it. "I may not remember everything, but I know you're angry with her for leaving you then and not choosing you now."

"This is fabulous wine. When I met Dalvarn of the woodland elves, he was at the height of his fame. People of every race, elves, humans, dwarves, paid ungodly amounts for a bottle of this finery." He took another sip. "I hope you weren't saving it for a special occasion. Dalvarn got out of the business at least three hundred years ago and his posterity doesn't quite have the magic touch he did."

That wine had been sitting there for hundreds of years and Thane only planned to open it the night he married Layala.

Wary of Hel's every move, Thane watched him walk around the room inspecting the décor, the navy-blue tapestries hanging at the sides of the open windows, the crystal chandelier above the desk, the Palenor flag pinned to the wall. Bookshelves full of Palenor's secrets and histories of this land.

Thane kept quiet, waiting for Hel to speak. Hel was trying to get a rise out of, goad him into another fight, but he wouldn't give in this time.

Hel brushed his dark hair out of his eyes and leaned against the windowsill, the night sky a backdrop to his eerie presence. They watched each other silently, both as if the other was a serpent and waited to see who would strike first.

"We played this game a lot as children," Hel said, breaking the silence. "It didn't help that Synick pitted us against each other. Once, he made us fistfight for dinner after not allowing us to eat for three days. There was a single place setting and two of us." He glanced away. "He believed that young males needed hardship and competition to grow stronger, and he wouldn't allow fullbloods from his house to be weak."

"I remember some of the training but not that specific night," Thane said. His "uncle's" methods were barbaric. He thought about the name Synick for a moment, and something occurred to him. "He wasn't our blood uncle?"

"No, he was a primordial god, one of the original seven gods of Runevale. We called him uncle because he was a close family friend. We're all Primevar and he took an interest in us—saw potential. He was our mentor."

"I know what we are—were." A side of the Runevale gods he'd chosen or... not one he chose but one he was brought up in.

"I think he believed if we hated him, we'd grow closer and stronger."

"It seemed to work."

"Well."

"Who won?" Thane asked.

He smiled as if reliving the memory. "You let me win. You were always stronger than me physically and a better fighter. I could outdo you in magic but in this particular instance, magic wasn't allowed. I was so angry with you for letting me win too. You deserved to eat that night, not me. But if Synick knew you purposefully pulled back, he would have made you run laps around his territory the rest of the night while cracking a whip if you should slow. So, I ate."

Thane tried to conjure something of that time to his mind but not much came. "We were the same age," he mused. A moment of celebrating a birthday flashed across his mind, a party they shared together as young ones.

"Born on the same day. But my mother, your blood aunt, left me on your parents' doorstep with a note. I never knew her. To this day I don't even know who my father is."

"Did she say why?"

He lifted a shoulder. "Does it matter? She abandoned her child."

Thane rubbed his forehead; a brief image of Hel's mother and Thane's Runevale father came to mind; they were twins. Black hair, blue-green eyes, striking and beautiful. A memory came to him then, standing beside the table with his arms behind his back, while a younger Hel and Synick ate. Those hunger pains and the smell of roasted meat flickered to life even now. He sighed and then clenched his jaw trying to resist feeling the nostalgia of their time and wanting to ask Hel to go grab a drink like old times. His threats a moment ago were overshadowed by the memories. "What of your family here?"

"Don't try to find my weaknesses, *Thane*. I don't have any. You'll never be able to defeat me. I could kill you with barely more than a thought if I wanted."

113

"I wouldn't go down like that. You know that." Which was probably the reason they hadn't fought again.

"Even so, there isn't anyone you can threaten to use against me. I cut off anyone I cared about a long time ago." His glare was cold, unfeeling. "Besides, soon enough you and I will be dealing with a bigger problem."

"You keep dropping hints like that but haven't said. So, what problem?" With Hel and the pale ones, and a mysterious past tearing him and Layala apart, he had plenty to deal with already.

Hel shook his head. "You don't get a free pass. No one was there to hold my hand to help me. I was alone here for years. Besides, Synick wouldn't have that. If you want to know what's coming, you'll have to remember that you are the god of war, and if I must drag you through the depths of the underrealm to do that, I will. Forewarning, it will hurt."

Thane's skin prickled and the hairs on the back of his neck rose. It wasn't even Hel's threat that worried him. He could take pain. It was what was coming, the same foreboding feeling that had plagued him for weeks now. Before today he thought it was the impending arrival of Hel, but that dark pit in his gut was still there. The bodies being torn apart must have something to do with it, but what?

CHAPTER 10

LAYALA

Layala woke to her head throbbing and blurry vision. Pushing herself up in bed, she pressed her hand to her temple and blinked several times to clear her sight. What the hell happened? It was dark, only a single candle lit within her chambers on her bedside table. The quiet sizzle of the wick was the only sound.

The last thing she remembered was... She flew out of the bed, grabbed the dagger off her hip, and whirled around the room, searching for Hel. The chair against the wall sat empty, the shadowy corners too. How did she get up here?

The last thing he said came to mind, "Go to sleep, little rabbit and dream of me."

Her dreams... It was like she watched Hel and Thane from above. Talking about a murder of a primordial god and a weapon given to—the night goddess. It was confusing and familiar all at once. Had he shown that to her? It wasn't as if it could be a memory, she wasn't there. Was it to throw in her face that he and Thane were close, or was it a clue to something more? Was he insinuating that she murdered this Synick, and if so what did that have to do with now? That voice at the end, "Trespassers are executed in my territory, Hel," that voice was hers.

Heart thundering, she crept to the door and slowly pulled it open a crack. Piper stood against the opposite wall with her arms crossed. Her chin jerked up and she rushed to her. "Laya, are you alright? I saw that the katagas serum didn't work and I ran. I wanted to get Thane, but Hel trapped all of us inside the throne room somehow. I'm sorry. I shouldn't have left you to fend for yourself."

Gaining control of her rapid breathing, she nodded. "It's alright. It was the right choice. Where is Thane now? Is he still trapped?"

"I'm not even sure. He sent his mother away, sent all the guards outside and told Fennan and Leif not to come near this wing of the castle or near Hel. He told me too. I just didn't listen."

"You didn't see which way they went?"

"Hel said something about Thane owing him a bottle of wine. I can think of a few places they might be. Let's go."

Having drinks like two old friends? Her stomach ached at the thought of the elf she loved dining with the Black Mage. When she saw them together in the dream, they were close.

Maker above, everyone thought Tenebris was the evil one, but what if Thane joined with him too? What if that had been his plan all along? She couldn't imagine she'd been played for a fool this entire time, but it felt like a serpent coiled itself around her stomach. Had Thane known that he and Hel were related before? Her breaths came faster.

Did he use her to wake him?

"No. I—I have to get out of here."

Piper's brow furrowed. "And go where?"

She slowly backed further into her room; her fingers scraped against her scalp. *It can't be true.* But she couldn't deny that since the day Hel woke things were different. He wouldn't make love to her and wouldn't marry her. Her backside bumped into the window ledge, and she turned.

Piper followed her into the room. "Laya, talk to me. You're panicking. I can see it."

I must get out of here. I have to think.

"I want to be alone. With the snap of his fingers, Hel put me to sleep. It was that easy. I just need to get away from him." She snatched a cloak draped over the back of the chair and shoved the window open.

"Hel isn't the only danger. There are radicals in the city who've hated you since you were born, people who want to string you up and hang you from a noose because you woke the Black Mage, thanks to the *Palenor Scroll*, and not to mention the pale ones, it's too dangerous. At least we know Hel doesn't want you dead." Piper pressed her lips together and shook her head. "I never thought I'd say this in a million years, but he wants to protect you even if it's in his own twisted way. You're safer here."

Even Mathekis, the pale one general, had told her long ago that she didn't need to fear Hel. He also said she'd one day stand at his side and that thought made her panic even more. "I'll come back." She used her vines to build an escape and then shattered them before Piper could follow.

Guilt would eat her up if she looked back so she kept her eyes forward. Wind tore through the loose strands of hair around her face as her quick feet carried her across castle grounds. The guards on patrol watched her go by with wary looks but none of them spoke. With a burst of speed, she ended up at a small grove of bushy horse-chestnut trees and stood at the edge of the castle grounds.

This part of the deep ravine didn't boast powerful or loud waters fifty feet below, more of a slow melodic dance. It would still be one nasty plunge to the bottom she wasn't sure anyone would survive, but the waterfall, and impressive whitewater currents were half a mile up as was the bridge to cross. But Layala had her own way now. The first time she'd created the bridge she was terrified she'd fall, which brought her magic to the surface easy enough. Simply standing at the edge of the cliff was enough for her magic to break free, to assure its master wouldn't die.

Magical black vines grew from her feet and tore across until they anchored on the other side. This part always made her nervous. *Just run as fast as you can*, she silently prepped herself. She could grow several and create an intricate bridge with no risk of falling but that took time and something about running over this made her feel alive. Her stomach tickled as she quickly sprinted across her makeshift bridge. On the other side, standing in knee-length grass, she turned with a triumphant smile and with the flick of her fingers the vine vanished. For everyone's criticism of her magic, at least she'd learned to make her vines disappear on her own. She checked the area to make sure guards didn't see her. The bushy horse-chestnut trees provided ample cover and she didn't believe she'd been followed.

After she slipped her cloak on and pulled up the hood, she started toward the city. The Valley was notorious for architecture reflecting the grace and precision of the elves, with intricate patterns, delicate carvings, and sweeping arcs adorning many structures. Even at night a sense of tranquility washed over her, accompanied by the fragrance of blooming flowers and the crisp scent of the surrounding woodland.

The high elf city had a delightful blend of natural aromas, tinged with hints of magic and mystique. The air carried the gentle perfume of jasmine, lavender, and wild roses, inter-mixed between the houses and buildings. Wisps of aromatic incense wafted from open windows and drifted through the air, offering a soothing and calming ambiance despite the danger of pale ones lurking in the dark beyond the city limits.

During the day the main streets bustled with an array of charming shops, each offering unique and exquisite wares. The storefronts were adorned with shimmering crystals and sparkling potions from the many magical plants in the Valley, each offering remedies for anything from sleepless nights to faster-growing hair.

At night, however, the streets were quiet, the shop windows dark with closed signs in the doors. She ventured deeper into the city with more shops dedicated to craftsman-ship. Elven artisans renowned for their exceptional skill and mindfulness to detail, highlighted their mastery in delicate elven jewelry, intricately woven tapestries depicting ancient legends of kings and wars and rare creatures like unicorns, and finely made swords. Her father would have had his smithee and storefront here. She wondered which building was his from all those years ago.

The melodies of elven harps and flutes drifted from taverns and other gathering areas at this hour, adding a serene and melodic backdrop to the city's soundscape. Layala pulled her cloak tighter as a pair of elves strolled by. They talked quietly to each other and didn't seem to notice her presence. She hurried past the grand library where sages and scholars gathered within, their tomes containing secrets and lore spanning centuries. She'd snuck in there for several nights to read alone, looking for answers of the old gods, of the night goddess, but even the oldest of books and scrolls didn't have answers.

Past the library the scenery began to change. The human district lacked the majesty of the elves. Many of the buildings were made of red brick, and the flower gardens contained weeds. The wrought iron fences surrounding the trees along the streets were rusted in places and needed a good polishing.

She paused in an alleyway, watching one door in particular. Pipe smoke rolled out the entry of the old red brick building into the cool evening air. Rambunctious music from tambourines and harmonicas with steady foot stamping drifted out as well. The orange light from within gave a familiar sense of nostalgia. Many nights she'd ventured to the Smoky Dragon back in Briar Hollow.

A tall balding man with a crooked nose stepped into the entryway, belched loudly then rubbed his protruding belly. "Best drinks in the Valley," he crooned and swayed down the quiet cobblestone street, whistling.

Layala stayed in the shadows. The building across from the establishment had a hanging sign of a five-petaled pink flower that read below the blossom *"Nerium Oleander"*, the most poisonous flower in the world. In the day, remedies and tinctures were sold, and at night, it was a gambling den. The new human establishment in the Valley was opened by none other than Aunt Evalyn.

A quiet wind brushed down Layala's spine despite her cloak, and the sound of leaves skittering across the stone in the alley behind her made her shudder. Gripping the hood of her cloak, she tugged it back slightly and turned. The alley was dark and there were no shapes or shadows but despite what her eyes told her she *felt* someone. Maybe it was all talk of cloaked figures and a feeling of dread, but she felt like someone was around every corner out to get her.

She shook her head and stepped into the firelight produced from the torches mounted on the buildings, lining the street as far as she could see. That itch at her back, the tingle of her spine made her turn once more. Again, no one stood in that alley, but Layala learned to trust her instincts long ago. She hurried across the street and stopped outside *"Nerium O"*, as she and Aunt Evalyn called it for short. The west side of the Valley, on this street alone, was for the humans.

The elven guard didn't patrol here, and if the humans saw her, she wouldn't be welcomed. It wasn't that most humans in Palenor hated the elves. In fact, many unexpectedly praised and worshipped them for their beauty and grace, but as with everyone in these times, they feared the pale ones and it was a curse synonymous with the fair folk.

With a deep breath, she slipped inside and was hit with pipe smoke and loud chatter. It took a moment for her sight to adjust to the new brighter light, but she spotted Aunt Evalyn behind the bar top pouring a drink. As if sensing her presence, Aunt Evalyn's brown eyes snapped to Layala, and she pushed the glass toward the customer and waved her over.

Keeping her hood up, Layala casually walked along the outside row of the gambling tables. A woman in all black with bright red hair that looked like a human Piper, laughed, and raked in her pile of winnings from the center of the table. The rest of the players, four men, all threw their cards and moaned about women being bad luck.

"Bad luck for you," the woman said.

All five of them turned and watched Layala walk by as if they could sense she wasn't one of them—an outsider. For this reason, if Layala came here it was usually during the day when the place was mostly empty save for a few customers.

When Layala stepped up to the bar top and placed her hands on the smooth, glossy surface of the black stone, Aunt Evalyn grinned and rested her hands over Layala's. "About time you come and see me."

"You can come see me too, you know."

Aunt Evalyn waved a hand. "Bah, you know how I feel about that family. Thane, I can tolerate. The other two, not on your life."

Layala chuckled. "Ugh, they are the worst. I can barely handle them myself." She was reminded of the *lovely* notes Talon and her friends left and rubbed her temples. A white fluffy dog trotted out from behind the countertop, tail wagging, tongue sticking out. "Hello Dregous." Layala rubbed his head. "You're such a good boy. I missed you. Are you keeping Aunty Evalyn out of trouble?" He barked once and rested his chin on her thigh. "Of course, you are."

"Need a drink? I'd need an entire bottle after a day of dealing with her royal majesty and her royal majesty junior."

"Not tonight." She couldn't take the risk of her senses being dulled in times like these.

Aunt Evalyn cocked her head to the side and brushed her black curls behind her rounded ear. "Are you and Thane doing alright? I don't even know what you've been up to lately."

Layala just shrugged. They certainly weren't what she wanted them to be. She didn't want to tell Aunt Evalyn the Black Mage showed up today or she'd lose it, and they hadn't spoken much about her possibly being a goddess reborn though Aunt Evalyn knew. She wasn't sure what to think about it. She only said, *"If you are a goddess it still doesn't change that you're my Layala".*

"You know you can come visit whenever you want and talk to me about anything. My door is always open, and you always have a bed upstairs if you need a night away."

"I know."

Aunt Evalyn nodded. "If you're too busy, feel free to say no, but I could use a little help. I'm running low on certain plants I use for my remedies. You were always my gatherer. Now I'm left to do it myself. Or use my worthless apprentice who doesn't know a purple pansy from a deadly nightshade."

Said apprentice hustled around the room delivering drinks and clearing plates. She may not be good at identifying plants, but she was a phenomenal waitress. Her long blonde braid hung to her low back and swayed with her agile steps as she swooped up empty mugs. She had a gap between her two front teeth but that didn't stop her from showing off her radiant smile.

Layala did miss the simple days of scavenging the woods for plants her aunt needed, and now that was a dangerous task. She didn't want Aunt Evalyn or her apprentice doing it. "I'll do it. You shouldn't be going outside the city."

"I must on occasion. How else am I supposed to get the things I need?"

"Hire an able man to do it or at least to be your guard. I'll pay for it."

She scoffed and gestured around the place. "I got plenty of coin."

"And I might take you up on the offer of staying the night, although..." Layala glanced at the man down the bar on her left. He watched her warily through a side eye but wouldn't look directly at her. "It's not like it was in Briar Hollow. You've seen the papers."

"No one is allowed to speak ill of you in my place or they may find a dash of Nerium O in their drink."

Layala laughed at that. "Have you heard any rumors about who Telvian Botsberry's anonymous source may be?"

Aunt Evalyn picked up a dirty glass from the countertop and dunked it into the basin of bubbly water beside her. "There's been plenty of talk, but no one seems to know who."

"It could be Varlett," Layala murmured. "Based on some of the information, it must be her. At least one of the sources."

Aunt Evalyn bobbed her head. "I wouldn't put it past her if she's still around working with the Black Mage. But the latest story makes me believe the source may be someone in the castle. Perhaps a maid or guard."

"Why do you say that?"

"Have you not seen it?"

Layala shook her head and the pit in her stomach that seemed to linger all hours grew heavier. She tugged it out from behind the counter and set it down in front of Layala. The headline jumped out: **Trouble in Paradise?**

Our High King Thane fought hard to win the heart of Layala Lightbringer. Last Summer Solstice the two could be seen laughing and dancing together. They fought in Doonafell side by side and the two were so in love that even a broken mate bond couldn't separate them. It seemed they were devoted, that the stars aligned, and the Maker brought them to be together despite wars, and her destiny for darkness, even with the rumors of her being the Black Mage's true mate... or so we thought.

An anonymous source claims that no one has so much as seen them kiss. Shouldn't she be attending breakfast with the royal family or at the very least, her betrothed? What about important meetings she seems to be absent from? Does she still wear her engagement ring? Why aren't there wedding plans? We know with the war things aren't ideal but we in Palenor have lived and wed and cele-brated through the fight against the pale ones all our lives; it's nothing new. I know if my betrothed was mated to the Black Mage, I'd call off a wedding, too. The question is, why isn't she out of the castle yet?

~Telvian Botsberry

LAYALA LOOKED DOWN at her purple lily ring and pushed the paper away. If she had to wager, it was Talon or one of her friends.

"Is it true? Are you and Thane…"

"Things are complicated with all that has happened."

"I told you almost killing his sister was a bad move. You know what that did? It showed you don't trust him. That you don't believe in his decision making or that he could have saved me. You took the matter into your own hands against his family."

Layala sighed. She hadn't trusted him to choose Aunt Evalyn and her over his family. "I did what I had to. You're alive, aren't you? And it's not like you raised me to be compassionate. You raised me for revenge—against them."

She gave her one of those stern mother looks and sighed. "And then you fell in love with Thane. But I am thankful to be alive."

"Besides, she's not the only reason. You *know* the reason. And it isn't because we don't love each other. I would die for him still. But it's like we've taken several steps back and are still friends but not—lovers."

"He's not going to let you go, Laya. I've never seen anyone more in love than that elf," she said with a reassuring smile.

Layala wished she could see it that way. Oh, she knew he

loved her, but he also loved Piper, Leif, Fennan, and his family. And she felt like she was slipping into the category. "I started training with Mage Vesstan and—" she clamped her mouth shut, almost letting slip the most feared name.

"I'll take another drink, Evalyn," the man down the counter said, tapping his empty glass with his fingernail to make a pinging noise.

"Be right there," she said and locked her deep brown eyes onto Layala. "And who else?" The suspicion in her voice made Layala certain she couldn't let it go.

"The most deadly flower in the world," said a deep familiar voice that sent a chill down Layala's spine. "How fitting."

Aunt Evalyn's eyebrows shot up in surprise. Layala turned just as Thane slid into the stool beside her. His bright green eyes trailed over her, and he lowered his voice, "I couldn't find you and it worried me."

He wore a light gray cloak, but his hood dropped around his shoulders. Although his dark hair covered his ears there was no mistaking one of the most beautiful elves in Palenor for a human. Everyone in the room stared at him. Even if they didn't know he was the High King by sight, they knew he wasn't one of them.

"Are you having me followed?" She told him Aunt Evalyn opened her own place, but she didn't remember mentioning the name. She thought about the presence in the alley. Was it him or someone else?

"No, but Piper should be with you."

"I ditched her. It's not her fault. How did you find me?"

"I know, and I don't think you'll hear the end of it for a while. As far as how I found you, I'm simply drawn to you wherever you go," he said with a playful smile. Of course, he'd want to flirt now and dodge the truth.

"I think there's a lot you aren't telling me." She thought of the dream she'd had of Hel and Thane—War in Runevale, the scenery and names mentioned vaguely familiar. They'd worked together to break into the goddess of night's territory. Their easy comradery like two brothers, made her sick. "I need you to tell me the truth about something."

His expression was guarded but he nodded. "Alright."

"Did you know before we went to the Void?"

"Know what?"

"Did you remember him before? Did you want to wake Hel? I know you were close with him at some point."

"No." Thane shook his head, eyes locked onto hers. "Are you insinuating I used you to wake him up? Layala, I didn't know then. And besides, I want to be with you. Why would I wake up your husband?"

Heat crept up Layala's neck and she stared at him. But he hadn't been with her since. "He's not my husband."

Aunt Evalyn approached and pressed her palms on the counter. He smiled at her, all tension melting away. "Evalyn, it's good to see you as always. You're looking extra pretty tonight. I like the new beads."

"Well, thank you," she beamed, touching the turquoise beads around her neck.

"Do you have anything good?"

"That depends on what you mean by good. Do you want to be knocked on your ass or do you prefer something light?"

"It's probably best if Layala doesn't have to carry me home."

She smiled and it deepened the wrinkles around her eyes. It didn't matter what she claimed, Aunt Evalyn had a soft spot for him. She didn't smile at anyone but her closest friends like that. Aunt Evalyn turned around to the shelf behind her, grabbed a green bottle, and the sound of a cork popped. Purple wine filled the tall-stemmed glass and she set it before Thane. "Be right back." With a few hurried steps she stood before the other patrons waiting for service.

He took a sip and set the glass back down. "It's good."

"Why are you here?" Layala asked.

His brows lowered ever so slightly. "I told you, I was worried. Piper said you took off. This city is dangerous."

"I'm fine."

"I don't want it to be like this anymore."

"Like what?"

He sighed. "Us avoiding each other. Keeping secrets..."

"You're the only one keeping secrets. But it's not like it's the first time." He didn't tell her their mate bond needed to be consummated in love. He'd lied and kept things from her in the past.

"That's a low blow." Thane frowned. "I want to be close to you again."

"You could have fooled me. It feels like you don't care about that aspect of our relationship anymore."

"Of course I care."

"Not enough to marry me. See, you called *him* my husband and that's why you won't marry me, isn't it?" she blurted out and then pressed her lips together. That dream and article weaseled their way into her head. But in truth, the fact that Thane was so keen on marrying her before all this made her question his love for her. It wasn't that long ago that in the dragon court he spoke about how anxious he was to make her his wife, and over three months had passed since.

"No. It's because you don't remember who I really am. I fought for you today, and I'll keep fighting. Haven't I done enough to earn your trust?"

"Haven't I? You're paranoid I was looking for him for reasons other than to take him out. Do you even want to take him down?"

"We can't kill him. It's complicated."

"Not to me."

"Everything I do is for you. Always. Killing Hel isn't in your best interest or mine. I hate to say it, but I have a feeling we're going to need him."

"For what? And why are we playing by his rules? I don't give a damn about his claim."

"Laya." He blew out a long breath.

"See, that right there is why things are like this. You won't even talk to me."

"I love you, and I want to marry you." He leaned in closer and lowered his voice, "But I can't be with you until you know everything. I'm doing it out of respect for you."

"Respect for me? No, this is something else."

"You won't even attempt to accept that you are Valeen."

Her breath caught. "I already told you why that is, Thane. But even if I wanted to, there is a wall there, a block." It was like Layala, didn't matter, and all he or Hel cared about was Valeen. She didn't feel like the goddess of night. She felt the same as she always had. She placed her hand on the side of his face, wanting to lean in. "But just so you know, remembering won't change anything."

"It might change everything."

And there it was. Layala dropped her hand and stared at the glass of wine before Thane, considering throwing it in his face. No one made her feel more in love and more furious. "You know there's a sign on the door that says no elves."

"You must have missed it."

"Will you just leave, please. I was having a good time until you showed up."

"Really? Because you looked miserable."

"If we weren't in public, I think I'd punch you."

He chuckled. "It's been a while since you threatened me. I think I missed it."

"Stop it."

"Stop what?" he said with a smirk.

She gritted her teeth. "Being—you. Stop flirting with me if you don't want to be with me."

"My dearest." He slid his fingers along the top of her thigh and leaned in closer. "I want to be with you." He leaned in closer, and closer until their lips were a moment from touching. Layala's core warmed and it pissed her off that with a simple touch and a few words he could make her melt. "Patience. That's all I ask for."

He had plenty of patience when it came to her and her attitude, so she owed him that at the very least. Even if they couldn't marry yet, why did things have to be so strained? It was like a slow torture. Her body ached for him, his touch, and his lips all over her, but he wouldn't even give her that lately.

Now he suddenly wanted to wait for marriage? Maker above, he wouldn't even hold her hand most days. It's like a part of him resented her but he wouldn't admit it. He'd relentlessly pursued her before and now they were becoming strangers again.

Despite her warring feelings, the intensity blooming between them grew with each passing second. It was torment not to kiss his lips when they were so close, and he smelled good. Not giving in, she started to lean away, and his hand wrapped around the back of her neck, stopping her escape as he finally pressed in, kissing her hard, weeks of built-up passion igniting in that moment. For all her snappy comments about telling him to leave it only took one kiss to melt into him. A moan escaped her, and in reaction, he stood. She blinked in surprise as he took hold of her hand.

"What's wrong?"

He tugged her off the stool and pulled her along the edges of Nerium O until they were under the night sky. "Where are we..."

Thane melted into the shadows, taking her with him and pinned her against the alley wall. Now this was what she'd waited for. The hunger in his eyes was reminiscent of times he watched her undress. His lips crashed into hers. Her fingers slipped into his hair, and his rough hand gripped her thigh. He pulled it up to his hip and leaned into her.

"Thane," she breathed. "Evalyn has rooms." His hot kisses trailed down her throat, and she shuddered. "Take me upstairs."

"You're so beautiful." His fingers dug into her hips, greedily pulling her closer. "I don't know if I can stop."

She pulled his lips to hers, pushed her tongue into his mouth. "There is no need. I want you. I want you now."

"Please, Laya."

His hands slipped under her top, his thumb grazed her breast and she moaned again. "Don't stop."

"Right here? We can't. Someone could walk down here any moment."

She wrapped her arms around his neck leaning into his touch. "Do I need to beg for you to take me to a room then?"

He pressed his forehead against hers. "Why do you have to be so tempting?"

"I need more than this," she whispered. "I need to be with you again, wholly. I want to be connected to you."

He shuddered and nipped her ear. "Laya, we can't. I want you to know who and what you're consenting to when you love me, when you marry me."

"I do."

"No, you don't."

She sighed, not only in frustration of her body's unmet craving but this argument. "I know who you are. You're my Thane. The Elf King who took me from my home and saved me from myself. You rescued me from your father at your own peril. You make love to me in bathtubs and whisper naughty things in my ear. You're the elf who loved me at my hardest and cherished me at my most vulnerable. *Nothing* stopped you before. Especially not another male." He made promises in the past about loving her in fields of wildflowers, of wedding vows, and being mated once again.

"I'm not *only* Thane Athayel," he said. "And that was before I knew better. I'm not doing this for him; it's for you. I won't have you angry with me in the future because I married you and it's not what you, and all that you are, wanted. You were once married to Hel, you loved him, you were mated to him, all things you don't care about now, but you will." He paused and looked down. His dark lashes glistened with tears in the moonlight cascading upon them. "I remember your wedding to him. I remember how it hurt to see that he made you happy and not me. I don't want you to resent me when I knew better, and you didn't."

Layala took a sharp breath. She didn't want it to be real. All she could see standing across from her in a wedding ceremony was Thane. "And—I left him for *you* according to him." She stroked the side of his face, wanting to beg him to see she loved him.

"Now that is a piece I don't remember. Hel says I tricked you, and I can't imagine that but... If I did, I won't again."

"Thane, that's not who you are. You wouldn't do that. And that was before. I loved you first here and now. He's horrible. I guarantee that's why I left. He's ruthless and cold and you're warm and kind and everything I ever wanted."

"If it doesn't matter when you remember, we'll marry, and I promise I will love you every night that you wish, and your bed will never be empty again."

The door to Nerium O swung open and a couple patrons stepped out, singing loudly. The drunkards couldn't carry a tune and swayed back and forth with their arms around each other's shoulders. "Hey, looky there," one of the men shouted and pointed in their direction. "A couple of love birds." They started making kissing noises and laughed.

Thane reached back and tugged out his sword, then stepped into the light of the street. "Might want to move on, boys."

"Oye, let's get out of here," one said and hurried down the street with the other quickly following.

Thane shoved his sword back in its holster and stepped back into the alleyway. Layala couldn't help but chuckle as she adjusted her crooked top, tucking it back into her pants. But the humor was lost when she looked up at him and the expression on his face said he still wanted her, but his body language shifted, and she knew his momentary lapse in resisting her was over.

"It's back to refraining then?" She groaned. He'd gotten her all flustered and aroused and would leave her wanting.

He turned away and ran his hand across his jaw. "I shouldn't leave Hel alone at the castle for long. He's opened up to me a little despite being a vengeful prick, but there's a reason he wants to train you and why he's here now. Something is coming and we need to prepare for it."

"What about a plan to at least trap him and imprison him?"

"I haven't worked one out yet but if we don't keep living life as usual, word is going to get out that something is wrong. I was able to send most of the guards outside for training but if anyone suspects Hel's identity..."

There was a leak inside their home, and if the people of Palenor found out that Hel was the Black Mage and he infiltrated the castle, they would panic. Thane was the one beacon of hope they had left. No one could know. "So, until we can figure out what to do about him, we have to pretend like he's a wanted guest. Your cousin."

Thane pursed his lips and slowly nodded. "Yes, I think we do."

CHAPTER 11

LAYALA

The next evening Layala stood outside at the edge of the stone circle on castle grounds. Begrudgingly, Piper was with her, but she wouldn't speak after getting ditched the night before. She sat on the bench with her arms crossed and a glare that might be cold enough to freeze water.

All the apologies in the world, even a cupcake from Tif didn't get Piper to cheer up. So Layala would give her a day to sulk. She approached Mage Vesstan who sat on the bench with his eyes closed, and by the sounds of snoring, he was fast asleep. How anyone could sleep sitting up on a hard stone bench was beyond her. Layala crossed her arms and watched a loud ribbiting toad jump from one lily pad to another. A second plopped into the pond to swim among the colorful fish. *What a simple life*, she thought.

The stone circle to the left of them hummed. Something about it made her wary. Was it the thing itself or the fact that the last time Layala stood at its center she'd nearly been suffocated by Hel? Where was he anyway?

The sun hung just above the mountains she stood below; Layala lifted her chin, closed her eyes, and let it warm her face. It was so quiet and peaceful here and she could see how Vesstan fell asleep.

"Oh good," Vesstan said in his feeble voice. "You're relaxed today."

Alright, apparently he wasn't asleep. "I went and saw my aunt last night. She often makes me feel better. I promised to scavenge for a list of plants for her after this. The task will take my mind off things." She'd have to stick close to the city with all the dangers on the loose in Palenor now.

"Excellent idea." He pushed up with the assistance of his cream oak staff and hobbled toward her. His long white beard swayed with each step. "We likely only have a few minutes before we're—interrupted."

"Unfortunately." Layala glanced over her shoulder. Birds sang evening songs in the willowy trees on the path leading to the castle. In the far distance servants and staff hustled about to ready the outdoor decor for the graduation ball of the new recruits. Thane insisted it happened to keep up appearances that everything was fine.

No one had seen Hel all day, but he was certainly nearby.

"Now, let's start with you standing at the center of the stone circle."

Layala heaved a sigh and stepped to it. "Why is this circle so important?"

"It's a conduit built a millennia ago. It aids in channeling your magic." He leaned his shoulder against one of the pillars and said, "Close your eyes. I want you to feel the energy around you." Mage training was so different from weapons and combat. She was used to aggression, ducking, diving, and moving in every way to take down an opponent.

Now it was, *"Feel the energy around you."*

Rolling her shoulders back, she inhaled and did as commanded. Listening to the pull of her lungs, the steady beat of her heart, and the sound of the wind rustling in the treetops, she settled into a quiet mind. Like a gentle touch, a hum emanated from the stones. It was much like the stone portals but unlike them there were no entities inside, no voices, and did not pull on her magic.

"Do you feel it?"

She nodded.

"Now let your power rise naturally, feel it, but don't use it yet."

Layala hadn't let her magic arise without provocation or need of it since she was a child. When she was threatened or angry and in battle it came easily, but not when she was calm. *Come on,* she coaxed. The warmth of it was there, deep inside that box she kept it trapped in, and she imagined lifting the lid and letting it free. It slowly crept out like a tentative child that had been punished. "It's a little harder when I'm not in danger."

"You act as if it's locked away. It should be as easy as breathing," said a deep, raspy yet rich voice. "It should always be there."

Her eyes opened in a snap to find Hel standing beside Vesstan. The changes in his appearance were minute, barely noticeable but there. She didn't know if anyone else would see it, but his cheeks were flushed, a sheen of sweat covered his brow. There were even slight dark circles under his eyes, and if she wasn't mistaken even his hair had lost some of its shine. She almost called him out on it but with his presence, the tingle of her magic flooded her body with ease.

"Ah, there it is," Hel said. "But I can smell your fear. You need to turn that off."

"I can't simply turn it off," Layala said through clenched teeth, but she wished she could, knowing he could sense it and that he triggered it.

Piper didn't so much as flinch at his arrival but almost looked amused. As if she was going to enjoy Layala's torture.

"Your magic should always be there, readily available, as much a part of you as your soul. You seem to be able to turn it off, hide it, so you should be able to do the same with your fear or anger or any other emotion."

Layala met his maroon eyes, and her brows furrowed, even they weren't as bright as she remembered. There was something wrong with him and knowing that gave her courage. "I'm not afraid of you."

"No?"

"No." Shit, they both knew it was a lie. She wasn't afraid of death, but she did fear the past they shared. Layala turned to Vesstan. "You know for most of my life I relied on weapons to keep myself safe, not magic."

Hel tucked his hands behind his back and interrupted. "I understand that but that changes today. You have an immense amount of untapped potential that you're not using."

Layala kept her gaze fixed on Vesstan. He stroked his long white beard and nodded in approval. "He is correct, Layala. There is no reason to hide your power now. You should be proud of it. You don't need to lock it away anymore."

Hel vanished and reappeared behind her, breathing on her neck. "What do I need to do to make you unafraid of me? Of anyone?"

Layala whipped around and stepped back. Her magic flared, warming her skin. He advanced on her and for every step he took, Layala moved back. "Keep still, little rabbit, I'm not going to hurt you."

"Said the wolf," Layala challenged.

He let out a dark chuckle. "You're making this too easy."

"Layala, you're allowing him all the control," Vesstan said in the strongest voice she'd ever heard him use. Her pulse thudded in her throat, but she froze, anchoring her feet in place. Would he trap her again so she couldn't breathe? Those maroon-red eyes beheld such malice, such hatred that she didn't want to look into them but the longer she did the more she felt like she couldn't look away, as if he held her there by magic.

"Get on your knees." Hel's command pressed upon her like a weight. Every part of Layala protested but she lowered down to one knee at a time. Her cheeks burned with shame as he smiled down at her. He held out his hand and put it in front of her face. "Kiss the knuckles of your true king, little rabbit."

Layala's muscles strained and protested as she fought to stay in place. His dark brow lifted as he waited. Unable to fight the command Layala pressed her lips to his warm skin, and she shuddered, feeling the tingle of his magic on her mouth. Layala's eyes lifted, and the smug look made her furious. *I'm going to snap your neck,* she silently vowed. *I'm going to destroy your world and everything you care about, Hel.*

He pressed his finger under her chin and with barely a nudge she was rising to her feet. "Good girl. Now, remove your clothes."

Layala felt that power wash over her, and she gulped. Sweat dampened her back almost immediately. This. This was why she feared him. The control he had over her.

"You don't have to do that," Vesstan called from the left.

Piper was up on her feet now. "Laya, you're strong enough to resist. You're the stubbornest elf I've ever met."

"Take them off," Hel said again.

Layala's chest heaved up and down in panicked breaths as her fingers began working at her belt against her will. *No no no*, she screamed at herself, and she gritted her teeth, and fought with everything she had to stave off that command. Every muscle battled against her but the tingle of Layala's magic pushed back. Sliding through her veins, across her skin to force Hel's magic out.

"No," Layala said and dropped her hands to her sides, balling them into fists.

He grabbed her chin with one hand and squeezed. As he stared at her now, he looked more amused than anything. "Take. Them. Off."

While touching her, his command was impossible to resist. Tears burned Layala's eyes as her weapons belt dropped to the ground with a clank. She began to lift her top and it rose above her navel.

"Stop." His hand dropped to his side, and he shook his head. "Look how vulnerable you are. I could get you to do anything I want. And there are others who would do far worse than me."

Who would do worse? "I'm trying," Layala bit out.

"No, you're not. Because you won't try to be Valeen." He crossed his arms. "Who was the first person you ever loved?"

He meant from before, but she wouldn't give him anything. "My aunt, Evalyn."

"Wrong."

"Certainly not you, if that's what you're getting at."

"Not me," he said with a shake of the head.

Thane? No... there was someone else, not a lover but family maybe. She couldn't recall.

"Look at me."

She turned her head, met his stare. The hate was gone, his features softened.

"In the tower, I put you in that red dress for a reason. It's what you wore the first time I saw you, remember? It was at my Uncle Balneir's party. War's father."

Layala shook her head.

"You hadn't left your territory in a thousand years. You hid away from everyone."

"I don't want to hear this," Layala snapped.

You were the most beautiful being I'd ever seen. You still are, he said in her mind.

"Don't try to win me over with flattery. It won't work."

Vesstan cleared his throat and tapped his staff once on the stone. "Perhaps we should get back to magic. Layala, will you do something simple for me? Grow a blossom in your palm."

"Did I say you could speak?" Hel glared at Vesstan. "We'll get to magic when I say so."

"Don't talk to him like that."

"Are you going to stop me?" A serpentine smile crossed his lips. "I'd love for you to try."

Layala jerked her sword free and held it ready.

"No, you don't get to rely on a sword today, love." He flicked his wrist and it ripped free of her hands and flipped end over end into the growing shadows of the setting sun.

Seething, she clenched her hands at her sides. He wanted her to attack him, so she'd look like an incompetent child. If only she could turn to shadow like he suggested.

"Control, little rabbit."

"Stop calling me that," Layala snarled.

"Then stop acting like one. You need to be calm and controlled in any situation." He appeared to her left and circled, trailing his fingers along her shoulder blades. She shuddered and hoped he wouldn't take control of her again. "Against any foe, so you can have a focused mind. There are gods on Runevale who would break you in seconds—who would love to humiliate you. Some could command you to jump off a cliff and you would if you don't gain surety in yourself. You are the goddess of night—one of the most powerful beings in all the realms. You fear no one and are never commanded by anyone."

Layala lifted her palm again and stared at it, ignoring Hel even though he was toying with a piece of her hair now. To spite him she thought of a flower, simple magic, as Vesstan said. She hoped it pissed Hel off she'd listen to the old mage over him. Her power bloomed in her core, and she mentally lifted the lid of the box, and the warm sensation of it trickled out into her body. *It's alright, we don't have to hide anymore.*

In her mind, she pictured a midnight lily blooming but without the deadly vines. Above her palm a spark of a dark cloud started and grew into a swirling mass. Inside a bud grew, and she couldn't help but smile, and then it opened into a full dark purple lily. With a single breath she blew away the cloud and grinned triumphantly at Hel.

Vesstan gave her a modest smile and a barely perceptible nod. Even Piper looked proud.

However, Hel looked less than impressed. "You made a flower. Congratulations. I'm sure your enemies are quaking in their boots."

"I stayed calm. I win."

CHAPTER 12

LAYALA

Layala slid open the stable doors and was hit by the smell of hay and manure. The training session didn't open her up to any new powers but her one triumph of the night was that her magic flowed freely within her even now. She'd spent most of her life trying to hide it, wishing she didn't have it, and it was strange to feel its strong companionship not under threat. She walked away from training with the confidence that she didn't need to keep it locked up anymore. All the times she was told to hide it or pull it in, even Fennan had told her to rein in her magic once in the battle outside Doonafel because the pale ones could sense it, but now she was free to be herself. Why hide from Hel and his minions when he was already here?

Fennan, Leif, and Piper were at a meeting with the new training recruits, and hopefully she wouldn't even notice Layala's absence or there'd be another day of silence. Thane was in a meeting with the night guards explaining new rules and where they were expected to be, and how to prepare for the upcoming graduation ceremony so hopefully he wouldn't realize she was gone either. He had plenty on his plate and being her personal guard didn't need to be added to it. She'd insisted on training with Hel and Vesstan without him so he could resume his kingly duties, and with his mother gone, the ceremony was now his responsibility along with a hundred other decisions to be made.

Last she saw, Hel was right beside Thane introducing himself as the High King's cousin to the guards and acting like he was simply a wealthy lord from the countryside. His audacity made her want to gag.

Three stalls down she found Midnight. He neighed loudly and stuck his head out of his stall window. Layala smiled and rubbed the white star on his forehead. "Hi, boy. Want to go for a ride? We must help Aunt Evalyn tonight."

He threw his head up and down excitedly and she unhooked the latch and swung the door open. She grabbed his dark brown reins and bridle off a hook to the left and slid them over his head. Maybe this new confidence made her reckless. Thane's voice warning her to not go out alone echoed in her mind. She ignored it.

After Midnight was saddled and ready, she hopped on. They trotted off at a casual pace and once they reached the bridge, a set of guards stepped away from their positions off to the sides and approached. "Lady Lightbringer," they both said, and a glance of confusion passed between them.

"I'm going out for a night ride. I should be back in an hour or so."

"Would you like an escort? It's dangerous."

"No, thank you. I'll be fine."

The two guards exchanged wary glances, no doubt questioning if they should allow her to go and what might Thane say or do if they did. "Lady, the High King asked us not to let you go off the property without an escort."

"I said, I'll be fine." She nudged Midnight's sides and rode past them.

They argued behind her, "We can't let her go."

"Are you going to stop her? She's called *Fight*bringer for a reason."

"Do you fear her or the king more?"

"Her."

"Coward."

"I don't see you chasing after her either."

She laughed quietly to herself and nudged Midnight to go faster. His large hooves clopped on the stone bridge and the heavy sprays of mist from the massive cascading waterfall assaulted her face. With a small, wooded area to the north in mind, she rode the trail that led up and out of the Valley. At the crest of the hill, she tugged back on the reins, turning him toward the castle. Midnight stopped and dug his front hoof into the dirt impatiently. "Just a moment, Midnight."

The moonlight illuminated the outline of Castle Dredwich. Torches lit up arched windows from within and shadows of passing elves walked by on occasion. Her home suddenly felt foreign and invasive. Like it wasn't home at all and never was. Nibbling her lower lip, she tugged on the reins, tearing her sight away from it, and kicked Midnight into a canter until they raced down the trail, wind tearing through her hair. His deep breaths shot out in huffs, and the pounding of hooves disturbed the quiet of night. Glowing eyes of little critters among the trees spied with curiosity. A pink pixie darted in front of them leaving a glittering trail of dust. The tiny creature cursed as she and Midnight sped by. "You have the entire sky!" Layala shouted back at it. As if the thing couldn't fly higher.

She let the feeling of freedom and escape rush through her, savoring being alone until they came upon the small wood at the Valley's edge. Not far away were rows of corn in a field and to the left of it a thatched roof house and a square fenced area with a handful of sheep. A single cow among the sheep lifted its head from grazing and mooed. She'd passed this farm on several occasions. Every time one lantern sat in the window while the female bounced around the kitchen. Why did they take the risk of being out here alone?

Layala dropped to the soft grass and ran her hand across the shiny black coat of Midnight's neck and then pulled the list out of her pocket and scanned it. She needed to make this quick. "Alright, Aunt Evalyn wants deadly nightshade. Not sure who that is for, but I don't ask. Lillian thrope root, good for stomach aches, pottifer leaf—ugh, does she know how hard it is to find?" Layala looked up at the oak trees and the variety of foliage growing along the forest floor. Wildflowers and sprays of baby's breath, a patch of forget-me-nots. Seeing the blue blossoms made her smile. She used to place that particular flower at her parents' memorial once a week. *I haven't thought about my parents in a long time*, she thought and that made her chest ache. Lifting her chin to the night sky, she searched among the stars; were their souls out there somewhere? If she'd once been Valeen but had passed on and was reborn, where had her soul been all those years. Questions she supposed she might never know.

Layala gripped the leather reins and tugged Midnight along behind her. As luck would have it, she found the Lillian thrope not even a foot into the wooded area. It was a blue weed that grew two feet tall and boasted long serrated leaves with gold spots. She dropped down to one knee and carefully pulled three of them up by the roots. Then tucked them in the pouch on Midnight's pack. Several feet over, among bunches of green weeds and foliage, she discovered the deadly nightshade with its star-shaped purple blossoms and near-black berries.

She pulled it up by the roots, plucked the berries and put them in a small glass container and placed them into the pack as well. Her foot hovered over the stirrup when a faint odor hit her. One might be able to say it was the farm animals lowing in the field not far off if she didn't know better, but that rotten scent was distinct to one creature in Adalon. Anger and frustration bubbled up in her chest.

She couldn't think of pale ones without Hel coming to mind anymore. And she'd stood there helpless as he mauled her with magic, and nearly made her undress with a simple command. *Maker above, how can I be so pathetic?*

Midnight lifted his head from nibbling on grass and nickered in alarm. She patted his neck again. "I know, boy. Time to go hunting." She pulled out her sword and turned to the horse. "Stay."

Moving like shifting shadows, she raced down the shallow hill and pressed her back up against the house. She slid to the side of the window, debating if she should warn them. A female hummed a tune Layala didn't recognize, and a moment later she heard a male say, "Whatever your cooking smells delicious."

"Mama, mama," a small child cried. "I heard something in my room. I'm scared."

"You're supposed to be asleep," the mother chided. "I don't want you to come out here one more time."

"But I heard something!" the child wailed. "What if it's a monster!"

"Back to bed."

Shaking her head, Layala crept to the corner of the house and peered around it. If only they knew how right the child was but if she alerted them, they might only get themselves killed.

Two pale ones were at the fence line only fifty yards away now. One of them threw a rock at a sheep and sent it scurrying. The small herd bleated in alarm and trotted as far away as they could get. Both monsters cackled and hopped the fence.

Reaching a hand into her belt, Layala pulled a throwing star. She waited until they were close enough that she wouldn't miss. The moonlight glinted off the star as it soared through the air and struck a pale one in the center of the throat. Soundlessly, he clawed at his neck and then tipped over into a dark heap.

"One down," Layala mumbled with a smile. Thane asked her why she did this and part of her did it for exhilaration, danger. Yes, originally it had been to hunt down Hel's location, but she knew where he was now and yet here, she was almost giddy at the thought of the fight.

"Pale ones!" the male voice bellowed from inside. "Get in the room with Hannah and don't open the door no matter what you hear."

Layala stepped out from the shadows and trudged toward the remaining pale one. The black under his eyes and mouth appeared darker and more sinister in this light. A low rumble escaped his throat and he slowly backstepped in retreat.

"What's the matter?" Layala cooed, lifting her sword. "Scared of a little she-elf?" She swung, her blade cut through the air with a whistle and clashed with the enemy's. He pushed back, sending her stumbling a few steps. With a snarl, she threw out her hand and her vine shot up from the ground and impaled him straight through the gut and drove him onto his back into the grass, circling around him until his body could no longer be seen among the coils and thorns and black blooming lilies.

A scream rent the night air, a slice through Layala's chest. She whipped around to face the house. There was a third she missed? The child! She sprinted down the path to the front door and found the father bleeding out in the entryway.

No.

"Help them," he gasped, holding his hand over the gaping wound in his stomach and the obvious bite mark on his shoulder.

Shit, he would turn if she didn't end him. Her hands shook but she leapt over the elf. Right now, she had to save the mother and child. The table was overturned, food scattered across the floor as she dashed through the living room. *Hurry hurry hurry.* Shoving through the door at the end of the hallway she found the room empty, with the light curtains blowing in the breeze. Her feet flew across the floor, and she jumped out the window without looking. Already outside the fenced area surrounding the property, the mother dragged the small child along beside her... but where was the pale one? A quiet rustle made Layala drop into a squat and a blade passed over her head and crashed into the house.

"Pesky little elf," the pale one sneered, trying to pull his embedded sword free. "You ruined my supper."

Layala shoved up, punching her blade through his belly. He roared and a wave of rotten breath spilled across her face. *Ew.* Holding back a gag, she shoved her weapon in further. *Die, you bastard.* Cold, greasy hands grabbed her face and the pale one slammed his forehead into hers.

The impact cracked loudly, and seeing stars, Layala stumbled back. *Not good, not good.* The world spun around her, and she lost her balance, falling onto her backside. She scrambled backward throwing out her magic, a protective shield, but she was seeing double vision and—where did the creature go?

A long shadow cast across her and she focused her power to hold her invisible shield, the same power she'd used against the dragon prince in the arena, and a fist collided a mere foot from her face, reverberating off her magic. She blew out her breath. Maker, that was close. The pale one screeched in rage and despite the pain throbbing in her head, she smiled.

The pale one stepped in front of her with an ax in both hands and swung. The impact hit like he'd struck a boulder. He hit again and again; the wrath on his already putrid face grew with each strike.

"You can't hide in there forever!" the creature bellowed. Her sword still protruded from his gut and black blood poured down his thighs and over his ankles... *Get up, get up.* Keeping her magical shield intact, she slowly pushed to her knees and then rose up. The ax fell to the ground beside him with a thud and the pale one roared and screeched, clawing with his bare hands to break through now.

"Not the most intelligent thing, are you?"

She pulled the dagger from her hip and the pale one stopped. *Well, that was easy.* She smiled and took a step toward him. He retreated back, afraid—no, terrified. Maybe he finally realized who she was and that he was about to die. She lifted her arm, aiming the point of her dagger at his forehead. As easy as it would be to spear him with her magic, this felt more satisfying. Knife throwing was something she'd done her entire life, and she never missed her mark.

"Master," the creature murmured, nearly stumbling.

Layala froze. *Master?*

CHAPTER 13

LAYALA

Gasping, she whirled around. Hel stood not three feet from her. And although his eyes were wild with dangerous hostility, he wasn't looking at her. "You dare touch your queen?"

The pale one took a step away, and then another. "Didn't know," the pale one said, bowing his head. "She killed others. Tried to kill me."

The brush of his cloak against her arm sent chills down her body as he stomped by her. His alabaster fingers grabbed the pale one around the throat and lifted his massive body off the ground with such ease. "Then you stand there and die." Black blood leaked from the pale one's eyes and he let out a high-pitched shriek before he fell to the ground in a lifeless lump.

Layala gulped, and like a statue she stood there, staring at his back and the way the silvery crescent moon outlined his form perfectly. It was as if she'd watched him like this a thousand times, as if she'd memorized him the way she had her home in Briar Hollow, and yet she couldn't recall a single thing about him.

He turned to face her. "Didn't your mother ever tell you not to go into the woods alone at night? Oh, wait, I guess she couldn't because you didn't have one..." he said, and she wanted nothing more than to slap him across the face.

Bastard. He was the root cause of why she was dead, why Layala never knew her mother. "I had a mother, but she died."

"I meant as Valeen."

"Why are you following me? Just leave me be. I had it handled."

"Aren't *you* looking for *me*? That's why you come out here every night, isn't it? You want to get me alone and take advantage of me, don't you?" He put a hand to his chest. "I'm not that kind of elf, Val. You'll have to at least buy me dinner first."

Layala scoffed and scrunched up her nose. The audacity.

"Well, if you're not up for a midnight romp, then you want to talk. So, talk."

"I saw you a couple hours ago, you know, when you commanded me to take off my clothes. If I wanted to talk I wouldn't have left."

"I did that to prove a point. And you know with the old mage and War around, excuse me, *Thane*, you can't say how you truly feel about me. I've always wondered—who's a better roll in the sack, me or him?" He rubbed the thin white scar across his chin, and the action reminded her of how Thane often had the same habit. It made her shudder. "It must be me. He's so—formal. Translate that to *boring*."

"A better—ugh. Considering I wouldn't touch you even if my life depended on it, we'll never know."

"Oh, you know. And one day you'll remember."

Layala narrowed her eyes. "You know what, something's

coming to me." His scarred eyebrow raised ever so slightly, and he leaned a little closer. "Thane's is bigger, a lot bigger, and he knows how to use it better. No wonder I left you."

Hel's jaw muscles twitched, and his trembling fingers curled into fists, but his anger vanished as suddenly as it came. A civar appeared out of thin air, already burning, and he clasped it between his fingers. "Liar," he said just before he placed it between his lips.

The thin line of smoke from it wafted her way. An image flashed across her mind of a male standing on a balcony with his back to her. He was entirely naked, and much of his body was covered in runes and other tattoos. The sweet smell of his civar wafted to her through open double doors. The night sky was full of waving colors. She blinked several times, clearing the thought. *What was that?*

With her stomach twisted into knots, Layala dropped her gaze to the grass. And for the first time since the fight started she heard the luminor crickets chirping and the sheep bleating quietly from somewhere near. The silence between them lasted too long and she knew without looking that he watched her and that made her skin crawl. "I was out looking for something and happened upon your creatures. So obviously I killed them. Even one less makes Palenor safer."

"They're yours too, you know. You could command them if you wanted."

She lifted her eyes to him. "What?"

"Haven't you ever wondered why they're drawn to you?"

Yes, she thought but only clenched her teeth tighter together. Although lately the use of her magic hadn't brought them to her. She wondered if it was because they weren't close or if he'd commanded them not to.

"Because they are mine."

She watched him skeptically, thinking there was more to that statement. There wasn't. "Well, I'm not you."

"Clearly." He smiled slowly, reminding her of a wolf ready to pounce. A very beautiful wolf. "You'll get it one day." He took a deep pull of the smoke and blew a puff into the night.

Layala shook her head and turned away, stalking up the side of the house. She needed to put down the father left dying in the doorway before he had a chance to turn and get up.

"Where are you going?"

Layala halted and whirled on him. "Actually, I do need to talk to you. There was a lady slaughtered by a beast of some kind. What other evil thing have you created now?"

"I don't know what you're talking about. The pale ones may exist because of me but I don't have any beasts. What did it look like?"

"I never saw it. Only the damage it left behind. But even the pale ones admitted they weren't the ones to do it."

Hel's perfect lips twitched into a slight frown, but it wasn't much of an emotion to get a read on. "That could be a problem."

"What is it?"

"I don't know for certain, and even if I did, I wouldn't tell you."

Layala groaned and started off again. It wasn't like he'd been forthcoming about anything since he arrived. She glanced back to make sure he wasn't following her, and he was gone, thank the Maker. As she turned back around she skidded to a halt and stopped millimeters from a blade sinking into her throat.

"I forgot to tell you the first rule of training. Never turn your back on your opponent."

"That's my dagger," Layala breathed. He'd taken it right out of her hand without ever touching her.

"It certainly is." He brushed it under the left side of her jaw. It was a caress, gentle and seductive. "I'm sorry, love, but I can't wait any longer."

"What are you talking about?"

"You remember the tower, don't you? How you woke me?"

"How could I forget?" she drawled. She'd sliced open her hand and dripped her blood into his mouth, breathed life into his lungs.

"I have a theory. This will only hurt a little." He dropped the blade to her wrist and sliced open her flesh.

"Ouch." Layala brought her cut hand up to slap the blade away and he grabbed her arm. Before she could move, his tongue slid across her fresh cut and his mouth closed around it, like a lover's nibble. A flood like a sedative hit her hard as his magic overwhelmed her, holding her in place.

"Stop," she said weakly. He gripped the back of her neck and pulled her closer, flush against his hard body, sucking blood from her wound. It hit her like a slap; all the weakening signs she'd picked up on, the dark circles, the tremor of his hands. Her blood had given him life and now... Holy Maker above.

"Get off me!" she jerked her dagger back from his hand then drove it straight into his side, shoving it all the way to the hilt. She was so startled that it went in, she froze rather than pulling it to strike a second time. Her magic lashed out, slamming into Hel like a war hammer and sent him stumbling until he fell onto his ass and caught himself with his hands behind him. Under the pale light of the moon and stars, his eyes shined like garnets once again, his black hair gleamed, and scarlet glistened on his bottom lip.

Layala slapped her hand over the small cut on her wrist and fell back against the house where the sharp knots of wood jabbed into her shoulder blades. "You need my blood to stay strong, don't you?" her voice came out as a whisper.

He stood and for a moment he looked apologetic. "It appears to be an unfortunate side effect for both of us. It seems the cost of waking me was your blood, therefore the cost of sustaining me is your blood. It's not something I anticipated, but magic often comes with a price." He jerked her dagger from his side as if it was nothing more than a small inconvenience. The wound closed in moments; the only trace that it was ever there was the blood glistening off his tunic.

He tossed her dagger back and her senses sharpened enough to catch it by the handle. "So, without it you'd die?" She dropped her hand from her wrist; there was very little blood and much of it was dried already.

Hel's fingers trailed the side of her face and she jumped at how fast he went from being several feet away to touching her. "We'll never find out."

Layala grabbed his wrist and shoved his hand back at him. "Don't touch me or I'll—" she breathed heavily, mind racing. What could she do? He was more powerful than her in every way even in a weakened state.

"Or you'll what? Threaten me with a good time?"

"If you want my blood from now on, you'll have to ask me for it, or I won't give you what you want. Ever." But she'd found his weakness. Maybe the only one he had. The only unfortunate thing about it was he appeared to be able to go a long time without needing her blood to rejuvenate. Two months had passed between waking him in the Void and now.

"You don't even know what I want."

"For me to remember you."

He laughed, and Layala's brows furrowed in confusion; he kept calling her his queen, protected her against his own.

Hel shoved his finger against her forehead. "I couldn't care less if you remember me, but you do have something in that pretty little head of yours that I need which requires Valeen to come out and play, not Layala."

Layala slapped his hand away. "If you ever want to get whatever knowledge I might have, start treating me with respect. At this point, even if I remembered, I wouldn't tell you."

"You'll get my respect when you earn it." He shoved his forearm into her chest and pushed her up against the side of the house. Layala glared defiantly as he leaned in inches from her face. "And you *will* tell me Val, or I'll kill *him*."

"No, you won't," Layala challenged, searching his beautiful yet harsh face, his thick dark brows tugged in, red eyes glowing. "Some part of you cares about him."

"I'd love nothing more than to prove how wrong you are about that." His hand snaked around her bicep, and he jerked her to his side. They started toward Midnight. "Shall I nail him to the wall and let you watch him suffer for days? Or let's get really creative—"

"Wait!" Layala tried to pull out of his grasp, but he only gripped tighter. "I don't remember anything, I swear." Her eyes darted toward the cluster of pines and oaks nearby. Warmth flooded her chest and down her limbs and her vines quietly wrapped around his ankles, halting him. She had to distract him, lead him away from Thane.

He looked down and then over at her. "You're being ridiculous. You know this won't—"

More vines coiled around his body, but it was the sweet but deadly spray from the opening lilies that made him shut his mouth. Without waiting to see if they'd affect him, Layala sprinted for the grove of pine trees. With arms pumping, and her elven feet gliding over the grass, she burst through the tree line, weaving between thick trunks, and leapt over mossy logs. If she kept going, she'd hit the unnamed forest soon enough and with it being nighttime... *maybe I can't get rid of him, but perhaps the beasts can.*

CHAPTER 14

HEL

H el clenched his fists at his sides and pushed his magic down the vines holding him in place until the ebony tendrils burned away into nothing. If he'd known she'd put up this much of a fight he'd have started their training this way. "Come now, love, the game of cat and mouse never ends well for the mouse."

Her shadowy form disappeared into the woods and Hel smiled. What fun this would be. With deliberately slow steps he followed her. It was only fair he gave her a marginal head start. It was not as if he could lose her trail. Now that he'd had a taste, the smell of her blood was like a siren's voice pulling him to follow. He thought back to their first confrontation and how differently it had gone...

The Past

"Trespassers are executed in my territory, Hel." Her sultry smooth voice washed over him like midnight rain on a hot summer night. No one's voice had ever felt like a feather sliding down his spine. His body shuddered with pleasure despite the sharp blade she held to his throat.

"It's a good thing I'm not trespassing then." He slid his gaze over to Valeen's placid face. She was even more stunning in her own territory. Her midnight purple bodice adorned with stars and moons around the low V-neckline fit like a glove. The sleeveless top wrapped under her arms and hit just below her ribs revealing a thin line of skin. From her rounded hips down, he couldn't help but drag his eyes over the black pants that fit in a way they could have been painted on her form. The colorful lights above shone off the moon and stars crown resting on her beautiful waves of ebony hair.

"Get out." She lowered the blade, Soulender, and pointed to the darkened spot in the wall he came from.

"I gave that to you as a gift and you would use it against me?" he tsked. "Have you used it against anyone else as of late? Synick perhaps?"

Her fury-blue eyes narrowed. "You attempt to break into my land and now you're here to accuse me of crimes? You're the thief, not I."

"I'm standing inside your walls. I would say it was more than an attempt. And you stole that from me. Seems we're both criminals."

The corner of her mouth turned up. "You said it was a gift." With the gentleness of a lover's caress, she slid the point of Soulender from his shoulder to wrist and a chill ran down his spine. "And you're only inside because I allowed it."

"Is that so?"

She met his stare and he'd be damned if it wasn't the most stunning thing he'd ever seen. "Leave. Now, before I have to do something I don't want to."

"Why do you hide in here? What are you afraid of?"

Her palm pressed flatly against his chest, and she backed him toward the wall. "I fear nothing."

They both stopped at the House of Night's edge. The pounding of War's ax crashing into the barrier sounded dull and far away although he was merely feet from them. "Get rid of that dagger. If anyone suspects you killed Synick—"

"No one but you and War knows I have it. If anyone suspects it was me, it's only because of the two of you. Tell your Uncle Balneir that you spoke to me, and I had nothing to do with it."

"You're quite demanding, aren't you."

"I'm not some silly girl to be trifled with. Get out of my territory or I'll cut off your pecker and every time you wish you could feel pleasure, you'll think of me."

"Oh, I already think of you, especially when it comes to pleasure."

"You think you're so clever and witty, god of mischief," she said with a chuckle, looking at him from boots to face. "I'll admit, you are quite delicious, and in my younger days I may have been tempted but when you're as old as I, the years tend to whittle out the stupid. I have no interest in you or your cousin or any of the Primevar. I've given you ample time, little boy. Leave."

The flush that filled Hel's cheeks came swiftly. "Tell me why you did it or I'll go back to my uncle with a very different story, and you can expect an army at your wall within a fortnight, and this little boy will destroy House of Night until there is nothing left. Soon no one will know that you or your precious territory ever existed at all."

The tip of the dagger was at the base of his throat in an instant. "You have no idea who you're dealing with. It was easy to kill your so-called uncle, a Primordial, said to be the best warrior the Primevar had, and I didn't even break a sweat. I can do the same to you just as easily."

Clenching his teeth together, Hel grabbed her wrist and pushed back though he was barely able to move her. "I don't like being threatened and that's the second time."

"Then do something about it," she challenged in a voice that sounded like she might start laughing at him. As if he was nothing more than a pitiful human and posed no threat at all.

The magical barrier finally cracked wide enough for War to stumble through, wild-eyed and ready for battle. A quick look between the two of them and he charged. His ax came down with blurred speed at the dagger threatening Hel's life. Valeen jerked it back and spun away, shifting entirely to shadow, and reappearing fully behind War. Standing opposite to them, she raised her chin ever so slightly and leveled Soulender at her waist.

"Why are you just standing there?" she curled her fingers on her left hand beckoning them forward. "Let's see what the best of the Primevar has to offer."

Hel and War exchanged a glance. She wielded a weapon that could end them forever. Any power Hel or his cousin possessed could hurt her but never kill her. She was a full-blooded Primordial goddess.

"Scared?"

War grinned and rested the length of his ax against his shoulder. "It's unfair for two large powerful males to fight a single female. I'd feel bad."

"Oh, gods, here we go," Hel murmured.

She came at them in the wrath of darkness, blanketing them in a cloud so thick Hel may as well have been locked in the blackest of dungeons where no light ever showed.

War cursed. Served him right. Hopefully, he got stabbed at least once for his comment.

Hel waved his hand blasting forth a ball of light that burned away the dark veil. Valeen was inches from him with the dagger leveled at his chest. "Shit," Hel backpedaled then dodged to the side barely missing a downward hack. She was out for blood, and this was no longer a game.

War took advantage of her occupation with Hel and swung his weapon at her. She turned in time to block it with her armored forearm and then drove the dagger at his belly.

"Damn it, goddess," he snarled, shoving his hips back, barely escaping her strike. "We didn't come here to fight." They went at each other, weapons flying at speeds difficult to track.

"No, you came here to steal this back and try to kill me for revenge."

War kicked his leg out and caught her ankle, tripping her up, but she dropped into a squat and grazed the dagger against his inner thigh. War dove and rolled out of the way, then threw out a blast of power that slammed into her shield with a crack and the impact lit up like a bolt of lightning.

Hel stepped back several feet to observe and folded his arms, assessing the goddess of night. She was better at combat than he anticipated, given that to his knowledge she'd never participated in any wars. She ducked and weaved, flipped and bent in ways that were incredible to miss War's weapon. There was no doubt she was able to take out Synick. But no one was better than War at combat. She was mistaken in thinking Synick had been the Primevar's most elite warrior.

Hel watched him pull back at least twice when he could have knocked her in the head. His downfall was having a soft spot for females, even for one that wanted to kill him apparently.

"Come on, War. Stop playing around," Hel said.

Their weapons clashed midair, and they stared each other down. "I'll back off if you will," he said, barely breathing heavily.

She shifted to shadow and Soulender whooshed through the air and sliced across War's shoulder, cutting into the thick fabric of his *leathers, but no blood by the looks of things. In a blink, she was gone in a flash of darkness and appeared before Hel; Soulender pierced his chest.*

Mouth dropping open, heat flared in Hel's body, panic filled him. He didn't want to die— couldn't die. His hand wrapped around the blade and both she and he looked down... it didn't go through. His eyes flicked up to hers, her chest rose up and down rapidly as she blinked in confusion. After a moment she bared her teeth, and she pushed harder—to no avail. Hel slowly smiled.

How was this possible? She'd caught him by surprise, and he should be dead. That was the true weapon, and he didn't have the time to put up a blocking shield.

The frustration fell from her face to one of confusion and she backed off, letting the dagger hang at her side. After a moment she brought it back up to eye level to inspect it, and Hel tugged his shirt down. A tiny bead of blood welled up from where the blade struck, and from there a new mark slowly appeared, the outline of a lily on a vine. "Well, that's interesting."

Before Valeen could attack again, Hel flicked his wrist, forming an impenetrable bubble around her, trapping her inside. She flipped the blade over, continuing her inspection of it. She seemed as baffled that the blade hadn't done its job as he was and didn't appear to notice her cage yet.

War slid his ax onto his back and cautiously walked around her then stared at the new mark beside many others Hel already possessed. "New shielding magic? Have you made yourself invincible now?"

Hel tugged his black shirt back up and looked Valeen over. "It wasn't me."

War's brows furrowed. "Perhaps the Maker spared you and that is a mark you are favored."

"Perhaps." He might believe so if he didn't see the same mark on

Valeen's shoulder that hadn't been there moments before. Did it mean they were to be sworn enemies marked to kill the other? Or something much deeper he didn't dare fantasize about. It was absurd.

Valeen lifted her hand and pressed it against the invisible bubble. "Let me out." Her voice was venomous, deadly.

War took a step closer to her and held out his palm. "Give us the dagger first."

She laughed and slid her hand along the length of the dagger, and it vanished. "No one will ever find it but me."

Hel was familiar with making things disappear into the aether, another realm, or simply sending something back to the place it belonged but to be able to do such a thing was a rare gift. One thing was for certain, no one would find that dagger unless she willed it—it could be anywhere, at any time, in any realm.

War slowly walked around her. "Do you have the sword of truth?"

"No. I couldn't find it."

"Why did you kill Synick?"

She tilted her head to the side, looking him up and down. "He murdered someone close to me. It's an offense punishable by death in Runevale if he wasn't a Primordial. I also suspect he's been stealing from my territory."

"Can any of this be proven?" Hel asked. Truth was he believed it without question. Synick prided himself on his variety of "stock" and had no qualms with murdering those lesser than him. It made perfect sense he'd take from House of Night if only to boast. She was one of the few who wouldn't sell or barter her people to others.

"Considering he is the head of the council—excuse me—was," she smirked, "I didn't bother going the standard route. He would lie, manipulate, and deceive as the rest of you do—as he has always done."

"We're not all like him," War said firmly.

"So, you're telling me you don't treat your people like cattle? You don't scheme to see who can have the most powerful bloodline or pit people against each other? I find that difficult to believe given who trained you. Your father and mother may be good people, War, but Synick was a piece of shit."

"I rule in Ryvengaard and no, I don't do those things. The dragon shifters follow me out of respect. And we're in agreement about Synick. Yes, he trained us, but we don't hold the same moral values."

She looked at Hel, and he sighed. "You know why people follow War? It's because he's a god and he could kill them with little effort. It's the same reason the people in my territory do as they are told and the same reason your people admire you. They revere and fear us. I give them small gifts of magic; they worship me."

She rolled her eyes as if she wasn't a goddess herself, revered and admired by others. "Exactly as I thought." She glanced down at her upper arm and did a double take. Her fingers ran over her skin, harshly rubbing at the new lily mark there. "What did you do to me?"

"I was hoping you could tell me."

She jerked her head up and shoved both palms straight out in front of her. A powerful blast shattered that bubble and sent Hel and War flying backward. It wasn't until he was on his ass outside the barrier to the night territory that he realized Valeen said she feared nothing, but that lily mark terrified her.

"VAL," Hel called in the darkness of the forest. "Come out, love, I promise I won't bite."

CHAPTER 15

LAYALA

L ayala pressed back into a wide tree. The decaying, knotted branches hung around her in gnarled and twisted ways. Every rustle of a bush, every hoot of an owl, or snap of a twig sent a jolt of panic to her already racing heart. *This was a bad idea. Leading him in here might get your ass killed too.* Beady glowing eyes seemed to peer out from every direction watching the new intruder. She was allowing the past to get the better of her. This forest reminded her of giants and the near death of Thane, the moment they'd been ripped apart. And to top it off, she was being stalked by the most deadly being in Adalon.

"Valeen," he called again, closer this time.

Dropping into a crouch below a bush, Layala took in deep cleansing breaths and searched the darkness around her. A centipede half as long as her skittered over the toe of her boot. Holding in a scream, she shot up, and flung out her leg, sending the thing flying. *Disgusting.* After a moment there was a sudden crawling sensation on the back of her neck. *Oh, it better not be...* She slapped at whatever it was and whirled around to a thick web entangled in her hair with a group of spiders as large as her head sliding down from the treetops. She squealed and slapped at her head then took off east. *Maker above, why did I come in here?* She leapt over downed trees and darted around mid-sized boulders, hoping it would lead her out but still away from Hel. This was worse than the dreams he'd haunted her in months before. *Damn spiders.*

Low-hanging tree branches whipped her in the face and across her body as she sprinted. One sliced open her cheek and she hissed at the sting but quickly swiped at it with her shoulder and kept running. Nothing in this area looked familiar, and there was no path in sight. The smell of a bog hit her moments before she stumbled into thick mud that quickly rose around her ankles. *Get it together, Layala!*

But there were things worse than her own death in life. Like watching him torture and kill Thane.

"You're letting fear get the best of you again." Hel's voice echoed all around the area making it impossible to know where he was now. "You can't hide. I can hear your racing heart."

Damn elven hearing. If her own thundering heart wasn't so loud she could hear him too. Layala glanced back. He was somewhere close now, but his form was not among the fog, the thick twisted branches, the tall ferns, or the little glowing eyes in trees. A clicking noise from a bird pecking echoed in the forest. There were no luminor crickets here, no other light than the meager amount that showed through the cracks in the canopy of trees.

You got yourself into this mess. Now you'll have to get out of it. She threw out her vine, wrapped it around a thick branch above and swung across the mud pit. Her legs carried her so fast everything around her became blurry, and her eyes burned with tears from the speed. The stomp of something colossally heavy shook the ground, and Layala skidded to a halt. She waited until a giant scorpion, half as tall as the hundred-foot trees, came into view, then waited until she spotted Hel too.

His taunting smile faltered when he realized she'd led him into a trap. With a smirk, Layala took off, running directly at the giant scorpion's pincers. It let out a high-pitched shriek and swiped at her; she dove through its open pincer and dodged its massive legs stamping and quaking the ground. Her feet carried her faster and faster, getting her out of harm's way. She darted to hide behind a massive decaying tree trunk. The beast lost sight of her and turned its attention to Hel. *Let's see you get out of this,* Layala grinned and ran without looking back.

She finally burst free from the unnamed forest out into the open and sighed in relief at the moon's light shining across the land and kept jogging into the field of waving golden grain, a small bit of comfort. After getting far enough away from the woods that she felt safe, she slowed and finally faced the forest. A wail sent a shiver down her spine. It didn't sound like a dying man. The openness of this area gave her no place to hide and nowhere to run. The castle was at least fifteen miles from here.

The breeze carried with it the faint smell of sweet smoke and a shiver ran down her spine. Layala gulped at the feeling that scent evoked in her. Had he taken down the scorpion already? He was going to be pissed now. She whirled around to run then felt *his* presence behind her. Every muscle in her body froze. There was no point in fleeing now. With a deep breath, she readied herself to face him and with a slow turn, she found Hel standing right behind her and jerked back ever so slightly.

"Boo. That was clever, Val. I'm proud of you." He smiled as if this was the most fun he'd had in a long time. "Oh, did I spoil the game? If you want to keep running, I'll turn around and count to thirty. Hide and seek is my favorite pastime."

Layala's brows furrowed, and she clenched her hands at her sides. She would no longer be his source to laugh at and make fun of. Turning on her heel, she started toward the castle. Showing her back to him was the biggest move she could make.

He appeared in front of her, eyes glowing red. "You didn't learn to not turn your back on me last time?"

"Don't you dare touch me again," Layala said and pulled a throwing star. The pointed metal was slick in her damp fingers. "This horseshit of you treating me like a puppet is over."

"I guess we're back to where we started." He took a step closer. "Or you'll what? Try to kill me?"

Breaths coming faster, Layala put the star's sharp edge to her own throat. "No, but I could kill myself." Even she didn't know if she'd do it.

His jaw muscles feathered, and his eyes darkened. "You wouldn't."

"I *will*."

They stared each other down for what felt like too long. "I think you're lying," he said. Layala pressed the steel star harder, its point piercing her flesh and slowly slid it; warm blood oozed down her throat and the sting made her wince.

His eyes blew wide. "Don't."

"Then stay away. I swear I will end my life, Hel. Then eventually you'll die too because you won't have my blood to keep you going. You won't get my memories. Your life will be over."

His throat bobbed and his gaze flicked from her bleeding neck to her face. "Valeen—"

"It's Layala."

In a flash, he vanished and reappeared before her and ripped the star from her hand and threw it far into the shadows of the wheat stalks. His warm hands gripped her face and he said with a shaky voice, "Don't you ever do that again. Not ever. Gods, you drive me insane."

"Do you even care about me at all or only yourself? From the moment I met you, it's my wife this or my wife that and then you treat me like I'm the dirt on your shoe."

His hands dropped to his sides and the fear and worry etched around his eyes turned harsh, lethal. "I don't really care about you. You're only a means for me to get what I want."

"The feeling is mutual." But a sharp sting in her chest, like an old wound acting up again. As if the goddess deep inside wouldn't stand for that, Layala shoved him hard in the chest. "Except, I'm the reason you're alive. You should be worshiping the ground I walk on, you bastard."

"You're the reason I'm mortal and trapped in this godsforsaken realm in the first place!"

Layala shoved him again, and he allowed it. She didn't know where this sudden burst of confidence came from, but she let her fury fly. "Oh, I'm sure you had absolutely nothing to do with it. You're just Mister Innocent. Poor, poor, Hel, a saint among heathens." Layala laughed. "What a joke that is. You're the worst of us all. A demon, the lowest of all creatures."

"Stop," he said.

She smacked him across the face. "You hate me? The sight of *you* disgusts me. How dare you try to make me undress! How dare you touch me with your filthy hands! I am not your plaything! And if you ever do any of that again I will find everyone you ever loved or cared about and destroy them and nothing in any of the realms will be able to stop me." Even Layala was surprised at the surety in her own words. She grew bolder still and went to shove him again and he grabbed her wrists. There was a long stretch of silence where he held her, and she stared up at him. Was there something there? Some familiarity other than his resemblance to Thane? The red color of his eyes seemed wrong. Shouldn't they be turquoise, like a warm ocean?

"You should know you already took everything I cared about a long time ago." He stared down at her and his jaw flexed. A desperate desire flashed in his features, but it wasn't her bloody neck his eyes fell upon, it was her lips, even if everything else about him said he hated her.

"And what was that?"

"You and him. You should go back to the castle. You're bleeding and every predator in the area can smell you."

"I am a predator."

The corner of his mouth tugged up ever so slightly. "Go," he prodded and dropped his hold on her.

She took one step away, then two. He didn't move but he watched her like the hunters he spoke of. There was no warmth there, no sign they were ever mates or lovers, just coldness in the beautiful planes of that face.

Well, she wasn't going to wait around and argue about it, so she started off toward that farm to get Midnight before she went home. To her astonishment, Hel didn't pursue her and when she glanced back, he was gone.

Layala stood in front of the gold-framed mirror in her room and dipped a cloth into a basin of warm water. With a squeeze and twist she wrung it out until the droplets splashed quietly. She dabbed it along the gash she'd put in her own neck. The line was angry red but crusted over and healing. Stray hair escaped her braided black hair like a halo of frizz, and all over her face and hands were little splotches of dirt from the unnamed forest mixed with splatters of black blood from pale ones. She mopped her face clean then glanced down at all the blood staining the collar of her blue shirt. She unfastened her thick bodice and dropped it, then with a sigh, she tugged her shirt over her head and tossed it to the corner.

A quiet knock sounded on her bedroom door. Ugh, who could it be? If it was Talon leaving another note she might not be able to keep herself calm. Or perhaps Pearl was back from her time off helping Reina's son. Another knock, more urgent this time.

Layala hurried to her dresser to find clothing and something to cover her wound with. She pulled out a thin, almost sheer white scarf. No, that was suspicious, and it might not cover well enough. There must be something with a high collar. There were several tops, long sleeve and short, and as she tugged them out, she found they all had V necks or round collars. Cursing, she shoved them back in and closed the drawer. Then the door opened, and Thane stepped inside. The candles in the room gave off enough light there was no hiding her wounds now.

His bright green eyes trailed over her, standing in her bralette, pants, and dirty boots. He quickly closed the door behind himself with his brows lowered in concern. "What happened to your neck? I thought you were training with Vesstan."

She swallowed hard not knowing what to say.

"Layala," he urged, closing the distance between them in four long strides. His calloused thumb ran across the thin slice. "What is that from?"

She didn't dare tell him about her confrontation with Hel or he might go after him, and she knew how that would play out. "I encountered pale ones at a farm. They killed the father—the mother and child got away." At least, she hadn't seen them when she went back for Midnight, but she'd been in her head so much thinking about her incident with Hel she didn't check to see if the father was truly dead... he'd been bitten.

His face pulled down into a scowl. "You could have been killed."

"I promised Aunt Evalyn I'd get her her list of plants." Layala cursed under her breath remembering she only retrieved two items on the list. "I wasn't looking for trouble."

"But it found you, Layala. Even I wouldn't go out to fight pale ones alone. One mistake is all it takes. You know I've lost friends to them. You've seen what they do." He shook his head and then ran his hand down his face.

"I didn't go to fight," she said, softening her voice at his worry. "It was for Aunt Evalyn. I can't risk her going out on her own if I don't do it. I'm not afraid to go out there. I don't want fear to rule my life."

"And it shouldn't have to but you're not immortal anymore." He shoved his hand into his hair. "I love you more than anything in all the worlds." He took her hand and kissed it then fixated on the wound on her neck. "Every time you sneak away, and I come to find you gone, it scares the shit out of me. All the things that could happen to you flood my mind. Like this." He lightly brushed her wound. "What if you don't come back one day and I find your lifeless body? Do you have any idea what that would do to me?"

Tears burned her eyes. "I—I'm sorry."

"You're slowly killing me." He slid his palm against her cheek and turned her face to look at him. The anguish in his voice, in his eyes, slammed into her. "You running off every night putting yourself in danger while looking for him. It's almost more than I can bear."

"I never meant... You know I wasn't looking for him for any other reason than to end all this. Can't you see that with him here?"

"I saw the way you looked at him when he first arrived... it was how you used to look at me."

"No, no that's not it at all. The only reason I have changed is because it's difficult to be around you with the way things are between us." It wasn't because of any memories of him.

She refused to believe the image of Hel's naked ass was a memory, no matter how good he looked. At the uncertainty on his face, Layala rubbed her forehead and threw herself back on the bed. Then she reached down, tugged off her boots and tossed them on the floor.

Thane sat down at the end of her bed but kept a careful distance.

This being afraid to touch each other was getting old. This wall between them seemed to only be growing thicker and taller. To chip away at it, Layala moved closer and pressed her palm against the side of his beautiful face. He closed his eyes and leaned into her touch. "I'll try to remember, for you. So we can be together. I just wish it didn't have to be this way because it doesn't."

"Laya, I love you, but I'm confused right now about you and me. There is a whole other person inside you waiting to come out."

"It doesn't have to ruin what we have now," Layala whispered. "You promised you'd love me in every life and in any realm... has that changed?"

"I will always love you." His chest rose sharply. "But I'm afraid you may not, and I'm trying to prepare myself for that possibility."

Hadn't she shown him over and over that she loved him?

She'd risked her life on countless occasions, and gave him everything, her heart, her body. She'd give him eternity as mates if he'd allow it.

"It's you that I want. It's always been you." She leaned in to kiss him and he pulled back. It would be a lie to say the rejection didn't sting. His eyes dropped to the lily mark on her shoulder and his silence, his action said more than words. "You don't want me anymore?"

He twirled a piece of her hair around his finger but wouldn't look at her in the face. "It's not that I don't want you. You know I want you, Laya."

Layala pushed his hand away and stood up. "If you still want me, then prove it. You pinned me to the wall in the alley then left me even more confused than before."

She stepped between his thighs. There was hunger in his eyes again. He drunk her in, and his tongue swiped across his lower lip. Then his hands slid around her waist, his fingers pressed into her flesh.

"You're pure temptation, Laya, and determined to ruin my vow," he admitted and tugged her onto his lap. "You're right. I shouldn't have left things that way."

She straddled her thighs around his waist and wrapped her arms around his neck, leveling her breasts in perfect reach of his mouth. He leaned forward, kissing the tops of her half-exposed breasts. Layala gripped him harder and threaded her fingers into his long hair.

His lips worked up her collarbone, her neck, until they reached her ear. "Maker above, Laya. Your body is perfection. You are perfection." His mouth moved back down until he wrapped an arm around her back and flipped her over onto the bed and he kissed below her navel. Goosebumps spread over her skin. "You want to feel the pleasure deep inside?"

"It's you I want. Not just the feeling." She lay back as he climbed over her and arched into him. His mouth trailed down her belly and his fingers played with the waist of her pants, where he continued his kiss.

"Only do this if you won't leave me broken, Thane. Promise me right now to be with me every night. That pushing me away is over."

"Laya," he breathed and lifted his chin. He stood upright and blinked as if coming to his senses. "No sex but," he smiled deviously, "I can delight you in other ways."

This was about so much more than pleasure and intimacy. Their entire relationship was about love and giving in because of that love, not lust or just wanting to feel something. She frowned and pressed her barefoot against his chest. "Promise me it all or you get nothing. Not even the satisfaction of watching me finish."

The expression on his face was like he was torturing himself as he took a step away. "If that's your requirement, then I'll hold true to my word about waiting for your sake."

She knew it was noble, virtuous even, but she wished he was more of a scoundrel at that moment. "Fine. Goodnight then."

With the back of his sleeve, he wiped sweat from his brow and cursed under his breath. "Goodnight, Laya."

CHAPTER 16

LAYALA

Light tapping footsteps hurried down a dark corridor. Dim glowing orbs hung along the center every few feet above her head. She made a quick turn and shoved through a door with etchings of the moon phases and stars surrounding it. A young blond man with waves past his shoulders and wearing round gold glasses looked up from the papers on the desk before him.

He stood upon seeing her and dipped his head. "Valeen," he said in reverence. "You appear troubled."

She closed the distance between them, lifted her right arm and tapped her fingers against her new mark. "What is this? We had two intruders at the border. When I tried to stab one of them in the heart, I couldn't. And this same mark appeared on his chest beneath my blade."

The man's blue eyes lifted and the bump in his throat bobbed. With furrowed brows he raised a hand toward her arm. "May I?"

"Yes."

His light touch moved over the lily mark on her upper arm at the base of her shoulder. "It just appeared you say?" She nodded. "I've never seen one like it..."

"You know what it means?" she suspected, but she needed to hear it from someone else.

He raised a finger, turned away and hurried over to a bookshelf that lined the entire wall. His fingers skimmed over the titles until he plucked a brown book with gold lettering. The sound of him hurriedly flipping pages filled the silence between them. The longer it took him the more sweat covered the back of her neck.

"I read about this before." He looked up from the pages. "Is he a god?"

She nodded.

"Then I assumed you had a weapon that could truly kill him." He cleared his throat when she stared. "There are a couple accounts of this happening before. When two people are destined for one another, they cannot kill the other, and a mark appears on their flesh. In this case, it looks to be yours on the arm of the attempt and his on the wound."

"What do you mean destined for each other?" she snarled.

"In this story, once they met, they were drawn to each other. It didn't matter if they tried to stay away, they always seemed to end up in the same places. They eventually became— lovers." He turned the book around and handed it to Valeen.

Her eyes fell to one line. Soulmate—an unbreakable union formed by the All Mother. The perfect match to the soul. *Slowly shaking her head, she looked up.* "This can't be. He's—" she nibbled her lip, hesitant to admit, but finally said, "not one of us. The All Mother wouldn't bind me to one of them. He worships the Maker not her. And especially not someone from his House."

"I've never seen a mark form on two people like this myself. But that account says there have been others, and some have been *enemies. I don't think everyone tries to kill their mate so there isn't a mark formed that way but for you..."*

Valeen's heart crashed hard against her chest. She scanned the page in disbelief and read: Once soulmates become one body, they become of one mind, and thoughts can be heard and spoken when desired. Mates are eternally drawn toward one another. Their mark is unique to them and may appear in many ways, however, it is typical when they become one flesh.

"I suppose it could have been worse. It could have been his wretched mentor."

"His mentor?" The blond man's eyes narrowed. *"So, it's Hel or War, isn't it? I saw something between the three of you at the party."*

"Don't ever speak of this to anyone. Ever." She slammed the book shut. *"This is simply a new tattoo. That is all."*

He bowed his head. "You have my silence, goddess."

LAYALA SHOT up in bed with a sweat-soaked brow. The morning light and chirping of happy birds outside the window were a stark contrast to the dream. Maker above, it felt too real to be only a dream. It was a memory. *Did Valeen—I, try to kill Hel before? Was that how the mark on my arm truly formed?* She blinked several times trying to clear her blurry morning vision, not to mention confusion.

She pushed her unkempt hair back and smoothed down the fraying pieces and meandered over to the dresser. A black short-sleeved top with silver swirls around the collar and the matching pants would be perfect for the day.

With a quiet click Tifapine stepped in through her newly installed miniature door, standing a foot and a half tall. She carried two rolls half as big as her and wore a grin only the happiest of gnomes had. "Mornin'," she said and wiggled her eyebrows. "I got into the kitchen and made some rolls. My recipe is better, but I won't be giving away my secrets. Anyway, I saw this strange—I will admit, very *attractive* new elf downstairs talking with Thane. They look oddly alike. He has shorter hair and creepy red eyes, but they could be brothers." She tore into the roll with her teeth and said with a muffled mouthful, "Is that his cousin I heard the staff talking about? Is this the same elf who carried you up here?"

"Yes."

"Scandalous."

Well, that news ruined Layala's morning. She blew out her breath and stepped into her pants and slid on her top. "His name is Hel, and it's not scandalous. We were training with magic, and I passed out." She considered using his title, but Tif would probably scream.

She narrowed her eyes. "But isn't that," she lowered her voice to a whisper, "the Black Mage's name. Zaurahel—Hel. I hear you all talking, you know. I thought it was strange Queen Orlandia left too."

Layala frowned and nodded. "Yes."

"So, you mean to tell me, the Black Mage is dragon's fire hot? No way." She shook her head and took another bite. "It wouldn't be fair of the Maker to do such a thing. He should be hideous, as hideous as he is on the inside."

Good lord, of course she'd find Hel attractive. "Well, it seems the Maker has a sense of humor."

"I hate to be the bearer of bad news, but have you seen the *Palenor Scroll's* story today?" She nodded toward the bedside table.

Layala's stomach dropped, and she turned around, starting for the folded-up paper on the nightstand. "No." Then a quiet knock came from somewhere in the bathroom and she paused.

Layala's brows pulled down and the hairs along her spine stood. "Didn't you say Thane was downstairs?" She listened for something else and watched the entry for a moment. It was nothing. Just her paranoia at work again.

"Yep," she said and happily chomped into the second roll. Layala wrongly assumed that was for her. "Should I just tell you? I'll just tell you. Telvian Botsberry wrote that he speculates that you are meeting with the Black Mage in secret places when you sneak off castle grounds at night, definite implication there, and Thane is too busy with the war and pale ones to know what you're doing. He said you'll be the fall of Palenor."

Layala's jaw dropped. "You can't be serious. I'll cut his hand off for writing such lies."

"Oh, can I come?"

Three aggressive pounds on the door made Tif shriek and fumble what was left of her roll. She barely caught it before it hit the ground. *Who could that be?* Thane certainly never did that, and the guards wouldn't dare. They walked on tiptoes around her lately.

"Open this door right now!" Talon's shrill voice sounded muffled through the barrier.

Layala sighed. She was supposed to have left with Orlandia, and she'd actively avoided Layala for months. The door flew open before Layala could get two steps and Talon marched in with her fists swinging at her sides and a scowl to rival a bear. With her heel, she kicked the door shut and turned on Layala with a pointed finger. "It's all your fault!"

The little gnome in her red hat glanced between the two then scurried under the bed in a flash.

"What are you talking about?"

"Thane kicked Vyra and my friends out of the castle and ordered me confined to my rooms. Not only that, but he also tried to send me away with my mother in the middle of the night. She said it was getting too dangerous to stay here but I know it was just a conspiracy to get me to leave my friends. Today he finally let me out and yelled at me for not leaving with her." For once, her usual perfect brown curls were falling out of her updo, and bits of frazzled hair stuck out here and there. "All because you can't take a little razzing. It's nothing less than you deserve after what you did."

"I'll say it again. I am sorry, Talon, for hurting you. I truly am." Layala supposed this was long overdue. She'd apologized months ago when they first arrived back, but they could only avoid each other for so long in the same household.

Her soft ivory cheeks reddened, and she stamped her foot. "Hurt! After I tried to help you escape, you repaid me by almost killing me! I saw the end, I couldn't breathe. I couldn't even swallow. I went cold, and I couldn't stop shaking. You better thank your lucky stars that my brother had the ability to save me!"

Layala frowned as the image of Talon suffering in Thane's arms flashed across her mind. It hurt her to see Thane with such terror in his eyes, but the worst part was she didn't feel bad about it. Not really. Aunt Evalyn was alive because of that move, and she knew Thane could save Talon. It was a risk she would take again if given the chance to redo it. "I am sorry. I won't ever hurt you again. And by the way, I haven't told Thane anything about your *little razzing*. He was truly trying to send you away for your own safety."

"Oh, yes you did! He shoved one of the notes in my face and yelled at me in front of my friends then made them leave. I've never been more embarrassed in my life. And I'll have you know it wasn't me who wrote them all. Everyone hates you. You're a disease in this place that we can't wait to flush out. You should hear the things the guards say about you behind your back. Even everyone in the city hates you. No one can understand why their High King keeps you around."

That stung the most; it was true after all. She stayed for Thane, but could their relationship survive the eternal invisible mark branded on her for waking the Black Mage? Even if not everyone believed yet, they would. What if she ruined Thane's life and his rule?

"You're right to be angry with me. Everyone is, but I am trying to fix it. I'm going to stop the Black Mage."

"You can't stop him!" she crowed. "No one can except maybe my brother but I'm doubtful of even that. He's the Black Mage, the most powerful mage in history. And what can you do besides grow some weeds?"

That was a gross understatement of her power, but she had a point. "I'll talk to Thane about letting your friends back inside. Just stop with the petty notes, alright? And if you are the *Palenor Scroll's* anonymous source, stop it right now."

Her brow lifted. "That's not me. It's Mother letting slip details to her servants but what can you expect, you're the reason her husband, my father, is dead." She didn't appear particularly sad about it.

"Orlandia?" Layala muttered.

"She'll keep doing it too. And I wouldn't be surprised if she comes back for the celebration ball." Silence lasted a full five seconds before Talon continued on, "And fine. If Vyra and all the others are allowed back, no more notes about you being fat or that you're a pariah in our society or a—"

"You're pushing it, Talon. I only have so much patience for your mouth."

She swallowed and took a step back. Good, she had some

fear of Layala still. But then Talon's shaky arm rose to point, and she sputtered, "Buh—buh—behind you!"

Layala caught sight of a shadow in her peripheral and whipped around, barely catching the wrist of the female wielding a knife aimed at her heart. *Holy shit!*

Talon screeched, ran toward the bed, and dove on top, pulling the blankets up to use as a shield. "Get her!" she wailed.

Instinct kicked in and Layala shoved her knee into the assailant's gut and then twisted her weapon arm. She rolled with the move and swung Layala around until she smacked into the wall. The vase on the shelf fell and the fertility fern collapsed and both shattered spilling dirt and glass across the floor. *Damn, she's strong.* Layala kicked back, nailing the woman in the stomach, and ducked under another strike, then bobbed out of the way of the blade as it sliced at her chest.

The brunette maiden was not an elf, nor did she look entirely human; there was something oddly animalistic about her. Brown leopard spots spilled from the top of her left brow around her temple and across her cheekbone. She bared her teeth, showing elongated canines and swung at Layala in rapid succession, the woosh of the blade cutting through the air with sharp whistles. Layala backpedaled toward the windows to miss each one, but all came dangerously close.

She threw out her vine; it wrapped around the assassin's wrist and tied her to the bedpost, forcing her to drop the dagger.

"Don't bring her near me!" Talon rolled off the bed and picked up a glass of water and chucked it at the woman. It knocked her in the side of the head; she turned with a menacing growl.

"You should have shut that one up yourself," the woman said with a sneer at Talon.

"Who are you?" Layala demanded, throwing another vine around the woman's waist, and hooking it around the bedpost.

Another dagger appeared in the woman's freehand, and she launched it at Layala. She threw up her arms and the blade stopped mere inches from her forehead. In her moment of distraction, the bedpost cracked and snapped in half, allowing the woman to break free. With blade-tipped boots she kicked Layala, driving her toe into her ribs. Layala barely felt the stab and cracked her fist straight into the woman's nose. She stumbled back a few steps, and with blood leaking out of her nostrils, she let out a wail that sounded something between a dying cat and a wolf howl. Right before her eyes, the woman's body shifted into a giant tawny cat with black and chestnut brown misshapen spots. She was at least the size of her human form in length and came up to Layala's chest in height. Her long canines dripped saliva and with her ears pinned back and huge black pupils, she had murder in mind.

Layala's heart crashed wildly, and she would have done anything for a sword at the moment, but she'd left it and all her weapons in the bathroom to dry after she'd cleaned them, and this beast stood in the way. Damn it all. "Where is the guard?!" Layala shouted at Talon and backed toward the window until she bumped into the ledge. With her hand behind her back, she felt for the window latch.

"I sent them away so they wouldn't hear me raise my voice and tell Thane. But you can handle—uh whatever she is, right?"

"I thought I could only grow some *weeds*?" Layala snapped.

The cat-woman let out another fearsome cry and lowered into a crouch, flicking her long tail back and forth. A moment later she pounced at Layala. She dove to the left onto the bed and rolled across it while the feral shifter hit the window, chomped at the green draping vines, rag dolled a stalk and tore it free. It hit the ground with a plunk. Then she turned and prowled onto the bed. Trembling, Talon latched onto Layala's shoulders and ducked behind her.

"Back toward the door," Layala said, watching the predator's light green eyes for signs she might pounce again. The moment they ran, the chase would be on. "Slowly."

Talon let go and her footsteps slammed as she sprinted for the door.

"I said, slowly!" Layala shouted and the cat leapt from the bed and soared through the air. Her front paws crashed into Talon's back taking her to the ground with a thud. Talon screamed loud enough to hurt Layala's ears; there was no way someone wouldn't hear and come running. The cat raised her head, teeth bared. Layala snatched the woman's dagger off the ground, and in three steps drove the blade into her side. The cat wailed and turned, slashing her massive, clawed paw at Layala.

"You came for me. Leave her alone!" Layala curled her fingers and called to her magic; it coiled out of thin air and wrapped around the assassin's neck. *Squeeze tighter!* she silently commanded. The cat wildly clawed at the black vine, and rolled around on the ground, writhing and moaning. After a few moments, she shifted back into her human form. Layala squatted down and jerked the dagger out of her side. "Who are you? Who sent you?"

Her face turned a dark shade of purple, as the magical vines squeezed harder. Her ragged breaths became shallower with each passing second. But Layala needed her alive. She needed answers. The vines loosened and she grabbed the woman by the crown of her head, gripping her hair. "Tell me who sent you and I might let you live."

She spit and a spray of saliva and blood hit Layala on the

left cheek. Layala recoiled for a moment then punched her again. The woman's head flew back and bounced off the floor then she laughed revealing red-stained teeth. "You're not what you once were, Valeen. Not even close. You're doomed like all the times before."

"Valeen?" Layala whispered. She grabbed the woman by the shoulders and shook her. "How do you know that name?" Pain seared Layala's thigh. She gritted her teeth to keep from screaming, and found claws embedded into her flesh.

"Release me or I'll tear your leg off."

The claws sunk deeper, and she began to pull, dragging them like blades down her muscle and flesh. Layala let the vines fall loose, the claws retracted, and she knocked Layala in the chin with a hard punch. She shoved her off and sprinted to the window, shattering the glass as she pounced through it.

The bedroom door burst open and slammed against the wall. Thane came through first and Hel trailed right behind him. They stood next to one another, surveying the disaster.

"There's no way the princess put up this much of a fight," Hel said, leaning up against the wall.

Thane rushed forward. "What happened!"

"A psychotic wild animal woman," Talon wailed, peeking out from covering her face. "She almost killed me."

Thane looked to Talon cowering on the floor then Layala and dropped to her side. He lifted his hand toward her waist where her black top was half covered in blood. "What is she talking about? Who did this?"

"I'm fine." She pushed his hand away.

Hel watched the exchange, and Layala immediately regretted showing their less-than-perfect relationship in front of him. She didn't want to reveal the strain between her and Thane even if there were rumors. But he seemed less interested in their interaction, and more so in the bloodstain that blossomed all over her shirt from the rib wound. Whether it was because her blood was his life source, and he was worried about losing it or he was worried about *her* she didn't know. Either way, she quickly folded her arm over her belly.

"You need healing balm." Thane touched the five puncture marks in her thigh, and she winced.

"I'm alright. I promise," Layala said with a half-smile, trying to reassure him even if it hurt like hell.

He nodded but still looked concerned. "So, what happened?"

"I don't know what she was exactly. She looked almost human, but she changed into a huge cat."

Thane's brows furrowed and he glanced back at Hel. "A feline shifter? But they're from Ryvengaard." He looked back to Layala. "How did she get in here?"

"It's not difficult to deduce," Hel said, tucking his hands behind his back and walking forward. "The assassin is a chameleon of sorts. Her skin can change to blend into her surroundings. She likely came in through a window and by the state of the room," his gaze swept across the broken vase and snapped bedpost, "there was a struggle. Layala obviously came out on top, although it should have been much easier than this. And you shouldn't have let her get away."

"I didn't *let* her," Layala balked. And if she was able to change her appearance to blend in, she might have been the one stalking her in the alley outside of Aunt Evalyn's place, Nerium Oleander. "She called me *Valeen*," Layala said, and swallowed the nervous lump in her throat.

"I'm sure she did because if she's a shifter that wants you dead, she was sent here."

"Sent by who?"

189

"This is the first assassin?" Hel asked.

"Yes..."

"They don't like when the three of us get together." His gaze fell to the window, and he pressed his lips together. A big silver owl sat perched on the tree branch staring inside. *How odd*, Layala thought. *It's morning and owls tend to only come out at night.* "They know we'll want revenge and they're going on the offensive," he finished, but was that what he truly meant to say? With his hands tucked behind his back, he began to pace. "I need you both to get your shit together faster. Our lives depend on it."

"When you say 'they', who do you mean?" Layala asked as she watched the owl spread its wings and take off. Although she had a feeling she knew.

He stopped and turned his head to look at her. "The Council of the Gods, love. They declared war on us a long time ago."

"Us?" Layala drawled. "There isn't exactly an 'us'."

She hoped Thane would back her up on this, but he was busy inspecting the broken window. "This was the bigger problem you kept hinting at," Thane said. "You could have simply told me."

Hel chuckled. "I knew you'd figure it out sooner or later. And Val, you know what they say, the enemy of my enemy..."

"Is my friend," Layala breathed. She didn't want to admit he could be right.

His smile widened making the dimple on his cheek deepen, and Layala's breath hitched. For all his wickedness making him ugly on the inside, he truly was beautiful, like gazing up at the vast starry night and the wonder that came with heavens.

Hel's voice whispered in her mind, *Careful staring like that, little rabbit, you might give the wrong impression.*

CHAPTER 17

THANE

Thane stepped out of the bathroom after discovering the broken windowpane the assassin used to reach through and unlatch the window's lock. Must he place bars on the windows? Or maybe Hel could set a shielding spell of some kind. Atarah, the keeper of the mage's tower, did once say "If he could think it he could do it as long as he had a rune to hold the spell." And from what Thane remembered, Hel was capable of just about anything.

Not only did he have to worry about pale ones and radical elves who may hurt Layala, now the gods' council sent assassins. The broken bedpost left splinters across the floor and sharp edges on the stump. Broken glass, and scattered bits of crumpled paper from the terrible notes Talon, and others, left the room in shambles. He inspected Layala for what felt like the hundredth time to make certain she wasn't going to suddenly drop to the floor from a lethal wound. The tiny pink scar across her neck from the blade that could have ended her life was almost invisible now, but the blood staining her shirt was something he could help with.

His sister looked like a pathetic child still whimpering on the ground while conversation went on around her. He stooped down, grabbed hold of her arms, and raised her up. "Come on, enough of that. You're not hurt, are you?" Talon gripped him around the waist and held onto him like her life depended on it. Groaning, he unlatched Talon's arms and moved her away a step. "Please go and find Fennan and tell him to put the guards on high alert. Tell him there's been an assassination attempt."

"Sure, but I'm writing to Mother too. She'll probably be over the moon when I tell her Layala was the target. She'll only be upset that the assassin didn't get the job done." Talon grew an almost comedic grin.

"Talon," Thane snapped.

"You know, princess," Hel said. "A mouth like that is bound to get your neck snapped. If you think Valeen will tolerate such disrespect once she remembers, you're dead wrong. Emphasis on dead."

Thane pursed his lips. Would Layala change so much? He feared who she might become; if the last battlefield was any indication, she'd have no remorse for taking lives if it gave her what she wanted. Seeing her and Talon together again reminded him of all the blood, his sister's ragged breaths, and her at death's door in his arms because of Layala's hand. In some ways, she chose her aunt over him that day even though he'd always chosen her.

There was nothing he loved more than the elf standing there watching him with those pretty blue eyes, searching his face as if she wondered what he might be thinking. It was torture distancing himself from her. Maybe it was the wrong decision. Maybe she'd always be the same, and nothing would change.

Talon stared at Hel, and the smug look she usually wore vanished. Her throat bobbed and she took a half step to put herself partially behind Thane. "Who are you?" she asked softly instead of her usually rude demanding tone.

"You know exactly who I am. I can hear it in the pitter-patter of your rapid heart. I can smell it in your fear."

With a trembling hand, Talon gripped Thane's arm. He nudged her toward the door. "Talon, go find Fennan. Now."

"I'm not going out there by myself," she hissed. "What if the cat-shifter is out there?"

"I'm the most dangerous thing in this place, sweetheart," Hel said with a dangerous smile. "You should listen to your brother."

Talon sucked in a quick breath, and hurried out the door, slamming it behind her.

"I've always despised entitled princesses, even if she is your sister," Hel murmured. "Or now that you're remembering, what is she to you?"

"She is still my sister, always will be," Thane said. He'd already considered this as memories of his first family on Runevale came to mind. He loved them too, but it didn't change that his elven family was still family. His elven mother still carried him in her womb, birthed him, and raised him.

"Huh," Hel said and carried on, "what did the assassin look like? Be as detailed as possible."

Layala stood up and her face contorted from putting weight on her leg. "Leopard-like markings on the side of her face. Wildly curly brunette hair. She bore a rune mark, twin diamond shapes, one slightly higher and to the left of the other. Her light tan leather bodysuit cut from her shoulders to her ankles. I've never seen the fashion before. A brown belt around her hips with turquoise beads... the rune mark, what is it for?"

"If it's the one I'm thinking of, it allows non-gods passage through realms. We could travel anywhere at will through the portals. It's part of being keepers of the realms, but most can't."

"If the gods are keepers of the realms, why don't we ever see them here?" Thane said. "They—we used to come, but we haven't seen anyone for—"

"Two thousand one hundred years," Hel said. "When we were cast out." His red eyes flicked to the window once again. Either he was worried another assassin would come through or something else out there bothered him. "Something barred them after that. They can't leave, but they can communicate and send others."

"How?"

"I don't know."

Layala lifted her shirt, revealing the wound on her lower left rib cage. It was smaller than Thane anticipated, and that lightened some of the weight off his chest. She dropped it back down and limped into her bathing room, and with a quiet splash of water, she wrung out a cloth. "Did it have something to do with us? If it was only after our banishment, it must be somehow."

Thane and Hel exchanged glances. She'd said that without any eye-rolling or denial. Her quiet steps pattered across the stone, and she appeared in the archway from the bathing room to her chambers, holding the cloth against her ribs. "Why are you both staring at me like that?"

Thane shook his head and stood. "I can get healing balm out of my room."

Layala dabbed at the wound on her abdomen. It was the most crucial of the damages to her body, but as of the last few months her injuries healed faster. This wouldn't last more than a day. Even her leg punctures would scab and heal over in a few hours.

"I'll be fine." She gestured toward the broken window. "So, who was that?"

Hel glided over to Layala's bed, fell back, and put his hands behind his head as if it was his own place of rest. "By your description, the beads are a dead giveaway, a servant from the House of Fury. Bitch must be on the council now, or she's just *furious* she can't leave."

A female flashed across Thane's mind. The House of Fury was for the goddess of fury. He knew her, at least in some capacity.

"The shifter is indeed originally from Ryvengaard, home of the shifters, as well as beasts one might only believe existed in nightmares. But her kind are humanoid as you saw, and without war and disease, they'll live a few hundred years. She only lives longer because of the undying waters in Runevale. It's a real treat she shifted on you."

"Ass," Layala murmured. "She could have killed me, you know."

"Looks like I'll be keeping a closer eye on you then. Real close. I may even sleep in here and warm your bed since *he* doesn't. Nights must get lonely, love."

A rush of angry heat flooded his cheeks. "You'll stay away from her," Thane said, stepping closer to her, grinding his teeth. "The only thing you will do is help her with magic and remembering. It's all you're good for anyway."

The corner of Hel's mouth twitched. His eyes danced with mischief; he'd gotten the reaction he wanted. "Magic is certainly my talent, but you know what I'm also good for?

Making her moan my name. I would give her such a high her skin would light up like the stars. Bet you don't do that."

Thane charged ahead, fists ready to fly until Layala jumped in between them, holding out her hand to him, and the other at a smirking Hel. He hadn't so much as moved on the bed, his hands still tucked behind his head, ankles crossed.

"He's just being an ass, his true talent." She glanced over at him. "Besides, if his lovemaking was as grand as he claims, I wouldn't have forgotten all about it."

"Help, I'm stuck," a tiny gnome voice called from the canopy above. Tifapine poked her head out from her perch then ducked back in.

"What is that and why is it here?" Hel asked.

"Her name is Tifapine and she's my gnome. Leave her alone or I swear on the Maker..."

He grinned and then laughed. "Why would I hurt her? She's cute. Like a little fluffy kitten. And you're Drivaar, Valeen, you praise the All Mother. If you're going to swear on anyone, it should be her."

"It's Layala."

"Whatever. Besides, I'm not in the business of killing small helpless creatures. What do you think I am, a monster?"

"Considering you cursed the elves, I have a hard time thinking of you as anything but a monster," Layala snapped.

Maker, they bickered like an old... he stopped that thought before it could finish and lead to other things like Layala moaning Hel's name rather than his, and distracted himself with trying to recall different houses in Runevale; House of Night, House of Fury, House of Spring... There must be hundreds named for the god or goddess who ruled their own territory.

Tif poked her head out again, this time with a smile. Was she even stuck?

Hel rolled out of bed and casually strolled past. Layala was the only thing stopping Thane from getting in a good punch. "I told you already. I didn't create the curse; it was a natural consequence of the balance of magic. They wanted more and more, and I gave it to them. I mean, gods they made me filthy rich, but then one day they started coming to me as white as snow and calling me master with bad habits of wanting to eat people. I was surprised myself."

Thane bristled at how he spoke of them so casually. After fighting the pale ones for years, losing friends, watching people get eaten as he said, how could he speak of it as if they weren't destroying Palenor? As if no one mattered. *He doesn't care about Palenor or anyone but himself. Remember that.* "If that's true, can you even end the curse?" Thane asked.

"I'm sure I could find a way. But why would I? I'm going to need them." He stepped out into the hall and gave a small wave. "I hear there's a ball coming up. I need to find a date. See you around."

Thane stared at him, *Need them for what?* With a wave of his hand, Thane pushed magic out and the door closed. It took all his restraint not to chase him down for a brawl. He knew Hel's games, knew he said things just to get a rise out of people, and most of the time Thane didn't let it bother him, but when it came to Layala he didn't always think clearly.

Layala tugged her top off and tossed it into the pile of dirty clothes. "I don't believe him. He must have had something to do with the curse or why would they be loyal to him? If it's the All Mother's balance of nature, wouldn't they simply be cursed?"

"I don't know," Thane said truthfully. "But I think

knowing that the pale ones are, in part, his fault, is a punishment. If you knew it was your fault the elves were cursed, you'd feel horrible." The old Hel, the one from his memories, his brother, would hate what he'd become even if he never admitted it.

"That would only be a punishment if he felt remorse or had a conscience, and I don't believe he does." Layala tugged on a fresh top and peeled her pants off. The sticky blood made them difficult to remove. She pressed the wet cloth over the four red lines.

"Let me heal that for you."

She frowned as he went to his knee before her. "You don't need to inflict pain on yourself to heal me when these will be gone by tomorrow."

Ignoring her, he pulled a dagger from his boot and cut open a thin line on top of his wrist. With the tip of his finger, he swiped the blood, drew the healing rune on her body and then whispered the spell to heal while pressing the dagger into the top of his arm. He endured the pain with a straight face to heal her.

When the four lines were pink, Layala snatched the dagger out of his hands. "That's enough or you'll need a healer."

"I heal faster than you."

"Yeah well, I still don't like when you do that." She sighed and handed him back his weapon. "But thank you."

He smiled. "You're welcome."

She slipped on a clean pair of pants then took her weapons belt off the wall and tugged it around her hips. "If Hel is bringing a date, I can bet who it's going to be, and I don't want her anywhere near this place. Maybe we should cancel it."

"We can't break tradition. All members of the army get a graduation ball when they finish training. It gives them something to celebrate after all their hard work and I can't take that from them when morale is already down."

"And if we did cancel, people would wonder why. Telvian Botsberry would have an abundance of theories no doubt."

"Exactly."

"Did you hear what he said about me?" Tif slid down the draping green canopy of vines and swung onto the bed. "He thinks I'm cute." She brushed crumbs off her chest and then twirled one of her brown curls around her finger.

After all that was being discussed, that is what the gnome had to say. "I thought you were stuck."

"Oh, I only said that as a distraction. I was scared you were going to fight, and I didn't know what would happen. He could really hurt you or if Layala got in the way, she could get hurt and she was already bleeding and injured from that crazy cat lady."

Clever little gnome. "Well, don't get any ideas about him being your friend," Thane said firmly. "Besides, he was probably lying about you being cute. You need to be careful around him. In fact, avoid him at all costs."

"Why would he lie about thinking I'm cute? I think you're jealous."

Thane laughed and folded his arms. "Why would I be jealous of that?"

"You've never said I'm cute." She put a hand on her hip. "Now you're mad I think he's cuter than you."

Layala chuckled and slid her sword holster over her shoulder and dropped her sword inside.

"How swiftly your loyalty changes, gnome."

"I'm loyal to Laya."

Layala smirked at that.

"Fine, I admit you're cute for a gnome," Thane said with a

smile. Tif giggled and blushed, and was about to say something, until he went on, "When you don't open your mouth."

"Uh!" she scoffed. "You're a turd. A big stinky one. And he is better looking than you." She stuck out her tongue. "By monumental amounts. You look like a bridge troll compared to him."

"You know, when you exaggerate like this, I know you're lying. I've been around you long enough."

"Alright, do I need to separate you two?" Layala ran a brush through her long black hair. "What is it with you two bickering all the time?"

Tif pointed at him. "He started it."

"She's like an itch that won't go away."

Tif squealed and a tiny pillow flew through the air and nailed Thane in the face. "Insult me again and I'll put itching powder in your underwear. I know where to get some. Then you'll really be itchy."

"Do that and you'll never see the light of day again."

"You wouldn't."

Thane laughed and scooped up the pillow and tossed it back at her. It flattened her completely on the bed. "Of course, I wouldn't. But you wouldn't put itching powder in your High King's underwear. Don't take everything I say so seriously, Tifapine."

With her red hat sideways and her curls pointing in all directions, she stood up with a grin. "Alright, maybe you're just as attractive as the Black Mage. Even a smidge more. His eyes are a little creepy, and I prefer long hair." She glanced at the mess. "What are we going to do about this? I'm much too small to clean this up on my own, and Pearl is on leave."

"I'll get guards and other maids in here to take care of it." He looked at Layala who was now tying her hair back into a braid. "What are your plans today?"

"I was going to watch the new recruits, but Hel just reminded me I need to see the dressmaker in town for the ball."

Thane rubbed between his eyebrows. "We have a dressmaker here." Why did she insist on making his life difficult? Couldn't she just stay here at the castle? She'd be safe watching the recruits.

"I know, but she doesn't like me anymore, and I'm afraid she'll make me an ugly dress."

"You have dresses in your closet."

"Thane, I've worn them all. I want something new. It's a girl thing, you wouldn't understand."

"Then I'll fire the dressmaker and get you a new one."

"By today? I'll take care of it. You can't do everything."

"You need to bring a guard. I'll send Piper." He pictured another assassin following her around and shook his head. "Never mind, I'll come with you."

"You're supposed to make sure the new recruits are ready to graduate tomorrow and so is she. There are patrols all over the city and a ton of people around. No one will attack me in the open."

He had the sneaking suspicion she might have other plans she didn't want him to know about. "Laya." She was like a wild mustang, incapable of being domesticated. He needed to make sure she was at least watched over by someone. If she was going out into the city where any number of people hated her, she couldn't go alone. The *Palenor Scroll* only fueled their skepticism of her. Many of the people who once praised her now thought of her as a curse and the ones who wanted her dead before were now radical. He didn't tell her how many times he had to have the guards clear a mob on the other side of the bridge, demanding that Layala be turned over for a trial. The

Black Mage may be enemy number one, but Layala was runner-up.

"Don't worry, Thane. I'll be alright." She smirked and winked at him. "I can hold my own, you know. They call me 'The Defeater of Dragons' now.

DEFEATER OF DRAGONS OR NOT, Thane couldn't leave her alone after the gods' council sent an assassin. He hurried down the stairs and told the guards at the front door to fetch the maids and get her room cleaned. They didn't question, just moved. Then he raced outside to find Piper; he'd have to take her place today.

The morning dew had burned off the grass and the ringing of metal on metal rang out in the otherwise peaceful air. Thane didn't typically hang around too much for training. It made them nervous to have their king watching but today he needed to be there. They couldn't be skittish pups when it came to a battle he'd oversee.

Piper knocked one of the recruits upside the helmet and then shook her head. "What is wrong with you? The grass isn't slick, there is no mud; why are you falling down? You fall down, you're dead. Graduation is tomorrow and the enemy will show no mercy."

Fennan's and Piper's team looked to be in a skirmish and Leif waited on the side with his team behind, grinning like he was the champion of the world.

"You're a sad lot, aren't you?" Leif jeered.

Fennan smiled and jogged over to Thane's side. "Despite Piper's attitude, the majority are ready. Some are better than others."

"That's how it always goes. I'm better than you," Thane said with an eyebrow lift and a smile.

Fennan shoved his shoulder. "You're better than everyone. No need to rub it in." After Tenebris's guards had shaved off his hair, he'd let his shiny black curls grow back out and they now reached past his ears. He even wore braids with gold jewelry weaved in them.

"I know this is her break from guarding Laya and I'd do it myself, but I'm afraid if it's me, it will land me in hot water, and Laya and I are already having problems."

"What is the issue with you two lately? You went from barely being able to stop touching each other to hardly looking at each other."

"It's complicated."

"Always is with you two."

"Enough about my love life. What about yours?"

"We have bigger problems. How are we going to get rid of our—unwanted guest? I can't believe he's just here introducing himself to the staff and guards like he's family. What does he want?"

Thane ran his hand through his dark hair and gritted his teeth in frustration. "Well, katagas serum doesn't work so at the moment, I have no idea. He needs something from Layala. I can't say more than that."

Fennan's jaw muscles twitched, and he stared ahead at the elves in mock battle. "You can't or won't say more? I've been your friend your entire life. You can trust me."

"It's not that." Though those words did bring a flash of Aldrich's face to mind. No one had seen or heard from the weasel since he snuck off at the battle at the Void. Thane tried not to think about him or what he might be up to. Hopefully held up somewhere in the human lands begging for scraps.

"Then what is it? You can't say he needs something from Layala and leave it at that. She is my future queen and my friend, and I care about her, too. She already woke him up. What more could he want from her?" His reddish-brown eyes widened, and he turned to Thane. "He's not here to claim her as his wife, is he? I mean, all that stuff about her being his true mate the papers are talking about is a farce."

"I don't know what it is he wants from her. He won't say. I think taking her away may be his end game, but right now he's pushing for her to remember being the goddess Valeen."

"Isn't there a book or scroll in the mage's tower about him?"

"I found something in my father's study, but the book is enormous, and I've barely made a dent in it. So, I haven't found anything yet but I'm working on it. Everyone has a weakness." Thane waved at Piper. "I'll take over her team, assess every-one's readiness, and see if anyone needs to be held back for the next round of training."

"She'll be pissed you're taking her away on the last day," Fennan warned.

"This is more important, and I'm her king and she'll follow my orders without question."

Fennan let out a short chortle. "If you say so."

Piper jogged over and tugged her Raven wing helmet off. Her red hair somehow stayed slick and smooth in her braid. A smudge of dirt mixed with the freckles on her left cheek, and she smiled at Thane. "Hi, Thane. It's good to see you out here to watch us for the final day." She gave Fennan a brief, very formal nod and then looked around behind them like she was searching for someone. "I was hoping Layala would join too."

"I need you to follow Layala for me. She needs a new dress

for the ceremony. She said she'll be fine on her own and doesn't want to bother you since you're training but—"

"It's dangerous for her to be alone." Her mouth twisted into a frown, and she glanced back at her team fighting in the skirmish. "I'm not going to sneak around behind her back if that's what you mean by follow. She purposely ditched me the other night. I'm still a little mad about it."

"Perhaps I implied that you had a choice," Thane said. "You don't." He hated when he pulled rank on his friends, but this wasn't a time to test his patience.

Piper leaned back slightly, clearly caught off guard by the forcefulness in his tone. The blush on her cheeks from the heat of the day deepened. "So, it's an order?"

"It's an order," he ground out. "Whether you sneak behind her back or not is up to you. But you will go be her bodyguard; that is your primary duty, one you accepted and swore to uphold. An assassin got into her room, managed to stab her, and cut up her leg, and she sneaks out of this castle alone whenever she feels like it with no backup. I know she's not the easiest charge but she's still yours."

Piper's face fell and her shoulders sagged. He'd clearly struck a nerve but everything he said was the truth and sometimes it hurt. "An assassin... Of course, High King. I will do better." She dropped her gaze and dipped her chin. "I will protect her with my life."

CHAPTER 18

LAYALA

Layala hurried down the steps to the front entrance where the morning sun shined bright and glorious. The guards standing on the sides of the bottom steps dipped their heads as she passed. "Lady Lightbringer," they acknowledged.

"Good morning," she said brightly, with forced enthusiasm. "Did you see which way the elf with shorter dark hair went? He's probably smoking." She smelled the sweet scent lingering in the air now.

"Toward the stables," the guard on the left answered. Maker above if they only knew who walked past them earlier.

In the distance, Hel led a monstrous all-black horse with a white star on his forehead out of the barn doors. The bastard thought he could take *her* horse? And why would he even need one when he could just poof into thin air and reappear where he wanted? This was deliberate.

She started off in a determined march, quickly turning into a run.

Hel pulled himself up into the saddle as she drew close. He tossed down the end of the civar, blew out a puff of smoke, and nudged Midnight into a walk.

Layala snatched the reins on the left side and pulled Midnight to a stop. "Where do you think you're going with my horse?"

"To find my date." His mouth twitched and she swore he was trying not to smile. "Jealousy looks good on you, love. Pouty lip and all."

Layala glanced around to make sure no one was in earshot. "Call off the pale one attacks. Send them back to the Void."

The leather saddle creaked beneath him as he shifted his position. "And why would I do that?"

"They're killing people."

"Tell you what, I'll get them in line when you tell me what I need to know? Deal?"

"I have no control over remembering anything. It could be months—years before then."

He shrugged and leaned forward in the saddle.

Midnight started walking and Layala pulled back on the reins again. "If you want to be allies against a greater enemy, you can't let them keep killing our people and destroying Palenor. And if you want to pass off as Thane's cousin and not the Black Mage here in the castle, so every single elf here doesn't try to kill you in your sleep or poison your drink then stop them. Please." Her voice cracked on the last word, and she cringed internally.

"You know what doesn't look good on you? Begging." He turned away, and with a nudge from Hel, Midnight took off, kicking up bits of grass and dirt in his wake.

Out of breath, Piper stepped up beside Layala. She grabbed Layala by the shoulder and turned her. "Are you out of your mind? Why would you try to stop him from leaving? I thought he was going to hurt you, and it would be my fault for not protecting you better."

"He stole my horse."

"It's a damn horse. It's not worth putting yourself in danger like that."

Layala shrugged Piper's hand off her. "Thane sent you, didn't he? I told him I'd be fine."

"You know, you're being a real jerk lately. You take no consideration of how any of us feel, namely me. And why wouldn't you want your friend to go dress shopping with you, unless you are planning something else?"

Layala blew out a breath, tearing her gaze from Hel's back. Thane must have gotten on Piper about not watching her closer. It wasn't her fault an assassin got into the castle. "Sorry, Piper. I didn't mean to take my frustrations out on you. And I know it was wrong of me to leave you the other night. Things have been hard for me lately and I'm not always in the best mindset. I'd love for you to come."

"You better. I can't presume to know what you're going through, but I am here." Piper started for the horse barns. "And don't worry, we have other horses. Let's go."

"Piper, are you excited to buy a new dress? I thought you hated dressing up."

She looked over her shoulder with a grin. "I like to look pretty sometimes too."

"For a certain elf?" Layala teased.

"Hush."

HEL

HEL FOLLOWED the golden shimmering line he cast to track the assassin. She couldn't be far given that he heard the glass shatter during her escape. He inhaled deeply and caught her scent too. A quick nudge with his heels brought the horse into a gallop up the trail leading out of the Valley. She'd have been smarter to hide within the city among people where he'd have to be discreet.

The golden line and her scent led him to a small, wooded area with tall grass and widespread oak trees. He dropped to the ground. "Here kitty, kitty. Why don't you come out and play?"

Bent grass and smears of blood led him further. A broken tree branch and matted down area showed a struggle. He smelled her before he saw her. Dragons could never be mistaken for anything else. They smelled like smoky mountains and this one in particular like lust. Out of the corner of his eye, he spotted golden hair shimmering in the light cascading down between the trees. Varlett stepped into view holding onto what could only be the assassin; her face contorted with pain, one eye swollen, busted lip, and she arched her back. Only then did he realize Varlett had her talons dug into the woman's spine.

"Look what I found," Varlett said. "Naughty cat, trespassing where she doesn't belong."

Varlett's scaled skin was black as pitch, glimmering in the daylight, and her golden eyes more reptilian than humanoid.

"Has she talked?" Hel asked.

"Not a word." Varlett twisted her arm slightly and the cat shifter hissed. "Although we haven't gotten to the fun yet. We were about to get started."

Hel folded his arms and looked at the assassin up and down. Layala did a number on her face. Even if she wasn't nearly as powerful as she once was, the elf was scrappy, he'd give her that. But this cat still came much too close to getting her mission accomplished. Had Layala been a less experienced fighter, it would be over—again. "Who's with you? I know you didn't come alone. They always send backups."

She snarled in return.

"You know it doesn't bother me in the least to torture you, and I have many ways. Maybe I should start with a burning sensation, akin to fire ants biting you all over your body." He smirked. "Yes, that sounds fitting of the crime."

She squirmed and wriggled in Varlett's hold, breaths rushing in and out. Then the screaming started. The wail sounded like a dying cougar. "Stop! Stop!"

He cupped his hand to his ear. "I can't hear you?"

"Stop! Please!"

"I didn't hear names or numbers." He intensified the magic, and she wailed again, half cat call, half human scream.

"They'll kill me!"

"It's true, they would, but trust me when I say I will draw it out and you'll know what true pain feels like."

"I can't, my family!"

"Tell you what, if you tell me now, I'll let you go." He withdrew the magic and waited. "You have three seconds. Three. Two—"

"Alright, alright." Sweat soaked her brow and by this point she had little color left on her face. Hel seized his magic and waited. "I was sent by the council. They said to take out Valeen first, then War and then it would be easier to get to you. You seem to give up when they're gone."

He stared at her with disdain. Varlett tightened her talons and the woman screeched. "Who else is here?"

"I don't know!"

"I will tear your spine from your body if you don't know anything."

"They are sending someone eager to see you fall. And he's evil, pure evil. I think he may be an immortal. I don't know his name."

"Gods can't travel outside of Runevale," Hel said. "We know this, or they'd be here."

"I don't know what he is, I swear on the All Mother. They just said he couldn't be killed and that we should stay out of his way. Of course, they offered a reward for whoever got the task done first." She gulped. "There also may be a couple others like me here. I haven't seen them, but even if they aren't here now, they'll keep sending assassins until you're all dead. They have spies."

"Thank you for being so forthcoming," Hel said, and gave a curt nod.

Varlett shoved her hand the rest of the way through and pulled out her heart through her back. The woman fell to the ground with a thud and the heart plopped beside her. "Well," Varlett started, then licked blood from her fingers. It always unnerved him when she did that. It made him think of the beast she was inside and could transform into.

"Could you not," Hel drawled.

She smiled, dragging her tongue even slower over her now fleshy palm. No more dragon scales. "Baby, if you want some, say it."

"Get some manners."

She dropped her bloody hand to her side and her reptilian eyes dragged over him. "You look refreshed. It was her blood, wasn't it? I knew it, fucking underrealm. She's your godsdamn lifeline still?"

Hel didn't like Varlett knowing his weakness, even if she'd always been loyal. "It doesn't change anything. It's just another reason we need to keep her safe from the council."

Her eyes narrowed; the slits even seemed to sharpen. "So, you took her blood. How did she react? How is Thane handling you?"

Hel chuckled. "She didn't like it if that's what you're wondering. And he's... both angry and curious. He remembers more than her. Not everything, which makes it fun."

Her talon slid along his throat, eyes fixed on the vein.

"Don't even think about it."

She pressed up on her toes and she kissed the side of his face. He never let her kiss him on the mouth even if they did other things. "Just a little taste of your blood? You know what it does for me."

She got a high off him. It gave her a temporary boost in magical power, but his blood or any part of him wasn't something he gave away lightly. He turned and started back toward the horse. "Clean up this mess and find yourself a new gown."

"She's not... affecting you, is she?" Varlett called. "You promised."

He swung up into the saddle. "She's a means to getting what I want."

"She better be. And who could the immortal the assassin spoke of be?"

"There are only three others I know of that are considered immortals who are not gods, and they come from the underrealm."

LAYALA

A BELL chimed and a strong scent of floral potpourri hit Layala as she stepped into the dressmaker's shop. Extravagant gowns hung in racks on every wall, aligned by color, darkest shades on the left side and white on the right and every color in between. Four of the most elegant dresses were fitted to mannequins around the large, open room. Skylights in the ceiling brightened the white stone floor and brought out the specks of crystal in the squares. To the far right, a three-step raised circular platform waited, half surrounded in mirrors, and a large dark brown armchair was set off to the side for a spectator. Layala took a step closer to an ivory sparkling ball gown on display in the window. It was adorned with thousands of silver crystals, and it glittered in the sun as radiant as a lake on a summer day. The train ran at least three feet with trails of shining silver whirls.

"It's gorgeous," Piper said. "It would be a perfect wedding dress."

"You should try it on," Layala said.

"I won't be getting married anytime soon. I was thinking for you."

"At this rate, I won't be either," Layala mumbled.

Piper's brows tugged closer, and she opened her mouth to speak but another voice interrupted.

"Good morning, ladies." Stepping through sheer curtains, a slender elf in fine off-white robes with a green trimmed neckline and dark hair pulled half back, strolled out from a back room. He clasped his hands before him, and his brown eyes gave both of them a head-to-toe scrutinization. After a moment, he wrinkled his nose. "How can I help you?"

Both Layala and Piper wore pants and carried more

weapons than most males, not the typical attire for a maiden elf in Palenor. Upon looking down, Layala noted the trail of dirt they left in their wake across the white floor. With a blush warming Layala's cheeks, she cleared her throat. "We need dresses."

"I can see that."

"For the graduation ball. Something elegant but not typical." Layala tapped her toe on the floor scanning the room for something she had in mind. Most were pastel colors like Robin egg blue or soft yellow, pinks, and lavender but there was a group of deep maroons and blacks. "I need something—black. Something striking and bold."

"There's not time to make something new so it will have to be off the rack." With a finger tapping his chin, he circled around Piper first. "You'll be easy to fit—waist probably twenty-four inches, hips thirty-six. You're average for a maiden of Palenor, if only a little stockier. I have just the thing too with that red hair."

"Stocky?" Piper balked. "I'm not stocky."

"I can tell in your shoulders you use those weapons you have on, and swinging a sword has made your back a little broader as well."

Piper's jaw dropped and she gave Layala a *is he serious* look.

He turned to Layala and raised an eyebrow. "And you are a little—curvier than most I dress. I'll have to make adjustments for your wider hips, behind, and bust. Though your waist is still petite it will take adjustments as well. Don't take that as disrespect. It's simply a fact."

Layala was used to hearing she wasn't as thin and willowy as most of the she-elves so it wasn't a shock but apparently Piper hadn't heard that she wasn't. "You're strong, Pipe. Nothing to be ashamed of."

"No shame, I'm rather sure you both get plenty of attention. Beauty and grace with an edge. But I bet you probably scare off all the males with those weapons," the elf tailor said and smiled, but let out a long breath when he scanned Layala's form again. "Come, come, let's get your measurements for certain." He turned and his cloth boots barely made a sound as he started toward the back of the store. "Amelia, we have work to do! We got hips and shoulders!" He clapped his hands and the sound of it echoed off the high ceiling above, then waved for them to follow him.

"Maker above, could he make it any more obvious that we're not small enough for his tastes?" Piper said as they trailed him through a sheer curtain. "I wonder if he knew who you were if he'd make such rude comments."

"Please don't mention my name," Layala whispered. "What if he's a radical who wants me dead?"

Piper leaned in closer. "It's not like he'd be much of a challenge, if he was."

A few minutes later, Layala stood in her undergarments behind a red velvet curtain. It was a small room with a single mirror and skylight above to give plenty of light. A female with straight blonde hair and a plain look about her for an elf stepped inside with a black gown draped over her arm. She reminded Layala of a mouse, timid and afraid to make eye contact.

"Mr. Drenovan said to put this on you first." The tailor's assistant produced a black corset from underneath the gown, and already Layala knew she'd be struggling to breathe. "It will help with the fitting." Her gaze fell to Layala's shoulder with the lily mark and flicked away as if she'd been struck.

"That's fine."

Layala braced herself as the assistant began jerking at the

laces, closing in the bodice tighter. The assistant avoided looking her in the face and kept her concentration on her work. Layala cleared her throat quietly, disturbing the silence, "Have you dressed many maidens for the graduation ball tomorrow?"

"Several, Lady, but less than usual."

Thane probably didn't allow as many attendees this time around with his strict rules on which families could attend and which couldn't be based on ties to certain radical families and those most loyal to the previous king. "Have you ever been to the castle?" In the mirror's reflection, the girl's cheeks pinked, and she gave a big jerk at Layala's upper back. Layala's breath hitched at the constriction. "Not so tight, please."

"Apologies, Lady, but we need a dress to fit. There's no time to sew you a new one." She gave another quick pull and Layala felt like her breasts were pushed up to her neck now. "And no, I haven't been to the castle. I'm a tailor's niece."

The corset cinched to the point Layala swore her ribs would crack but with assistance, she stepped into a black dress, pulled it up past her hips, and up over her bust. Two long strips of fabric tied crisscross against her chest and around the back of her neck.

The tailor's assistant started on the buttons that went up the back. "I can use extenders where they don't reach but it's going to fit."

"Whatever you need to do."

Sunlight crept out from behind white puffy clouds and cascaded down from the skylight above creating a warm glow in the dressing room, lighting up Layala's skin and giving a golden shine to her raven hair.

"Why did you want black? That's usually the male color. It's not typical for maidens and the ball is supposed to be celestial themed."

"I need to feel like someone else." She didn't need to be Layala. She needed to embrace the goddess of night. After that dream she had, she wanted more knowledge. It was like having a lick of the best cake then having it snatched away. But as she stood and watched herself hoping for something to show like the vision of a naked Hel on a balcony or her dream, there was only this room and the tailor's assistant.

"Come out here and let me see when you're dressed!" Piper hollered.

The tailor's assistant stepped back and swept her arm out indicating to Layala that she was finished. "I'll leave you to decide how you like it." With quiet steps she disappeared through the swish of the curtain.

Layala tugged her hair loose from her braid and ran her fingers through her strands pulling it to the front to flow down over her breasts. Carefully, she stooped down and reached into the pocket of her pants and pulled out a tin of lip balm. It was a dark cherry red and it stained her lips with a couple swipes.

"Layala, the ball isn't today. You don't need to look perfect," Piper called again but more forcefully than before. Her guard had no patience.

"I'm coming." She twirled around to check her rear, the seam looked like it would rip if she bent over too far, but it hugged her rump and along the back of her thighs nicely, from there the fabric flowed out. It wasn't exactly a good gown for agility but excellent for making Thane think twice about his abstinence from her.

Layala gripped the velvet curtain, tugged it aside and stepped out. Piper stood before a mirror adjusting the folds of her forest-green ball gown. "I love it," Layala said. "That color is gorgeous on you."

She turned and inspected the back where it was left open in

a V all the way to an inch or two above her rear. "Thanks. I don't know about the back." She ran her hands over the sequined sleeves. "Or the long sleeves. I might get too warm. It's going to be inside."

"You must wear it. I've never seen a prettier dress on you."

She smiled and it lit up her face. "Thank you. I like yours as well. How do you feel about it?"

"I do like it but it's a little tight," Layala said, placing her palm on the snug bodice. "I can barely breathe. Perhaps I should try on something else."

"You look striking, and it hugs your curves, which I'll admit I'm a little jealous of, but you'll want to be able to move easily in case something happens. Let's see what else we can find." They started toward the front of the store again. Piper cleared her throat and said slowly, "So... I don't want to pry so feel free to tell me to mind my own business but what's going on between you and Thane? I mean even before Hel showed up. I've been meaning to ask but I've been a chicken. At the first day of training, you said you felt he doesn't want you anymore... And the way he yelled at you the night we got caught. I haven't seen him that upset in a while. You know he kicked both Leif's and my ass in training the next morning. Leif more than me of course."

"He's hurt, I think, that we went behind his back more than anything." And nothing had been going on between them. That was the problem. "Maybe you should ask him what's been going on between us."

Piper gave her a pointed stare. "I'm asking you."

"He..." she thought of the night he had her pinned on the bed then pulled away and told her she would have to wait. Layala glanced around and closed her mouth when the tailor's assistant entered the dressing area and dipped into a curtsy.

"You have another guest waiting for you."

"Another guest? For us?" Layala asked.

"Were you not expecting someone else? He said he's a friend of yours."

"Do you think Thane sent someone else to look after us?" Layala asked, peering at the sheer curtain that led to the front but only shadows could be made out.

"It's probably Leif or Fennan," Piper said. "Although after an assassin, I wouldn't be surprised if it's Thane himself."

Layala swept her gaze around the many dresses and gowns and stopped at the window to check on their horses. Midnight's eyes were closed and his head low. He looked like he fell asleep despite groups of elves walking by him on the crowded road outside. The faint chatter of the teeming streets, the slamming of a blacksmith's hammer hit rhythmically from somewhere nearby. *Wait...* Layala's heart quickened. *Midnight is outside...* Suddenly Piper gripped her wrist like she might tear it off.

"Ouch," Layala protested, shooting her a glare.

"Well, it's certainly not Thane."

Layala followed her friend's line of sight and found, in the oversized armchair with a lit civar between his fingers and a wicked grin, the vilest person she'd ever known.

"Hello, love." He smiled. "You should see the look on your faces. Were you expecting someone else?"

CHAPTER 19

LAYALA

The floral scent of the potpourri lingering in the shop's air had masked the smell of the civar now hitting her senses. Layala glanced back at the tailor's assistant through the curtains, but she hadn't followed and hopefully she stayed in the back. How did he find them? She was certain he went in the opposite direction. Both Layala and Piper had been on high alert as they went through the city in case they were tailed by an assassin or—him. No one followed close behind.

"Stay here," Layala breathed and for Piper's safety, Layala made her way across the white glittering floor, bare feet silent as the night. She swallowed hard and stopped before Hel. He wore his perfectly tailored black suit with a deep red undervest. His wavy hair curled around his face in a perfectly tousled way and there wasn't even a shadow on his clean-shaven face, but there was a small dark stain on the collar of his top and she wondered whose blood it was.

"Mmm I do like it. Give us a turn." He twirled his hand in a circular motion, waving smoke everywhere. "Your ass looks phenomenal."

"Why are you here?"

"War may think the redhead is a sufficient guard for you, but I do not."

"I thought you were finding a date," Layala snapped and crossed her arms.

"Didn't take long, love."

Light footsteps interrupted them. "Oh, I see you've met Mr. Black." The tailor shop owner, Mr. Drenovan stepped out from the back and clasped his hands together. With a grin he hurried across the floor and stopped next to Layala, waving a hand toward Hel. "This nice fellow offered to pay for both your dresses as long as he approves."

Layala turned to the owner. "You can tell Mr. *Black* I don't need his charity."

"Uh," the elf stuttered, and with eyes so wide they might pop out of his head, he looked back and forth between them unsure of what to do. "Mr. Black?"

Hel flicked a gold coin at Mr. Drenovan, and he caught it with glee. "Tell Miss Lightbringer I'll be paying either way." *That's what good husbands do,* he whispered in her mind.

Her teeth clenched together, and she wanted to take the burning end of that stupid civar and shove it into his eye. *Not my husband,* Layala thought, narrowing her eyes at him.

He smirked. *You're learning, little rabbit.*

Her throat went dry, and she coughed. He heard that? *Stay out of my head.*

I can only speak to your mind and vice versa. I can't read your every thought. Although your face gives everything away well enough.

After biting the coin and inspecting it thoroughly, the shop owner turned to her with arched brows. "Miss Lightbringer?" he asked, realizing the significance of the name, and surveyed her with new scrutiny, going from face to body, stopping on the lily mark. "Miss Lightbringer! Why didn't you tell me who you were when you came in? Can I get you a glass of wine, perhaps a few hors d'oeuvres for you and your friends? We have outstanding chocolate from only the best in the Valley, and a variety of nuts from all over Adalon. Maker above, if I'd known I'd have the future queen of Palenor in the shop I'd have set up much differently and had dresses ready for you!" He placed his palm flat against his chest. "It's dreadful what the *Palenor Scroll* writes about you, dear. I don't know why His Majesty allows it."

"He's not a tyrant like his father. He allows freedom. The *Palenor Scroll* is allowed to write what they please."

I'm certain if War wanted to stop it, he would, Hel whispered to her mind. "A glass of wine would be wonderful, Drenovan," Hel said aloud with a charming smile.

"No, thank you." Layala shook her head and scowled at Hel. "We need to be going." She needed to get this maniac out of here before he killed someone. Gah, *I should have listened to Thane and used the house tailor, even if she is Orlandia's loyal dog.*

"Wine please." Hel's voice sounded a little different, more resonant, and his eyes seemed to glow a light brighter. "I don't need to be going anywhere. I'm rather enjoying myself." He lifted his hand and curled his fingers at Piper. "Come here."

Layala's heart thundered in her ears, drowning out the sound of the busy streets that idly played in the background. "Don't..."

"Don't what?" Hel stared at her through the smoke rising out of the civar between his lips.

Grinning, Mr. Drenovan clasped his hands again. "I'll be right back with the wine, Mr. Black."

Piper stopped at Layala's side and even if she looked terrified, she lifted her chin slightly and stood tall. Hel patted his lap. "Hello, Red. Have a seat."

"No." Layala grabbed Piper's wrist and tugged her slightly behind.

"I didn't ask for your permission," Hel said, then looked at Piper. "But let's make this into a training session, shall we? Turn yourself into shadow and I won't make her sit on my lap."

"I can't."

He raised a brow. "Fine. Come. Now." His voice took on that same resonant tone, and Piper stepped forward.

Layala grabbed her arm and jerked her back, but she pushed forward, trying to get around Layala, as if in a trance. "Give me a second to try."

"Fine. Stay where you are, Red."

She froze.

A stare down ensued, his malevolent red eyes locked on hers. Causing a scene, not complying, could result in Hel killing one or more people, the shop owner, and his assistant to start. Her magic reacted to her racing mind, warming from her chest down her arms to the palms of her hands. Her gaze flicked to the window, many people passed by and if she used her magic here it would give them more reason to fear her. Glancing down at her hands she imagined them turning black, shifting to something not solid. Nothing happened.

"Time's up."

Layala growled. "Don't command her like she's one of your toys."

"You don't want to play this game with me. I make the

rules. I said turn into shadow, and I wouldn't command her, but you can't, can you?"

Piper stepped forward and gave Layala a half smile. "It's fine, Layala. I don't want him to hurt anyone else."

"Piper, no," Layala said quietly, but in a couple strides Piper turned and sat on Hel's lap.

He wrapped his arm around her waist and pulled her closer. "Now Miss Lightbringer, I promise I won't break her fingers or her neck if you try on that dress." He pointed to somewhere behind Layala. "And don't try anything stupid or I'll be forced to do something regrettable to your friend."

Waiting behind her on a mannequin was a dress that hadn't been there before. It was midnight purple, a shade or two away from black, with tiny silver stars along the bodice with a half-moon placed at the center of the sweetheart neckline. The solid deep purple skirt flowed wide. Along the back of the shoulders and down the back was a sequined drape. It was one of the most beautiful dresses she'd ever seen.

Hel snapped his fingers, and the dress came off the mannequin and floated to Layala. "Take your time. I have lovely company," he said, and stroked his finger down the side of Piper's neck. She slammed her eyes shut but was controlled enough she didn't flinch.

Layala snatched the dress and hurried to the back. "Help me get this on," Layala commanded the tailor's assistant and dashed behind the velvet curtain. She peeled off her black dress and corset, counting every second she was away and stepped into the new one. A horrifying image flashed across her mind: Piper left on the floor with an endless stare just like the guards he killed days before.

Of course, the dress had a lace-up back and couldn't just be slipped on. "Faster."

"I'm trying, Lady Lightbringer."

The girl jerked and tied, breathing rapidly. Was this dress one she'd worn before? She stared at it in the mirror. It looked familiar though she couldn't say why. Even the feel of it gave her the sense she'd worn this exact dress and it fit her perfectly.

"Done," said the assistant, then she stepped back. "Wait, where did you get this? It's not one of ours."

Layala shrugged, picked up the front of the gown and moved. The sound of the fabric swishing with each step echoed in her ears. She steadied her breathing and calmly stepped through the curtains to the front of the store. The more she panicked, the more he would enjoy torturing them.

Piper still sat upright on his lap, no blood in sight. "I'm alright," she mouthed.

It was so quiet in the room her elf ears heard both their hearts beating and the shallow pull of their breaths. At first, Hel's stare worried her; his pinched expression made him appear irrationally upset. But the longer she watched him she wondered if he wasn't angry, but sad. As if seeing her in it broke something inside him.

Hel's red eyes slid along every curve, as if drowning in her. His throat bobbed and he lifted his eyes to meet hers. "Do you remember that dress?"

So, she *had* worn it before. Layala shook her head as she slowly walked toward them. She caught sight of herself in the mirrors behind the raised platform and stopped. It felt like something was missing, but what?

"Wear it to the ball tomorrow or little Miss Red will pay the price."

"Why do you always resort to threats? You could have just given it to me as a gift. It's a beautiful dress. Perfect for the occasion." The better question was why would he make a commotion out of her not wearing it? It was a dress, and this ball wasn't anything special. Balls, parties, and festivals happened quite often in Palenor. Orlandia found every occasion to invite friends and to dress up. The Spring Equinox would be soon, the second largest festival in Palenor apart from the Summer Solstice celebration. They missed the Winter Solstice on their travel to the Void from the dragon court months prior, but no doubt there'd been a party.

"And you'd accept it as a gift from me, would you? No, you forget I know you. To you, it's been a few days since I came into your life, but I've known you for *years*. You'd refuse to wear it simply because it was from me. Even if I'd packaged it up nicely with a bow and gave it to you with a smile and a box of your favorite dark chocolate truffles."

Layala's mouth twitched. *I really am as stubborn as a mule.* "Why is this dress so important to you?"

"You'll figure it out, love."

Mr. Drenovan hurried into the room grinning from ear to ear. "I've got the wine!" He sang cheerfully. "Wow, I must say Lady Lightbringer, that dress is stunning on you. You look like... a goddess." He brushed past her and handed the long-stemmed glass to Hel.

Odd choice of words, Layala thought.

"I hope this is to your liking, Mr. Black."

Hel finally tore his gaze from Layala and tipped the wine back. It was gone in moments. "It is." Then he pushed Piper off his lap and stepped away. His hand ran through his dark, shaggy hair and shoved the empty glass at the tailor.

Layala watched him carefully, his tense shoulders, the slight narrowing of his eyes, the hard line of his lips. He was upset, but why? Maybe it made him think of who she was and the goddess he lost.

Still smiling, Mr. Drenovan said, "I will have the dresses packaged and sent to the castle at once."

"Thank you, Mr. Drenovan," Hel said and headed toward the exit. Hopefully he'd keep walking and leave them alone. The door opened with the chime of a bell, but he paused in the doorway, looking over his shoulder. "Get changed, ladies. We need to get back to the castle. I'll be waiting outside."

THANE

THANE SAT at the desk in his office, leaning over the book he discovered behind a hidden bookshelf in his father's old bedroom. It was the first he'd found with tales of the gods and goddesses of Runevale.

The curtains were pulled wide, allowing an abundance of light into his office. The smell of fresh-cut lemons for the tea in Fennan's hand lingered in the air. Fennan sat in a leather chair with his feet propped up on the side table and a book in his lap, a white teacup in one hand. The final matches for the new group went well. Most of the recruits were ready to go out and join the ranks save for a handful. So, the three of them bathed and changed into fresh clothes filling the room with a variety of fragrant soaps.

"What if we put a large dose of katagas serum in his drink? The smaller doses on the barbs aren't enough but something more?" Leif asked as he paced back and forth. The sound of his boots hitting the floor had become calming rather than irritating. "And we want him dead, right?"

Thane looked up from the page. It would be difficult to explain to them why they couldn't kill him in a way they would understand. To them he was the Black Mage, the creator of the pale ones. To him, Hel was his family.

Fennan scoffed. "Of course, we want him dead. What kind of question is that?"

Leif stopped at the window and sat on the ledge. "What if he dies and magic disappears entirely from everywhere?"

"I don't think that's how it works," Fennan argued. "He's given the title because that's his affinity, not that he created all magic."

"You don't know that," Leif fired back.

"I believe Fennan is right in this regard," Thane said, rubbing his scruffy chin. He needed a shave. "Mages can use his spells but not everyone can. He isn't in charge of who is born with magic and who isn't, but he can gift magic to others. Hence the runes."

"So, when he died, elf mages stopped being born?" Leif crossed his arms.

"That's part of our curse," Fennan said. "The Maker took away our magic for what we've done. And we thought Layala and Thane were mages, but they're not, are they? They're elves with the power of gods."

"Yes," Thane agreed. "But I think it would have been the All Mother who took magic away, as she is the balance in all things. It wasn't Hel's doing even if he played a part. The large dose of katagas serum will not work. Besides, trying will only anger him enough to kill someone I care about, and at this point he's playing nice."

Thane glanced back down at the page. *Only two weapons can kill a god of Runevale, a dagger known as Soulender, and the Sword of Truth. Soulender was given to the Drivaar from the All Mother and the Sword of Truth to the Primevar gifted by the Maker to keep the balance between the two sides. During the wars the Primevar attained both weapons, effectively calling a treaty between the sides where peace lasted until the Great War of the Realms and both went missing.*

Thane's body stiffened. Hel was looking for something. Something Valeen had... Did she know where one of these weapons was? Was that why the assassin wanted her dead? Another thing Thane couldn't figure out was how the gods were able to end their lives the first time. It was evident the gods didn't use either weapon or Layala, Thane, and Hel wouldn't be alive here and now. They'd have been gone for good.

"Listen to this," Thane said. "Remember I told you he wants to go back home and that he was being punished. This says it right here, "and Valeen, Hel, and War had their immortality bound up and were slaughtered for their mutiny, murder, and crimes against the council, forever punished to live and die as mortals but never go to Serenity, the realm of everlasting peace where souls go to rest. Never privileged to be gods again," he held up his finger, "*Unless* they prove themselves worthy."

"According to whose standard? What is worthiness?" Fennan asked.

"It doesn't go into more detail," Thane said, and leaned back in his chair, closed his eyes, and got lost in what felt like a dream...

The Past

A single tear rolled down Valeen's flushed cheek. She was on her knees before the eleven council members, and he, beside her. Rows and rows of levels went up toward the golden, domed ceiling where people from all over Runevale hung over railings to watch their demise. It was unprecedented to see gods being punished, and to have a primordial goddess bound by magic and on her knees was unheard of. His mind raced on how they could get out of this. Every exit was covered by guards. Hundreds surrounded them in the rows of benches and even people standing in the aisles. If he had more time he would work his way out of the bonds around his neck, wrists, and ankles.

War turned his head slightly to his father standing in the front row to the left; not a member of the council but they wanted to vote him in to take the place of a member Valeen had killed weeks prior. Look at me, Look at me. But Balneir wouldn't meet his eyes. Don't let them do this, he silently pleaded.

War leaned forward slightly, to peek at Hel on the other side of Valeen. Hel's spine was erect, his chin held high. Not an ounce of remorse or fear showed in his features but when did he ever show how he felt? If anyone could get out of these bonds and escape it would be him, but it wouldn't matter. He wouldn't help War or Valeen, not after everything...

"You will answer for your crimes," said Percillia, the council leader. "You were ordered to stand down. Your wars spilled over into Ryvengaard, Adalon, and Vangra, not to mention the chaos and destruction you have caused here in Runevale. You were ordered to hand over Soulender and you refused. All three of you are sentenced to exile by execution."

"You can't do that," Hel snapped. "You don't have the weapons to do so." His voice echoed in the vast chambers.

"We cannot kill your immortal souls, but we can kill your body if your immortal strength is drawn out and held. The council has decided you are henceforth stripped of your immortality, where it will be bound, and you will be mortal. Where you will live and die again and again until we decide enough is enough. May the All Mother and the Maker have mercy on you."

Sweat slid down the back of War's neck. With the combined

power of the eleven council members, they could do this spell. He'd seen it done once before. Their immortality would be kept within a magical object. "No," War said, rising to his feet. "Punish me. I am at fault. I'm the one who fell in love with Valeen and turned her against Hel and convinced her to come with me. I'm the one who started the wars. I took Soulender from the vault and killed Synick alone. These crimes are all mine. Let them go."

The crowd behind them gasped at his admission.

Pricilla's sharp eyes narrowed. The members of the council looked amongst each other. "If you produce Soulender and the Sword of Truth, we will show leniency."

That was what this was truly about. Power. Whoever held those weapons had the ability to kill a god. He had no idea where either weapon was and even if he did, he wouldn't give it to them. If they had the opportunity, they'd use them. This spell to bind their immortality was their second-best punishment; it allowed them to be reborn and perhaps one day come back.

Hel looked over at him, jaw muscles flickering. Hatred burned in that gaze, but he also silently pleaded with him not to tell. He assumed wrongly that War knew. Valeen never told him where Soulender was.

"No," War said. And the people in the crowd murmured.

Pricilla's sleek dark brows arched. "You'd rather be mortal, cursed to die and be born again and again than give us the weapons? The weapons belong to the council for protection and balance. Soulender has been grossly misused." Her icy blue eyes cut to Valeen.

"It won't matter how many times I live and die; you will never get Soulender back," Valeen said resolutely.

"You would use the weapons against us," War added.

"Stand down, War," his father said firmly, stepping out of line. His gentle face pleaded with him to be quiet. "If you prove yourself worthy, you may come back someday." He meant if they gave them

either weapon, they could come back. If he convinced Valeen to hand Soulender over. No one knew what happened to the Sword of Truth but Synick and he was dead.

War dropped back down to his knees beside Valeen. He should have never taken her to his home that night... She turned to him, bottom lip trembling. "I'm so sorry," she whispered.

His throat burned with emotion. "This is not your fault."

"I'm scared," she whispered. And he wished he could take her into his arms and carry her away from all this. "What if we never find each other?"

"I promise I will find you. I'll always find you." He turned to Hel. He pretended not to watch them, but he would be able to hear every word they said. His chin was held high and jaw tight. "Hel, will you forgive me?"

"Forgive you?" Hel set cold, unfeeling, unflinching eyes on him. "No, but I too will promise to always find you, War, to torment you for the rest of time. You are no longer my brother."

"Hel, please," Valeen pleaded. "Don't blame him. He's your best friend, your blood. We should have stopped this a long time ago. I never wanted any of this to happen."

"Oh, don't worry, love. I'll be sure to find you, too. See you on the other side." He stood and said loudly, looking at each member of the council. "You're making a mistake, for I am the god of mischief and magic. One day I will come back here, and I'll end all of you. There will be no more gods of Runevale, save for me and whom I choose. That's not merely a threat; it's a vow." He smiled, deadly, lethal. "Your actions today will give the goddess of night, the god of war and myself a common enemy. I wouldn't want to be on the wrong side of the three gods most likely to end you all." The chambers burst into chatter and murmurs. Some people even hurried for the exits. "That's right, run cockroaches, I'll be back."

. . .

THANE WAS PULLED from the memory when Fennan said, "You should go rest, Thane. You've been under too much stress lately."

He opened his eyes and blinked rapidly at the bright light. Had he dozed off? "You're right." Thane pushed up from his chair and stepped out of his office into the hallway, closing the door gently behind him. Then he leaned back against the wall and closed his eyes, clenching his hands at his sides. The pain of losing her, of watching the hurt on Hel's face flared up inside his chest.

He knew what happened after; a spell drew out Valeen's immorality, a shimmering white essence pulled into a vial around the council leader's neck, the core that made her body strong and impenetrable to weapons, disease, poisons, and time, the magic that made her unable to truly die. Then an ax came down on the back of her neck. It was the only time he'd ever seen Hel shed a tear, and the only moment War had ever given up on a fight...

How many times over the last two thousand years were they reborn and killed? Did the council recently find out who they were reborn as, and that's why they only now sent an assassin? They'd never sent anyone before today... in this life. Hel was right. They didn't want them together. They feared what the three of them might do.

Holy Maker, what if every time they rejoined, they were assassinated? He'd thought the gods abandoned this realm but —the ravens that followed him, the silver owl he'd seen out the window—his Runevale father's messengers watched him all his life.

His heart lurched into his throat, and he shoved off the wall and moved toward her bedroom across the hall. Where was Layala—Valeen, gods he didn't know what to call her. He threw open her door and found her room empty. The cleaners went through and stripped the bed, replaced the frame with a new white one, cleared the dirty clothes, swept the splinters of wood and broken glass, scrubbed the blood off the floor. It looked as if the assassin never came but she did. And Hel—he promised them torment. He whipped around—Piper was not an adequate guardian for what was coming. *How could I be so foolish?*

CHAPTER 20

LAYALA

Layala stepped out of the dress shop into the afternoon sun. The bakery down the street brought with it the smell of sugary cakes and cinnamon twists, and her mouth watered at the delicious scents. Baskets of colorful flowers hung from the cream and gray buildings in this section of the city. Many of the shops on this street painted the ornate trim of their storefront a bright color of blue or green; the bakery was trimmed in light pink. Vendors didn't shout in the cobblestone streets to get patrons as in other cities. It had a formality everyone seemed to inherently understand. Soft harps and flutes played, bringing a feeling of peace and harmony.

Groups of elves in fine clothes walked conservatively and serenely along the side paths of the main street. Offering waves and smiles to each other as they passed.

Two human street cleaners with a hand-pushed wagon, creaky wheels knocking over the cobblestone, stopped to clean up the horse droppings. The younger boy was first to pull his shovel and started whistling on his way over.

"Good day to you," he said, tipping his brown hat. His eyes stuck on Layala's face as if it was the first time he'd ever seen an elf. Layala wondered if she had dirt on her cheek like he did. He shook his head, pulling his stare, and went to work.

Whether it was customary or not, Layala pulled out a couple bronze shepins from her pant pocket and held it out as they began to shovel their horses' messes.

The younger boy, probably in his late teens, nudged the other, a man with graying hair at his temples and robust chest and shoulders. They stopped shoveling and both appeared too stunned to speak or move, as if she offered them poison.

"It's a tip," Layala said. She always appreciated a tip for her work in Briar Hollow. "Thank you for cleaning up our mess."

"Oh, no, miss," the older man shook his head and waved his hand. "It's our job to do this. You don't need to pay extra."

"Well, now I must." She smiled, walked straight up to him and he froze like she might hurt him. She pulled open his front pocket, and the coins clinked when she dropped them in. The younger boy's mouth hung open, staring at Layala again.

"Thank you, miss," the man said, patting his pocket. "You're most gracious and kind."

"You're welcome."

Layala turned around to find Hel already mounted on Midnight and looking down the street. Layala wanted to drag him off her horse, but it wasn't worth causing a scene.

Piper stepped into the stirrup and swung her leg over. "You don't have to do that, you know," Piper said.

What was wrong with showing a bit of generosity? Thanks to Thane, she had more money than she could ever need.

Layala hopped on her borrowed gray horse and settled into the saddle. "I know."

"She has a soft spot for the less fortunate," Hel said, pulling on black gloves. "Don't look now but there are two males watching us. In front of the bakery, sitting at the table. They haven't taken their eyes from you since we stepped out."

Piper and Layala immediately spotted them. Their plates of food hadn't been touched and both of them glared with definite disdain.

Hel rolled his eyes. "I said, don't look."

"They're elves," Layala mused, ignoring him.

"Zealots who think Layala should die for her dark magic. The group has been around since she was born," Piper added. "See the bit of green sash poking out of their shirt pockets? It's one of their codes."

"And why aren't they being arrested?" Hel asked.

"They haven't committed any actual crimes," Piper said. "None of them have ever attempted to hurt Layala."

Hel grunted and nudged Midnight forward. "I don't like that. If it were my city, there would be no zealots and the *Palenor Scroll* would find someone else to harass."

"You'd create more with your brutality," Layala argued, trotting up beside him. The people walking the streets moved around them like water over rock. "I'd rather prove them wrong than right."

"I know you would, love. That's where we differ."

"And why is it that they immediately know who I am but not you?" Layala complained. She stared down the two zealots as they passed them, so they knew she knew who they were.

"People are funny like that. I'm sure they sense something is off about me, yet they wouldn't ever suspect the *Black Mage* would simply ride down the street on horseback. But you are betrothed to their High King, so they know you're here in the Valley. If these zealots are anything like people I've dealt with before, they know exactly what you look like, probably have drawings of you, and spread word about sightings. I'd bet Telvian Botsberry is one of them." He turned to her with a wicked smile. "I did like that last story of his. *'Layala Light-bringer sneaks out every night to meet with the terrible Black Mage.'* I wonder what they might be doing in the dark?"

"It better not be you," Layala glared. "Some of the details from the anonymous sources are too right. Talon says it's Orlandia letting slip secrets to her servants but I'm not so sure."

"It's highly likely to be her given that you and War killed her husband. And I have better things to do with my time than stir up petty drama among the elves."

Layala glanced back at Piper; a crease formed between her eyebrows as she searched the crowd. Those two zealots were... face down on the table. Layala tugged back on her horse's reins and twisted around to make sure she wasn't just imagining things. Both were slumped over; one of their drinks was on its side, dripping liquid all over the tabletop onto the ground. People walked by the table not seeming to take notice or care until a waiter tapped one of them on the shoulder and got no response. "They're not moving."

Hel glanced back. "Oh them. That's because they're dead."

Piper's mouth dropped and then she smiled, and when she noticed Layala looking at her she started coughing as a cover. Was she seriously amused by this?

"Did you kill them? How?" Layala whispered, kicking her horse back into a walk. He hadn't even looked back during their conversation.

"Well, they didn't die of natural causes."

"You can't go around killing people, especially in public."

"They had it coming and so does anyone else with a green sash in their pockets that I see. Publicity is necessary to send a message."

"He's not wrong," Piper chimed in.

"He was threatening you not even ten minutes ago," Layala said.

"Well, I've said the group should be wiped out for a while now. Thane doesn't want to be seen as a tyrant like Tenebris. I've told him we could take a small group and get it done in secret, but he won't give me the go-ahead."

Hel laughed and turned in his saddle to look at Piper. "Did we just come to an understanding, Red?"

"I think this is probably the only thing we agree on."

"You're both confusing." Layala forced herself to keep a straight face but some sick part of her deep down relished in the fact that Hel killed them. Someone stood up for her and with how many people hated her and wished her dead, it struck a chord. It wasn't that Thane wouldn't, but being High King came with responsibilities and consequences Hel didn't have to think about. For Thane, people had to cross a line before he'd take life. Hel wasn't burdened with such misgivings.

"We got sidetracked. So, what are these better things you have to do besides stir up drama?"

He chuckled, bringing out the dimple on his cheek. "Save your ass, for one. Plan the demise of others. Get your and War's memories back. Even if I'd like to snap his neck, I need him."

I knew it, she thought. *His threats to nail him to a wall weren't legitimate.*

"For what?" Layala was surprised he was opening up to her

some and even more that she could have a conversation with him that didn't involve threats.

He looked her in the face. "I'm not sure how much to tell you. You don't even believe you are who you truly are." He tore his garnet eyes away and gripped the saddle horn tighter. The horse hooves clopped along the stone. "But we've been through this before. We can do it again."

"What do you mean?"

"I mean this isn't the first life we've lived since we were banished from Runevale. Every time you, War, and I get together, they send someone to kill us. It may or may not have something to do with my threats of revenge. But they always start with you." He flicked a stray piece of hair out of his eyes. "I think so that War and I will suffer more... Then they get to us eventually, and we start this all over again."

Layala's chest constricted. "How many times?"

"I remember Runevale, and twice before this. It's why I did something different this life."

"The Void..." The black bubbling tar, the decaying earth, and wall of black mist came to mind. But surrounding Hel and his tower was a lush reddish garden.

"Yes."

"The goddess in the stone and scepter said it made you stronger."

"Much. The land decayed because it was strengthening me, and with each passing year in my sleep my magic grew stronger. I may not be immortal anymore but close."

"What of the jungle there surrounding you? It didn't decay."

"I don't truly know. It must have come from my subconscious."

"So why didn't the council kill Thane or me this time before I could wake you?"

"My theory is that since you and Thane didn't use your powers often, the council didn't know until recently. They don't know when or who we'll be born to. We may always look the same, but they can't come here themselves anymore. They can only send spies to watch for signs."

"The owls," Layala mused though she didn't know how she knew that.

He nodded. "Owls, crows, people. The crows and owls are likely War's father, and he wouldn't send assassins, so if he knew, he kept it quiet. Thane's elf father might have been a prick, but his true father is kind." He took a deep breath and looked up as if he might find him among the clouds. "But before, none of us ever lived much past our early twenties, about the time when memories started coming back. We'd find each other and then they'd find us, but in this life something changed. I was here three hundred years without finding you or War. I didn't remember who I was until I was almost thirty. And once I did, I earned the title of Black Mage. And about twenty years later, the curse came. It wasn't that the Runevale gods didn't send people to assassinate me. They certainly knew who I was, but by the time they did, I was much too powerful. And I was asleep for so long, they wouldn't know when I'd wake."

"Where were you in the two months since the tower?"

His red eyes found hers. "Learning what happened over the last few hundred years."

"Was that you who warned me I was in danger in my room? Was it an assassin?"

"Yes, and yes."

"Were you there?" Layala balked.

"No, I happened to be doing a scrying spell to check in on you. I felt something wasn't right."

"A scrying spell? Like you watched me through a crystal ball or something?" Layala's brows furrowed. So, he could spy on her from afar at any time? A chill ran down her spine.

"Or something."

"You haven't watched me..."

"Undress? Bathe? Touch yourself while thinking of me?"

Layala gasped at the audacity. "I would never do that and think of *you*."

With a chuckle, he said, "No. I don't watch you in private moments. I'm not a pervert. I do have *some* morals."

"You better not watch." She scowled at him and then to move the conversation forward, she asked, "Who decides when and where we're born again?" He was finally opening up to her, giving her the answers she desperately needed.

"I don't know. I assume the Maker. The fates."

"The All Mother," Layala added.

Hel smiled at her. "Possibly."

Layala couldn't stop herself from inspecting the curve of his strong jaw, the perfect slope of his nose, his luminescent skin— it all made him impossibly beautiful, and that smile. She wanted to hate him for everything he'd done, but she found herself admiring.

"I like to think that fate played a hand in this life. That the Maker and All Mother thought it was unfair they killed us before we ever got to really live. Everything happened this time for a reason. You being hidden away with a human woman, Thane's elf father being jealous and hiding his magic. I planned to have Mathekis train you when you were old enough and protect you, but this worked better. You were supposed to be kept safe by King Tenebris and his wife. He and I made a deal. I had not the faintest idea War would be his son or that he'd bind you together as mates with my spell."

"I can't believe you trusted any of them, especially Mathekis."

"Mathekis isn't like the others. There was another god, a demigod, that was banished in the same way, and I believe Mathekis is him though he never told me so. He has the persuasion gift that gods do."

"I know about his gift from personal experience," Layala murmured. And it made sense that all the other elves lost their magic except for Mathekis.

They went quiet and the sounds of the city filled the silence; chatter from the elves moving from shop to shop, horse hooves clattering, somewhere nearby soft string music played by a band. The spray of water from a stone fountain in the center of the street ahead crashed into the gathering pool. Children splashed at its edges and tossed coins to make wishes.

"Do you remember anything yet?" Hel asked, but he didn't sound hopeful.

Layala shook her head even though the dream she had of talking with the blond male about her mate mark still was very fresh in her mind. The moment of realization of her past-self recognizing Hel as her mate then and now felt private and not something she wanted to share with anyone yet. She certainly didn't want to admit aloud that he very well may be the perfect match, created by the All Mother herself.

They trotted down busy streets, turned here and there to make their way out of the city. It was only when they rode out into the open that the three of them relaxed some. Piper kicked her horse and rode up beside Layala. "I don't think we were followed."

"So, Red," Hel started. "How is it that you were dubbed

Layala's bodyguard? You've got the ruthless part down, if you're willing to kill a group of people who haven't harmed Layala. But I'm certain there are better choices, although War is the jealous type. I'm not too surprised he chose a female."

"The High King's name is Thane and I'm plenty capable," Piper said.

"Piper is one of the best warriors in Palenor," Layala said. "I would choose her any day."

Hel's eyes dragged over her as if assessing her in a new light. "Perhaps I should make you a mage. Do you want magic, love? I don't make this offer lightly. It would make you a better bodyguard for her."

"The Maker took our magic away for a reason," Piper said, though she tore her gaze away and stared off as if deep in thought. Magic must be tempting to someone who didn't possess it.

"True, there are no natural-born elf mages anymore, but I can give you power like you never dreamed, Red."

"No one wants your deals. It's not worth the price of possibly becoming a pale one," Layala said.

"Suit yourselves. I'll be close enough to be your bodyguard from now on anyway." He shrugged. "Oh, his ears must have been burning."

Thane raced toward them on Phantom in a full gallop. The pounding of the hooves was like thunder, as was the murderous look on his face. He roared up to them, jerking back on the reins so that Phantom reared with a cry, and slammed back down. His windswept hair and venomous scowl passed between each of them.

"She's fine, as you can see." Hel's tongue quickly swept over his bottom lip. "She has been in my *very* capable hands. We even found the perfect dress."

Thane's jaw muscles flexed, and he pinned her with a stare. "Are you alright?"

"Yes." She gave him a reassuring smile. "Nothing happened."

His tense posture relaxed with his shoulders falling slightly forward. "You can't keep leaving. You must stay. We have to stay together. Please listen to me for once. It's much, much too dangerous."

"You've remembered something important," Layala assumed.

"I remember the day they killed us the first time." His gaze passed from her to Hel. "And I know it happened again and again."

"We were just discussing that very topic," Hel said.

Thane set his jaw firmly, and the cold glare he leveled at Hel sent a chill across Layala's skin. "I also remember the promise you made me," Thane said, deadly, lethal.

"Don't worry," Hel purred. "So do I."

CHAPTER 21

THANE

T hane bounded down the front steps of the castle. The birds chirped happily with an exceptional sunrise, painting the horizon with pinks and salmon and blues. The morning dew created a fresh aroma in the air, and he took a deep breath. Layala, Piper, Leif, and Fennan already waited for him. Seeing them all gathered in their training leathers reminded him of old times.

Layala smiled at him; genuine and warm. "Good morning."

He thought she was still upset with him about leaving her unsatisfied on her bed but by the way she smiled at him now, maybe she finally understood.

"Good morning." He smiled back. "This is a rare occasion. I didn't expect everyone."

"We decided it was needed," Piper said. "It's been too long."

Leif grinned. "The good ol' days."

Thane rolled his shoulders. "I say we run around the

grounds once then go to the training yard for sparring. I've missed the last few days and I'm getting antsy."

"Fine by me," Fennan said.

"Let's roll out." Piper was the first to move.

The rest of them went after her, flying across the grassy landscape, weaving around flowering bushes, and gardeners tending to them. A few guards stopped and bowed as he passed and although Thane had another level of speed he could tap into, he didn't.

Fennan reached the training yard first and plucked a sword from the wooden barrel. "Leif, you up for the challenge?"

"Always am."

For training, they typically used blunted blades to avoid accidents or—with the glower on both Leif and Fen's faces—purposeful injuries. There was still some lingering competition over Piper even if she didn't give either of them the time of day anymore. Maybe this was a bad idea.

Leif snatched up a sword, red hair moving in the breeze, the celestial tattoos on his face scrunched with his scowl, and without waiting for Thane to start the match, Fennan swung. Their swords rang out, over and over, clashing and clanking. Grunts and snarls erupting along with bits of grass and dirt flying.

"Have they been like this since we got home?" Layala asked, leaning closer to his side.

"Pretty much since they fought over Piper the first time by the portal on the island."

"Let's not talk about it," Piper said, folding her arms.

"Neither of them is competition for you, War, but I know someone who is."

Thane, Layala, and Piper whipped around to find Hel approaching wearing a dark gray tunic with intricate designs around the shoulders and over the chest as well as thick black leather pants for fighting. His sleeves were rolled to his elbows revealing the many runes and tattoos on his forearms.

"I'm a little hurt that I'm not a part of the club."

Layala blew out a long breath and narrowed her eyes. "Our training isn't until the evening."

"I'm well aware."

Thane had a hunch he'd show up, hoping he would even. He was tired of the elusive games and Hel holding all the cards. "Now that you're here, I challenge you to fight, a sparring match. And when I win, you'll give me some answers."

Layala's eyes widened but she pressed her lips together and didn't protest.

Hel looked bored when he said, "You know this will be a repeat of last time."

Thane smiled, ready for a challenge. "What happened to me being stronger and a better fighter."

"Well, that was then, let's see if it's still true."

"Swords?"

"I think we might be tempted to do more than just spar if we have swords," Hel said, narrowing his eyes.

"Alright then." Thane rolled up his own sleeves and took a few steps back. Even if Hel was strong in magic, no one was a better fighter than Thane. With confidence, he moved into a fighting stance and held up his fists.

"This fight stops when one of you is injured or taps out," Layala clarified. She glared at Hel. "You must agree to the terms."

"Agreed."

Thane nodded. "I agree."

With bloody noses and hair miffed, both Leif and Fen

stopped their own bout. Fennan spit bloody saliva into the grass. "Let's bet. Five silver on Thane," Fen said.

"I won't bet against him," Leif said, taken aback.

"I will," Hel said with a smile. "Five silver it is."

"Done. Thane is the best fighter in all of Adalon."

The confidence of Fen only fueled Hel's entertainment. His eyes sparkled with joy and with a mischievous smirk, he said, "I hope you have five silver to spare."

"We'll see."

"Say when," Thane said, drawing Hel's attention back to him.

Hel lifted his palm and said, "I promised to drag you through the underrealm, and I always make good on my promises."

In a flash, Thane was plunged into darkness, as if he was falling through worlds; the sky and landscape around him dropped at a blurry speed then it halted, and he stood in a dark forest with blue light. Massive trees with roots twisting and growing ten feet out of the ground stood all around him. Black-capped mushrooms with tops that reached his shoulder grew in bundles. Sleek dark vines hung off trees, moss covered fallen rotting logs. A black pond bubbled to his left and smelled acrid. Was this real? Could Hel truly transport him to the underrealm and was that where he stood now?

A serpent slithered past his boot, and he jumped back. It was as thick as his thigh and Thane couldn't see the end of its length.

"Do you remember this place?" Hel's voice echoed all around him as if he was in the branches above.

"No," Thane said quietly, unsure what he might draw if he made too much noise.

"You've been here before. You wanted some answers, some insight, you can have it."

A twig snapped and Thane whipped around, reaching back for a sword—he didn't have one. "You tricked me," Thane snarled. "We agreed to a sparring match."

"You didn't specify what kind of sparring. This is how we spar with magic. Not every spell is a physical attack... Have fun."

So, this was an attack on the mind, an illusion? His magic flared within him, and he pushed at the surrounding forest, but it didn't go away. This place reminded him of the unnamed forest, as if a piece of this land had somehow spilled over into Adalon. A clicking noise like the clacking of pincers made Thane dash out of the clearing and crouch under the group of protruding roots that formed a cage around him. One he could easily slip through but something larger than him wouldn't.

"War!" Called... Layala. "War, where are you?" She stepped into the blue light cascading down between a break in the trees. With weapons strapped to both thighs, a sword on her back, a gold dagger on her hip, black boots with the moon cycle in silver going up the outside in a vertical line. This wasn't Layala. It was Valeen.

Thane crept out, watching her carefully in case this was a trick. A smudge of dirt across her cheek and the sweat beading on her brow appeared real enough. She held a small brown bag in her hand. "Where is Hel?" she demanded, looking him up and down.

"I don't know."

"He was with you two seconds ago."

Thane noticed a ring on her left hand, a pear-shaped black diamond with two sparkling, crescent moons on either side.

"We need to get out of here. We've spent too much time already."

"How?"

She narrowed her blue eyes at him and in a blink, she had her golden dagger out, a forearm slammed into his chest, and she shoved him against the tree. The tip of the blade pressed against the base of his throat. "Who are you?"

"It's me. It's War." He held up his palms to show no threat. He didn't know if he could die in here, but the sharp point of the blade felt very real.

"Tell me something War would know then."

Thane cursed in his mind.

"Are you going to kill my cousin?" Hel said, appearing behind them. "I know he can be annoying, but I don't think we should gut him and leave him in the underrealm. It's a bit harsh, love."

"I don't think it's him. He asked me how we could get out."

"The door, obviously," Hel drawled. He gestured to the right and in the distance covered in vines and steeped in weeping branches stood a rounded archway with a barely visible door where dim light shone around the edges.

"Exactly, *War* knows that." She pressed the blade harder.

"Well, tell us something only War knows then." Hel's smile was all feline and shadows. "Or we'll leave the imposter here. For instance, why are we down here?"

Thane clenched his teeth together. Whatever was in Valeen's hand no doubt, it was small, but he had no idea what it was. "To find something?" And Hel knew that. Valeen pressed her blade until the sting of it burned, really and truly. "Wait! Wait. I fell into some of those mushrooms. It's messing with my mind."

She pulled the blade back. "Why didn't you just say that, you fool?"

"Because it's messing with my mind," Thane snapped.

Hel smiled and slowly shook his head. "Clever," he murmured.

"Let's go before we have to fight our way out or worse, get trapped here." Valeen started off, and Thane hurried to catch up to her side.

"So why are we here?" And as soon as he said it a memory flashed—"*Bring me the ring of a demon prince or I'll expose you. All it will take is one whisper to destroy your world. I know you killed Synick.*" He'd overheard someone—a female blackmail Valeen. "*And if you kill me, I've set up for the truth to come out about what you did and what you have in your possession. Theft of the most coveted weapon, and the murderer of a primordial, it's enough to get you exiled forever.*"

"A demon prince's ring?" Thane balked. He wasn't even entirely sure what a demon prince was but there were stories in the oldest of books about demons and what they could do.

Hel quirked an eyebrow. "So, you do remember."

"It's coming back. Damn, mushrooms."

Valeen skidded to a halt, and both hands snapped out to grab Hel and Thane by the front of their shirts. "He's here."

Thane didn't like the way she said that. He glanced back and in the shadows fifty yards off, a pair of red eyes watched them. An eerie tingle ran down his spine.

Valeen lowered her voice. "*Nothing* can escape this realm." To add to the chilling warning, the scream of some helpless creature being assaulted by something that shut it up quickly, echoed throughout the forest.

"We shouldn't be here in the first place," Hel murmured

and turned to Valeen. "If you had just told me who was black-mailing you, we wouldn't be in this mess."

"We'd be in a bigger mess because you'd have done something reckless," Valeen whispered. "We're here now anyway."

Thane's magic flared again. "We can destroy him. There are three of us."

"A prince of the underworld?" Valeen hissed. "Are you mad? They'll send legions to attack the realms. Protecting the realms is more important than anything. It is our duty."

"I thought they couldn't get through the door," Thane said.

"If we kill the demon prince, they'll find a way." Hel's jaw muscles flexed. "Even if it's five thousand years from now. Demons never forget."

"And once they notice one of their rings is missing?" Thane whispered.

"I knew I smelled outsiders," a demon cooed in a gravelly voice, creeping out of the shadows, far enough away he wasn't an immediate threat but close enough Thane could see every detail. He stood at least eight feet tall, with curling black horns growing out of the top of his head of white hair. He was humanoid, with striking features, gaunt cheeks, a dark blueish-gray complexion but the veins going up his bare arms were lighter, and his fingers ended in snow-white nails that were pointed like talons. His deep blue cloak floated behind him as if air pushed it to ripple and wave though there was no wind to speak of. "The gods don't belong in my world. You may rule in the other realms but not here."

When he walked forward, his blackened, dirty bare feet didn't touch the ground. He floated above the craggy forest floor.

"It was a dare," Valeen said, tying the small brown sack to

her belt. "To see if we could sneak inside without you knowing. Looks like we failed."

He let out a low, menacing growl. "You know better than to trifle with me and my brothers over a dare, goddess. This is not your playground."

"You know how we arrogant, asshole gods like to test one another," Hel said, waving his hands around as if it was all a simple misunderstanding. "And to come here is the greatest test of bravery. It's a testament to your power, demon. We'll be taking our leave now."

"You don't come to the underrealm unless you're dead. Since you are not, you don't get to leave without payment." His red eyes fell to the golden dagger on Valeen's hip. "I'll take that."

"If you come near me, I'll cut off your head with it." She scowled at him with such steely assurance Thane believed her. "You may rule the underrealm, but I rule the night. I do not fear the dark, demon, I was born of it."

Hel leaned closer to Thane bumping his shoulder into his. "Gods, I love her," he whispered with a sly grin.

Thane smiled and although this felt real and dreamlike at once, he began to think this had all happened before, that he was awake in Hel's memories somehow, but it also reacted to who he was in the present. Hel certainly was the god of magic.

"A hair from the primordial goddess's head then."

"No," Hel said, immediately, and stepped forward—the move was a threat of its own. "You will not touch my wife's hair."

Thane instinctively knew or remembered that a hair with the correct magic could be used to track someone anywhere at any time, maybe something even worse. Other pairs of eyes began to pop up in the shadows, watching, waiting. Something growled, gurgly and wet. The thick air smelled of rot and although it had been cool when he arrived, the temperature began to rise as if the presence of so many demons produced heat of its own.

"We need to leave," Thane said through clenched teeth, heart hammering. He tried to tell himself this wasn't real, and he was standing in the training yard back at Castle Dredwich, but he wasn't sure if this was entirely true. He could *smell* them, *feel* the heat on his skin. Even Hel promised that getting his memories back would hurt.

"We *cannot* open the door," Valeen snapped and jerked her sword from her back loose; the golden blade glinted off the dim light. "Not until we know we won't be followed."

Thane reached back and found he suddenly had a weapon —two. A sword and an ax.

"But we need to get closer to it. We're three hundred yards away." Hel grabbed Valeen around her waist and tugged her backward. "Demon bites are poisonous even to us."

"How do you even know that?" she questioned and the three of them sprinted for the door, jumping over, and slipping through massive protruding roots and tangled vines.

"If you won't give it freely," the demon prince called, "I'll take your blood instead." He raised both hands and the hundreds of eyes that lurked in the shadows sprang into the pale blue light. The pounding of beasts bounding after them thudded loudly. Thane didn't dare look back as he sprinted.

The three of them made it to the door and whirled around, weapons ready. Hel's fingertips sparked with bright white volts, black shadow rolled off Valeen making her difficult to see, and Thane held an ax in one hand and sword in the other. A dog-like beast crept toward him, all black, no hair, the hump of its shoulders behind its head reminded Thane of a bear but its slender sleek body had rib and spine bones protruding. Its massive jaw with three rows of hundreds of serrated teeth dripped saliva that sizzled and burned the ground with each drop.

"And the reason I know, love," Hel began, "is because this isn't my first time here."

She glared at him. "You came here alone?"

"Not the time for arguing," Thane said. The beast lunged toward him, and he swung, cutting its head clean off. It plopped to the ground and bright green blood spurted out, pooling around it. More came, Thane went into a frenzy, cutting through demons, with his blades like slicing through warm butter. Volts of lightning lit up the darkness, Valeen shifted to shadow, disappearing, and reappearing to cut down demons.

"They just keep coming!" Hel hollered.

A great troll-like beast, twelve feet tall, a protruding gut with slashes of scars across its gray skin, no eyes, no ears, horns that dropped the length of its body. With each step the ground shook, bringing it closer. Even the dog-like demons began to whimper and back up. It bellowed, spewing saliva, and showing off thick tusks.

Thane felt something touch his foot, a boney hand wrapped around his ankle. The decrepit body of a nude male, lying on his belly, crawling toward him. "Take me with you. Free me of this place."

Thane's nose scrunched up at the sight of him. He kicked his hand off. "Don't touch me, demon."

"I'm not a demon. I'm a prisoner here, one of the damned." His voice was weak. "You are a god, a hero. Free me."

"Don't listen to it," Hel said and stomped on his head, cracking the skull with a snap. "It's deception."

The dog demons crept in again, jaws snapping and snarling, as the giant troll stomped closer.

"I'll take out the troll," Thane said. "You two wipe out the rest of the dogs so we can get out of here." Without waiting for confirmation, Thane sprinted, and with a leap, he soared through the air, sword, and ax gleaming. The curved blade of the ax embedded in the troll's neck. Thane grunted trying to pull it free, but the troll's hide was thick and stiff. Thane's eyes narrowed—the skin began to grow around his weapon, as if his body absorbed it. *What in the realms?* The troll bellowed again, spraying bits of goo all over Thane, and grabbed him around the waist, like he was a toy, squeezing so hard he thought his ribs would snap. *Can't breathe. Can't breathe.*

With a deep roar, Hel appeared in the air, and came down with a sword, straight through the troll's arm. Thane fell with it and crashed into the ground. He rolled out of the hand's grip onto his knees and threw out his hand. A wave of his magic rippled out, hitting the troll. Its skin began to peel off as it burned again. It cried out, writhing and hit the ground and convulsed, forcing the trees to sway with its thrashing. Until it stopped and was nothing more than a pile of goo and bones.

Hel laughed. "Remind me not to piss you off."

"I wasn't going to give it my ax." He picked it up out of the sludge and—

"War, behind you!" Hel cried lifting his hand, but pain lanced his calf.

A demon dog sunk his teeth into Thane and snarled. He gritted his teeth and sliced it in half. *Shit—shit, poison.* Valeen met his stare and with more fury than he'd ever seen, she let out a warrior's scream and a wave of black whooshed out. Thane turned and curled in on himself. Hel followed as the blast rocked them like the clap of a massive ocean wave. But there was no water and it suddenly smelled of charred flesh and earth, but it was quiet. No more snarling beasts.

Thane opened his eyes to find the ground was scorched, the troll's body was ash, the trees around them nothing but charred stumps. A small circle around both he and Hel were the only things left untouched for a hundred yards or more. Thane stood, brushing off the ash and soot from his shoulders. His calf pulsed with a strange heat that slowly began to creep through his body.

"Now!" Valeen said and shoved open the door. Hel grabbed Thane's arm and dragged him toward the door. He stumbled through into bright light. The venom of the demon pulsed through him, making the world around him spin. He slumped to the floor and then everything went dark.

THANE WOKE up lying in the grass, staring up at a blue sky and the faces of Layala, Hel, and his friends hovering above him.

"Thane, are you alright?" Layala asked. "What happened?"

"One minute you were standing, the next you hit the ground like a tree in a windstorm," Leif said.

"I told you he was fine," Hel said and stood.

"What did you do to him?" Fennan glared. "He looks confused."

"Just a little magic."

Thane blinked, shielding the bright sun with his palm. His calf still ached, and he shot up, pulling up his pant leg. There were no marks. "Was that real?"

"It happened a long time ago," Hel said, crossing his arms. "And do you know what happened after?"

Thane's brow furrowed. "Yes..."

The Past

Valeen pressed a cool damp cloth to his forehead. "Are you sure he'll get better on his own?"

"He's immortal, Val," Hel said. "It will take time for his body to push the poison out but yes, he'll be fine."

He stared into her worried eyes. A halo of light like a starburst glowed all around her. She was so beautiful, so lovely, and he couldn't think of anyone he'd rather take care of him at this moment. It was wrong to think such things, to feel this much fondness toward Hel's wife. He couldn't say he was in love with her, at least he'd never admit it, not even to himself, but he thought of her more often than he should. He blinked, trying to clear the haze but it only worsened, and he was scorching, sweat covered his entire body and he wished he could jump into an ice bath.

Valeen lifted the cloth to Hel, and he touched it and frost spread over the surface. She pressed it flat against his left cheek and he leaned into it. Would it be alright if he... his hand brushed her fingers then he slipped his palm into hers and held it like she was his anchor to this world. "Thank you."

"Of course," she said, giving his hand a squeeze. "You'll be alright soon."

In the corner of the room a pair of big red eyes glowed in the shadows. Panic jolted him out of his haze. "They're here!" He shot up, nearly knocking Valeen off the bed. "Hel! The demons are here!"

Hel whipped around, hands sparking with bright light. The demon hound prowled from the shadows, more grotesque than before with chunks of exposed muscle and bones, scars across its body, larger teeth.

"There's no demons." Hel turned back, closing his hands at his sides; the magic flared out. "It's the poison, it isn't real."

"It's right there!" he pointed and jumped up. He grabbed his

blade from the bedside floor and charged. He hacked at it, cutting a round table in half, splitting the wood with a crack.

"War!" Valeen shouted. "There is no demon!"

But it was there. He saw what they could not. A trick of the demon. He swung again as it lurched at him, cutting down into the armchair. Sprays of dust and fluffs of cotton wafted into the air. Valeen stepped into his path with her palms up. "War, there are no demons. I made certain we were not followed."

The demon hound growled and barked, going for Valeen with wide acid-dripping jaws. "No!" War charged, knocking her aside, and hacked at it. His unsteady momentum sent him stumbling and crashing through the wall, and into a cool, darkened hallway. An arched window in the stonework to his right revealed the sparkling night sky filled with waves of colors. He pushed to his feet and stumbled back, catching himself on the stone wall before he fell again.

Now the demon prince sat in the window, laughing at him. "And I thought the gods were powerful. If they're all as weak as you, I should bring my legions to take whatever I want."

War roared and charged, driving his legs hard and fast. Until an elbow hooked under his chin, and wrapped around his throat, and he suddenly couldn't move. Paralyzed completely from head to feet. "Release me, demon, or I'll destroy your realm! We'll see how your demons fare against dragon fire and the strength of the gods!"

"As mighty as you are, they certainly should fear," Hel said with a chuckle. "But I am not a demon. I'm your cousin. And I'm sorry I have to do this, but I can't let you hurt Val and destroy her home. Go to sleep."

War sagged into him and there were no more demons.

"I THINK he's back in some sort of trance." Leif waved his hand in front of Thane's face.

"I'm fine." He blinked several times and pushed Leif away.

He sprang to his feet where he and Hel met eyes and shared an unspoken understanding. Even if they hated each other now, even if they loved the same goddess, they were once as close as brothers and that bond could never truly die. Hel showed him the past to prove that they could fight together, and he showed him the beast that was rumored to be roaming Palenor, and maybe without saying it, that Hel believed a demon prince was here to assassinate them.

CHAPTER 22

LAYALA

The afternoon of the graduation ball, Layala paced her room waiting for it to begin. She'd been dressed for hours in the gown Hel made her promise to wear. Tif whistled from her perch and swung her legs over the edge. "That dress is so beautiful. Wow! You'll certainly be unmatched if that is what you were going for. Those look like real diamonds and the drape is like something I only dreamed of. Mama would say I was only pretending I was rich, but I wish I could have one to match. We'd make quite the pair; a jumbo and a gnome."

"Thank you, Tif. We'll have one made for you later if you want. Now, I want you to stay away from the party tonight, in case something bad happens, even if the food will be tempting. I know you're braver than you used to be so please listen to me."

She gripped one of the green vines draping over the bed and slid down, landing on the cushion of a pillow. "Course, my lady. Besides, when are lady's maids invited to balls, especially gnome lady's maids?"

A mask showed up in her room that morning to perfectly match the dress. She didn't know how it arrived on her vanity, but she knew who sent it. It would cover around her eyes and forehead. It was made of lace-like material with one side dark purple curling up higher almost like wisps of smoke, the other half a glittering silver, with a starburst at the center.

As the sun dipped behind the horizon, Layala moved in front of the body-length mirror, inspecting her reflection carefully. In Pearl's absence she didn't style her hair as often and left it combed and down. The mask would be enough to cover the loss of an intricate style.

She stepped in front of the mirror to tie the mask on, and wondered yet again why this gown didn't trigger her memory? Why was her goddess side so elusive? She needed to remember Valeen... become Valeen. Her relationship with Thane depended on it, not to mention perhaps her life.

Thane told her he suspected a demon prince would come for her and he was immortal. And though he didn't go into detail about what this demon was capable of, she knew both him and Hel were nervous.

After their sparring match, Hel's demeanor shifted toward Thane, as if he saw him less of an opponent to torture and more as an ally he would need.

But as she watched the sequins sparkle on the bodice in the dying sunlight and peered at her own blue eyes through the stars and moon mask, nothing came but a feeling of dread.

Even if she and Hel had a moment of reprieve where he spoke to her in a casual conversation and seemed like a normal person rather than a murdering mad elf, she still hated that he manipulated her into wearing this dress. Even if it was beautiful, the most beautiful gown she'd ever worn, ever seen, her defiant side wanted to change into something else and burn it just to spite Hel, but she couldn't chance Piper's life. *Wear it or little Miss Red will pay the price,* he'd said.

Tif slid to the floor and scurried to Layala's side. "You really think the food will be good? Perhaps cakes, rolls, maybe even cookies? Oh, and I bet Thane serves the best wine at these events too." Her eyes seemed to double in size at her own descriptions.

Layala laughed and stooped down to pat Tif on the top of her red hat. "Don't even think about it. Now, there are protective enchantments on this room, so it is safe in here. As long as you *stay* here."

"No need to worry about me. After that cat woman came in here, I've had my guard up. Got me a butcher knife stashed just in case." A butcher knife would be almost as big as her.

Three firm knocks hit the door. Layala picked up the front of her dress, unsure who to expect. She opened it to find a note. She was hesitant to open it at first even if she hadn't gotten any new threats recently.

I can't wait to see you downstairs. Meet me on the dais. ~Thane.

She smiled and despite his frustrating vow to keep his distance, she couldn't wait to see him either. She turned to set the note inside and caught sight of a small triangular-shaped box that looked like a deck of cards. "What's this?" she murmured.

She scooped it up and read, printed on the glossy black box in gold foil lettering, *gods and goddesses.* Underneath a note was attached. *Don't start expecting gifts from me, but you need this. ~Hel*

Layala rolled her eyes and set both notes and the box on the dresser. She'd have to look at it later, but her curiosity was certainly piqued.

With a nervous smile, Layala looked down at her dress one more time as she arrived at the double entrance doors to the ballroom. The guards stepped away from their positions and held up their hands. "Invitation, please."

Layala lifted her mask, "It's me."

The guard dipped his head apologetically. "Welcome, Lady Lightbringer."

The plucking of a harp, flutes and other string and wind instruments in a lovely tune drifted out from the ballroom. Rows and groups of standing and dancing guests dressed in their most luxurious attire filled the room. Some maidens wore white gowns with golden suns and masks to match. Others dark blues and purples with glitter shaped like starbursts. Not everyone wore celestial-themed attire, but many did, making it easy for her to slip in amongst the crowd unnoticed.

Navy-blue tapestries trimmed in gold draped over the large, rounded windows encrusted in gold trim. Crystal chandeliers with hundreds of burning candles drenched the room with soft light. Layala scanned the crowd for Hel, nerves making her stomach tense, but among the many masked males in nearly identical suits, it would be hard to find him. Who was his date? He could enchant anyone to hang on his arm, even Piper or... Aunt Evalyn.

Although the thought of him stepping in with Talon on his arm just to piss off Thane almost made her giggle. Layala didn't see either of them yet, but she spotted Piper next to Leif, the two redheads were hard to miss standing against the wall on the left side of the room. Her green dress stood out right away as did her peacock-feathered mask. She laughed at something he said and gave him a small push on the shoulder. Leif might be a bit uncouth, but he was always good for a laugh.

Thane stood alone on the dais, hands resting at his sides, looking in her direction. Even if no one else noticed her entrance, he did. She smiled and warmth seeped out from her chest. Maker, he was beautiful. An off-white jacket, black pants, a golden mask with half a sun flaring out on the left side of his face brought out the flecks of warmth in his dark brown hair. A golden crown adored his head tonight even if he preferred his dark silver one.

Layala moved along the outside edge of the room, heels tapping lightly as she crossed the glossy pearl floor. She lifted the front of her dress and one of the servants took her gloved hand and helped up the steps.

Thane met her at the top. Her eyes followed the outline of his suit, cut perfectly, bringing out his broad shoulders and trim waist. She expected Thane to smile and tell her how beautiful she was, or at the very least greet her, but with his hands fisted at his sides, and the firm set of his jaw, he didn't appear happy to see her.

"Is something wrong? I know the other night wasn't... ideal. I just want you to know I understand even if I don't agree." They hadn't talked about his willingness to please her but not go any further and how either of them felt about it.

His long stretch of silence while inspecting every inch of her might make a girl blush, if he wasn't clearly annoyed, maybe even hurt, while doing so.

"Thane?"

"Go back upstairs and take that dress off," he whispered, a little more snappy than usual.

"Why?"

"You don't remember that dress, do you? Tell me you don't remember it, Laya." The wild look in his green eyes, brought out even more by the mask, made her step closer to him and grip his hand.

"No, but I'm assuming you do." And Hel knew it would have an effect on him.

"That bastard." He turned away and swore again. "Just when I think maybe the ice is melting and he isn't such a prick, he does this."

She gripped the lapels of his suit jacket, turning him to face her again. "Talk to me about it. It's alright."

Staring down at her with agony he said, "That is the dress you wore the day you *married* Hel. You know what this is? Him reminding me yet again, you loved him first, you married him first. So, wear something else, anything else."

Layala's jaw dropped. Somewhere in the back of her mind a different tune apart from the music in this room played. The ghost of warm hands slid across her waist. "*Everything that is mine is now yours, love—my territory, my power, my heart, my body, my soul, yours forever,*" and that deep, soothing, honey-rich voice wasn't Thane's. It was Hel's.

Layala shook her head clearing it away and said, "As much as I'd like to change, he said if I don't wear it, he'll hurt Piper. So, remind him, I left. Remind him who I'm with now. I bet he's watching."

Thane glanced about the room but didn't stop in any one place among the hundreds in attendance. Once he turned back to her, he smiled. "I like that idea."

Now calm and composed, Thane dropped his bright eyes to her mouth. His big hands gripped her waist and pulled her into him. A moment later their lips met. The kiss was soft at first, appropriate for a public setting and then, it deepened. His tongue explored her mouth, making her heart race. His arms wrapped around her, possessive and wanting more. When they finally pulled apart, he smirked and adjusted her mask. "You do look very beautiful. It's going to be difficult to stay out of your room tonight. It's difficult every night."

Layala chuckled. "You must like pain."

"Apparently so. But waiting will make it that much better. All the built-up tension," his finger lightly trailed over her collarbone, "the nights I spend dreaming about what I will do to you when it's time. If you'll have me then."

Layala shuddered at his touch and brought her arms around his neck. "Your teasing is the sweetest torment," she said. "I like this side of you much better. I don't like broody Thane. You're supposed to be my bright sun, and I the moody, temperamental night. Teach me another dance?" She might remember the steps of the Kenatara from the Summer Solstice festival, but she thought that it might be only for that day.

"I'd love nothing more. Listen to the music, feel it and I'll guide your steps." He cupped her waist with one hand and took the other into his grip. "Right foot back," he stepped forward and she stepped back, "left step, right step, forward." He led every move, but never took his eyes off hers. "Very good. You're a natural. It must be all your years of fight training footwork."

She leaned in closer and whispered, "I missed this. I shouldn't have been sneaking out at night. I shouldn't have gone after Talon. I don't deserve you, Thane."

"Don't say that. I am far from perfect. I shouldn't have ignored you. The past few weeks have been very confusing for me. I'm trying to make peace with that life and this one, and somehow bring them together. I have two sets of parents, and I remember a life and side of me that is hundreds of years old, and then short lives in between this life as an elf. Here I was raised to protect you and be a king and fight pale ones who happened to be created by my closest friend, my *brother*. And then dealing with the guilt of somehow taking you from him. You were the only person he ever truly loved and it's all messing with my head."

Layala nibbled on her lower lip. "I don't think I had parents before..."

"No, as a primordial, you wouldn't. You were simply created. Hel and I are third-generation gods, I suppose. I can't fully remember."

"I think... I think I've missed you more than just these past weeks." For a moment she saw him dancing with her, but it wasn't here, and everything faded away...

The Past

They danced under the bright stars and three moons, and colorful streams of light waved across the sky. "You know," he said, "I didn't think I'd ever see you again let alone be invited into the goddess of night's home for a party."

"Think of it as a truce," she said, pushing back against his hand on her lower back, forcing them to stand further apart. It was too intimate otherwise, closer than customary. "I don't want a fight with you or your cousin."

"It's been six months, if we were going to come back for a fight, we would have." War's smile was devastating and would bring a lesser goddess right under his spell.

"And why didn't you? I murdered your uncle. A primordial. A crime that would get me exiled forever, if and when you could detain me, that is."

He chuckled and lifted his shoulder as they turned. "Neither one of us wanted to fight with you or to see you fall."

"Is it that simple?"

"It's that simple."

"If I were a male and not a beautiful goddess?" Her eyebrow ticked up.

He laughed. "Then I wouldn't have lied to my father and the council about you having nothing to do with my uncle's death and we'd be at war right now."

"So, either you're what the humans refer to as a 'gentleman' or you're a filthy-minded male and thought by sparing me war you might get something else from me."

His throat bobbed and she noted the shine on his forehead. "Maybe I'm both." He spun her around and out and she whirled right into Hel's chest.

"HELLO, love, did you miss me, too?" Hel said very much in the here and now. Layala blinked several times, taking in his masculine scent, then pushed off his chest. Varlett's elbow was hooked around Hel's and the venom in her stare made Layala step further away into Thane's strong arms.

A long, shiny black dragon talon trailed down the collar of Hel's black suit coat. "What a lovely little party," Varlett said. Curly black horns protruded out of her golden hair. Her ebony mask was outlined in silver beads that matched her dress. "Thanks for the invitation, most High King."

CHAPTER 23

LAYALA

T he room was suddenly too hot, the chatter of the voices all around louder and encroaching like she'd been thrust into an echoing cavernous tunnel. Layala pressed her clammy hands against the bodice of her gown and looked around for an escape. Seeing Varlett, the horrible way she smiled, her beast like eyes, it brought the most terrible times of her life flooding right back. Being starved as she was held prisoner, Varlett's bloody hand shoving through Thane's torso right after she broke her mate bond to him. Her dragon form crushing Layala into the ground, stealing away her chance to end King Tenebris, and forcing her to wake Hel. She was either going to explode with anger and level the room with magic, or she must leave. Her hands began to tremble, shadows seeping from her fingertips. *Shadows, shadows, shadows.* She clenched her fists and willed her magic back.

"You remember Varlett, don't you?" Hel asked, watching her carefully through a simple black mask of his own.

"How could I forget?" Layala tried to keep her voice even, but the venom seeped out. "You're not welcome here. Leave."

"That's no way to treat a guest, Layala," Varlett said, pulling her arm free from Hel, and brushed her long golden locks over her shoulder. "You don't want to cause a scene, do you? They're already watching." She grew a slow smile and the slits of her eyes sharpened. "But it's not me they have their eyes on, or me they fear, it's you. They're waiting for you to *snap*." She clicked her fingers and cackled. "Go ahead, give them what they expect, *dark* mage."

"Your control is slipping, *Laya*," Hel said, using the name only those closest to her did. "You haven't been training on your own time. Maybe you should go stand at the pond with the old mage and take some deep breaths."

"Screw you."

"Anytime," he purred.

Thane pressed his big hands on Layala's shoulders and nuzzled his scruffy cheek against the side of her face. "Come on, let's finish that dance outside on the balcony." He slid his fingers down her arm and clasped her hand, fingers inter-twining.

Hel's eyes dipped to their hands. "Yes, better take poor Laya out of here. We wouldn't want her distressed."

"*Hel*," Layala snarled as a warning. "How could you bring her here? She tried to murder Thane and it would take all night to name all the other things she's done to us."

His grin vexed her even more. "Are you upset with my choice of a date? You left me, you shouldn't care who I fuck."

Layala's body flared with heat. "Don't get too attached to that bitch, she'll get what's coming to her soon enough." She swung her gaze to Varlett. "Mark my words, dragon, your days are numbered."

Varlett's upper lip curled, her fingers grew into long black talons, and she took a step for Layala, but Hel jerked her back to his side. "As much as I love a good girl fight, now isn't the time. We have an audience."

"If you touch her Varlett," Thane snapped. "I'll tear your arm off." Thane tugged on her hand with enough force she couldn't resist, and it was only a few long strides to the double balcony doors and the cool night air hit her face. Layala took it in, rushing over to the stone railing and gripping it. The stone beneath her fingers cracked with spider-like webbing, and with a start she let go.

Lifting off his mask he leaned his back against the stone barrier beside her. "You'll get your chance at her one day, but not tonight."

"Why in Maker's name did he bring her? I hate her. I *haaate* her, Thane." Layala stared out over the landscape, the pink weeping lilac swaying in the breeze, and up at the mountain looming above. "She threatened to cut out my tongue and *eat* it. She almost killed you. She murdered my friend Ren. She's insane."

"We knew they had some kind of history. I expected it. I don't know why you didn't."

"I thought he'd bring Talon or something to piss you off."

"Getting in *both* our heads seems to be his goal tonight. He's the god of mischief. It's what he does. It's a sort of show to let us know even if we're on the same side against the council, he's still Hel. But remember, us being together gets in his head too, so it's not all one-sided," he said with a sly smile. "I bet watching me kiss you in front of everyone got to him, even if he says he hates you now, he doesn't."

"How much more do you remember about him?"

He exhaled slowly and glanced up at the night sky. Luminor

crickets chirped below and the music from inside drifted out through the doors. Layala expected Hel and Varlett to darken the doorway at any moment.

"I remember much of the time we grew up together, fighting beside him. The younger years." He half smiled. "There was this time we went to a mountain notorious for giant eagles. And when I say giant, I mean a wingspan of at least twenty feet, talons much like dragons, beaks perfect for tearing flesh. We dared each other to steal an egg and whoever got one would get bragging rights. To make it more challenging we decided against magic and climbed the steep cliffs by hand to invade their nests." He chuckled at the memory. "I got up top first but was caught by a mother bird and she knocked me out of her nest, sent me freefalling from what must have been a thousand feet. I couldn't levitate then and as a god it wouldn't have killed me, but it would have hurt for damn sure. Hel grabbed an egg, tucked it under his arm and jumped after me. When he caught me, he gripped my arm and in a puff of smoke we were back on the ground. He handed me the egg and said I got there first."

"So, you see him as your friend, and he wasn't always a monumental ass, is what you're trying to say."

Thane let out a soft laugh. "Yeah, I guess so." He was quiet for a moment then said, "There's something about Varlett that bothers me, other than the obvious reasons. You've been around her more than me but when I see her, I think she reminds me of someone I knew but I can't place."

Thinking back to some of the things Varlett said to her, she wondered if it may be true. "She told me once that she knew you even better than I did... she said I would remember something I saw between her and Hel." Layala pressed her lips together.

"And that would only be possible if she knew us from before," Thane finished. "Even if it was any of the three lives we lived before this."

"But she's not a god. How could she live that long?"

"I believe most dragon shifters can live thousands of years if they take care of themselves... or maybe that's only in their home world," Thane mused, tapping his chin. "Ronan said the only dragon old enough to remember Ryvengaard was losing his mind, which would mean none of the dragons are over two thousand years old except for the one that paints but no longer speaks."

"And Varlett," Layala said and gritted her teeth.

"Varlett is a master sorceress. She must have found a way to preserve herself here."

"It's probably all the blood she drinks, although it wouldn't surprise me if she drank it just because she's sick in the head."

"Remember, she is a dragon. They like raw meat and blood wouldn't be that far off."

"I'm going to kill her," Layala promised. "One day."

"I love it when you're vicious." The corner of Thane's mouth lifted. "Let's go back inside and make sure those two aren't causing any problems. And I'm sure the boys and Piper would love to see you."

On the way back inside, Layala beamed at Thane. "When we danced, I remembered something about you and me from before."

He smiled. "Tell me."

THE SWISHING of ballgowns and the shuffle of feet to a slow intimate melody filled the ballroom. Seeing the elves move with such unison and elegance captured her attention. Hair pulled into braids and lovely styles in various shades from the blondes to red to black as coal. She spotted Leif in the crowd. With his copper-brown skin, fiery red hair, and tattooed face, dancing with an unknown lady. To Layala's surprise, Fennan and Piper danced. She flashed perfect white teeth, enraptured with whatever Fennan was telling her. Whether Piper would admit it or not, she still loved Fennan. Perhaps she'd get some wine in her and get Piper to confess and give Fen another chance.

The two Layala wanted to find the most among the crowd, she didn't, and that made her nervous. Not that Hel had done anything that would risk revealing his identity, but he always had a trick up his sleeve.

Then she spotted a little red hat poke out from behind the blue tapestries in the corner of the room, closest to the side doors. That gnome never listened to anything. She knew the most feared mage in history walked these halls, that assassins might come, and still Tif disobeyed. What happened to the days she was terrified of jumbos?

"Ugh, Tif is down here. I told her to stay upstairs."

The gnome slunk out from behind the tapestries and headed for the table with the food... of course.

"She's your lady's maid," Thane said and then kissed Layala's cheek. The warmth of his lips lingered on her skin. After her retelling of the memory of them dancing together from their previous life, his mood lifted all the more. He was all smiles, and it didn't look like even Hel or Varlett could bring that down. One brief recall obviously wasn't *everything,* but it was a step. "I'll grab you a drink. Wine?"

"Thanks for pawning the argument off on me. And yes, a glass of wine, please."

Thane chuckled. "I'll be waiting for you over here."

Layala hurried across the glossy floor, nodding at guests, and smiling as they greeted her and dipped into curtsies. No one stopped her. Unless invited, it wasn't customary to approach royalty in Palenor. And ever since Thane threatened everyone at the Summer Solstice festival last year, most guests steered clear of her.

Tif was almost at the tables and Layala close to blocking her path when hands slid around her waist and wrist and swung her around. Her heart lurched and she nearly jerked away but Hel gripped her firmly. Seeing him, her curiosity and anger simultaneously piqued.

He didn't ask, didn't so much as whisper a word as he pulled her into the sea of dancing couples, blending into the steps without missing a beat. If it wouldn't cause a scene, she'd smack him and tear out of his arms. With worried wide eyes, Layala searched for Thane; Varlett slid between him and Leif.

"Don't worry, she won't hurt him," Hel said. His black mask brought out his red irises.

Layala glared, trying to pull her hand out of his. "She almost killed him. I don't trust her. Let me go."

With his palm on her lower back, he tugged her closer as they stepped in smooth unison. "She won't. I forbid it."

"She told me you and her had a falling out because she craved more power and so did you. What makes you think she'd listen to you? She cares about herself."

"That isn't why." He flashed pretty white teeth. "How did War like your dress?"

"He said I looked beautiful."

"It looked like he said a lot more than that. He remembered. Did you?"

Her brows lifted, realizing he'd watched them from the

crowd. Layala searched his piercing eyes, more maroon tonight rather than such a deep red. As if under a spell, she found she couldn't look away, and the longer she held his stare, the faster her heart beat. "No."

"You know why I think that is? Why he's remembering and you're not? Yes, he's a few years older than you in this life, but he believes he's War. You still want to be Layala Lightbringer."

He was right. She wanted to only be in love with Thane, only to be High Queen of Palenor, not goddess of night, not Queen of Villhara, or previously married to Hel. Even if she knew it to be true now, she didn't want it to be. That meant she shared a bed with this ass before.

"What did you do with your crown I gave back to you in the tower?"

"It's hidden away where no one will find it."

"Maybe instead of hiding it you should put it on."

No, she wanted Palenor to be her home. "What do you want from me?" she asked. "What from my memory is so important?"

"I want you to look at me and see me."

Layala tilted her head slightly. She knew that wasn't the truth, at least not the whole truth. "I do."

"See *me*, Val. Not the Black Mage, not a stranger. I want you to remember the last time we danced together, and you wore that dress. I want you to know why when I look at you, I die a little inside, and..."

"...And?" Layala sounded breathless.

"And why sometimes I wish the council would have had a weapon to kill me for good and put me out of my fucking misery."

Layala squeezed his hand gently. "Don't say that." Everything inside her was screaming at the thought of him dying even though she would have done it herself not long ago.

That vulnerability she witnessed for the briefest moments faded and the smug mask returned. "I'm much too bitter and vindictive to die now, love."

"Help me remember. Tell me something—anything. Make it feel real."

"Anything?" he asked with a mischievous quirk of his scarred brow. Being this close she realized the thin white line reached from the top of his brow to his temple. She dreaded what might come out of his mouth next, and he started laughing. "That frown is going to give you wrinkles. I'll tell you one thing; you kissed me first."

Layala scrunched her face. "That doesn't sound right." She wasn't one to make the first move. Unless she'd been different before. But wasn't her soul, her personality the same?

"You practically begged me, and when I wouldn't, you shoved me up against a wall, and planted the hottest kiss I'd ever experienced in my five hundred years right on my mouth. You got handsy too, copped a feel of the goods. You even told me I was a big boy."

Layala smiled and shook her head. "You're lying. I know you are."

"How do you know?"

"Because I wouldn't do that or say that."

"Are you sure?"

"Yes."

"Then, what happened?"

"We..." was it dark? A garden of jasmine and tall bamboo, the sky was filled with strange colorful lights. No, a dark castle... Layala slammed her eyes closed trying to find that time, but it wouldn't come forth. "I don't know. But not that. There were no walls to shove you against."

His eyes glittered with delight. "So where was it?"

"Was it a garden like the one you put in my dreams, where you *tormented* me? Chasing me like some wild beast." A good reminder of who she danced with.

"I didn't put you there. You put *us* there. We certainly kissed in that garden and a lot more, but not for the first time. And I don't remember any chasing."

"Well, you did."

"*Well*, why did you run?"

"You scared me."

He paused only for a moment. "Anyway, what happened when you kissed me first and said I had a big dick? I want details," Hel said, changing his steps to match the new song. Layala only noticed the switch in music because his movements slowed. This song was gentle, more romantic.

"I didn't say that!" Layala whisper-shouted and glanced around at the other guests. No one seemed to pay particular attention to them.

He smiled ever bigger, bringing out his dimple. "What did you say then?"

"I don't know."

"Yes, you do."

"No, I don't, Hel."

"I like it when you say my name. Say it again."

Layala scoffed. "Don't make me regret dancing with you."

"I don't recall asking." He adjusted his hand on her back, only moving his fingers but the touch sent goosebumps rising on her flesh. "But you haven't left yet. Why is that?"

She finally looked from his eyes, pinning her gaze into the

rune peeking out from the collar of his high-necked top. "What is that rune?"

He lowered his chin to find the one she stared at. "It's a shielding rune so I can't be tracked by anything or anyone."

"And that?" She lifted her hand off his shoulder and ran her finger over the small one just behind and below his left ear. Goosebumps rose under her fingers, and he missed a step for the first time but recovered quickly and cleared his throat. "It allows me to walk through solid objects."

"Like walls and doors?"

"And people or their weapons."

"So, if someone strikes you with a sword—"

"If I see it coming, I could change, and it would go straight through me. I got the idea from you actually, when I saw you turn completely into a shadowy mist. That time in the tower a few months back wasn't your first attempt to kill me, you know."

That's how we found out we were mates, wasn't it? She thought.

He smirked. *Yes. But neither of us knew it at the time.*

She hadn't meant to let him hear that. A flush worked its way up her neck, spilling into her cheeks. Luckily her mask covered half her face, and the low light wouldn't make it so noticeable. She thought about her dream and the words she read: The perfect match created by the All Mother.

His soft voice entered her mind, *Ah there's that lovely blush again. It makes me notice things I shouldn't, like the curve of your collarbone, and what the low neckline of that gown would do to me if I was still in love with you.*

Layala cleared her throat. "Back to your magic, couldn't you make yourself impenetrable to weapons?"

"My, aren't you full of questions. I could and I did. But

magic like that I must consciously think about or activate, so I pick and choose based on the situation."

"Interesting. Who was more powerful, you or Valeen?"

He tilted his head slightly. "You mean, me or you? And that's a tough one. I don't know."

"How did you find out you needed runes in the first place? Did you simply draw a symbol one day and found it magical?"

"No. As a child my magic was untamed. Random things happened often, like me suddenly turning invisible and unsure how to turn back or setting fire to the dining room tablecloth. Once, when War and I were sparring with no weapons, we must have only been thirteen, I thought about how it would be nice to have a sword and as I swung a fist at him, my arm turned into a sword. He dodged at the last moment, and I drove it straight into a wall and got stuck. My Uncle Synick back-handed me so hard for losing control of my powers that I flew at least twenty feet and hit the other wall and cracked it. Back then our bodies were nearly impenetrable, but it still hurt. After that my grandmother, the goddess of wisdom, found a way for me to harness my magic in runes on my body. A way to trap them so they didn't come out unbidden."

"Your grandmother is the goddess in the stone?"

"Yes."

She didn't see that one coming. That meant she was Thane's grandmother as well. "I'm a little confused how that all works. The primordials were created but not born."

"Yes, and they are the strongest of us all. Most of them had children with each other, and the Maker and All Mother also created a second generation of gods to procreate and soon there were thousands."

"I don't," she stammered, "I mean, we don't have any..."

"Children? No."

Layala sighed in relief. "When did you discover you could grant magic to others with them?"

"It wasn't too long after I started using runes. I tested it on War of course. He wanted wings like the dragons but it's different with others. It comes with a cost if I'm to give to them. For me, it's only my own energy, strength."

"He doesn't have wings now."

"No, the magic I gave him didn't transfer over with this life."

"What was the cost?"

"It was an experiment. I couldn't figure out why when I put the symbol on him nothing happened. So, I wrote down what I wanted to happen and offered a life, a rabbit. It wasn't enough. So, I got two, and wrote the symbol in their blood and set it aflame. It burned the symbol into his skin and worked." He suddenly smiled, slyly. "I think someone is getting jealous."

Layala found Thane watching them intently from near the drink table. How long had she been dancing with Hel? The worried expression on Thane's face made her stomach turn. Then Varlett leaned close to him and said something, and he turned with a glare. They started quietly arguing.

"We're done." Layala pulled her hand from his and stepped back. "Was this all just to piss him off? Like the dress and bringing *her* here?"

He frowned but didn't say anything. Layala shook her head and stepped around the dancing couples, murmuring apologies for getting in their way. Once she broke free of the crowd, Hel caught up to her side.

"Certainly, it was to make him jealous, but I also wanted to talk to you. I like talking with you."

"Stay away from me. I can find my memories on my own." His hand brushed hers and she jerked away. "I'm going to

Thane because I love *him*. I've *always* loved him. And I will always choose him."

Hel grabbed a passing maiden and snapped her neck so fast Layala barely heard the pop before he shoved her limp body into Layala's arms.

Layala gasped and gripped her under her arms and around the middle like they were hugging. "What is wrong with you?"

"Better get the body out of here before someone thinks *you* killed her. Right now, she simply looks a little drunk. The *Palenor Scroll* would love that story," he said and stuffed his hands into his pockets then left her standing there with a dead girl in her arms.

CHAPTER 24

LAYALA

Layala didn't even have to move before Thane was at her side, taking the dead girl out of her grasp. "It's alright. I have her."

Tears burned her eyes and she backed away. He killed an innocent girl because of what she said, because she pissed him off. "I need some air."

"Go. I've got this," Thane reassured her. Fennan, Piper, and Leif rushed over, surrounding him while she hurried out of the ballroom. She dashed through the torchlit corridors and made a turn out a side door into the fresh night air. Crickets chirped and torches lit the path ahead to a small white gazebo surrounded by red and white roses. It sat empty, thank the Maker. A quiet refuge for her at this moment.

The benches inside were comfortable and made of cherry-colored softwood. She leaned back and observed the little fairy lights twinkling in the rafters of the gazebo. A warm breeze wisped her hair around her face, and she closed her eyes.

"It's intriguing to find you alone out here. Almost as if it was supposed to happen."

Layala's skin prickled as Hel's voice trickled down her spine. She gritted her teeth and shot to her feet, ready to give him a piece of her mind, but as she turned left and right, he was nowhere to be found.

"Over here," he said from behind.

She twirled on her heel and his shadowy hooded figure waited near the tall bushes about ten yards out. Out of reach of the torchlight. The hair on her neck and arms lifted. Why would he hide? "Hel, what are you doing?"

"Come have a walk with me."

Something wasn't right. She scanned the area, looking for guards or party guests and found them utterly alone. "Why don't we go back inside?" One foot moved back, then the other. She didn't want to run but staying felt foolish.

"Come, sweet Layala." He didn't move from the shadows.

Alarm bells went off in her head. Hel would never call her sweet Layala. This was a ruse of some kind. The council's assassins... she turned lifting her dress and dashed out of the gazebo, running down the pathway. Until someone grabbed a fistful of her hair and jerked her to a halt. She plucked a throwing star from the folds of her dress, whirled around, and nearly fumbled it in shock. The creature holding her must be over eight feet tall with huge horns curling out of long white hair, blue-gray skin covered lean muscle, creepy bright red eyes, different from Hel's, there was no white at all.

For one moment, recognition flashed across her mind, she'd seen this beast before.

"Hello, goddess." His voice was gravelly and had a deep bass. "Remember me?"

Layala tried to jerk out of his hold, but he gripped her

throat with his other hand and lifted her off the ground. She wanted to scream for help but couldn't get air. She kicked wildly, and jammed her throwing star into his arm but he didn't flinch.

"And they said it would be difficult to get you alone and kill you." He let out a rough cackle and squeezed harder.

Hel, I need you! He's choking me!

Magic rushed to the surface of her skin and vines ripped out of the ground, coiling around the monster's legs and up his body. Another shot up from the grass jamming straight through his arm like a spear. With a roar, he dropped her. She hit the ground and gasped for air but coughed from the brutality of his hold. She struggled to her feet in the gown, and it ripped under her foot, but she managed to move forward to the castle.

A sharp blade embedded in the back of her calf, and she went down with a scream.

She rolled onto her side, jerked the blade free and jammed it into the thigh of the beast already hovering over her.

"You're not invincible anymore," he said with a raucous laugh. "Just a sad, pathetic, mortal ripe for the slaughtering."

Layala scrambled back as he moved forward like the dagger sticking out of his thigh didn't bother him. More vines shot out of the ground, and they slammed into him but couldn't penetrate, so she twisted them around his legs to at least hold him back long enough to let her get to her feet and run.

Get to the door, get to the door. The injury to her leg caused her to limp but didn't slow her down much. She slammed into the castle's side door, stumbled through, and crashed into Hel's chest. "Hel," she breathed. "You came."

He caught her around the waist and steadied her. The flare

in his eyes was pure panic. "Who was choking you? Who hurt you?"

Layala stared at him for a moment, then turned back to point but there was no one there. "He was... there, right there." The mess of her broken vines was scattered all along the path, but the creature wasn't trapped in them. There was no sign of him at all.

He gripped her chin, forcing her to look at him. "Who was it?"

"I don't know." She could barely catch her breath. "He was huge, massive horns, red eyes. His skin was a strange bluish-gray."

"Fuck." Hel slammed the door shut without ever touching it and led her over to a stone bench in a nearby alcove. "Where are you hurt?"

After sitting, she lifted her dress to show him her bloody calf. With a frown, he crouched and lifted her leg to get a better look at the wound. With his palm hovered over it, a warm glow and heat brushed her skin. By the time he moved his hand the wound was healed. He reached up and touched her neck, sending a chill through her. She couldn't see it, but it was bound to be bright red and maybe already bruising. "Who was he?"

"Who I feared would come. The demon prince from the underrealm."

If he was immortal as Thane said, how could they ever beat him? And if Hel feared him... Layala gripped his wrist as a warmth emanated from his hand over her throat. "We can't kill him?"

"You don't need to worry about that right now."

With a shuddering breath, Layala leaned back against the wall. Even though she was healed, and nothing hurt, the buzz of the fight still coursed through her veins, her hands trembled from it. "He sounded like you." She gulped. "He imitated your voice somehow."

The fury rolling off him was palpable. "And you went to him?"

"No. I was about to tell you what a complete asshole you are, but who I thought was you, wouldn't come out of the shadows."

He rose out of his crouch and sat beside her on the bench. "Fuck," he murmured. "When I heard the terror in your voice... Gods, I haven't been that scared in a long time. I forgot what fear felt like."

The pessimist in her wanted to say it was because she was his life source, but it was more than that. Even she couldn't deny it. "How did you know where I was? At that moment I forgot to say."

"I didn't. I just followed my... instincts."

They sat quietly for a long time. Neither of them felt the need to speak or fill the silence. All that was needed was the comfort of two souls who felt like they didn't belong, and the soft music from the ballroom drifting from several hallways over.

"Thank you for coming," she whispered.

He nodded as he stood then held out his hand. "Let's get you to your room, love."

LAYALA'S BATH smelled of lemon and thyme. Wisps of steam rose around her, curling the hair around her face. All she wanted was to relax tonight. After the disaster at the masked ball, and five nights of mage training with Vesstan, and only him, nothing could be better than this. *No thinking of male elves who insist on torturing me in one way or another*—that thought only brought to mind how Thaneless her bed had been and how much she wanted his lips all over her at this very moment.

She couldn't believe the fortitude he had to stay abstinent this long when all it would take was opening the door to her room and there she was, waiting, and willing.

Layala lifted the box of cards Hel left and popped it open. If she had patience, she'd look at each one, but she shuffled through until she found Valeen. The tickle in her stomach was either nerves or excitement but she didn't know which. Much like the statue she'd seen, the image painted on one side was of her sitting on a throne, legs crossed. What she'd mistaken for snakes were black vines wrapped around her arms with blooms at her shoulders, the night crown adorned atop her flowing black hair. The card, like the others, was outlined in a decorative golden border and at the top it read: *Valeen* and the bottom: *Goddess of Night*.

Tif's hands then face popped up over the lip of the tub by Layala's shoulder. "Oooo, pretty... That's you."

"I believe it is," Layala murmured. She reached over to the small, rolling table beside her and plucked a glass of blush wine off it and brought it to her lips.

"Can I have some? Just a teeny-weeny thimble?"

"Sure. Why not?"

Tif pulled a thimble out from behind her as if she'd been waiting to ask all night. "It will be a girls' night tonight! We should have invited Piper and Aunt Evalyn."

"It's a girls' night every night for us, Tif," Layala complained and took a long gulp of wine. "Next time I'm going out for girls' night. I'll even take you with me."

Layala tipped her glass and filled Tif's thimble. The little gnome grinned deviously. Layala picked her up by the back of her dress and placed her on the side table so she could sit rather than stand on whatever thing she'd dragged in there to reach the top of the tub.

"We go out and I'll yodel!" With her legs spread and both hands wrapped around the silver thimble she tipped it back for a drink. "We could do a duet! I bet you can sing. You just look like one of those elves who has a lovely voice."

Layala chuckled. "I can carry a tune, but I don't know if it's lovely," and took another sip of wine. She turned the card over; her brows rose. A description was written on the back.

The goddess of night is said to be created from a fallen star and an ancient flower that blooms only at night, not born of another or formed in the womb, making her one of the seven primordials. She is night personified, riding a white chariot pulled by two onyx, winged horses.

Powers: Her powers are of the strongest among the gods. She can manipulate darkness and shadow as well as turn into a shadow form herself to slip through the attacks of others. Levitation in this form is possible as well but she does not fly over long distances. She can form light, illuminating the dark like the stars and moons and even conjure the moons' power to produce a shield or attack. Serpent-like deadly vines with poisonous blooms to impale or trap her enemies. As with all the gods, enhanced speed, strength, and persuasion over lesser beings.

Layala blinked and reread the section. This was certainly more power than she expected. She'd produced a shield and of course her vines but turning entirely to shadow, and levitating were difficult to fathom. Also persuading people with words like Hel and Mathekis?

She read on: *History: Valeen is one of the Drivaar, who worship the All Mother. She ruled the solitary night territory also known as*

House of Night alone until she met her mate Zaurahel or Hel, a Primevar, the group believes in the superiority of the Maker, he is the god of magic and mischief. When they combined their territories, it became known as Villhara, where she became queen and he king over both.

No known children. It is said she left her own night territory and her mate for his cousin, the god of war, to rule over Ryvengaard with him, causing the great war amongst the realms. Later she was punished by the Runevale council, and her immortality bound, to die and be reborn again and again.

With a groan, Layala tossed the card and downed the rest of her wine. She pressed the cool empty glass to her forehead and shut her eyes. *Did I leave Hel because I loved War more? Was it because Hel was a complete bastard, dick, ass, prick...* she ran out of names to call him. She couldn't accept that she simply cheated on Hel with his best friend, his cousin behind his back. It wasn't like her or Thane. Something else must have happened.

"Look at these," Tif said, holding up the card for Hel and War. "It says, the extent of Hel's powers are unknown, making him ranked in the top three amongst the Runevale gods despite not being a primordial... What's a primordial?"

"It's the original gods not born from anyone but created by the Maker and All Mother." Layala rested her arms on the edge of the tub. "And War?"

"It says, War is known for his brilliant mind and prowess in battle. He is not a primordial either but born of two gods, Balneir and Rivenna. Second generation gods." Tif chewed on her lower lip, "War is said to be the only god Hel trusted or cared for until Hel met his wife, Valeen."

"Oooff." Layala cringed at the betrayal.

"Don't be sad," Tif said, setting the cards down. "Will you sing a song for me?"

The wine made her feel up to it. "Something fun? Or romantic or—"

"You pick."

"Alright." She started humming first, swishing her toes along the surface of the water. Steam curled around her face, and she inhaled the wonderful, scented soaps from the tub. A tune began to form. Words drew from her lips; she didn't know from where, but the song was sad, melancholy, and in a language she couldn't understand, but somehow she got the feeling of broken hearts and goodbyes. She might not consciously know the language but some part of her did. Her voice lilted off the bathroom walls, the perfect atmosphere for singing that made her voice sound clear, lovelier, and tears sprang to her eyes. *Why am I crying?*

Tif pressed her hands flat over her heart and closed her eyes. The final word fell from Layala's lips, and she blew out a breath and plunged under the water where the silence became peaceful. She popped back up, and Tif was wiping tears off her cheeks.

"I knew you had a good voice. Although we could work on your higher register." She put her hand over her stomach. "You gotta really breathe deep and sing from down here."

Layala swiped water off her cheeks and giggled. "Singing hasn't been a priority of mine. But I liked to sing as a young girl. Aunt Evalyn was always humming or singing something."

After her fingers and toes were pruned, she finally rose up. Rivers of water rolled down her body splashing into the tub as she wrung out her hair. She reached for a towel on the nearby shelf, but it was empty. "Where are the towels?"

"Umm, well I spilled something earlier and had to use

them. But I promise I'll bring them back, freshly washed, and dried."

"I need a towel now, Tif, not later. Am I supposed to stand here and drip dry?" She sighed, remembering she left one hanging on the back of the chair next to her vanity and she stepped out of the tub getting water all over the floor. A chill ran across her body from the cool air on wet skin. She hurried into her main room, turned her head, and screamed. Layala slapped her arm across her breasts and a hand over her groin, then turned away.

"Get out!" Layala hollered.

Hel laid sprawled across her bed, a civar between his lips, ankles crossed as if this were his room and his bed. With the flick of his wrist the towel on the back of the chair appeared around her shoulders.

"I didn't look," he said as if he were about to laugh. "I know if I did you'd gouge my eyes out. Probably with your nails."

How did he know she was thinking exactly that?

"I saw you do it once to a peeping tom. Not pretty."

Layala snatched the edges of the towel and wrapped it around her body, then she whirled around, wet hair flying out and slapping against her skin. "You can't come in here whenever you feel like it!"

He didn't move, didn't so much as tilt his chin down to see her standing wrapped in a towel. "When you didn't answer the door, I got worried. Would you have preferred I entered your bath chambers or waited here?"

"When someone doesn't answer the door, it means they don't want to be bothered, not to come in. I locked the door for a reason."

"I can walk through walls, remember? Locked doors are worthless."

He snapped his fingers and in an instant with a quick puff of air she was fully clothed, and dry, even her hair. In astonishment, she touched the clothes; her usual style of black pants, boots, a long, belle-sleeved top, this time in a royal blue and a black vest, weapons belt on and all. He'd done it before, but she was still shocked by it.

He sat up and blew out a stream of smoke, staring into her face and—seeing too much. "A lament for my broken soul," he said.

"What?"

"It is," he cleared his throat, "an age-old song you were just singing." He lifted the *Palenor Scroll* from the bed beside him. "How have you been the last few days?" he asked conversationally. "I apologize for missing training, but we'll get back to it, I promise." She hadn't seen him since he escorted her to her bedroom door after the attack. Layala eyed the *Palenor Scroll* in his hand. She'd avoided it as much as possible; it only upset her.

"Where have you been?" she didn't want to say she was worried but a small part of her was. Maker above, how could that be possible?

"Miss me?"

"You know what, never mind. Leave, Hel. I don't want to deal with you tonight. I want to relax."

"Notice how there hasn't been any pale one attacks lately? Perhaps I do have a heart after all."

She narrowed her eyes at him but wanted to smile. He'd actually called them off.

He set his feet on the floor and started reading from the paper in a voice that sounded mocking, "*Layala Lightbringer: The Bell of the Ball. Many of us watched the High King and his betrothed kiss and dance on the dais, the dream of many maidens in*

Palenor. To win the heart of our warrior king, who pledged himself to the Lady Lightbringer as a child, our strong, noble leader who —blah blah." He held up his fingers with the smoking civar. "*He whispered in her ear, held her close and if they missed a step, no one saw it. But that isn't the true story of the night, is it?*"

Layala took in a deep breathing waiting for the bad news.

"*Who was the mysterious masked elf she danced with for two songs in a row among the many coupled dancers?*" He mockingly gasped and smiled. "*We don't dare presume it could be the Black Mage inside our own Castle Dredwhich but who could it be?*" He chuckled and looked up from the paper. "Two songs in a row, what a scandal." He took a pull from his civar. "The obsession these people have with you is fascinating. They proclaim you are evil and wicked and to hate you but it's clear they love you."

"At least 'the dead elf maiden in Layala Lightbringer's arms' wasn't the headline," Layala said. "I can't believe you did that."

"I mean, is it really unbelievable?" he drawled.

With a glare she snapped, "No, actually. Not at all."

"Anyway, she wasn't an elf," Hel said and set the *Palenor Scroll* aside. He stood and flicked his civar into the air where it disappeared. "You didn't see her rounded ears? Or notice the tattoo on her wrist? She was an outsider."

Layala thought back to holding her but hadn't noticed any of her features at all. "Was she human?"

"I didn't look that long."

"So, she could have just been an innocent human."

"When do humans ever get invited to the High Elf King's parties?"

Unless they were servants, never. And the maiden's dress was much too fancy to be a servant, that much she remembered.

"The better question is why didn't *Thane* tell you she might have been an assassin? Oh, right because he's afraid you might grow a soft spot for me."

Layala rolled her eyes. "You don't know if she was or not. You snapped her neck and threw her at me because you were pissed off."

"Because you said you love Thane? I can see that you love him, and I know you have for a long time. It's not a surprise. But I watched that girl watch you for nearly an hour. It wasn't random."

"So now you're supposed to be my hero?"

"Hero?" His eyes darkened and he sauntered toward her, stopping inches away; the curl of his magic slid along her skin, catching her breath. It wasn't dark and frightening but sensual as if it wanted to wrap around her and know every part of her being. "No, love, I'm certainly the villain. I'm everything from your darkest nightmare. I will do things that will break your heart. I will kill whoever I need to fucking kill, and if it's a sweet innocent human by mistake, then it's collateral damage, and I won't give it a second thought." He leaned in closer, his breath brushed against her ear. "The truth is you need me. If I had a heart like you and War, we'd be doomed to repeat this all over again and again and again. The Council of Gods has no mercy, and neither will I."

He leaned in even closer and inhaled deeply, sliding his nose, lips along her neck. Her skin pebbled with the sensation of his light touch, and he slipped his arms around her waist. The most terrifying part of this scenario was she didn't pull away and didn't want to.

"There was another story. Did you see it?" His breath on her skin made her shudder.

"No," Layala whispered, afraid to hear it.

"Telvian Botsberry found half-dead, unable to speak because his tongue was cut out, unable to write because his hands were cut off. I suppose he shouldn't have been telling and writing lies about a certain someone. He won't anymore."

Her eyes widened. "You did that?"

"You're still my wife, and I won't allow it any longer."

Either it was the wine or something else, but her magic wanted to dance, desired to seek out Hel's power. It warmed her from the inside, tingled along her arms and felt too much like lust. Because it wasn't only her magic that liked his arms around her. Her body reacted to his touch, craved it even.

His chest rose and fell faster under her palms. His hands slid up her back, entangled in her long locks. "Your magic calls to me. I can feel it brushing against my skin like a lover's caress."

She swallowed hard. "Please let me go."

Ever so slowly, he uncoiled his arms from around her torso, then appeared by the door in an instant, breathing heavily like he'd ran for miles. He gave her one last long look and then he was gone.

CHAPTER 25

HEL

Hel took in a deep breath, closing the door behind him and rushed across the hallway to the room he'd taken up. Then hurried out onto the balcony and pulled out a civar. Fuck. His heart raced and his mind even faster. The more he wanted to hate her, the more she crept under his skin, like an infection that heated his entire being. What a cruel thing indeed.

While he was out searching for the demon prince for days, all he could think about was the first time Valeen invited him to her home. When he started to fall for her hard and fast, catching feelings he'd never allowed himself before. She was sinking into him all over again, and he didn't want her to. He wanted to hold onto his hatred for her betrayal, for leaving him more shattered than anyone ever could have. He wished he could forget it all like her, to not feel the warring pain inside of wanting her so much his body could catch fire and hating her with the same amount of passion.

If only he hadn't gone that day, if only he'd turned down her invitation, would things be different now? But he fell for her story...

The Past

The garden at Valeen's palace was warm despite the territory's rumored perpetual night. Did the sun ever shine here to grow the thick bunches of jasmine over trellis arches and or the full and blossoming purple wisteria? Everywhere Hel looked, green foliage, fruit, and wild blooms grew in lush abundance. This garden rivaled even the gods of flora and nature. Despite the stunning scenery there was only one thing of beauty he cared to look upon.

Valeen's black gown hugged her curves. The back was cut low in a V ending just above her divine rump. Her black hair was pulled up in a high bun on her head with curls left down to frame her face. He hadn't seen her since the time she tried to kill him for trespassing six months prior. She danced with his cousin and then instead of accepting his invitation for a dance, she asked him to go for a walk in her gardens.

Neither of them had spoken since they stepped out from the party of onlookers and now walked alone, side by side. She kept her hands tucked close to herself and made certain to put a decent amount of space between them.

Hel wasn't sure if she didn't know what to say or if she waited for him to speak. She was the one to invite him and War here in the first place and he had yet to learn why. Did it have to do with the mark on his chest and her arm? In her halter top dress that revealed her shoulders, and arms, it wasn't as if she tried to hide it.

"Do you know why I asked you to come here?" she finally said. She stopped under a jasmine trellis and faced him.

"I'd like to think it's because I made such an impression you can't stop thinking of me, but I doubt it."

Her serious expression cracked into a soft smile. "You certainly made an impression, but I wanted to explain myself. After you and War did not come back for battle as you said you may, especially after what I did, I thought perhaps I misjudged you both."

"You don't need to explain anything. Your business is your business," he said, although he was practically frothing at the mouth to know.

"I murdered a primordial and I would have murdered you to keep it secret. You still think it's only my business?"

"I deduced you had good reason. I never liked him much anyway. Synick was a prick."

"The council wouldn't see it that way."

He shook his head and put his hands in his pockets to stop his urge to touch her. "No, they would not. But I'm not on the council, am I?"

"You know the story of the gods, of the primordials." It wasn't a question.

"We learn it in our lessons as children, but I'd love the story from you." It was always fascinating to hear a primordial speak of the time before they kept time, before there were other gods. Each told of their creation a little differently.

"As I'm sure you know, I emerged from white ash—remnants of a fallen star. I took my first breath in the dark, and for a moment there was nothing but the sound of my own breathing and my heart pulsing.

"Then there was light. Beside me in a bed of clovers lay another, hair so blonde it was nearly white, skin golden and full of luster, eyes of lavender rimmed in gold. My sister. For she was the day, and I, the

night. Though none of us primordials were related by blood. We didn't keep time; we simply were.

"With us was Elora, the goddess of wisdom, and Atlanta, the god of waters, Creed, the god of nature, Synick the god of elements, and Era, the god of time. We shared our talents, and our gifts freely. Elora gave us language and the ability to write and read. With Creed animals and nature became our friends. My sister Katana and I set the days and nights.

"We didn't know war or hate. We had no need to use our powers for fighting or evil. We didn't understand the concept." She paused and plucked a white jasmine blossom from the vine and looked at it lovingly. "Katana's favorite flower was jasmine. She and I were inseparable despite being opposites. She was all smiles and laughter, bright and happy. She could talk to a wall for an hour, I swear. I was more reserved, and I liked being alone under the stars as much as I liked company. And for a time, it was only us primordials.

"Until Elora opened a portal and we saw into other worlds. We didn't know what she'd done then but through a swirling pool we witnessed others like us, millions of others, people with wings who turned into giant beasts, fair folk with pointed ears who sang so lovely we were drawn to them, and many others different in some ways but we wanted to know them.

"The All Mother and our Maker came. They said if we joined with the other races we would learn pain, and sorrow but also joy and true love. That our powers were gifts others did not have and we should remain fair and just. They created us to be guardians and watchers over the realms.

"In time, other gods were created to join us. Like the goddesses of love, and fertility, and the gods of serenity, and truth, and many more. Not as powerful as the original seven but strong and gifted. My sister Katana and Atlanta fell in love and had many children. Creed, Era and Synick mated with several of the lesser gods, even

with the elves, fae, and dragons. And that's when the prejudices began." She frowned. "As you well know, Elora mated with Creed only to have a pair of twins and no others."

Hel nodded. "Elora was said to be jealous of his many other lovers. So, she only had my mother, and War's father."

"Yes, Elora the goddess of wisdom is too intelligent to be played for a fool, but she got what she wanted out of the relationship." Valeen pressed her lips together and looked at him but for only a moment. "I remained chaste. I didn't want children to bring into the power struggles. It became a competition to see who could create the most gifted and strongest, all to help the realms, they claimed, but I saw it as greed, and what this power did to the others. We were supposed to be the peacekeepers among the realms, and many of the others used the realms as their playgrounds."

"I always heard you remained chaste but," he cleared his suddenly tight throat and tugged at the collar that felt too snug around his neck. "Don't try to murder me again for asking but are you still? It's difficult to imagine—it's been thousands of years."

She arched her brow. "May I finish the story?"

"Please do," he said, tucking his hands back in his pockets to resist the urge to touch her. He didn't know why but he wanted to hold her hand or brush her beautiful golden skin.

"Your Uncle Synick had long desired me. He said we'd have the most powerful children, stronger than anyone. When I refused him, he grew angry. Somehow he got ahold of the Sword of Truth, the only weapon at the time that could kill one of us immortals. Instead of using it on me, he put it where it would hurt me most, the one I loved more than anything, my sister Katana."

Hel swallowed hard. Now that was one part of the tale he'd never heard before. There were stories of Katana's murder, but it was said no one knew the perpetrator.

"After I lost her, I shut myself inside my territory, cut off from the *other gods. I built my fortress, wards, and walls no one could cross. I hid away from the fighting, the bickering, the mating, and the scheming, and let my people, who I'd brought from other realms, prosper in peace and harmony.*

"*And for an age I made myself into a weapon. I learned cunning and guile, combat, and war. I studied the realms, the other gods— lesser and full-blooded alike, until I knew everything about them. I didn't need children to be the most powerful. I would forge myself into the greatest weapon and bide my time.*"

"*I am—*" somehow "*sorry for your loss*" wasn't fitting or nearly enough. He believed every word she said, felt it all to be true. This was why she hid away for so long, why she killed Synick—it wasn't murder, this was vengeance. "*Why doesn't anyone else know Synick killed Katana? We need to make this known so you can be absolved if anyone ever finds out.*"

"*They won't believe it. I tried to convince Atlanta and he didn't accept it. He said one of the primordials wouldn't do it—we were all too close, too connected. And that may have been true at one time but then, we'd grown apart. Atlanta believed it to be a jealous god, who would stand to gain from her death. When a primordial dies, their powers are transferred to others in their line.*"

"*He thought it was one of their own children? They couldn't have known that. No primordial had ever died before.*"

She lifted a shoulder.

"*But how did you know for certain it was Synick?*"

Valeen looked him straight in the eyes. "*Because he told me. He wanted me to know. He took pleasure in seeing me break. He said it would only be his word against mine and it's not as if the council would exile him—he was the head of the council. If I'd had a weapon to kill him, I'd have tried right then. It wasn't long after that Soulender was found by Elora, and Katana's death sparked the wars between the Drivaar and the*

Primevar. People started placing blame on our creators for giving us weapons that could kill immortals, and we chose sides."

"But you didn't fight in the battles."

"No but I do praise the All Mother and I believe she gave Soulender to us because Synick was given the Sword of Truth by the Maker."

"That is the story, but I never understood why he would do that. As if he wanted to spark a war?"

"No one knows. The Maker isn't evil. Sometimes I wonder if Synick got the weapon some other way. He claimed to have found it. But the Maker and All Mother haven't shown themselves since... I don't even remember how long it's been. I can't even recall their faces anymore." Her chest rose as she took in a deep breath. *"But they said we'd know pain and certainly, we do."*

"But you also know joy, happiness, and love, don't you? The bad times make you appreciate the good more and all that... or so they say."

She lifted a shoulder. *"I am not unhappy, but I don't remember the last time I truly felt something other than when I drove Soulender through Synick's heart, and that was glorious."*

Hel flicked his fingers and a civar appeared between them. *"These help a little with that."* Had she truly smiled or laughed or allowed anyone to love her? *"Want to try it?"* He brought it to his lips and breathed in.

"I gave up trying to feel better with substances a long time ago. It's fleeting, not real."

"You're better than I then." He blew out a cloud. *"Who was that blond male with you at the party?"*

"Presco, my dragon scholar." The corners of her mouth curved ever so slightly. *"Why do you ask?"*

His eyebrows raised and he shrugged. "Curiosity." It was much *too soon to admit he was jealous of the male who got to hang on her arm. "Did you explain your story to War?"*

"No, I'll leave that up to you." She let out a quick breath. "I also wanted to apologize for my reaction to you and for stabbing you with Soulender. I was the one who let you inside. I should have behaved differently. Since you were Primevar and so close to Synick—I prejudged you. I hope I am not wrong by trusting you enough to bring you here."

"I am nothing like him and I wouldn't say we were close." He took another pull on his civar. "And no harm, no foul. I apologize for making threats as I was the trespasser. You didn't do anything I wouldn't have." His gaze dropped to the lily mark on her arm, and he ran his fingertips over it. She jerked back in surprise, as if he'd shocked her. "You don't like being touched, do you?"

"It just surprised me. It's not customary to touch so casually in my territory."

"My apologies. But I suppose we should talk about the mark." Sweat dampened his lower back. "Do you know what it means?"

She shook her head. "You?"

"I've looked at many libraries, but I haven't found anything definitive. And I don't trust anyone enough to ask. Not even my grandmother Elora. She'd wonder why I was inquiring."

"Theories?" her eyes seemed to sparkle, and he had an inkling she was hiding something.

He smiled. "I have many."

The blond dragon scholar appeared from around the bend in the path and bowed to Valeen. He narrowed his eyes at Hel before facing her. "Goddess, I hate to pull you away, but guests have been asking about you, and War is, I wouldn't say under threat, but everyone is wondering why there is an outsider here."

"I'll be right in."

He bowed again and Hel watched him disappear. The dragon

certainly had feelings for Valeen. What he couldn't discern was if she shared them. Was this the male who broke down the chaste goddess's walls?

"Poor War left alone to defend himself." Hel chuckled. "But he loves attention. I'm sure he's enjoying himself."

They started back. "You and War are close friends?"

"The best. He's my brother. Well, cousin but you understand."

"I understand completely. Katana wasn't my blood sister, but she was still my sister."

Once they reached the double doors, Hel grabbed the handle to pull it open then stopped and turned to face her. He found his breath unsteady, even his hands trembled. As if her very presence ignited him with energy and made him want to shy away at once. No one had ever had this effect on him before. "Will I ever see you again?" He swallowed hard. "I would very much like to see you again."

He heard her heart beat faster, the only betrayal of any emotion. "Meet me at the cliffs of Amonlee on Luna's next full moon."

CHAPTER 26

LAYALA

Layala and Piper stood out in the training yard. The grass was damp from the rain the night before, which made it soggy under Layala's boots. Handfuls of other soldiers sparred in the area around them, their swords rang with metal on metal. Some laughed as they watched a pair of their buddies grunt and beat on each other in a wrestling match. A trio of soldiers shot arrows at bales of hay painted with red targets at the center.

Layala toyed with the throwing star in her hand and stared at the fake wooden soldier who was about to get a weapon embedded in its head. The breeze picked up pieces of her hair and brought the smell of the nearby waterfall.

Piper pulled back on her bow. "So, what's on your mind today? You haven't asked me to train with you in a while." The bowstring twanged and the arrow whistled, hitting the stuffed soldier in the chest.

"Well, you've been busy training others. It's not that I didn't want to."

"True but there's still a reason we're out here?"

Layala readied her feet and threw the star. It cut through the air and embedded in the stuffed soldier's chest. "I just needed to get my mind off things. Now there's a demon prince doing the bidding of the council because he wants me dead for stealing his ring. Something I don't even remember doing."

"And? I heard all about the demon from Thane and Fennan already, so I know there's more."

Layala laughed. "Fine. I hate Varlett. I hate her. I saw her in the hallway today and I want her gone. She almost killed Thane and stole my aunt which then made me almost kill Talon, just to name a few offenses, and I don't know what to do about her. And the way she and Hel touch each other, it's disgusting. I want to gouge my own eyes out thinking of them..."

Piper frowned and then quickly turned it into a smile. "We'll figure it out. We always do."

"What was the frown for?" Layala tossed another star and it hit with a thud.

"Um." Piper pulled back the arrow and released it. She faced Layala and let her bow fall to her side. "Why does it bother you that Hel and Varlett are together?"

"It doesn't."

Piper dragged her fingers through her loose hair. "You said you wanted to gouge your eyes out thinking of them together. I'm worried that this bond between you will cause problems. Have you been feeling drawn to him, or do you have any sense of loyalty to him?"

"Of course not," Layala said.

"I don't know much about mate bonds, but I know what it was like watching you and Thane together. He felt he loved you before he even met you. They're strong, powerful, and I'm sure hard to resist."

"Well, I love Thane. There's nothing to worry about."

"Have you two been heating up in the bedroom again? Perhaps sneaking off?" Piper grew a mischievous smile. "That kiss at the ball was pretty scandalous if I'm being honest."

Layala tossed another throwing star. "The kiss was all there was."

"And here I thought the *Palenor Scroll* was simply gossip. Seems there truly is trouble in paradise."

Both Layala and Piper whirled around to find Hel with a smug, arrogant smirk. He snapped his fingers and the throwing star from her belt appeared in his fingers. "You're good with these. But you need to practice magic. We've missed a few lessons recently."

"As you can see, I'm busy."

"Not anymore."

"Fine. Not here." The last thing she wanted was to be embarrassed in front of the soldiers when Hel made her look like an amateur.

"No, I thought we could try something different today." He grabbed her arm and suddenly everything was dark; she lifted off the ground and immense pressure crushed into every fiber of her being. She couldn't draw breath and just when she thought she was going to pass out, her feet hit solid ground and she greedily sucked in air.

"You could have warned me!"

The waterfall roared, cascading over the edge of the rocky gray cliffs below her feet. She was at its edge and the height, staring down at the seventy-foot drop, made her woozy. They stood on a wide patch of craggy ground. One side was a steep cliff and the other the river raged.

"What are we doing up here?"

"Training."

She turned and glared. "And that needs to be up here?"

He stepped closer to her, and she moved back, the rocks shifting under her feet. This was much much too close to the edge, and it brought flashbacks of falling off the cliff inside the prison cart. "That demon prince will rip off your head for stealing his ring and the gods only know what else he brought with him. You must become Valeen again."

"I can't."

"I'm going to push you off unless you tell me about the cliffs of Amonlee, in five."

"Are you insane?"

"Four."

"Don't you dare!"

"Three."

"Stop it! Stop counting." She held up her hands with magic flaring, and stepped hard to the right toward the river. She could get across the water with her vines.

"Two."

Vines appeared over the water like a bridge and as she made a run for it, he grabbed her upper arm and swung her back around, and she suddenly couldn't move. His magic snaked its way through her body and held her to his will.

"One."

"Hel!" she squealed.

He backed her to the cliff's edge and shoved her. A scream caught in her throat until his hands closed around her wrists, dangling her upper body over certain death. The wind whipped up around them, blowing her hair wildly. Sprays of mist wafted all around. Her heart crashed in her ears. His hold on her was the only thing keeping her from falling.

"The cliffs of Amonlee, Val."

"It's where we met up alone for the first time!" she shouted over the cascading water and wind.

He smiled. Maker above, she was on the verge of falling to her death and he smiled like that?

"And what else?"

"Let me up and I'll tell you."

"Ah, ah, ah, that's not how this works, love."

She wracked her mind for the memory. *Amonlee, Amonlee,* she chanted. *What the hell happened in Amonlee?* She closed her eyes and felt the sun on her skin, the smell of salt air and florals. Eyes flashing open she blurted out. "You brought me flowers and we swam in the sea."

"Our first date." He jerked her up into his chest and wrapped his arms around her completely. Together they backed to the center of the small rocky platform they stood on. "You know I wouldn't have let you fall."

She shoved him hard in the chest to get him to let go but he didn't move. "No, I don't know that."

"Val, come on. I saved your ass against the demon. I came *running* when you called."

"It's Layala."

"See, this is why you can't remember and it's going to get you killed."

"Just because you won't kill me, doesn't mean you won't push me off a cliff and save me after just to scare me."

He laughed. "You're impossible sometimes." A mischievous smile spread across his face revealing his dimple and pretty teeth, then he moved her back one step, two.

"What are you doing?"

"Well, you said it. I'll push you off and if you can't save yourself, then Hel will swoop in to save the day."

"Hel, I can't fly. And I haven't been able to change entirely into shadow, just remnants." A gust of wind rushed around them and Layala gulped. But that sparked a memory. "Wait, take off your shirt."

He stopped and tilted his head to the side, peering down at her. "That's a bit forward, love."

She pulled out of his grasp and pressed a palm against his chest to put him at arm's length. "As if you wouldn't take the chance to get naked with me," she said and immediately regretted it.

"I wouldn't actually." He glanced down at his nails as if he were bored. "You don't do it for me anymore." He looked up with the barest hint of a smile. "But I will say the whole damsel in distress thing you have going on is more appealing than I thought it would be."

"Damsel in distress?" she scoffed.

"It's not as if I want to be your bodyguard and mentor so don't get any ideas about us being friends. This is only out of necessity. It should be War doing this but then it would be the blind leading the blind."

"We're certainly not friends. You don't need to worry about that." She rolled her eyes. "And just take off the shirt. I think I remembered something."

"I'm only doing this because I'm intrigued." With a snap of his fingers, his shirt vanished and he stood in only a pair of black trousers and boots. He stuffed his hands into his pockets but left his thumbs out.

Holy gods. His body was defined but not overly so, lean but full in the chest, shoulders and, arms—perfect. Rune marks and decorative tattoos covered a good amount of his skin but with plenty left exposed, raw. She regretted asking him to stand there half naked.

"It's rude to stare, you know."

Layala cleared her throat and stepped around him and found what she was after. Along his back on either side of his spine a pair of black feathered wings marked the length from his shoulders to the base of his hips. "Wings," she whispered and couldn't stop herself from running her fingertips over the marks. Goosebumps rose under her touch, and she smiled.

Then, she shoved him hard in the back and sent him stumbling off the cliff.

CHAPTER 27

LAYALA

What did I just do? Layala rushed to the edge. Hel fell, dropping like a stone, the wind doing nothing to slow him down. With his arms held wide and his legs straight out he looked almost like a five-pointed star. *He can fly. He can fly.* She reassured herself, heart crashing into her ribs. *But why isn't he stopping?*

"Hel!" Layala screamed. He couldn't die, right? Their mate bond kept them from being able to kill each other or was it only the first time? A way to tell them they were mated so not to harm the other.

He dipped below the ravine that split the castle grounds from the rest of the Valley and would hit the water in seconds and surely it wasn't deep enough. "Hel!" Layala concentrated and drew vines out of the side of the ravine to create a net to catch him below. It would hurt when he hit but at least he wouldn't be dead.

Massive white wings appeared out of his back and caught the air, lifting him up out of the shadows and into the open. Sunlight shimmered off the pearl feathers with an iridescent hue. Layala slapped her hand over her chest and finally caught her breath. He soared upward, beating his great wings every few moments but also gliding on the lifting air.

Looking at Hel, one would think he'd have chosen black wings or even a deep red, since he favored the colors but somehow, the white wings suited him, a contrast to his dark side. Watching him fly over the backdrop of the Valley, where the roofs of the houses sparkled in gold and the charm of Palenor from this view high on the cliffs, drew her deep into a memory...

The Past

The light blue waters of the Eversent Sea lapped gently into the high rocky cliffs of Amonlee, reddish-orange by nature. This cove made the waters gentle and perfect for swimming. Valeen sat with her legs dangling over the edge, a hundred feet or so from the rocks below, kicking her feet slowly. She used to do this with her sister Katana many years ago. It was still one of her favorite places in all of Runevale, in all the realms. The salt air smelled of driftwood and seaweed and brought back a nostalgia of giggling young ladies who dared each other to jump. Sunlight sparkled off the white-capped waves, calling for her to delight in the warm replenishing water.

"Hello, Hel." She turned her upper body to watch him approach. Rather than his usual black suit, he wore a loose white button-up top left open to reveal his sun-warmed chest and dark runes. A petal of the new mark created by her peeked out. His sleeves were rolled as well as his dark pants, revealing bare feet and ankles, and showed even more runes. A casual look she didn't expect of him, and it let her

see that perhaps there was more to him than shadows and mischief. She wanted to know what more there was to him.

"The sunlight suits you," he said with a charming smile. He looked around at the tropical palms and lush green grass that grew to the edge of the rocks. "I've never been here. Nice choice. I expected darkness, maybe even a cave with bats."

She laughed. "I may be the goddess of night, but I love the sunshine and the sea as much as the stars."

"Noted."

"And how can you have missed the most beautiful spot in Runevale all these years?"

"Well, perhaps fate was waiting for me to be invited by a certain someone." He dropped down beside her, leaving enough space they didn't risk touching but close enough they could.

"Perhaps." She looked into his beautiful blue-green eyes, much like the water below.

"Are we sure Atlanta won't come with weapons and threats for trespassing on his territory?" Hel asked, even if he didn't appear concerned.

"He told me I'm always welcome here. It used to be Katana's territory, too."

"I wasn't really in the mood to fight today, so that's good news. But I think you and I would make quite a team." After a moment of silence, he reached over and took hold of her right hand. She almost drew it back but out of curiosity, let him turn her hand over and trace the lines of her palm with his fingertip. The light touch sent a chill through her body despite the warm air. "Hmm, interesting."

"What are you doing?"

"This is your love line; it's long and straight, then it splits."

She smiled but had no clue what that meant. "Alright, what does that mean?"

"You will have two loves, but I think at different times."

"I think you're making this up as you go."

He chuckled. "Palm reading is something my tutors taught, but I'm with you on it being made up." He moved his finger to another line and his brows furrowed. "Here's the lifeline. It looks to fracture, which for an immortal that can't be right. I probably need to brush up on my readings. It was one of those lessons I didn't take seriously." He released her hand; part of her wished he wouldn't have. "We know you're on your first life but what about loves?"

"Are you asking if I've ever been in love?"

"When you put it that way it sounds too personal for our first date."

"This is a date?"

"Certainly." With a wave of his hand a bouquet of wildflowers with sprays of baby's breath and decorative greenery appeared. He leaned it toward her. "See, I even brought flowers."

Taking them in hand, she smelled the colorful blooms taking in the rich florals. "Have you been in love?"

"No."

She didn't know why but she hoped he would say that. "Why? You're beautiful, charming, powerful, you can't tell me you haven't had your fill of ladies."

He was quiet for a moment, watching the waves roll in. "I've never trusted anyone enough to let myself fall in love."

"Why?"

He turned to her with a smirk and that dimple. "How about you ask me something simple, like what my favorite color is?"

"Fine, what is your favorite food?"

"That's not simple, that's hard. Excruciatingly hard. How could I choose? I do love grapes. Well, let's narrow that down to fermented grapes."

Valeen laughed. "Wine isn't a food. I should have known you'd be a lush."

"Hey now, no need to take digs at me. I haven't been drunk in ages. I don't know if I can get drunk—it doesn't affect me much."

"I think that's how it is for most gods. But I have some drink that would knock you on your ass guaranteed."

"It's probably best I don't ever drink it then since I'm such a lush," he said, making her laugh. "You have one of the best laughs I've ever heard. It's like velvet and joy and an endless night."

She couldn't help but stare at him and the way his dark hair moved in the breeze. His light blue-green eyes popped against dark lashes. He was much different than she expected. She expected someone militant and stiff, like Synick. "Do you want to swim?"

"Trying to get me naked already?"

Valeen set her bouquet beside her, stood, and tugged the bottom part of her dress over her head and dropped it next to the flowers. This left her in a plum purple suit that cut high in her hips but covered her torso and revealed only a bit of cleavage then tied around her neck. She glanced down at Hel to see if it gave the effect she wanted. His mouth hung open and his eyes trailed up her long legs. She smiled. "It's rude to stare, you know."

He jumped up and tugged off his shirt. "I just didn't expect you to wear that. I thought it would be a full-body suit. You seem so very —prim."

"I am very prim," she said with a smile. "But we're swimming."

Suddenly huge white feathered wings shimmered into existence from his back. Now it was Valeen's turn to gape. "You have... wings. I've never seen that before. Well, except dragon wings but yours are feathered and gorgeous."

"It's magic, love, for which I am the god of. I can do pretty much anything I want."

"They're stunning. I almost wish I had a pair myself."

"I could give them to you."

"Perhaps another time." Then she leapt off the cliff into a dive.

She hit the warm water and kicked back up to break through the surface. Hel jumped and with his massive wings spread wide he dropped into a glide and landed on a boulder a few feet away from Valeen. He crouched and with his wings half spread he looked like a statue.

She smoothed her hair back and waded in place. "So, your favorite color is red, and you don't like water." She tapped a finger against her lips. "You're good with a blade but prefer magic. You have a type, not physically per se but you like the chase, the ladies you think are hard to get. Then once you have them, you get bored, and move on looking for the next high. You vowed to never marry or if you do it's for power, but there's a small part of you, somewhere deep down that wants love. Real love."

He tried not to smile. "How could you know all that?"

"Because I've known many males like you. I'm old, remember?"

"You've never known anyone like me, love."

"We'll see." She raised a brow. "You're not coming in?"

"You just said yourself, I don't like water."

"Come and swim."

He smiled and tucked his wings before they shimmered out of existence. "I'll go in there for one thing."

Valeen kicked her feet up and floated on her back, staring at the white puffy clouds. "Name your price."

A moment of silence passed. "A kiss."

Her heartbeat picked up and she pressed her lips together forcing back a smile. "Well, if you want one, you'll have to catch me."

"But then I might get bored," he teased.

"I very much doubt that. You can never really catch the night." She flipped over and dove underwater. Groups of colorful fish swam away as she went deeper. Long strands of seaweed danced in bunches and shells and other colorful creatures scattered across the sandy seabed. She kicked around to see if he'd jumped in yet. He had not.

Hands closed around her waist. She twirled around and there he was. Blowing bubbles out, he grabbed her hand and kicked up, bringing them to the surface. "That was too easy."

He didn't lean in for the promised kiss, but they held each other's stare. The gentle waves lapped against his back and pushed him into her. His big hands slipped around her waist, and his eyes fell to her lips. An energy buzzed between them, an invisible cord pulling, winding taut.

"Too easy," she repeated, and reality crashed down. A flash of Synick pinning her against a wall filled her mind, pushing in for a kiss, pleading with her to let him have her, begging for a union. "Give me an heir, the most powerful heir in all the realms." And part of her wished she would have, then Katana would be alive. The thought made her sick.

Hel and Synick looked nothing alike, sounded nothing alike, but they were of the same House. He was Hel's mentor.

Shifting into her lighter, half-shadow form, Valeen rose out of the water and then turned entirely into shadow and reappeared fully on top of the Amonlee cliffs. She snatched up her dress, left the flowers, and marched for her chariot. Too easy, she repeated in her head with a scoff. And he was right.

She slipped her light purple dress overhead, stepped into the chariot and picked up the reins. "Boys, it's time to go home." The two geldings stomped and tossed their heads, ready to take flight.

Hel appeared fully dressed and dry in his usual black suit right next to her in the chariot, shifting the weight. "If you don't want to give a kiss, I won't ask for it. It must be special to you and I'm not yet. I'd never want to make you feel uncomfortable with me." He smiled trying to turn the conversation lighter. "But I would accept a replacement price for getting me into the water. Would you go on another date with me? I'll plan this one."

Staring straight ahead she said, "I think this was a mistake."

What was she thinking even coming here to meet him? She should have never invited him and his cousin to her home. He was Primevarr, and she swore she wouldn't get involved in the mating for power games and for all she knew, that's exactly what he was after, just like his uncle was. Hel had no children yet.

He folded his arms and leaned back against the chariot. "I've upset you. I didn't mean you were easy... it was a foolish choice of words on my part, Valeen."

"No, it's not anything you did or said. We," she finally looked over at him, "are not compatible. We're too different. I shouldn't have agreed to... a date."

"You don't know we're too different. You're making assumptions."

"I know enough." She tapped the reins on the horses' backs, and he grabbed hold before they could move.

"You know what I think? I think you're scared. You're scared that I might be the one to change your world and drag you out of the uptight and lonely state you've been wallowing in since your sister died," he leaned closer—too close, she heard his heart beating, "and you're even more scared that mark on your arm means exactly what we both know it means. And I'm not Synick." He stepped back and out of the chariot. "Goodbye, Valeen."

"Wait," she started.

He vanished.

Layala blinked rapidly, pulling herself out of the memory. Holy Maker above. Her mind reeled at being sucked back into the here and now. She could almost taste the salt on her lips, smell him as he leaned in close and his words—*You're even more*

scared that mark on your arm means exactly what we both know it means. Shit. Shit. It was like history repeating itself. He was so —not Hel in that memory. Sweet and playful.

The thrill of that day with Hel on the cliffs made her feel a fondness she didn't want to. She'd have to fight to hold her tongue now rather than demand to know what happened after he vanished. At this very moment, she felt pulled to that time, wanting to fall back into those memories, and discover how she could merge then and now.

Still gliding on his wings, Hel flew in wide circles below. *Is he leaving me up here on purpose?* She shook her head. *Of course, he is. I just pushed him off a cliff.* But Layala thought back to that memory, *Valeen—I could fly, or at least hover... I rose right up and out of the water without wings, without anything but my power. And then somehow shifted to another spot.*

Layala took several steps back and inhaled three very deep breaths. *You can do this. Embrace the goddess. It's time to accept it. I am the goddess of night.*

Before she changed her mind, she ran. *Magic don't fail me!* And in four strides she leapt off the cliff. Her stomach felt like it dropped out of her. The wind whipped wildly past, so loud in her downfall she heard nothing else, not even her own screaming. Her magic flared, tingling all over her body, vines broke free, crashing into the rockface to get a hold. But that's not how she wanted her magic to show itself. *Stop falling. Fly! Hover, something!* Tears streamed up the sides of her face into her hair.

She did not stop.

A body slammed into her, and strong arms wrapped around her torso. "Are you fucking insane?" Hel shouted, sliding his arm along her backside, and hooking behind her knees, where he promptly pulled her tighter to him. "Were you testing me?"

"What? No."

"I told you, I won't let you die."

"Are our lives tied together like the mate bond you created? I know you need my blood every once in a while but that's different."

He let out a huff. "No. They're not. If you die, I won't. That particular stipulation is something only in the bond I created. Death isn't a consequence for most gods. But for mortals I thought it was poetic."

A closet romantic.

I wouldn't go that far, but I have a few different sides, love.

A quick dip from a gust of wind made her wrap her arms around his neck for assurance, even though he held her tight. "So, is all this truly only because of something you need from me?" She sounded disappointed even to her own ears.

He was quiet; the whistling wind filled in the silence. "You're my wife and my mate. I care about you. I always will. So no, that isn't the *only* reason." His eyes fell to her, and he gazed for far too long. It was intimate, almost as if he was afraid to admit what he said and wanted assurance that he hadn't made a mistake.

She couldn't take his penetrating gaze any longer and blurted out, "I think I can fly, like you said. I thought my magic would save me if I jumped."

"Don't use my crazy methods on yourself, alright." He shook his head. "You can't remember who you are. You're not ready. We have to take this one step at a time."

"But I do remember. I remembered something." Mistakenly, she peered down and the distance to the ground made her feel woozy. She was used to riding a dragon which felt secure and much like straddling a giant horse. This did not feel like that. "Will you take me back down?"

His huge wings disappeared and before they even began falling, he stood on solid ground with her still in his arms. The jump happened in an instant and left her nauseous.

"What did you recall?" he asked.

He set her down and she wobbled, pressing a hand over her queasy belly.

"Are you alright?" He gripped her arm.

"A little dizzy." She took in a deep breath and the world stopped wavering. "I'm alright."

Hesitantly, he let go of her and pushed his hands into his pockets.

"The day on the cliffs of Amonlee. I remembered it like I was there now. It's how I knew you had wings."

"So that's why you pushed me." The corner of his mouth curved up. "And here I was thinking you thought you finally had your chance to take me out and took it."

"It wasn't my intention. I just wanted a little payback for all the torture you've inflicted on me."

"It scared you, didn't it? My impending death."

She hated to admit it but relented, "Yes."

"I saw the safety net you created for me, and heard you scream my name. It did make me sort of miss you screaming my name in other ways."

"I thought I didn't do it for you anymore?" she countered.

"I think we both know that was a lie. I'm ready to take a roll in the sack if you are."

She flushed and lightly smacked his arms. "Are we so sure we can't kill each other?"

"Plotting my downfall still, I see."

"I should be after that sexual comment, but that's not why I ask."

"No?" His brows lifted. "Dare I say you care for me?"

"Don't push it," she said, and he laughed.

"Neither of us has dealt a lethal blow aside from the first time. It could be that the All Mother intervened the once. I don't know how these things work. There's only one way to test the theory, and I'd rather not." He still stood shirtless, hair windblown and disheveled. He looked good like that. "Anyway, don't jump off any more cliffs until we've worked on your ability. We should work on it last. It will be the hardest and take the longest."

Layala wondered why if Thane had been able to fly once to save her, why she couldn't do it to save herself. "I saw on my card," Layala started, and his brow quirked, "the cards you gave me. I can produce light with the power of the moon?"

"Yes. I've seen you produce a shield; it's the same type of power. We'll do that tonight."

She clapped her hands together and bounced on her toes. "Great."

His dark brows pulled closer. "You hate my training."

"It's not so bad. I want to learn. I want to remember."

"This is very—unlike you."

"Well, I can't keep resisting it. Like you said, it puts me in danger."

"When you do remember, you're going to hate me more. Because old you despises me even more than new you."

That wasn't true. Remembering made her hate him less. It revealed a side of him she didn't see now. A funner, relaxed version of Hel. Even if he wasn't the same person anymore, there was a glimmer of hope for him.

Layala tore her gaze from his and looked toward the castle. From this side of the ravine, she couldn't be sure if they had a new training exercise or what was going on, but the guards ran toward something. And she hadn't noticed it before, but dark storm clouds had rolled in overhead, blocking out the sun. It must have come in fast. She had just marveled at Hel flying in the sunshine.

"Whatever this is." He motioned back and forth between them. "This momentary comradery we have, it won't last."

"It could."

"You won't say that forever."

"We could call a truce now and make it hold even later."

"A truce," he said flatly.

"Yes, a truce between you and me and Thane. That even when we remember we won't fight each other."

"Isn't that what we're doing now? You're the only one of the three of us that doesn't remember who you are."

"I mean not a temporary truce. One that lasts after you get whatever it is you want from me." She sighed, annoyed that he still wouldn't tell her what that was. "I've heard of the wars we caused. The fighting between realms when people chose sides. We could promise to never let that happen again."

Layala held out her hand to shake on it, and he only stared at it. He wasn't willing?

"You don't know what you're asking for."

"A promise not to go to war with each other when we no longer need each other."

"You realize I still have an entire army of cursed elves. Aren't you going to work that into the deal?"

"If we don't fight then you have to release them from their curse, and that would mean now. It's their nature to kill and infect mine and Thane's people. Our people. They're your people too."

"I can't do that."

"Why not?"

Screaming pierced the air. Layala whipped around to face the castle grounds. This wasn't a training exercise. The guards were actively fighting something.

CHAPTER 28

THANE

Thane's back began to ache after sitting at his desk for so long. The wooden chair was uncomfortable and his neck stiff from the hours leaning over the book he found in a hidden room behind his father's bookshelf. There was hope that something in these handwritten accounts could trigger a memory but so far there was nothing but stories of appearances the gods made and lore he couldn't decide if it was myth or real.

He had to figure out why Layala—Valeen left Hel in the first place. In his own memory before the council, he said he turned her against Hel, convinced her to go with him and leave Hel, but he wouldn't do that, would he? She must have left him because she wanted to not because he tricked her.

Did he truly fall in love with his cousin's wife and steal her from him? With all he knew about their friendship, he couldn't imagine it. Hel was his brother, Valeen his friend. But how could he have turned her against him? What could he have said? It made him ill to think he'd betray them both like that. Poring over the pages for hours didn't recall the memory of why Valeen left Hel, but it did bring back something else...

The Past

War walked the path through the front grounds of his manor in Ryvengaard. High walls surrounded the property, so high in fact one could see nothing but the tops of trees on the other side. But such was common in a place with shifters. Dragons could fly, yes, but shifters of all kinds called this realm home, along with beasts, and flora and fauna twice the size of any other realm. Even the beetles grew to reach his knees in height.

The king of the dragon shifters, Zeir, strode toward him with his advisor at his side. Both males were over seven feet tall and broad. Zeir wore a long blue tunic that reached mid-thigh, with the sigil of his house on the chest, a red dragon. War had never seen him without his royal robes, a white fur-lined velvet material that draped around his shoulders and to the back of his knees. "High praise, god of war," the king said and dipped into a bow, as did his advisor. Zeir's shoulder-length white-blond hair fell forward.

"King Zeir, what brings you here today? Your correspondence didn't reveal a topic. Only that it was important." He and the king had become friends over the last century, but the young king still regarded him in awe each time they met up.

"Can we walk and talk?"

War nodded and they started side by side down the pathway, leaving his advisor behind.

"How are you?" Zeir asked. "It's been a while since we simply talked."

"Things are stable at home, and the realms are in order. I'd say, for now, everything is well."

Zeir smiled. "I meant how are you?"

"Oh," War said. He'd been busy watching the tensions grow between the two feline shifter clans. When time had no consequence, one day ran into the next. He never stopped to think about how he was. "I'm fine. And you? How is your family?"

"That's what I wanted to talk to you about."

War paused and faced the king. "Did something happen?"

"No, nothing like that." He waved a dismissive hand. "We've been friends for a long time. And yes, you have friends but no one to share your life with."

War shifted, knowing where this was going.

"I don't offer this lightly or without much deliberation. My daughter Varlett fancies you. You've known this for a while I'm sure. She is of proper age now, and I believe she will grow to be a powerful sorceress. You saw her potential yourself in the last battle. A match between the two of you would secure your ties here in Ryvengaard as well as strengthen my claim on my title. I wouldn't be challenged as often for my position."

These things were true, and yet his mind drifted not to the dragon princess but to the goddess of night. He couldn't even fathom why. She was Hel's wife now... This was an advantageous match, and Varlett was a very gifted sorceress for her age. In time she'd be one of the most dangerous dragons in Ryvengaard.

If he was to rule this realm and the dragons properly, it made sense he'd wed the princess. Although Varlett was still very young, only thirty-three. She was mature enough, but there was something about her character that always made him want to watch his back when she was around. He was five hundred years old, and dragons didn't usually match make until they hit at least a hundred. With a lifespan of a few thousand years, they tended to let their younger years be for play and discovery.

"You don't need to answer now," Zeir said. "Just consider it.

331

You're a god and I know the intricacies you all have with who you mate with. But I believe Varlett would give you powerful children."

War had never cared about any of that. He hadn't thought of having children yet or even considered a wife. "Is she here? Have you spoken to her about it?"

"No, I don't want her to be crushed if you decline. And yes, she's waiting in your tearoom."

"What does she think we're in discussions about?" War glanced back at his manor. The tearoom could be seen from here. She was likely watching them now.

"About the potential of battle with the Varmoose clan. They've been testing my border security lately, but with the Drakonan's backing me, I doubt they'll attempt a battle."

War rubbed the back of his neck and tried to peer inside the window, but the daylight's glare made it difficult. "I'll take it into consideration."

"I know she's young but she's ambitious."

That's what worries me, *he thought.*

He stepped into the tearoom to find her inspecting the items on his bookshelf. Her golden curls tumbled down her back like a water-fall to her hips. She put a hand on her petite waist, and he couldn't help but follow the curve of her body. She was beautiful, and bronzed-brown skin against golden hair, as well as the two black dragon horns she let grow out of her head when most didn't in this form, made her unique.

"How did the chat with my father go?" she turned and tucked her hands behind her back.

War plopped down in his oversized sky-blue chair and poured himself a cup of steaming liquid. He needed its calming properties. "Battle strategies would bore you no doubt, but I enjoy them."

Before he could take a sip, she made her way across the room, took the tea from his hand, set it on the side table and hopped onto his lap. She straddled him, forcing her white dress to scrunch up to the apex of her thighs, revealing that she had no undergarments on. Pulse quickening, he swallowed hard and her talon slowly, gently, moved down his throat. Blackberries and spice filled his nostrils, her perfume. He set his jaw but didn't make a move. "Varlett, he could walk in here."

With the wave of her hand the door slammed shut, and a twist of her fingers the lock clicked into place. "You didn't care about that last time. Or the time before—or the time before that." Her lips gently pressed to his throat, trailing to his collarbone.

"Did you tell him we slept together?"

"No, why?" She palmed the sides of his face and pressed her lips to his. Her kiss was all-consuming and demanded more, always more.

Talons grazed his skin as hands slid up under his shirt, the tips dug into his chest. A sting burned his ear; her sharp teeth scraped his earlobe and he quietly hissed. "Because he proposed a marriage between you and me."

Whether she told or not, Zeir must suspect and that must be why he offered her hand. Most dragons didn't expect to marry their first sexual partner, but the rules were different for the royals. Maker, he knew it was a terrible idea, but her sultry voice, the way she always found a way to touch him in front of others but subtly, and then whispered promises of more once night fell, tickled the darkest senses in him. It wasn't love but they couldn't seem to stay away from each other once they'd had a taste.

She leaned away, licking the bead of blood from her bottom lip —his blood. She claimed the taste of it was euphoric, made her feel unstoppable, even one drop. The slits of her yellow eyes narrowed. "He proposed this today?"

"Yes."

Her feet slid to the floor, heels clacking quietly. She stood and

around her finger. His mind flashed to them naked, bodies moving together on that armchair with her moans filling the room, and his face flushed with heat again.

She tilted her head slightly, eyes inspecting him as if she could see into his thoughts. "You remember me now, don't you? I can see it in your face." In a flash, her hand wrapped around his throat and squeezed. She pressed in closer, whispered in his ear, "And from that blush you must remember that way I sucked you real good."

He shoved her in the chest, sending her stumbling back into the wall. "Don't touch me." The thought of them ever being together made him physically sick. In this life he'd only been with Layala, had waited many years for her. Gods, he believed she was all he ever knew, and that memory of Varlett ruined that.

She cackled and slowly shook her head. "And you remembered I like it rough too, I see. The noble, sweet Thane has a delicious dark side and not just on the battlefield."

"Get out of my castle. You're not welcome here."

"That's not what you used to say."

Magic tingled through his body, and the floorboards creaked from an invisible pressure. "Get. Out."

"I came to warn you there's a demon running loose on your grounds. I could help if you'll ask nicely." She clicked her long black talons together. "Lots of screaming and people dying."

Cursing under his breath, he resigned to deal with her later. The past, her drama, would have to wait, because the present needed him, needed Thane the Elf King not War. He hurried across the hall into his bedroom to grab his weapons. Without looking back, he felt Varlett's presence behind him. "I saw Hel and Layala together. You should be worried. And maybe you should stop being such a gentleman and stick that cock of yours where it belongs before she forgets how much she loves you. And I don't mean in me."

How did she even know he and Layala weren't sleeping together? He whirled around on her. Thane clenched his teeth and snatched up his sword off his dresser. "Stay out of my business."

"It was easy to get the little gnome to talk and that creature knows *everything*. You should keep a better eye on her."

"What did you do?"

"I bribed her with food and a little truth serum. She's fine."

Thane slipped his weapons holster on and looked her over. The dragon princess he once knew was long gone. "You almost killed me. You took Tenebris's side, and I don't know if I want to know how you and Hel ended up together."

"I could have ripped out your heart or tore through your vital organs, but I didn't, did I? I missed everything important. I knew you'd heal, and as far as me and Hel go, well, it should be easy to figure out when you consider your betrayal against both of us."

It couldn't be true. There was no accepting that until he knew for sure... but then again he would do anything for Layala.

He shoved past her out into the corridor and started down the steps. "So that excuses what you did? I'm not what I once was. I could have died in the forest."

Varlett easily kept up with his fast pace. "But you didn't. I watched you from a distance over the years. I knew of your incredible healing abilities even as an elf."

This entire time she knew everything. Knew him. Watched him. Gods, this was a nightmare. Thane groaned with the urge to punch himself in the face. "So, you broke my mate bond because?"

"If I didn't Hel would have lost his mind and done something stupid. Like kill you. And I wasn't sure if she would have been able to wake him with a spell like that bound to her." She shoved through the front doors first. "Plus, it was satisfying to watch."

"You two need to get over the past. Maker, it's been thousands of years. Move on."

A set of guards went running by and both Thane and Varlett sprinted toward the screaming. "Where is Layala?" Thane asked, frantically looking around for her.

"She's with Hel. He'll protect her."

CHAPTER 29

LAYALA

The screams rose and Layala stepped toward the ravine. "What's going on? Can you see?" She turned to Hel, and he'd transformed into the leather-studded armor vest he wore the first time she saw him. A black cloak and thick black pants.

Without saying a word, he grabbed her by the arm, and they appeared at the base of the front steps to the castle. "You need to get inside." He pushed her in the back toward the stairs.

Layala stumbled and caught her balance before she fell onto the steps. The quick shift wasn't as disorientating this time around. "I don't follow orders from you," she snapped and charged around him.

He appeared in her path again and stuck out his arm, catching her. "Don't make me do this the hard way. That demon prince and his hounds are here for you. Go to your room and lock the door. The wards I placed there will keep you safe."

She tried to peer around him, and he moved in the way. "How do you know it's the demon?" Layala faked going one way then darted the other and sprinted toward the snarls, shouts, and fighting. It could be pale ones and he didn't want her to know.

An arm snatched her around the middle, and in one quick move he threw her over his shoulder before she could fight back. "Put me down or so help me, I will—" the world spun and went dark again, and they ended up outside her bedroom door. Except this time the corridor walls seemed to be moving and nausea fought its way up to her throat.

Hel shoved down on the handle, pushed through, and kicked the door shut with his heel. With his grip ironclad on the back of her thighs, he moved swiftly across the room and tossed her down on the bed.

Oh, he was going to suffer her wrath now. She stood up, toe to toe with him though he was at least a head taller forcing her to look up.

"I've lost you three times," he said, holding up his fingers for emphasis. "I won't allow it to happen again. Stay here."

"Thane is out there!" Layala tossed her arm toward the window.

"And if you promise to stay, I'll go help him. If you don't then I have to remain here with you and babysit. The choice is yours."

"I'm not the weak maiden you believe I am."

"I never said you were, but I am not taking chances."

Layala stepped around him and peered out her window. The guards circled around a huge hunched-back black dog, as big as a horse with rows of sharp teeth, bright red eyes. It snarled, snapped, and grabbed hold of a guard by the leg and tossed him into the air. "Holy Maker above," Layala breathed.

And further down there was another. This one ripped a guard in half, blood pooled on the ground beneath it. And then she spotted Thane running toward the danger. With her palm flat on the glass she said, "Help him. Help *them*. I'll stay."

"If you're lying to me..."

She turned around. "I said I'll stay. Go."

"Don't set foot outside this room until I come back. Promise me."

"I promise."

He dashed out the door, and it clicked quickly closed behind him. Layala paced back and forth in front of the window, chewing on the corner of her nail.

A quiet rustle brought Tif swinging down a green vine from her perch, and she landed on the bed. "He frightens me and for some reason also gives me tummy butterflies." She scurried across the floor and climbed up to the windowsill. "What's happening? I've been napping—holy horseballs. What is that thing?" She pressed her face against the glass, palms flat on either side of her head.

"A demon hound."

"Ew, there's so much blood—is that someone's detached leg!"

Layala paced back and forth watching the soldiers take swings at the beasts. Varlett cast a rounded cage of black bars around the larger of the two. Weapons stabbed through the bars but didn't appear to penetrate the demon hound. It bit through metal swords, breaking them in half as if they were wood.

Thane dodged under a clawed paw and swung down at the leg, but his sword didn't cut through. He dove narrowly missing jaws, and Layala's heart jumped into her throat. What kind of weapons did they need to fight the demons? "Come on,

341

Thane, magic." As if he heard her, he held out his palm and the hound froze but nothing else happened. No skin peeled from its bones, and no roaring in pain. Others took turns stabbing and hacking at its hide.

A knock on the door made Layala jump. She turned and stared at the thick wood. All the guards were outside and everyone else had to be hiding.

"Don't open it," Tif squeaked.

Another three quick raps. "It's Thane. Open the door."

Layala sighed in relief and started for it then froze halfway. Only a moment ago she saw him fighting. Unless he could move through space like Hel now...

"Thane is down there," Tif whispered. "I see him."

"Layala, hurry. I need to make sure you're alright." Whoever it was sounded exactly like him.

Layala grabbed her sword from the holster hanging on the wall and readied herself. Her magic coiled through her, more intense than usual, vibrating in her veins. Even her hands trembled with the power. Her gut told her who it was waiting outside.

"Open this door or I'll tear it off the hinges." The voice was different now, deadly venomous and gravelly. She'd heard Thane sound ruthless, but this was not him.

"Maybe we should go out the window," Tif suggested.

"This room is warded. We are safer inside." Layala hoped Hel's magic could keep out who she suspected wanted in.

The door rattled and bowed, crashing like thunder. Layala's chest heaved up and down with heavy breath. *He's going to break in!* With a crack the door was torn away and left wide open. Tif screamed and the sound of her scurrying boots pattered across the stone floor. Layala gulped, leveling her sword at the intruder. The demon prince with his curling horns and glowing red eyes.

"Hello again, goddess." He scowled and stepped forward but as he tried to cross the threshold he hit an invisible wall and was halted.

Hel, Layala silently called to him. *The demon prince is outside my room.*

"What is this?" The demon prince placed his palm flat against it and pushed. "Let down the guard and I'll kill you fast rather than slow."

"You need to work on your bargaining skills."

"I already made a bargain. I kill you, and I get my ring back."

"They're lying. They won't ever give it to you. But I could get it back." Layala gulped. "I'm the one who was stealthy enough to steal it in the first place. I'll get it for you." She had absolutely no recollection of the ring, this demon, or where she stole it from, or who had it now.

"You're a goddess trapped in a mortal body with no access to Runevale. You can do nothing for me." He slammed his fist into the invisible shield. It made no sound despite the force he hammered with. "Let me in and I won't peel the skin from your bones. Let me in and I'll simply slit your throat. The longer you make me wait the more pain I'll cause, and I do enjoy inflicting pain."

"Go back to the underrealm."

He growled and his long nails tore at the wooden door-frame. He clawed at it like a wild animal digging for food, splintering pieces, shredding through it like paper. Layala backed further into the room, heart hammering.

"I will tear this room apart splinter by splinter, brick by brick."

"And you still wouldn't get to her," said Hel's smooth voice. Layala couldn't see him yet, but heard his boots coming down the corridor. Slow methodical taps. "But if you want revenge on a god, I'm a treat."

The demon pulled his glower from Layala and backed away from the battered doorway, turning his head slowly. "My fight is not with you Zaurahel."

"But you made it so when you came for her. You know that."

"Rumor was you dropped this one a long time ago." His cruel smile tugged at the edge of his mouth. "You know, you're looking more like me and my brothers than a god." He tapped the corner of his eye. "Makes me wonder."

What does that mean?

A wavy dark wooden staff appeared in his hand and a red blast of light shot out of the top, crackling and sizzling. Layala gasped and ran to the threshold of the doorway, preparing her shield. The magic hit an invisible barrier before Hel, absorbing the power, taking it in like a thirsty desert floor. The stream of scarlet grew thicker, the crackling louder and more intense. Heat bloomed from the energy blast, making Layala take a step back. To her astonishment, Hel almost looked bored in a casual stance.

Finally, the demon prince halted the flow of magic and his menacing scowl faltered to something akin to worry.

"See, you don't have your ring. We're not in your realm. And you don't instill fear into me," Hel said calmly. "You're going to have to do better, demon." A ball of swirling light began to form over Hel's palm, growing larger with each passing moment.

"This isn't over." The demon prince grabbed the edge of his

long cloak, whirled it around himself and vanished in a cloud of gray-blue smoke.

Layala turned and ran for the window. The demon hounds were gone. She spotted Thane squatting next to an injured soldier. Letting out a slow breath, Layala pressed her forehead against the glass. "He's alright." She found Piper uninjured nearby, as well as their other friends. Leif gripped someone's hand and helped them up. Fennan looked to be holding a compress over a soldier's thigh.

"Not a thank you or acknowledgment for coming to your aide?" Hel's warm honey voice snaked down her spine. "Typical."

Layala turned and tossed her sword on top of her bed. "Thank you. I wasn't sure if you'd hear me with all the commotion."

"I'll always hear you if you need me." His crimson eyes trailed over her from boots to thighs to hips. His slow inspection brought a warm flush to her cheeks. When his heated gaze finally made its way up to her face, he said, "Is that blush for me, love?"

She cleared her throat. "Don't be absurd. I'm hot from the demon encounter."

"That blood rushing to your cheeks," he moved closer, "the pounding of your heart. You're making this difficult for me."

"What does that mean?" She took a slow breath, trying to calm her heart but the closer he came the faster it beat. A slow *drip, drip, drip* came from somewhere.

"You don't see what I do." He lifted her hand and brought her fingers to his lips. A droplet of blood ran down her finger. "You don't understand how I can hate you and want you more than anything at the same time."

For some reason, she didn't pull away, didn't fight or protest. She stared into his eyes, entranced. His was equal parts danger and delight like the sweetest poison. His tongue slid across her middle finger, and then his lips closed around it. It was only then she realized one of the flying splinters must have shot out and cut her finger. It stung a little but the longer her finger was in his mouth the more it numbed, and a pleasant heat bloomed in her belly. She jerked her hand back and stepped away. This felt much too sensual, much more than him healing her injury, although that's what happened. The cut was gone, and he got another little hit of her blood to rejuvenate his strength.

Layala took a wide step around him and headed for the exit. "We need to check on the others." She stopped in the doorway and glanced back at him. "Will you use your magic to heal some of the injured soldiers?"

"Remember when I told you I wasn't a hero?"

"Please."

"Why should I exhaust my power to heal a bunch of elves? It's going to take a lot. What's in it for me?"

"My gratitude."

He smiled, bringing out the dimple in his cheek. "Tell you what, I'll save a few elves if you can tell me what happened next in our story."

"You mean after our first date? When you left me on the cliffs?"

"Precisely."

"Fine, after you heal at least ten elves, I'll tell you."

"Done."

CHAPTER 30

LAYALA

Later that evening, Layala sat at the dining table, staring over the lip of her glass of wine. All the mangled bodies, the screams and cries of the soldiers who'd been bitten and poisoned by the hounds haunted her. They had no cure for it and not even Hel's magic drew out the infection. Hel said they'd suffer for hours and hours before they finally died. As a mercy, Thane put down the three demon-poisoned soldiers.

Fennan tapped his boots under the table, scowling at Hel and Varlett across from him. Thane cut into his food, avoiding looking up. Piper and Leif on the other side of Fennan, picked at their food. It wasn't as if they hadn't all seen companions die or witness the carnage of battle. The tension in the room stemmed more from new threats, and two of them sat at their very dining table.

"I'll work on an antidote for the demon's poison," Varlett

347

announced, breaking the silence that had gone on for way too long, and sipped on her glass of what Layala assumed was blood. "I'm sure that won't be the last we see of them."

"That would be helpful," Thane said, finally lifting his chin.

"I'm sorry, but why are they eating with us?" Fennan blurted out. He'd definitely been waiting to say that for the last several minutes. "Why are we tolerating this again? Him, I understand. Kind of." He waved a hand at Hel then gestured to Varlett. "But her? She worked with Tenebris."

"Tenebris was a means to an end for me. Nothing more. And I did just save your ass," Varlett said, clicking her talons against her glass. "Or have you already forgotten you nearly got your arm ripped off?"

"I would have moved out of the way on my own. I didn't need your help." He leaned forward, rapping his knuckles against the tabletop, staring her down. "And one good deed doesn't absolve you from the host of offenses you've committed. I could list them out, but it would take all night."

"Whatever you say, elf." She lifted her brows and stabbed a cherry tomato with her talon and popped it into her mouth.

Thane cleared his throat. "Look, we need to come up with a plan to take out the demon and his hounds. That's why we're all here." Thane straightened his spine and set his fork down. "As we all witnessed, our weapons are ineffective against them. Even magic did little damage."

Hel pushed back from the table, stood up, and leaned over the back of the high chair. "Since you don't remember, I'll let you in on a little secret. They're weak against obsidian, and your swords are made of steel. And sunlight but that's not something you can produce."

Thane crossed his arms. "Obsidian is rare and more feeble."

"In Adalon, yes it's rare." Hel pushed the chair in and walked over to the long row of windows looking out across the castle grounds. "But that's what can kill them."

"So, I have to find enough obsidian to make us swords." Thane's hands curled into fists on the table. "That's just great."

"Can't you just poof swords out of thin air for us?" Layala asked. She'd seen him do that on several occasions with clothes and those civars he smoked regularly.

"I don't pull things out of nowhere. They're from a place I keep them. I call it the aether. And if I had obsidian weapons stored there I'd have *poofed* them into existence already." He sat on the windowsill ledge and crossed his arms. "And while you're collecting your obsidian, it's not safe for Layala here."

Thane shifted toward him. "It's not safe anywhere in Adalon. I've been protecting her all my life without your help. I think I've got it handled."

"Except if it weren't for me, she'd have been killed today and the other night."

Thane glared at Hel. "No, because I wouldn't have put her in a room by herself."

"Oh, you'd have kept her at your side fighting against demons you can't kill. Exceptional plan."

"And where would she go that's safer than here with me and her friends that will lay down their lives for her?" Thane asked, eyebrows arched. Layala swallowed hard. Yet again Thane and the others were putting themselves at risk to protect her. What if Thane was killed because of her, or Piper, Leif and Fennan? Any of the Ravens...

"With me of course. They've infiltrated Castle Dredwich twice now. They know where she sleeps, eats, her routine, everything."

"That's not happening," Thane's voice took on a sharpness that hadn't been there before. "She's staying with me."

"What's the matter? You two are on a relationship hiatus, aren't you?" His lips curled into a wicked smile. "There are no wedding plans. You called it off. You said you needed time. I'll give you time. Besides, she's *my* wife. It's not as if she went somewhere with me for her safety for a while, it would be improper."

The room went so quiet the only thing Layala heard was her own soft breath. The blood seemed to drain from her face rather than flush with heat. "Everyone out, except for Hel and Layala," Thane snapped. The chairs scraped against stone, footsteps quietly tapped on the floor, and the three of them were alone. Even Varlett left without protest.

Both Hel and Thane gazed at Layala expectantly. "What do you want to do?" Thane asked.

The fact that he even asked left doubt as to if he wanted her here. Did he want her to go? "Stay, of course," her voice came out weaker and with less conviction than she'd hoped.

"Do you really?" Hel drawled, pushing up from the window's edge. He sauntered back to the table. "This place is sucking the life out of you. The people in the city have turned on you. You can't trust the people inside the castle either." His garnet eyes flicked to Thane. "I'm not trying to be an ass for once but whatever is going on between you two isn't helping her remember. In fact, being here with you is keeping her attached to this life and this one alone. You want her to remember, don't you?"

Thane's lips formed a hard line.

"I'm not running away from everything and everyone," Layala said, before Thane could get any ideas about her leaving.

"And the last place I want to be is stuck with you and Varlett, only Maker knows where."

"She's safer with both of us to protect her, Hel," Thane said. "So why don't the three of us sit down, eat, and get past the bullshit."

Hel let out a "ha," and shook his head. "Get past the bullshit? You do realize we're all here because of you, right?"

"And we can't change it so let's move on and figure out our next offensive move."

Layala narrowed her eyes at Thane. "What did you do?"

"He manipulated you into leaving me, that's what."

Thane shook his head. "That's not what happened. And if she was truly yours I couldn't have manipulated her. She's a bloody primordial goddess. She's not a fool. Manipulation is what you're good at, not me."

Hel looked up as if the ceiling suddenly became his enemy. "Then tell me, cousin, what happened?"

"I don't remember yet, but I wouldn't trick her into leaving you for me."

"I remember perfectly well what happened but neither of you would believe me, so I won't waste my breath." His lip curled back, and he started for the door. "Your next offensive move, *Thane,* is to find obsidian." Then he vanished before he even reached the door.

THE NEXT MORNING Layala sat up in her bed, bleary-eyed and groggy. She blinked several times and the outline of Tif sitting on the pillow next to her slowly came into focus. "Tif, what are you doing? You know I hate when you stare like that when I'm asleep."

"This came for you. A bird named Sallow dropped it off while you were sleeping. I hope you don't mind that I read it even though it's clearly addressed to you."

Layala took the envelope and pulled out the paper inside. *Layala, I've been waiting a while for those items you promised to find. I'll have to go out tonight if you can't. I'm out of stock.*

~ Aunt E.

"I completely forgot about her. How could I forget?"

Tif tapped her chin. "Well, there has been a lot going on. Why, with the first assassin, demon hounds, the creep with the horns who wants to kill you, and Hel and Varlett here, not to mention the strained relationship between you and Thane. No one blames you for forgetting." She patted Layala's arm with a big smile.

"I need to find the rest of the list Aunt Evalyn gave me."

"Can I come?"

"It's too dangerous."

Tif folded her arms and stuck out her lower lip. "Too dangerous? I'm not the one Horns wants dead! You are. I could be your backup." She took her tiny dagger out of her dress and pulled it from the sheath. "I can give Horns the old stab, jab, duck, move. You know he's pretty big. I bet he has a large member I could easily slice, too." She waved the dagger back and forth with sound effects.

That statement brought mental images Layala did not want to entertain. "Gross, and no. You're good at hiding Tif, not fighting. And that's exactly what I want you to do."

"I can sneak attack from behind." She jumped up and parried the air. "Heeyaw!"

"Just stay here. I'll be back soon."

Tif let the dagger droop to her side. "If you're not back by nightfall, I'm telling Thane."

"I'll bring Piper."

"I'm pretty sure Hel and Thane said she's not a sufficient guardian. Not that she's not a good fighter but Horns seems powerful."

"She'll have to do."

FULL GRAY STORM clouds rolled in, darkening the morning sunshine. Rain looked to be threatening again but the rampant spring storms were not about to stop her mission to find the rest of Aunt Evalyn's list. She already felt horrible for forgetting, and she was out of time. Evalyn would go out by herself and that was too dangerous for her, especially with demons on the loose. Layala only hoped she wouldn't run into any herself.

Piper rode faithfully beside her but wasn't quiet about it. "Thane is going to kill me."

"Piper, it's fine. We'll make this quick."

"I might as well write the letter to my family for funeral arrangements because he's going to kill me."

Layala turned Midnight along an offbeat path and Piper trotted next to her on a roan stallion. "The pottifer likes to grow in the shade among thick underbrush, usually near ash trees, and the wood I know of is just northwest of the city."

"You mean where pale one's last attacked?" Piper rolled her eyes. "Yep, this solidifies my grave. It shall read: Here Lies Piper Fireheart, the fool who disobeyed her king."

"But Hel said he'd called them off so we should be in the clear in that regard."

They rode awhile before she pulled Midnight to a stop amongst the ashy white-trunked trees with round green leaves. "It should be around here."

Thunder cracked overhead eliciting a neigh from her horse, and with the lack of bright sunshine it felt more like evening than morning. Piper glanced around and hopped off. "Let's hurry before it starts downpouring."

They wrapped their horses' reins around branches and headed further inside the woods. Weaving around the close-knit tree trunks, they searched among the thick grass, the ferns and tall weeds for the plant with orange leaves. After about twenty minutes she found it. "Here."

The sound of raindrops plopping all around hit her senses before it dampened her skin and clothes. She quickly jerked the pottifer by its base and the snapping of roots followed. With a couple shakes the dirt clods dropped and with the plops came something else. *Thump, thump, thump... What is that? Not the rain, not the storm...* With her skin prickling, she turned in a slow circle.

"Piper, what is that?"

Piper took out her sword. "I'm not sure."

Thump thump thump—faster this time.

Footsteps.

Running.

Layala whirled just as a pale one leapt at her, taking her to the ground. It was a small child. Eight at most.

Layala screeched, shoving at her chin, pushing her snapping mouth away from her face. She'd never seen a child turned. It was assumed they couldn't survive the transition. The horrible high-pitched scream close to Layala's ear caused a ringing sound that deadened her hearing. She drove her knee up and tossed the girl aside. Her small body crashed into a tree. Before Layala could fully rise, the creature was scrambling back toward her.

Tears burned as she pulled her sword free. How could she kill a child?

"Stay back or I'll kill you."

She growled and dropped into a crouch, crawling on all fours toward her.

"Cut her down!" Piper screamed.

Hel said she could command them right? "I command you to stay put, child!"

The girl froze, tilting her head back and forth. *Maybe I can tie her up? But she's a pale one regardless. She could infect someone else.* Layala gulped, gripping her sword tighter. There was something familiar about the girl's dress.

"Fine, I'll do it," Piper strode forward and raised her sword high. "It's not a child anymore. It's a pale one."

Hot pain suddenly ripped into Layala's thigh. She screamed, then slammed her teeth together and brought her sword down across the back of the neck of another pale one, a woman... and a child, together... She sucked in a sharp breath. These were the two from the farm she tried to save.

She never put down the father.

Layala stumbled backward, clutching at her thigh. Blood oozed down her leg and teeth marks marred her flesh. *Holy shit. Holy shit... she bit me. A pale one bit me.*

Piper stood next to the dead child, her sword hung at her side, as she stared at Layala's leg. "Laya." Tears filled her eyes. "Layala!" she screamed, and those angry tears flooded down her cheeks. She dropped her sword and fell to her knees. "I failed you. Oh, my gods, I failed you. I can't—I can't. You know what this means." She was struggling to breathe.

Layala's chest pinched, and panic squeezed. "Get up. We have to get back."

Swiping her tears, Piper slowly rose. "There won't be much time. Maybe Hel can... Run!"

Turning, her feet flew over the ground, dodging trees, panicked breaths coming faster and faster. The scenery around her became a blur. *Holy Maker above, this can't be real. How long do I have?* Once she got to Midnight, she hopped on and she and Piper rode side by side. She pushed Midnight as fast as she ever had. His hooves thundered over the grassy plane around the Valley.

Once the castle came into view, she tugged back on the reins, and tore off her sleeve to use as a compress around her leg. If any of the guards saw a bite mark, she wasn't sure what they'd do or if they'd even hesitate to try and put her down.

Thane's face came to mind, and his words. "All it takes is one mistake." Tears blurred her vision crossing the bridge. She dropped off Midnight at the front steps, boots hitting the ground and dashed up the front entrance steps. The guards dipped their heads and pulled open the double front doors.

"Go get him!" Layala shouted to Piper as she made a left turn toward her wing of the castle. Piper nodded and took off straight ahead toward the training grounds.

Thane, I'm sorry. I'm sorry. He warned her. He begged her not to go out alone.

Layala dashed up the stairs that led to the bedrooms. She didn't stop until she saw his door. At the top she wobbled and pressed a hand on the wall. The corridor was a blur now, a hazy halo of light from the window at the end. A high-pitched ring flooded her ears. *I have to make it.* Shaking the fogginess from her mind she trudged forward. *Please be here. Please. I need you,* she thought.

Her fingernails scraped against the door as she pushed down on the handle and the door clicked open.

The light burst through the windows blinding her. Layala brought her hand up to shield it. "Hello?"

"You need me, huh? And I didn't know we were on 'entering before knocking' terms."

Layala stumbled into the room. "Hel, help me."

CHAPTER 31

HEL

Fuck, Hel knew something was wrong and didn't listen to that gut instinct. He caught her around the torso just as she fell into him. "What happened?" He swung his arm under the back of her knees and lifted her against his chest. She was feeble, lethargic. He smelled a coppery tang, but she wasn't bleeding profusely.

"She bit me," Layala mumbled, grasping at his tunic as he carried her over to the daybed in the corner of Thane's office Hel had taken up.

He laid her down and scanned her body, finding the wrap on her thigh. "Who bit you, Val?" He tore it free and ran his fingers over the deep puncture marks. He felt the blood draining from his face.

"The child was there, and I couldn't kill her, but Piper did." Tears slipped out of the corners of her eyes. Her body began to shake with her sobs.

He grabbed her face, forcing her to look at him. She wasn't

making sense. Her bright blue eyes were glassy, unfocused. "Did a pale one bite you?"

Her chin trembled, and she nodded. "Can you help me? I couldn't go to Thane. I couldn't make him do it if it's too late. He'd never forgive me. He already had to kill Osric."

"No one is killing you."

"I can't be one of them. You can't allow it." She grabbed his shirt, pulling herself up. "Give me my sword. I'll do it."

"Stop it." He uncurled her fingers and pressed her chest to lay her back down. "I'll fix this."

"What if you can't? Hel, please tell me you can save me." She threw her arms across her face and began sobbing into them. The beginning stages of the turn often resulted in hysteria. "I'm going to turn!"

Fuck. Hel clenched his jaw, sat on the bed, and pulled her arms down. "Look at me." Her wild searching eyes locked onto his. "Good. Now take some deep breaths. Better. You're not going to turn. You're a goddess. You're immune to it," he lied, but he needed her to calm down. If she had her immortal body it would be true, but Mathekis proved someone with the blood of the gods could turn when they'd fallen from grace. "And even if you weren't, I said I'd fix this. You'll be perfectly fine."

"I'm immune?"

Strands of ebony hair stuck to her wet cheeks. He gently lifted them away. "Of course."

"But I'm so cold." She dragged in a breath. "I might throw up."

He tugged up the blanket and tucked it around her shoulders. "Remember when I told you that you first kissed me and called me a big boy?"

"Yes," her voice trembled.

"You were right. It was a lie, but we did kiss."

"When?"

"You must remember, it was after the cliffs. You promised to tell me about it." He started to rise, and she gripped his hand nearly hard enough to crush a weaker elf's bones.

"Don't leave me."

"I'm not leaving. But I need to grab something off the desk, alright?"

"Don't leave me," she repeated, more desperate. "He left me, and he didn't come back."

He clasped her other hand, too. "I'm staying." Hel's throat felt thicker, and he cleared it. He needed to get to that desk, but he could spare a few moments to calm her. "Tell me about after the Cliffs of Amonlee." She closed her eyes and swallowed. The silence stretched long enough to alarm him. "Val?"

Glossy eyes settled on his face. "Why did you do it? I loved you more than anything. You were the love of my fucking life, my only true love, and you broke me. You destroyed me."

His brows furrowed. "What do you mean?"

"I thought what we had was real."

Hel's heart pounded. "It *was* real."

"I hate her. I hate you. I'm going to rip her heart out. And then I'm going to tear her head off."

"You're starting to hallucinate." And the rage of a new pale one was starting to take hold. "I need to help you. I must let go of your hand."

He pulled away and dashed to the desk, jerking open the drawer for ink. Several bottles rattled around inside. Then the door popped open, and War rushed in with Piper right behind him. His gaze swung from Hel over to Valeen. "No."

Hel snatched the ink and quill, spilling droplets over his hand as he slammed it down.

War's footsteps pounded across the floor, and he dropped

to her side. "Layala..." He lifted a lock of her hair; the front strands on the right side had turned pure white. He sucked in a sharp breath.

Hel started writing, *make time stop what has begun, bring back flesh anew*. Wait. That wasn't going to work. He scribbled it out. *Stop the change that has begun and—*

War's fists slammed into his chest, crushing him into the bookshelf. "This is your fault! Stop this curse! Stop it right now!"

"I'm trying," he said through clenched teeth.

"She's turning," his voice became hysterical. "You created this curse. She's going to be a monster. This is your fault!" He punched him in the jaw, hard enough for Hel to see stars and knocked down half the shelves behind him spilling books everywhere.

"I know!" Hel roared, head snapping back. A coppery tang filled his mouth. "Now let go of me before I can't stop it! If she turns fully, I can't turn her back. This curse is beyond me."

War dropped him, and Hel shoved past to get back to the desk. Half the ink bottle spilled across his unfinished spell. "Damn it, War. You fucked it up!" He grabbed a fresh piece of paper and dipped the quill again.

Stop the curse that has begun, bring back flesh anew. By blood and by fire I pay. Then he drew a new symbol. A wave of invisible power rocked the room, a signal it was ready. Both Hel and War hurried to her side. War placed a hand on her damp forehead and gripped her hand. "This better work."

Piper quietly sobbed at the end of the bed. "I should have seen the pale one coming."

"It will work." Hel tore open the fabric of her pants over the wound, leaving him plenty of space to work. Hand trembling, he cut his finger and in his blood drew the symbol over the bite wound. *This better fucking work.* With a flick of his fingers, fire ignited the blood symbol. The lesions began to close, like invisible threads sewed it shut and then her flesh was perfect with a brand-new blackened rune mark over her thigh as the flames died out. He looked at her face. The white streak of hair was still there. He didn't think his heart could pound any harder, but it did.

"Val, can you hear me?" Hel whispered.

Her skin still kept the golden hue, her lips rosy but that could change...

Her eyelids fluttered.

Say something, please. Talk to me.

"Why isn't her hair turning back?" War slipped his arms around her and lifted her onto his lap. "Please, Layala don't go where I can't follow. Don't leave us. I can't lose you again." He brought her up to his chest, kissing her forehead over and over.

Hel's eyes burned and he stood tall, legs unsteady. It must work.

A minute passed. Two.

His heart might stop.

"I swear to the Maker if she turns, I'm killing you right here and now," War snarled.

Hel swallowed hard, watching her for any signs of awareness. "I will let you."

"Stop fighting," she murmured, eyes fluttering open. "I'm alright." She finally lifted her head on her own. Her crushing blue eyes found Hel first and the corner of her mouth tugged up, then she lifted them to War. "I'm sorry."

A tear rolled down Thane's cheek and he squeezed her into his chest. "Layala," he breathed. "Maker above, Laya, you're alright."

She hugged him back and Hel looked away, a squeeze on

his heart cinched. "I'm going to get some fresh air." His boots tapped quickly as he moved to the balcony doors. He shoved them open and hurried to the railing, leaning his upper body weight against it. His shoulders sagged. *Gods, I almost lost her again and it would have been my fault this time.* With a flick of his fingers, a civar appeared and he took it between his lips. The sweet smoke wafted to his nose before he took a drag.

Murmured voices drifted from the room. A door closed a few moments later and then footsteps traipsed his way, too heavy to be Valeen's. "She went to bathe off the blood and change. Piper is with her."

Hel watched the two white swans slipping along over the water. Then a black feathered swan popped out from the reeds and joined them. War and Hel stood beside each other in silence. The sun peeked out from behind dark clouds. The smell of the fresh rain burning off drifted upward. It wasn't even noon yet and his life was almost ruined.

Now that his nerves had settled, he thought back to what she said about him breaking her, destroying her. They'd ruined each other all those years ago.

"She came to you first."

Hel pulled the civar and blew out a stream of smoke. "And?"

"She thought she was about to die, and she came to *you.*"

His heart skipped. "Because she needed me to help her."

"We almost lost her, Hel. Again."

"I was in the same room." Hel watched a set of guards walking the path far below.

"She's not safe here."

"As I've stated."

A long pause and then he said, "Take her away."

Hel stilled with his civar halfway to his mouth. He turned

and stared at his cousin, clearly so in love with Hel's mate. His bright green eyes were bloodshot. Shadows existed under them, shadows he hadn't noticed before. Dark stubble from days of not shaving grew unmanaged. Even his hair wasn't sleek and styled as usual. And in that moment Hel realized War was a better person than he'd ever be.

"I can't keep her safe here," War said. "But you can."

Hel turned away. "She's not going to accept it."

War grabbed him by the front of his shirt. "She almost turned into a pale one. You said you sent them away and told them not to attack."

"I did but many of them are barely more than rabid animals. They can't be completely controlled. You should know that as much as anyone." Hel's scowl traveled from the fist clenched around his top to War's face. "And let go of me."

His grip loosened and he dropped his hand. "It doesn't matter anyway. If that didn't get her, the demon prince will or another assassin and until she remembers, until she's Valeen again... you have to take her and keep her safe. Train her. Make her remember. You even said it yourself, I'm the one holding her back."

Hel took a deep inhale of his civar. *Fucking underrealm.* "I'll come back when she's ready." But taking her away meant leaving War vulnerable. The council might change their target. And even if he was still bitter at him for everything, he needed him.

He cared for him.

"I'll have to leave Varlett here with you. She might be the only one strong enough to help you fight a demon prince other than me."

"Fine."

"You must be the one to tell Val. She'll fight me."

He nodded somberly. "I will."

LAYALA

LAYALA QUICKLY TOWEL dried off and ran her fingers over the new rune mark at the top of her thigh. Was it permanent? It looked similar to a five-pointed star with a crescent moon through the center. If it was, at least it was pretty, and a permanent mark was better than being a pale one.

She shook her head at her own stupidity and slipped fresh clothes on. Piper left her to bathe alone but probably wasn't far.

On her way out of the room, she caught her reflection in the mirror and halted. *Is that...* she was inches from the mirror in a few steps, tugging at the white chunk of her hair, from the top of her forehead framing her face, all the way to the end of her strands at her hips. *How the hell am I going to explain this?* She groaned and tucked her hair behind her ear. Maybe Hel could fix it.

Piper paced the hallway and looked up with sorrow. "I'm so sorry, Layala."

"Don't blame yourself. If it's anyone's fault, it's mine. I shouldn't have hesitated." She sighed. "I need to thank Hel."

Piper nodded and slid down the wall to sit against it with her knees up to her chest.

She hurried across the hallway and into the room. The smell of Hel's civar drifted in from the balcony. The two of them stood side by side with their backs to her. For some reason she smiled. She stepped through the balcony doorway, and they turned at the same time.

"Feeling better?" Thane asked, but he looked sad.

"I am." She smiled bigger. "I'm sorry I scared you but it's alright. I'm alright. I'm not going to turn." She wanted to go to him and hug him again, reassure him with her body pressed against his but she stayed still. "Thank you, Hel. Really. You saved me."

He simply bobbed his head and turned back to look out over the castle grounds.

Thane stepped closer, took her hands, and led her back inside the room. The pain and confusion on Thane's face made her stomach drop. "What's wrong?" she asked. Had something else happened. Was this only temporary?

"Laya." His chin quivered but his voice came out strong, unwavering, "I've always done what's best for you."

"I know," she said, searching his face for a sign of where this was going.

"You're not safe here anymore."

"So, we can go somewhere else for a while."

He nodded solemnly. "Yes, you can."

"Just me?" Slowly it dawned on her. Oh gods, no. Desperation rose up in her throat. This couldn't be what she thought—he wouldn't. "Thane," she breathed on the verge of tears.

"If I stay here, the demon prince will think you're here too. He won't expect us to part. But you can go with Hel and finish your training."

"Don't do this." Layala's throat ached with raw emotion.

"You need to go." He tore his hands away. "I want you to go."

Tears silently slipped down her cheeks. The rushing of her blood pounded in her ears, drowning out everything. "You don't mean that."

His silence said more than words.

"Thane, I want to be with you. I want you. I remember some things. We can go together."

"This isn't about that anymore. It's about you staying alive. I know what it felt like to watch you die over and over. I can't do it again." He raked his hands through his hair. "I can't. Every time you die it's because of me. It's like the All Mother is punishing me for taking you from him. You must leave."

"That's not true. We always have a choice."

"Whether it is or not, you can't stay."

"But I love you."

"You have to go. Hel will keep you safe and help you become who you're supposed to be." A single tear ran down his cheek. "Leave Castle Dredwich. Leave Palenor."

"Thane."

"It's over between us, Layala." His face hardened. "Don't make this harder than it already is."

"This isn't what you want," Layala said, chest aching. Her heart felt like it might crack. She glanced toward the balcony doors left wide open for Hel to hear. "He's manipulating you, clouding your judgment. Can't you see that?"

"The only one who clouds my judgment is *you*."

Those words were a hot knife to the heart. On shaky legs, Layala backed away. It was true. All the pain and suffering Thane had been through, every self-sacrificing questionable judgment was because of his drive to save her, to protect her. She was his downfall.

She didn't remember leaving the office or walking to the corridor to get to her bedroom. Packing her bag felt like someone else, like she was a ghost watching herself move slowly around the room. Until she broke down and sobbed into the silk covers on the bed she'd never sleep in again. She pulled her lily engagement ring off and left it on the pillow.

CHAPTER 32

HEL

Hel pulled his civar from his lips and through a hazy cloud of smoke watched Varlett approach. Her heeled boots tapped lightly on the stone floor. Her reptilian eyes raked over him in a hungry gaze, and he wasn't certain in which ways she craved him. There were times he thought she might rather take a bite than ride him. The sitting room he waited in was one of many with wide-open windows overlooking the property, and fancy high-backed chairs with side tables and tea cookies.

"Valeen and I are leaving," he said before she made it to the seat across from him. He'd rather have a chair between them lest she might be tempted to do something rash.

She stopped and gripped the back of the cushioned chair. "For how long?"

"I don't know. Could be weeks, months, not likely years but..." he lifted a shoulder. "You'll stay here with War. Protect him. Take out the demon and any other assassin that comes for him."

Her knuckles turned white, and her black talons punctured and drove into the backrest of the cerulean cushion. "After all I did, after all the time I waited, you're just leaving with her? I waited over four hundred years, and I made sure she stayed alive for you." She shook her head, horns slowly grew out of her head, and smoke puffed out of her nostrils.

Here we go.

"No," she said firmly.

"Yes."

They stared each other down, seconds ticked by, and neither of them moved.

"I'm not bound to you anymore. You can't force me. I'm going with you."

"I never forced you to do anything, Varlett. Everything you ever did was because you wanted to. And you're staying and doing exactly what I said."

She tore her eyes away from him and gave a cruel smile. "It wouldn't matter what she did. You'll always be obsessed with her. It's all about precious *Val*. Even if she's a lying cheating whore, you can't let her go. And after everything I've done for you, proved to you my loyalty, loved you, even after all that you'd still choose her. Round and round we go, me chasing you, you chasing her, her chasing War. It never ends."

Hel rolled his eyes. "Stop it, Varlett. You're being dramatic. I need—"

"Something from her memory," she mocked. "You know what I think? I think you just can't stand to see her with him and even if you don't love her anymore you'll never let them be happy. And that means you never will be."

Hel took a pull from his civar. "You know me well, Varlett. You're absolutely right."

This was what they fought about right before he went into his long slumber. She went feral when he said he'd sleep until Valeen came back to wake him. Then she told him she never wanted to see him again and she hoped he stayed asleep for eternity. That was the truth of their falling out all those years ago. She told Layala it was about power because she didn't want to admit it was about her.

Varlett picked up the chair and threw it against the wall, leaving a chip in the stone and the chair in broken pieces on the floor. "Am I ever going to be enough for you? Are you ever going to love me and not her?"

Hel's gaze flicked to the window. The lush green bushes swayed in a breeze. "I've told you before." He slowly rose from his seat and adjusted his left sleeve. "I don't love you and I never will. But you know what I can offer you, if you stay loyal to me, you'll be at my side when I rule Runevale. The choice is yours. You stand with me, or you can go back to being a ruined princess in Ryvengaard, disowned by your father for turning your back on him and choosing me over him and War."

Varlett's eyes flashed with dragon's rage, but her talons sliced down the front of her dress, tearing open the fabric, exposing her naked flesh beneath. She pushed the ruined gown away from her body and strutted toward him. "Even if you don't love me, you'll make love to me before you go."

Hel held up a hand and halted her with magic. His gaze swept over her naked form and then he lifted his gaze to her face. "I'm not in the mood."

LAYALA

A FEW HOURS LATER, Layala and Hel stood at the portal inside the unnamed forest. They'd made it an hour before sundown. There were no goodbyes with her friends, no crying or asking if there was another way.

She didn't see Thane again before leaving.

Not a word had been exchanged between her and Hel since he saved her. Her bags were slung across her body. He carried nothing but the clothes on his back.

"Isn't Varlett coming?"

"No. She's going to help War."

Layala glanced back toward the direction of the castle. It was not even close to seeing distance and the thick gnarled trees would have blocked any view anyway. She wanted to protest, what if she hurts him? What if she is the one who tried to kill him and not the demon, but she clamped her mouth shut.

"Where are we going?" she finally asked. *Not the Void.* It dawned on her that he brought them here with his magic but if they were using a portal, it meant they must be going further than he was capable of taking them.

"To Ryvengaard."

THANE

THE DOOR CREAKED on its hinges. Thane stepped inside his room with his palm flat against his chest as if the pressure could ease the ache. Head pressed back against the wall, he shut his eyes and took deep breaths. She was gone. He sent her away. He sent the one he'd loved for millennia away with her—mate. Nausea burned the back of his throat.

"You truly are a fool." Varlett rose up from the chair in the corner of his room. The red liquid in her wine glass swirled as she stepped. "How could you let them leave together?"

The pain he'd nearly given himself over to vanished, replaced by a mask of placid. "I told them to go."

"I know." She stopped and popped out her hip, bringing the lip of her glass to her mouth. "Are you holding out hope she'll come back and still choose you?"

"Look, if you're not going to help then leave."

"And let the only thing that might possibly stand between them die? Besides, if you die, Hel will blame me. And as much as he says he doesn't care about you, he does."

"Why do *you* care so much?"

"If it isn't obvious then you're an even bigger fool than I thought."

Thane clenched his teeth. "He will choose her over you every single time. Who's the fool now?"

Her hand flashed out to strike him and he caught her wrist. "If you ever attempt to hit me again, I'll snap your neck." He shoved her into his dresser, rattling the candle sticks and other various items on top. "I am not the clueless elf I was six months ago. I am the god of war."

Varlett shrunk away from him, leaning farther onto the dresser but a smile slowly crept at the corners of her mouth. "Welcome back, War."

CHAPTER 33

LAYALA

L ayala was numb. The muted chatter, clinking drinks, and raunchy comments barely registered. The dim lighting coming from the candlesticks hanging from cheap metal chandeliers at least made her feel like she could sink into the shadows. This place was completely different and exactly the same as every other pub she'd ever been to. The patrons had horns and membranous wings and scales, or fuzzy cat ears and markings on their skin. There was even a male with golden feathers along the back of his neck that went under his collar. At another time she might marvel at the many new races and languages she heard but she didn't feel anything. She heard Thane's words, telling her to leave, that it was over, but it almost felt like a dream, one she was still trapped in. Gripping the metal handle of her mug, she closed her eyes then took a drink of ale. After only a few sips, it made her feel warm and fuzzy.

The walk here from the portal wasn't more than fifteen

minutes. She'd been in such a haze she didn't even remember what anything looked like outside, and it was dark anyway.

A giant of a male, a dragon shifter by the horns and talons, slid into the booth opposite her. She inspected him only for a moment to assess a threat but by the time she looked away she couldn't even tell someone what his hair color was if they asked. He said something completely foreign; words that rolled and others that sounded clicky.

Her heart was broken and left in another world. She didn't feel like talking until his talon slid across the topside of her wrist. "Don't touch me."

"Ah, Murlian tongue. No wonder you looked confused. How long have you been in Torp?"

"Is that the town we're in?"

He cocked his dark-haired head to the side. A massive scar ran the length of his forehead, down the side around his eyebrow and the bottom of his jaw. "Yes."

"About ten minutes then."

"You're an elf." He tapped his talons on the wooden planked tabletop and leaned a little closer, inhaling. "And a mage." He inhaled again, deeper this time. "Maybe even something more. Rare in Ryvengaard."

Layala took a long drink of the ale. "Yep."

"Come play a game with us. Let me and some friends show you our hospitality."

Hel told her to wait here. That he'd be right back. And she wasn't up for games anyway. "I'm good where I'm at."

"We'll bring the game to you then." He waved a hand and the group from three tables over stood. All five dragon shifters, at least seven feet tall, rugged looking with scars and unruly facial hair.

Layala groaned. She'd been in Ryvengaard all of twenty

minutes and already she had to deal with the local riffraff. One slid into the booth beside her, another next to his friend and the other two pulled up chairs at the end of the table. They smelled like booze, smoke, and trouble.

The shifter beside her took the pipe from his mouth and a bitter stench rippled out of his mouth as he spoke, "You alone?"

"I get it." Layala shifted away from him, resting her hand on the dagger at her hip. "I'm a beautiful girl, alone, much smaller than you lot. An easy target. But trust me, this isn't going to play out like you think."

"You hear that, boys? She ain't an easy target."

They all chuckled and Layala rolled her eyes. All she wanted was to be left alone. To drown in self-pity, was that too much to ask for? She wanted to finish this mug of ale in silence until she didn't think of Thane anymore.

"We don't want to hurt you, doll," said the shifter who first approached. "We just want to get to know the new girl and play a game as I said. Truth or dare?"

"Dare," Layala said, meeting his reptilian-like stare. Did heartbreak make one reckless? Or was this alcohol stronger than she anticipated? She glanced down in the mug to find she hadn't even drunk half of it.

The group laughed again. "She's feisty."

The shifter smiled. "Alright, dare. I dare you to go outside and find a rocktailed wyvern. Don't worry, they're little buggers, but do have a nasty bite. You're capable, right? If it's too much, we'll let you switch to truth."

He was goading her, and she knew it, but she was still about to take the dare. At least it would let her escape these assholes.

A smooth as velvet voice said, "Oh, boys." Hel tsked his tongue. "You picked the wrong target."

"Who are you?" the scarred leader asked.

"I'm the monster your mother warned you about. The reason you're afraid of the dark."

The group of them laughed, except the leader. He clenched his fists on the tabletop, assessed Hel from head to toe. "That so?"

"Most definitely."

"You don't look like much to me, elf."

"But you sense it, don't you? That I could end you with a snap of my fingers. And if I was a better person, I'd give you a chance to walk away, but seeing as I'm not..." He smiled. With a flick of his wrist five of their heads snapped hard to one side with a sick *crack*. All five bodies slumped forward, to the side or out of their chairs. The silverware and drinks rattled with the impact. Layala slowly poked the shoulder of the shifter beside her with his face smashed against the table. His pipe still burned from the side of his mouth, the embers sizzling the skin of his cheek. They were dead.

Except for the leader across from her. Hel's expression was wolfish. "*You* don't get off that easy." He dragged him out of the booth with ease that didn't seem possible given the dragon shifter's size. With the leader on his back, Hel stepped on his throat. He gripped his thumb and bent it back. "You can't shift, can you? Can't move. I bet you're terrified."

Someone at the next table stood and shouted, "What's going on over there?" And pointed angrily their way.

Hel glanced over his shoulder. "Stay where you are. All of you, or every single person in the room is dead."

No one got up, or even did more than sit there and blink. She wasn't sure if it was because of his gift of persuasion or if they were scared he'd make good on his threat.

A bright red serpent appeared around Hel's shoulders and

slithered down his arm, its tongue flicking out on the way until it made its way to the dragon and coiled around his neck. His eyes were wide with terror, his body frozen, as the snake opened its mouth, bearing huge dripping fangs and sunk them into the dragon shifter's neck.

Hel dropped his hold on him and reached his hand across the table to Layala. "Come on. Let's go."

The dragon shifter on the ground began to convulse and white foam dribbled out of his mouth and then he stopped moving, and the snake vanished.

Layala grasped Hel's hand and in a flash they appeared outside in the middle of the deserted dirt roadway. Pulling away, she said, "That was... Terrifying and simultaneously one of the most interesting things I've ever seen. But you murdered six people." She wasn't as horrified as she might have been even a day ago. In fact, she didn't care at all. Those men wanted to hurt her.

"More of an execution rather."

"They really didn't do anything except talk to me."

"In the book of Hel, that makes it justifiable."

"You're barbaric. You do know that."

"And you're not surprised, or at least, you shouldn't be." He started walking and she fell into step beside him. "Besides, they were mercenaries. You know what they deal in?"

"No."

"The barter and trade of poor girls like you. They spotted someone worth a lot of coin, and I don't even want to begin to imagine what they might have done to you if given the chance. I thought I showed restraint, actually. I could have been much more brutal, and took my time with each of them, but then I probably would have had to kill everyone in that bar, and there'd be no one left to serve us ale later. Gods forbid I'd have to pour myself a drink or make my own meal."

"Was that snake... real?"

"As real as anything else."

"What would have been more brutal?"

"Love, you know a quick death is the easy way. I could have nailed them to the wall by their wings, then cut off those wings, used magic to make them suffer with an immense amount of pain, and then sliced into a very important artery that would make them bleed out but slowly."

Layala simply nodded and stared ahead.

"No gasp? No, 'Hel, that is terrible'?"

Layala only thought about the mug of half-full ale she left behind. Pity. Her head already swam from it. Her legs even felt watery.

"Anyway, the bartender told me what those dragons did for a living. He also said that your old estate is only about an hour's walk from here. I couldn't remember its exact location. It's been two thousand years. I wasn't even sure it still stood."

Layala perked up at that, lifting her chin up toward him. "*My* old estate?"

"Well, yours and War's old Manor estate."

"Why would you bring us there? Wouldn't it be... awkward?"

"As opposed to watching you and him together in person for the last several weeks?"

"Maybe if you told me what it is I need to remember, I'll remember, and we can go back."

"You won't."

"How do you know?"

"What happened after the Cliffs of Amonlee? Where did we

get married? Can you levitate? Can you turn to shadow? Do you know the name of your sister and who she was?"

Layala stalled, putting a hand to the side of her head as if it would help her think. "I had a sister?"

"My point exactly," he said over his shoulder, never stopping his pace.

She hurried to catch up to him. "I know what happened after the cliffs."

"Why don't you tell me on the way then."

The Past

Valeen paced back and forth on the balcony outside her chambers. Three days before, Hel left her standing on the cliffside, leaving things more confusing between them than before she met him there. She knew it was foolish, wrong. She should have never opened this door. She should have left it latched, locked, and barricaded.

Now she couldn't stop thinking about him. Every moment of her day drifted to his last words, "You're afraid," and she was. She didn't believe she feared anything anymore, not death, not the loss of anyone or anything, but she was terrified of Hel.

She couldn't live life like this. She must confront him and put a closure to whatever she'd opened up. It was simply the unknown, the "what ifs" that ate away at her.

She'd end it.

Tonight.

Pulled by her winged horses, they flew through the darkened sky and across the border of her territory into Hel's where it was also night. If he had sentries in the trees below they didn't attack or sound an alarm. The lights of small towns and large cities glittered below in patches surrounded by trees of green and others with maroon and red leaves. It had been so long since she'd ventured this way, she forgot about the colors.

A castle built on top of a rocky hill a thousand feet from the ground level, was only accessible by the winding road up the side of it or flying. A thick fog surrounded its base, and seemed to grow thicker the closer she drew. With a tug, the horses took a downturn and glided over the wall and onto the stone courtyard. The guards didn't move from their posts. And there were several other carriages, some pulled by horses, others small wyverns, or hippogriffs.

She tossed the reins and hopped out, boots clacking with each step up to the front doors. This is a bad idea, she chanted with each breath. The two guards on either side of the front entrance bowed.

"Goddess," they said at once then quickly pulled open the heavy black double doors.

Music trickled out, soft and sensual with string instruments and deep, slow drums. Female laughter came from somewhere nearby. Valeen took a deep breath. She was dropping in on a party she wasn't invited to. She shook her head and turned around. It was stupid coming here.

"You're welcome to go inside, goddess," the guard to the right said, gesturing with his hand. "Zaurahel said you might come and to tell you he's in the grand ballroom."

There was no way he could know she was coming. She hadn't decided until an hour ago. But now she couldn't turn back. They'd tell him she came and left, and that made her appear weak.

"Thank you." She pushed her shoulders back and strutted inside past two thick, smoky black pillars, exotic potted ferns, and a pair of giggling girls, who appeared to be telling secrets. Their clothes were —minuscule. Scraps of fabric covered their breasts and round behinds.

She came to the top of a long set of stairs that led down into what she guessed was the grand ballroom. Couples danced in seductive *ways, grinding on each other, kissing, groping. It smelled like sweat and alcohol.*

Hel sat on a throne on a dais above the main floor but not nearly as high up as she now stood. With a beautiful maiden on each arm of his chair, both turned toward him. One curled her fingers around a lock of his thick dark hair. The other threw her head back laughing at something he said. His hands rested on both of their behinds.

Valeen's face flushed and something dark and dangerous deep inside wanted to go down there and rip both of the girls off his throne. She clenched her teeth—she'd never felt murderous toward random strangers. What was wrong with her? Why had she come here? She'd never been to a party like this. She didn't allow this sort of behavior in her home. It wasn't proper to act this way in public. This mark on her arm couldn't fate her to be with him in any way. It was a mistake. A dreadful mistake and so was coming here.

He finally looked up and they stared at each other from a distance. He had to be fifty yards away, but she swore she heard his heart stutter. He pushed through the two girls and got up, moving through the crowd, never taking his eyes off her. Valeen turned and hurried for the exit. She was a coward, but she felt more like a fool than anything. He didn't want anything from her but what his uncle did.

The guards opened the doors for her again, letting in the cool night breeze. She took the stairs two at a time and just as she reached the final step next to her waiting chariot, he appeared in front of her.

"Hello."

She halted before bumping into him.

"Do you often make a quick appearance at parties like that? Pop in for a flash and leave them wanting more?"

"I didn't think you'd be having a party. It's rude of me to intrude."

"Come back inside."

She held up her palm. "I'll go. I don't want to take you away from your... friends."

"We can stay out here if you'd rather. You came to see me, not them."

With her lips pressed together she nervously pawed at the ends of her hair. She came to put an end to whatever it was that they started but she was embarrassed now that he stood here before her. They hadn't started anything. It was one meetup. They didn't even kiss. So, what if they bore the same lily mark. He had a hundred ladies in there at his beck and call and she was certain he'd done much more than kiss at least some of them.

"I came to say—what I wanted to say is..." she chewed her bottom lip trying to find the right words. "I harbor no hard feelings and—"

"I can't stop thinking about you." He moved a step closer. "You're all I think about. I can't even sleep."

Her eyes widened and swallowed to wet her suddenly dry throat. "Oh." Gods above, could I be any more inane? "Oh!" she thought.

"All I've thought about is the kiss I never got. And the way you smile, and that purple swimsuit," his hands slid on either side of her face, inching into her hair, "and maybe if I just got one kiss my need for it would be fulfilled."

His touch was warm and intoxicating. "You'd want more." His need was oddly satisfying. She'd been told Hel never kissed on the mouth. Rumor was he found it too personal, more than just a need to satiate lust.

He smiled. "I think I would. Maybe we shouldn't." He dropped his hands to his sides and sucked in a sharp breath then let it out slowly.

"We definitely shouldn't."

"Nope." He tucked his hands in his pockets.

On a wild impulse, Valeen fell forward from the last step and *wrapped her arms around his neck. When their lips collided, his hands came free and gripped her waist, lifting her onto the edge of her chariot. They kissed and kissed, hands tangled in hair, tongues dancing tentatively. She felt like she was falling into an endless abyss that was him and she'd never escape. To take a breath, she pulled away and put her fingers to his mouth. "There, my debt is paid. I promised you a kiss in the water. But only one."*

His bright blue-green eyes flicked back and forth between hers. "Only one."

"I'm going to go now." She sounded as if she was talking herself into it.

"Alright." He carefully pulled his hands away as if it was a fight to do so.

She swung her legs around, dropped into her chariot and picked up the reins. After a moment she cleared her throat. "Well, goodbye then."

He grinned. His fingers gripped the side of her chariot as he leaned in. "I want more."

She laughed. "I told you you would."

"And then you said we shouldn't, but you kissed me, love. You changed everything in one decision. You should have left."

"I made my move. The next is yours then."

The horses tossed their heads impatiently and began pawing at the stone and they lurched forward. Hel started walking alongside the moving chariot. "Leave a way for me to get in."

She smiled and tapped the reins against the horses' backs, and they spread their wings. "A way through the wall has been open for you since the first time you came."

NIGHT CRITTERS CHIRPED and croaked in the shadows, and the pale light of two moons guided them out onto a path leaving behind the small town whose main street consisted of a pub, a post office, and an apothecary. Her body felt fuzzy and warm after thinking about that memory. She briefly touched her lips... Or was it the ale?

Layala promised to tell him about it, so she turned that intimate moment between them into as short of terms as possible, "Well, I came to your castle. You had a party. I was disgusted by the crude behavior, so I left. And then you chased after me, of course." Hel let out a "ha" and rolled his eyes. "And then I... kissed you. Maker above, it *was* me that kissed you first. But completely different from what you described. There was no 'big boy' nicknames or dick grabbing."

"Did you just say 'dick'?" His eyebrow raised. "Val, I'm shocked at your filthy mouth."

"Shut up," she drawled. "Besides, Valeen might have been a bit of a prude, but I'm not—as much. Cock is still hard for me to say aloud."

"*Valeen*," he drew her name out, "you naughty vixen."

"I think I'm drunk." The ground did appear to wobble. "I can't believe Thane ended our relationship. How could he?"

"You had half a pint of ale. It's the travel between realms." He grabbed around her bicep to steady her steps. She took note of his ignoring her comment about Thane. "And you don't need to refer to yourself in the third person. You don't have a split personality."

"Alright, I was a bit of a prude back then but now I'm not. Better?"

"You certainly lost those prudish behaviors over time. Wild cat in the sack."

Layala pulled away from him and smacked his arm. "Stop it."

He laughed. "What?"

"You know, for someone who claims not to care, you keep asking me to remember a certain kind of time spent together." She booped his nose with the tip of her finger. "Did I just boop your nose?" She cringed at herself and began to sway off the path into the tall golden grass.

He grabbed her arm again, tugging her close to his side. "Yeah, you did. And I bring up those times because it makes you squirm, and blush, and I know it will get under War's skin."

"Whatever. Are we almost there? I'm tired of walking. My legs are even tired of walking." She laid her head on his shoulder and felt his muscles stiffen up. "Maybe you can carry me. You're strong enough, right? You look strong enough."

"Plenty. But you can walk."

"Thane would, but he broke up with me so..."

"I was there, love."

"You smell nice."

"So do you," he murmured.

"You're a little bit beautiful."

"Just a little bit, huh?" He chuckled, and that was beautiful too.

"A lot of beautiful?" She tapped her chin with a finger. "That sounds strange. I think just beautiful. I can see why I fell for you the first time. And back then you weren't such a jerk."

"Yes I was, but not to you."

She abruptly lifted her head. "Why walk when we can fly?" Grinning, she stepped in front of him and placed both hands on his chest. "I want to see your wings again."

"There are massive things flying around here. Like dragon shifters, wyverns, and insects as big as you and me. Even the birds here are huge. It's better to stay low." He took her hands off his chest but kept hold of one and started forward. He glanced over his shoulder, checking the road behind them.

A pebble caught her toe, and she stumbled off balance and the only thing that kept her from falling was Hel's grip. She started laughing and said, "Can we go back and get more of that dragon ale?"

"Shhh." Hel held a finger to his lips. "You might as well be screaming 'Come and get dinner'."

"Oh, and I make a delicious snack." She lifted her shoulder to her chin and grinned at him then giggled, putting her hand to her mouth.

He deadpanned.

"But it's dragon tongue you want all over you now. I hope that bitch is jealous you and I are here together."

"Maybe the ale is stronger than I thought." He walked even faster, tugged harder on her wrist.

"What do you mean? I'm fine. Sober as a sailor." She brought her hand to her brow and saluted.

"That you are."

She looked up at him. "Maker, you two look so much alike. The same bloody beautiful mouth, and dark hair and just," she waved her hand in front of his face, "this. Different but similar. Why is that?"

"We're related. Obviously."

"But cousins don't usually look like brothers."

"Our parents were twins. We took after them."

"Really? Was it hard to tell them apart?"

He looked down at her like she was absolutely ridiculous. Maybe she was. "My mother and his father, oh yes, so difficult."

"I didn't know they weren't identical; you just said twins. Why are you being an ass? Never mind, don't answer that." She nibbled on her lower lip. "I hope Thane is jealous, too. How could he break up with me? After everything we went through. After he promised forever. He gave me his virginity. He waited for me. He killed his own father for me."

"I'm really not the shoulder to cry on, love. Besides, War was far from a virgin when he met you. Maybe in this life but certainly not before."

She considered that for a moment then went on. "How is it that if you and I are mates, he and I could, you know, do that and he does not die?"

"I implemented the infidelity clause in the mate bond I created. It doesn't come with ours."

"Bet that pisses you off."

He gripped her wrist tighter and pulled her to a stop, jerking her close—inches away. "I have been patient with you given the situation, but if you don't stop talking, you're going to see the side of me you don't like."

She smiled and ran her thumb over his lips. "Who said I didn't like?" She leaned in closer, felt the wisps of his hair brush her nose as she whispered in his ear. "I find your dark side sexy." Her fingers trailed along the side of his neck. "It might be the sexiest thing about you besides the dimple on your cheek."

She heard his heart beat faster; the slither of his magic enveloped her, thick and wanting. His hand was at her throat, his thumb, gently caressing her flesh up to her chin. "You're lucky I feel like being a gentleman tonight because I think your broken heart would give me anything I want, but I won't be your mistake, Valeen. If I'm ever going to have you again it will be when you realize that I'm the only thing you ever truly wanted, when your body begs for my touch, and you ask for more."

The ground suddenly rumbled with what felt and sounded

like something colossal landing. Hel's arm wrapped around her waist and a hand clamped over her mouth and they tumbled into the tall grass. *Don't make a sound,* he whispered to her mind.

He kept his hand over her mouth. His body was fully on top of her front, heavy and solid. A low grumble and stomps shook the ground. Layala tried to turn her head to see what it was, but the swaying grass blocked everything but the sky.

What is it? she asked silently.

A dragon. Fully shifted.

I can take down a dragon.

In this state, no, you can't.

Can't you just snap your fingers? Boom. Dead.

Full-shifted dragons are not that easy to kill.

Layala peeled his fingers away from her mouth. *Can't you snappity snap his neck?*

No. Stop asking questions.

His weight seemed to grow heavier the longer they lay there. And he was pressing down on her bladder. *Is it gone yet? I have to pee.*

He dropped his chin and glared down at her. *Are you five when you're drunk? Hold it.*

The sound of massive nostrils sniffing the air made Layala stiffen up and grip Hel tighter.

What happened to the poofing? Poof us!

My memory of the exact location is a little fuzzy.

"I smell you rats. Come out," said the deep rough voice of the dragon. "No one kills six dragons on Ryvengaard and gets to walk away." The stomping footfalls came closer. The snout came into view, blocking out the stars.

Get us out of here!

He can't see us.

He can step on us!

A giant paw lifted above them, Layala screamed, and everything went dark until a few seconds later her back was pressed up against a wall and Hel was flat on her front. There was no dragon. All around them was tall golden grass that reached her hips, and sparse trees on rolling hills that seemed to shimmer in the silver moonlight.

Hel looked up. "Well, we made it."

Layala pushed him off her. "You waited until we were about to get squished."

"I'm a bit disoriented from the realm switch, as well. At least I got us here."

The beige wall was at least seventy feet high, though bits of it crumbled and chunks of it were gouged. A massive hole she could easily get through was to the left. She slipped inside the wall and found an aged, but still standing manor.

Hel walked past her. "Let's go inside and see if it's livable."

She watched his back, the stealthy way he moved. The pale light from the moons shone down on him, bathing him in silver. That dragon encounter sobered her up quickly and she couldn't get her feet to move. She ran her hands down her face. *"I find your dark side sexy?" I'm so embarrassed. I could sit down and die right here.*

Hel glanced back with a smirk. "I won't forget it either."

CHAPTER 34

LAYALA

T he doors to the manor creaked as Hel pushed them
inward. With no overgrowth around the entry like on
other parts of the three-story house, or giant holes in
the walls, someone had to maintain the place. In fact, considering how old this place was, it was a miracle it even stood
at all.

A candelabra with six candles flickered to life on the entry
table to the right. Layala ran her finger over the surface of the
round table, leaving a streak in several years' worth of dust. Up
above in the high-domed ceiling was a tall crystal chandelier
with chunks hanging down or missing completely. Hel's gait
was silent as a ghost while he moved to peer around the corner
leading into another room.

Moving light came through an archway further ahead and
then a figure appeared. Male, tall, unkempt shoulder-length
light hair, wearing a night robe with fur trim. He might have

been a dragon or a different kind of shifter, but she couldn't distinguish any features to tell.

All three went silent as a staring match ensued.

"Valeen," the stranger finally said, adjusting his round golden glasses. "It's you." He dropped to a knee and bowed his head, setting the single burning candle he held on the floor beside him. "My Queen."

"Who are you?" Layala went to step around Hel, but his arm shot out blocking her.

"Prove to me it's you, Presco, before I tear your head off."

The male lifted his head. "You once promised me if I ever looked at Valeen's ass again, you'd, and I quote, 'tear my skull from my spine and set it on a pike and once it dried you'd use it as decor in your office'. Guess things never change do they?"

Hel slowly smirked. "It is you, you old bastard. You look good for your age. You could use a comb, however."

Layala glanced back and forth between the two. "What am I missing?"

"This is Presco, your old right hand. You're too-smart-for-his-own-good dragon scholar." Hel crossed his arms. "Have you been here this entire time?"

He stood up, bringing the candle with him. "Off and on to attempt to keep this place from falling into ruin. Valeen always said she'd come back one day. Then a couple days ago the goddess of wisdom sent me a message to come and wait here. She didn't say why but now I know." He started for a room off the hall and waved for them to follow.

Soon Layala sat in a dusty blue armchair with her hands folded on her lap. Presco lit more candles on the fireplace mantel and on various side tables, and found a seat across from her. "Good gods, it's been what, two thousand years and you both look exactly the same except you're elven. If the council knew you were here..."

Hel plopped down in the seat beside Layala, letting loose a puff of dust. "They knew we were in Adalon and killed us two other times after our initial exile. Hence why we are here now. Valeen needs to... train. By the way, she prefers to be called Layala now."

Presco stared at Layala for an uncomfortable amount of time. "I apologize for gawking; it is surreal seeing you again after such a long time."

It suddenly hit Layala she'd seen him before in her dream. He was the one who'd told her that her lily mark was a mate bond. He looked older, more rugged with less boyish charm, but he still held onto youth even if he had a few lines around his eyes and forehead now.

"So Layala," he said as if tasting each syllable. "You don't remember me. You don't remember who you are, do you?"

"Yet," Hel said, crossing his ankle over the top of his thigh. "It's complicated."

"I remember some things," Layala answered. "Not much, I'm afraid. But I've been informed of the major details like I'm supposedly a primordial goddess and he was once my husband."

Presco pushed his glasses higher on his nose. "Supposedly?"

"Like I said, it's complicated." Hel tapped his fingertips together, watching Presco with a predatory cognizance. He didn't trust him. Layala could see it. "Why aren't you surprised to see us together? The last time we saw you, we were at war."

Presco lifted a shoulder. "Well, Zaurahel it's not surprising to me in the least that you two would end up together again given the nature of your relationship."

"We're not together," both Layala and Hel said at once. Layala tucked her hair behind her ear and avoided looking over at Hel, though she felt the heat of his gaze on her.

The dragon scholar's eyes flicked back and forth between them. "At least you're not enemies anymore?"

"We're—reluctant allies with a common enemy," Hel offered.

Presco raised his eyebrows and slowly nodded. "Uh huh. Alright, well, where is War?"

"Thane is back in Adalon. We were going to get married until..." Layala trailed off and stood up. "I'm going to take a look around and see if anything jogs my memory. Is there a room I can stay in?"

Presco stood, holding his hand over his abdomen, a gesture of ceremony. "Certainly, Valeen, this was partly your house. Your room was upstairs, first door on the right. I brought fresh bedding for all the rooms."

"Thank you." She quickly left and found the stairs. They creaked as she headed up the spiral. She avoided touching the railing due to the cracking paint and dust.

"War is now Thane?" Presco questioned. "And a wedding?"

Hel's voice followed her up the stairs. "How about I give a quick version of the last two thousand years."

Layala came to the top of the stairs and paused before the first door on the right, left open a crack. The white paint peeled and chipped; the gold handle was round and partially rusted. She pushed it open, and a memory flashed.

"What is she doing here?" a familiar female voice hissed.

"She asked," War replied. His voice was one she knew all too well.

393

"So, you are at her beck and call? She is your cousin's wife! She's his problem, not yours."

She stood at the top of the stairs, listening to them argue with a single bag in hand.

"I know who she is," War snapped.

"This will cause a war. And not just between the gods. You rule Ryvengaard. You'll drag my father and the dragons into this. Take her back now."

"This isn't up for discussion." His boots stomped closer.

Valeen darted inside the room and gently shut the door.

"How dare you disrespect me like this. I am your betrothed and you bring the goddess I know you're in love with into this house? I'm just someone you like to screw. But her? That devious bitch has had both of you in her grips for years."

Her heart thundered.

Something crashed and glass shattered on the floor.

"Yes, throw a tantrum, why don't you, because you know I love that. And if you believe I'm in love with her then why are you still here, Varlett?"

LAYALA SNAPPED out of the memory. Varlett? Her stomach dropped. Varlett was War's betrothed. And they left them back in Adalon together. *This is why Varlett despises me. But how did she end up with Hel? Two scorned lovers joined forces?* She shook her head, trying to recall more. *What happened next? Why was I there in the first place?* Nothing came.

Starting around the room, she picked up a black winged horse statue about the size of her palm and wiped dust from its back. A second was on the vanity top. These were her horses, the pair that pulled her chariot, Starborn and... *Midnight.* Maker above, had Thane known that when he named her horse in Adalon? Some part of him must have. It couldn't be a coincidence.

She set the horse statue down. *I must remember him. I have to get back to him. Even if he said he wanted me to go away, that we were over, he didn't mean it, not really.* Still a little woozy from either the realm change, or the ale, Layala took off her weapons belt and sword and set them on the dresser top. Then meandered to the full bed pushed up against the far wall and flopped down on it. Without kicking off her boots, she picked up the throw blanket beside her and curled up in it.

She cried herself to sleep.

"I'M ASSUMING VARLETT LEFT?" she asked, setting down the white teacup. She and War sat at opposite ends of the dining room table with a healthy spread of fruits between them.

"She did." He cleared his throat. "Are you going to tell me what happened?"

"I don't want to talk about it yet."

"He's going to come here."

"I know."

"What do you want me to do when he does?"

"Tell him to go away. Tell him I don't want to see him ever again."

War looked down at his plate, tapping his fingers beside it. "You need to give me a reason if I'm going to do that. I can see you're hurt but you know what he is to me. You're putting me in a bad position."

The scenery of the dream shifted to a dark bedroom. It was night, a different place entirely.

A different time.

Floorboards creaked and her eyes shot open. Pulling a golden dagger from under her pillow, she whipped around, the point of the blade stopped at Hel's throat. "What are you doing here?" she snarled.

He held up his palms in surrender. "I came to sneak you out." She lowered the dagger and sat up. His gaze trailed over her bare shoulders along her close-fitting, silk night dress the color of crimson. It barely covered the tops of her thighs. "Well, damn, love. I wasn't ready to see you in that. It makes me think of what you'll wear on the night I make love to you."

She chuckled and shook her head. "You're confident, a little too confident, I think."

"Is red your favorite color, too?"

"One of them but I prefer purple."

He grinned. "After that purple swimsuit you wore, I think it's mine now, too."

She rolled her eyes and stood, going to her closet. "What do you mean sneak me out?"

"Break you out of your territory for some fun. You told me the next move was mine. This is my move."

She smiled, rifling through her hanging clothes. "I can leave whenever I want, you know."

He grabbed her wrist and snapped his fingers. She was suddenly in a tight-fitting black dress with thin straps and deep red whirls so dark they were barely noticeable. "It's much more fun if we pretend like you might get caught. I think Presco would be upset if you left without telling him."

"He'd worry."

Hel tugged her toward the open window that he must have come in from and said "Ready?" and they jumped.

Another jarring shift brought them stepping out of a portal to a large bonfire, drums and tambourines beating. Half-shifted dragons with wings protruding out of their backs danced and talked in gathered groups. There must be a hundred or more. She'd never seen so *many in one place before. A boar the size of a horse roasted over a smaller fire and the smell made her mouth water.*

She tugged her hand back from him and cleared her throat.

"You don't like me holding your hand?"

She half smiled. "There are people watching us."

"So can I grab your ass?" he said with a wink.

Her eyes widened and then she started laughing. "You're quite the tease, aren't you?"

War stepped away from a group with a golden goblet in hand, moving their way. "We're crashing War's party?" she asked.

"It's not exactly crashing when I was invited."

"He looks surprised."

"To see you."

Hel slipped his arm around her waist and tugged her flush to his side. "Dragons know how to party and so does War. If your last very formal event was any indication of how you've spent the last thousand years cooped up in your territory, you need this night."

Her heart fluttered at the warmth of his hand on her waist. "What's wrong with my parties?"

"Nothing, they're just formal. Proper. Too much talking and not enough inappropriate dancing." They strolled right by War. "We'll chat in a minute!" Hel shouted to him over the music.

War laughed and raised a glass to them.

With his hands on her hips, he slowly pushed them side to side. A flush worked its way up her neck, but she didn't stop him. Rather she began to sway with him and the music. She put her hands on his shoulders, and he smiled. The music was upbeat, the group of dragons started singing and moving their feet in unison, Hel did too.

"I don't know this dance!" she shouted over the music.

"Me either. Just go with it." He spun her around and dipped her low then brought her back up so fast her hair flung forward, half wrapping around him. She laughed and they circled and stepped.

His hands moved over her hot skin, daring on the edge of inappropriate but he never went too low, though his thumbs scraped under her breasts, and it caught her by surprise at how much she liked it. She threw her head back, looking up at the stars as they swayed with her. The two moons filled her with energy, with vigor, making her skin subtly luminate. She hadn't let herself feel so free like this in longer than she could remember. Her powers tingled along her body, a high of its own.

Hel's fingertips pressed into her upper back. She tilted her chin down, grinning. "This is wonderful. Thank you."

"You look good letting go. Beautiful. The most beautiful thing in the realms." His hands slid down to her ass, and gripped her, lifting her. She gasped at first then pulled herself closer, their lips a breath from touching. As if he couldn't take the temptation any longer, he kissed her. He was water and she was a desert that craved it. Her thighs wrapped around his hips, her hands caressed his face, tangled in his hair as their lips moved.

He held her against him with ease, with surety. Possessive.

His lips trailed down her throat, over her collarbone, and she curled tighter around him. Tilting his chin back up she kissed him, sliding her tongue between his teeth.

She finally pulled away and slid down his body. The funny thing was at the moment she didn't care if anyone saw them. If she was back in her territory, she'd be mortified. She never acted this way with anyone, and it wasn't wine or drugs that made her feel this way, but him.

He pushed his fingers into her hair and caressed her cheek with his thumb. "I think you might be my undoing."

The way he looked at her, like she was the only thing that mattered made her heart lurch. The way she suddenly cared about him made her nervous. The way her mind began to wonder if he'd taken any of those girls to bed that night at his party burned her with jealousy. It was too fast, too soon.

She said, "We should go say hello to the host."

"Alright." He slipped his hand in hers, intertwining their fingers and they made their way over to War. "Hello, cousin."

War tipped his goblet back and held out his other hand. They pulled each other in for a brief embrace and then he turned to her. "I did not expect to see you here."

"Hel is persuasive."

"I know," War said with a laugh. "I think he could talk anyone into just about anything."

"Is that so?" she said, raising an eyebrow at Hel. "Then I should be careful?"

"Most definitely," Hel purred and nipped her earlobe. "Very careful. I'm the bad guy."

Goosebumps rose all across her skin. "I'll make you yearn to do naughty things. I'll make you want to bring down those walls and call me things you never even thought of with anyone else like—'mine'. We'll get lost in other realms doing questionable acts like grinding at a party with dragons." He flicked a gold coin into the air. "And stealing their gold." He pressed it into her palm. "Something to remember this night."

Flushed and heart pounding, she closed her fingers around it. She didn't know what to say in response, so she looked at War. "Do you like it here in Ryvengaard?"

Hel let out a deep belly laugh, pulled his arm from her and brought a civar to his lips. "I say all that and you ignore it and ask War a question. I think I like you."

War smiled down at her. "He does like you. There's no thinking about it."

"I never could have guessed. You stole Soulender, one of the only weapons that can kill you just to lure me out so you could see me."

"When you put it that way it sounds a bit psychotic," Hel said, then blew out a puff of smoke.

"Then you let me get away with murder. So yes, I think it's safe to say you like me."

"Alright, don't rub it in. Or you'll figure out you've got me wrapped around your finger already and that would ruin my reputation." He ran his thumb over the lily mark on her shoulder. "I'm not supposed to like anyone. Except for War and my aunt. They were the only exceptions to the rule."

"You two grew up together, correct?"

War nodded. "Remember that time we snuck into Synick's wine stash for the party after our tutors? And he caught us on the way out, broke both bottles over our heads then made us drink until we threw up?"

"Ah yes, good times. Nothing like an ass whippin' to reminisce on. I still can't drink that flavor of wine."

"Were you closer with Balneir or Synick?"

"Balneir," War said. "My father was the one who taught us all the important things. Synick taught us to be tough, and how to fight but my father taught us how to care. And my mother taught us how to love."

"She is the goddess of love so I wouldn't expect anything else," she said with a smile. "I always liked her."

Hel looked toward the bonfire. There was a sadness in the depths of his eyes.

"And what happened to your mother?" she asked. "I haven't heard anything about her in a long time."

Hel forced a smile. "Don't know."

"I don't mean to be rude but in my research I never could find who your father is."

He took a long pull of his civar. "You're guess is as good as mine. She left me on War's parents' doorstep when I was a baby, and no *one has seen or heard from her since. I guess she figured her twin brother would take in her mistake."*

Her mistake... ouch. How could he think of himself that way? War and Valeen exchanged a look. War gave a slight shake of his head, a warning not to keep going down this path.

"I think even if she couldn't take care of you, you are her greatest blessing."

He huffed but gave her a half smile. "You're an optimist."

"Not always. Will you dance with me again?"

He tossed his civar and swept her up in his arms, getting a giggle out of her. "I thought you'd never ask, love."

LAYALA SAT UP IN BED, blinking away the intensity of her dream and tried to adjust to the bright light filling the room. She pressed her hand over her chest; her heart pounded beneath her palm. Holy Maker, she'd accused Hel of having mother issues, saying that if his mother didn't love him who else could, and she's said it to be mean, but she didn't know when she said it that it was true. Now she felt horrible. And kissing him, feeling the heat of his hard body pressed to hers, swaying with her, her body was warm and tingly all over even now.

How had he changed so much? How could his story be that War tricked her into leaving, and her memory be that he did something to make her leave? How had things gone wrong?

No. I can't let the past get to me. I can't feel things for Hel.

Thane. What is Thane doing now?

She threw herself back on the bed and draped her arm over her eyes, blocking out the sun shining in through her window. No, she couldn't think about him either. She'd start to cry again. She had to get up and do something, distract herself.

A knock startled her. "Yes?"

"I'm going out. I'll be back soon," Hel said from the hall.

Layala flew out of bed and practically dove for the door. She jerked it open. "Where are you going?" He was the perfect distraction.

He was already halfway down the stairs, but he stopped. "To check out the area in daylight."

"But isn't it dangerous to leave me here alone? We left Adalon because it was too dangerous..."

"This house is heavily warded against anyone who would wish you harm. I can feel the magic still in place from before. It goes out to the wall so you can go outside if you wish."

"Alright."

His eyes flicked over her, and the corner of his mouth tugged up. "What were you dreaming about?"

"Why do you ask?" She thought about how he'd swept her into his arms as his last act in the dream.

"You said my name. Well, moaned it more like."

"Goodbye, Hel." Layala closed the door, and she heard his laughter as he went down the steps.

CHAPTER 35

LAYALA

Layala stepped out the front door and stood in the morning sunshine. The warmth of it against the skin of her face brought a sense of calm to her already anxious morning. A piercing bird call made her jump, obliterating her moment of peace. A red-breasted robin-look-alike hopped along the unkempt path, pecking at the ground. Layala rubbed her eyes, sure she was hallucinating. The robin must be at least four feet tall with an orangish serrated beak that could tear a hand off.

She reached for the dagger on her belt and cursed realizing it was upstairs.

"Good morning, Valeen. Or would you prefer I call you Layala?"

Layala half turned, so she could still keep an eye on the bird. It hopped once more then flew away giving her a chance to think. If she was going to embrace her past shouldn't she go by her old name? At the same time, she didn't want to give up this life.

Presco stopped beside her. His golden hair was combed and tied back at the base of his neck. He wore a simple white tunic with a brown belt and pants. Round glasses reflected the sunlight until he pushed them up a notch.

"Valeen is fine." Although it felt strange to give up the name her parents gave her and everyone she loved knew her by.

"So, Hel cursed the elves."

Layala was surprised he'd tell him that.

"Word spreads through the realms. The elves have had a rough go the last few hundred years. I pity them."

"He claims he didn't create them, and that they did it to themselves, but I don't believe it. We all know if a spell of his isn't fulfilled people change. That's the consequence. He did that, not the balance of nature."

"He told me he meant for them to be loyal as the price for not fulfilling his stipulations but not the monster consequence. I really do believe that was out of his control." Presco slipped his hands behind his back. "It must have started from a single spell. It would have been a complex spell, not a simple one."

Layala chewed on her lip. "It must have been the mate spell that started it all. Those who were disloyal to their mate would be loyal to him." Layala thought back to Novak's death, the human man she loved before she ever met Thane and died because of that mate bond. If he'd been an elf, he might have turned rather than died and then he could have bit her. Was that how it happened? Then the curse spread through the bites and became rampant.

"What if we destroy the spell? Would it end?" But then that would mean she'd never be able to be mate bonded to Thane again. She didn't believe Varlett's lies about not being able to use it a second time. Everything Varlett said came into question. What were her true motives? Did she want Hel awake so that she could have her—former betrothed back? She avoided thinking about his name, either of them or it might send her into a spiral. Especially knowing they were together. *Now I know how he feels about me and Hel.*

"That may work but if I had to guess, the damage is already done."

"The goddess of wisdom said the key was his heart. I tried to shove a blade through it once. But I can't, and even if he, accidental or not, cursed the elves... I don't want to."

Presco looked down at her with his brows raised. "Perhaps the goddess didn't mean it so literally."

Layala opened her mouth to speak until Hel stepped through the hole in the property's surrounding fifty-foot wall and both Layala and Presco straightened. In silence they watched him approach. His eyes were more maroon today, softer somehow, and with the half smile on his face and skin almost glowing, his mood matched his appearance.

He pushed his hand through his shaggy, shiny black hair that curled at the base of his neck. "I get the feeling I've been the topic of discussion this morning." He set one boot on the bottom step and crossed his arms. "All good things I'm sure."

Presco forced a smile. "I'm going to continue cleaning up the house. There's years' worth of dust and cobwebs. I sneezed half the night. Not to mention the hole in the wall that let insects creep in." He disappeared inside and the door shut behind him.

"You're in a better mood," Layala said.

He started off to the left toward a small fruit orchard overtaken by tall grass and weeds. Layala hurried down the steps and caught up to him. He plucked a plump purple round fruit and bit into the soft skin. "I found a pretty farm girl down the road all too happy to tell me about the area." The purple juices from the fruit ran down his chin, though he quickly wiped it. "I might even go back tonight."

Irrational anger boiled inside her at the thought of it. "You're a pig." He plucked another piece of fruit and threw it. It careened at her face, and she barely snatched it before impact.

"And you're a little jealous."

She bit into the sweet, juicy fruit. "Hardly."

He chuckled. "Oh, I'm well aware of what jealous Valeen looks like." He leaned back against the tree. "Rosy cheeks, a scowl to rival a troll, and that wild look in your eyes."

"Maybe I'm annoyed I have to be here with you."

He tossed the fruit up and down. "I'll never forget the first time I witnessed your inner demon come out." He smiled and bit into the fruit. "Remember? We were at that upscale restaurant having dinner. The servant had brought our food. The music was soft, the lights were low, you looked stunning in that silver summer dress."

Layala could almost hear the music now...

The Past

The savory meat and herb-crusted vegetables smelled divine. In this establishment in Hel's territory only gods and goddesses were allowed, and the place was packed with beautiful people. They sat at a rounded table inside a horseshoe-shaped booth next to one another. A female sang on stage, a slow melodic song.

"Enjoy your dinner," the servant said and dipped into a sweeping bow and hurried off to another table.

Heads kept turning their way, eyes darted to her and away as quickly as they came. She tuned out any conversation nearby, afraid of what she might hear. "Why is everyone looking at us?"

Hel glanced around as if he hadn't noticed. "Because you're here with me. Away from your House. You know how the gods love something to gossip about."

"We should have gone to dinner in my land."

"We can leave if you'd like."

She picked up her fork and shook her head. "And then put a target on my back for showing weakness? I may have been out of the game for a while, but I know how this works."

His hand slid around the back of her hips, and he tugged her closer to his side. It was a purposeful move, not simply because he wanted her close. It was to show the others they were there together, and it wasn't for business.

Hel happily chatted about who of importance was at the place and who to watch out for. He put faces to names she'd heard or read about. So many new people from before she locked herself away. Halfway through their meal a demigoddess with stunning auburn hair and a deep green dress that cut in a low V down to her belly button stopped by their table.

"Hel," she said with a seductive smile.

"Lily," he acknowledged, blasé.

She slid into the booth beside him and nudged her shoulder against his. "I've missed you. You haven't been by the club in months."

"I've been busy."

Her gaze flicked to Valeen then she slipped her hand over his shoulder. "Stop by tonight then when you're done here."

He pushed her hand off. "I have plans and in case you haven't noticed you're interrupting our dinner."

Valeen set her fork down and straightened her spine. Lily was testing her.

"*But you don't mind, do you, Hel?*"

"*I mind,*" Valeen said.

"*I think you better go, Lily,*" Hel's voice took on a sharper tone.

Lily met Valeen's stare. "*It's nothing. Relax. You're as uptight as they say. I'm just saying hi to my friend. We meet often.*"

"*Really?*"

"*Oh yes.*" She smiled, and Hel stiffened, and his eyes flashed wide. An odd sudden reaction.

Valeen glanced down and found Lily's hand sliding up his inner thigh. He shook his head before she could move further. "*Don't. I'm with Valeen now.*"

"*You like it,*" she whispered and began to rub him slowly.

"*Lily, stop it.*" He snatched her wrist.

Valeen flashed into shadow and had Lily by the throat, dragging her out of the booth, and retook her solid form. She lifted her feet off the ground and held her by the neck. The room went quiet, even the singer stopped. Onyx shadows seeped out of Lily's eyes, nose, and ears.

"*Valeen, wait.*"

"*You think you can disrespect* him *like that?*"

"*I apologize. It was rude of me.*"

"*Rude?*" She brought her closer, gripped her throat harder. "*If you ever touch him again I will burn through your mind until you are nothing but an empty shell, unable to die but never live. He's mine.*"

Her mouth opened and more shadows rolled out. "*I'll stay away.*"

"*You better.*" She dropped her and shoved her onto the closest table, spilling their drinks, shattering glass. Her gaze swept around the room, and no one stared anymore. Lily quickly got up, not even taking the time to brush the mess of food off herself and scurried out the exit. After adjusting the hem of her dress at her thighs, Valeen *retook her seat, scooting up to Hel's side. Then leaned in and kissed him hard on the mouth to show everyone exactly what their relationship was so no one would question it again.*

Hel grinned at her. "I think I'm in love with you."

LAYALA TOOK another bite of her fruit. That jealousy flared in her now. She turned to face away from Hel so he couldn't read her easily. The pit of his fruit hit the ground with a thump and Hel brushed his hands together. "You *do* remember."

"I really don't know what you're talking about." She licked the sweet juice from her lips and shrugged.

Hel slipped his hand into hers, interlocking their fingers. She looked down at their hands clasped together confused. "Why are you holding my hand?"

Wordlessly, he pulled her along beside him toward the hole in the outer wall. After they were on the road, he said, "Are you hungry?"

"Yes..." The fruit was enough to make her stomach rumble for more but not satisfy. In a flash they stood outside the pub they'd been at the night before. The sudden change made her stomach twist and the ground spin. "Warn me next time."

"You'll get used to it."

Once everything stopped moving, she took in the small town, if one could call it that. There were three shabby buildings and a dirt road. In the light of day, the pub looked much larger; even the doorway was at least ten feet tall and nearly that wide. "I thought we were training today?"

"We will. But you're hungry and we can't have that if we want to make progress."

"Isn't it a bad idea to come back here?" But she didn't stop him from pulling her inside. The place was just as full as the night before with the majority of the tables filled with patrons. It smelled of roasted boar as well as raw meat. The sun shone in through the windows illuminating the smoky atmosphere.

They found an empty table and Hel gestured for her to sit. "I'll be right back."

He's up to something, she thought, setting down the pit of her fruit on the smooth wooden tabletop. Across the room, he stopped and spoke to a female waitress for only a moment before he abandoned her to slide into the booth.

"What are you doing?"

"I told her to bring us a couple drinks and breakfast."

"Thanks," she said slowly, still suspicious. "And they're not angry about last night?"

"It's a new staff. They won't know it was us and if anyone asks, I'll charm them into forgetting." His eyes leveled on hers. "I must say you look good today. Something about being in a new place makes you glow. You're even moaning my name and not his already."

Heat crept up her neck and she wished she would stop doing that. "You're dreaming, Hel."

"Ah, there's that blush again." He pulled a smoking civar out of thin air and brought it to his lips.

"Why do you smoke those?"

He shrugged. "It's a habit. I like the smell."

The waitress appeared and set the drinks down. "I'll be right back with your breakfast." She paused and smiled at Hel. "You're very handsome."

The way the lady spoke made her skin prickle. Like she wanted to mount him right there.

He leaned forward, propping his elbows on the table. "Thanks, love."

Smiling, the waitress squatted down to tabletop level,

reached forward, and took the civar from his hand. A moment later she brought it to her lips. "What are you doing later? I get off my shift after the rush."

A twinge of anger tugged at Layala's chest. She gritted her teeth and then quickly picked up her metal mug to find out it was ale again. Was she a dragon shifter? She looked human but doubtful one would survive in this realm. Even the birds were predators.

"Well," Hel plucked the civar back from the waitress's fingers and leaned back, "I'm teaching this one a few lessons and then I'm free."

The waitress looked over as if noticing her for the first time. "Is she your girl?"

"Nope."

She turned her attention back to Layala. "So, you don't mind if he and I meet up later?"

Layala took another long drink of ale and shook her head. "Not at all." The image of smashing her mug into the side of the girl's head flashed across her mind. *What is wrong with me?*

"And if we hump?"

"Excuse me?" Layala's brows furrowed. What a strange thing to say.

"You know what that is, right?" The waitress chuckled and stood up, leaning on the table.

"Obviously," Layala snapped. "And it's such a crude thing to say. Get some manners. You should go do your job and see if our breakfast is ready."

"Best go, love, this one has a nasty temper," Hel said and shooed her away. She quickly left at his suggestion.

With her jaw hanging open Layala scoffed. "I have a nasty temper?"

"It isn't a lie."

"You've got some nerve. And don't call her 'love', it's annoying."

He smiled and took another puff of his civar. "I can only call you that?"

"I'd rather you called no one that, least of all me."

"Least of all you, but I can't call her that." He chuckled. "Got it."

"This whole thing is you trying to make me jealous, isn't it? To make me angry so I'll use my magic. You told her to say those things." Layala shook her head. Well, he could do whatever he wanted with that girl. She was only here to train and remember so she could go back to Thane.

"I told her to flirt with me. If she wants to take me in the back and do improper acts, it's not my fault."

"Well, I'm *not* going to obliterate her mind for flirting with you. Sorry to disappoint. I don't care."

"I thought you didn't remember."

Layala huffed and took another drink of ale. She should throw this drink in his face and walk out. But then she'd get no breakfast, and it was her favorite meal of the day.

"It wasn't just jealousy that made me react that way when Lily had her hand on your, you know. It was completely inappropriate, not to mention assault. She deserved what I did and more."

Hel's brows rose in surprise. "Agreed."

"And if it were the other way around, you would have done worse."

He chuckled. "No doubt."

"Was that the first time you said you lov—" she clamped her mouth shut. That was not a discussion she wanted to have.

He looked at her knowingly but only said, "Better slow down on the ale. I don't want to have to carry you back."

"Don't tell me what to do. Or maybe I'll obliterate your mind. Then all my problems would go away. You wouldn't be dead but not alive either."

"Gods, you're mean. I wouldn't even do that to my worst enemy."

"Ha, that's funny."

The waitress appeared again, and set down the plate of roasted boar, chopped potatoes, and a side of fruit. "Enjoy." She turned to Hel. "So about later—"

"Look, lady," Layala started. "As you can see, we're talking, so come back when we're done." Layala was surprised at her own rudeness. Usually, she let things roll off her back.

The girl picked up the mug and tossed the contents in Layala's face. Cold ale washed down her neck and over her chest, dripping on the table. Fury burned hot and fierce in her chest. Black mist seeped from her fingers, and soon her hands shifted, then her arms. Still keeping their shape but see through.

"Now that was uncalled for," Hel said. "You'll have to apologize. I have this thing about people disrespecting her."

Layala shoved up from the table and half the room stared at her. The waitress just threw a drink in her face. She was dripping wet and now they waited for her reaction or waited to see what Hel would do. She wanted to punch her, choke slam her onto the table, and scrambling her mind almost filled her with delight, but then the waitress said, "What's wrong with your hands?" Shadows drifted from her fingers; the room began to dim as if the sun had gone behind the clouds.

Revealing to everyone who she was when they were supposed to be hiding from the council and a demon prince was not the best idea.

Stay calm. Make her apologize, Hel said in her mind.

Layala cut Hel a glare... was this training? Maker, it wasn't to get her to use her power, it was to see if she could restrain herself.

She pushed her magic down, thinking of the time she stood in the summoning circle, took a deep calming breath, and turned her glower on the waitress. "Bow and apologize. Now."

The waitress narrowed her eyes, looked over at Hel and then back to Layala. Hel took a pull from his civar and watched patiently.

Layala swiped her sleeve across her face to clear the ale then pulled out her sword. "You have three seconds. Three, two—"

The girl bowed her head. "I apologize, Miss."

Now what? Hel asked. *Mercy or not?*

Gritting her teeth, Layala pushed her sword back into its holster on her back. "Go."

Layala turned and left the building, taking in deep calming breaths. She stopped in the middle of the road. There were only a few people out walking about and none of them paid her attention, but she found a nearby tree and hid behind it, to test her shadows that came out unbidden. It was time she gained control of them. Her magic hummed and tingled. She imagined her fingers shifting first. Wiggling them before her face shadows crept out and her hand changed to a charcoal black before going unstable.

Feeling like someone watched, she glanced around the tree trunk, and Hel stood against the building, smoking. Leaned back as if he didn't have a care in the world. Prick. Even if his training methods were unconventional, he was good at them and testing her... *Control, little rabbit,* she heard in her head from the training sessions back in Palenor.

Getting an idea, Layala smiled to herself. She closed her

eyes and felt her whole body shifting. She was weightless, shadow, and she vanished reappearing on the side of the building, forcing herself to regain solid form. She peeked around the corner, and Hel shoved off the wall and trudged to the tree where she previously stood.

"Val?" he called, turning in a circle. The worried lines intensified. "*Layala*, this isn't funny."

She quietly laughed watching him panic and sink lower into the shadows of the building. *He must really be worried if he's using that name. Good.* He hurried back into the pub, and Layala took off running in the direction of the manor. If she went fast enough he might not see her round the bend. Two could play these games.

Tears streamed down the sides of her cheeks from the wind rushing by. Her feet pounded the uneven surface, but she barely made a sound. Everything blurred. It felt like someone tugged her hair behind her, but it was the pull of the wind. She'd never moved this fast. Not even close, like she was a dragon on a dive for prey; even her stomach tickled.

The giant wall came into view, and she finally slowed, sucking in deep breaths. Hel was nowhere in sight, and she smiled triumphantly. She hopped through the wall then silently cursed.

He sat in the middle of the front steps of the manor. Gritting her teeth, she strode forward and meant to march right past him until he said, "About time you show up. Perhaps you're a tortoise rather than a *little rabbit*."

"Prick," she moved around him.

"Asshole."

She stopped and did a full turn. He stood and slid his hands into his pockets.

"Did you just call me an 'asshole'?"

"What's the matter. Don't you like the taste of your own medicine?"

She didn't even know how to respond. Thane had never called her a name back. No one did except maybe Talon. With her fists clenched at her sides, she whipped around and marched up the stairs.

"You're going to run away from two fights today, I see."

Growling Layala turned and started back down toward him. "I didn't run away. I stayed calm and controlled. Just like you taught me, then left because I'm covered in ale, thanks to you getting in that girl's head. And this," she gestured back and forth between them, "isn't a fight."

"That was all her. I only told her to flirt with me." One eyebrow arched and he stepped closer. "But what if I did this?" He vanished and appeared behind her, sliding his hand around her throat. He leaned down and ran his nose and mouth along her neck. "You smell good."

Layala stiffened, her entire body tensed, goosebumps peppered her skin. Her magic didn't fight to break free, however, she took control of her breathing, pushed her fear and agitation down.

"Where is my little rabbit?" His hand marginally tightened on her throat pulling her back close to his front, but it wasn't uncomfortable.

"She's gone," Layala said.

"You've gained control. I'm proud of you. I think even just a week ago you'd have lost control of your magic back there, and we all know how you reacted to me touching you." He released her and stepped around. "You're not afraid of me anymore."

"No," she said and smiled.

He smiled back. "My little rabbit has outgrown her nick-name. Whatever shall I call you now?"

"How about my name?" she said flatly.

"Which one?"

She hesitated but said, "Val. I like Val."

"So do I." He went around her, his shoulder brushing hers as he passed. "It would be rude of us to leave all the cleaning and repairs to Presco. We'll be here a while so we might as well make it to our liking."

"I thought we were training?"

"We did. You passed."

CHAPTER 36

LAYALA

The afternoon was spent cleaning the manor. Layala started by wiping the tops of mantels in the dining and sitting areas. The dust was inches thick, and she had to dunk her cloth into the bucket after a single swipe. This was going to take days, if not a week just to clear the dirt out.

She enjoyed listening to Presco and Hel chat about dragon politics, how many kingdoms and clans there were now. Seven dragon clans with one king. And the king was now Varlett's younger brother.

Hel ran a broom across the floors. The swishes of the bundled straw scraping stone became a steady sound. This was the first time she'd ever heard Hel have a normal conversation that didn't include snide comments with someone other than her, like she would chat with friends. He laughed at appropriate times, had witty comebacks, or added to whatever Presco said. Their chatter flowed easily. She didn't know why it surprised her that he could be normal. Well, normal wasn't a word she could associate with him. He was anything but that.

Presco was an intellect and some of the things he spoke of went right over her head, like his comments about how magic interacted with cells within the body and mutated them beyond that of someone without the ability making them resistant to disease, illness, and injury. She didn't even know what a cell was, but Hel appeared to. And it was strange to see him doing housework. It felt like a task below him or at least he'd think so. And couldn't he use magic to spell the broom to sweep for him? Layala added to the conversation here and there when prompted but for the most part she listened and focused on her menial task.

She hadn't cleaned and done household chores since she left Briar Hollow and it felt strangely good. She felt useful. At Castle Dredwich servants did everything. Fennan even reprimanded her once for trying to saddle her own horse.

She giggled to herself thinking of the days when her maids wanted to help her take a bath and she couldn't even fathom the idea. Why would any adult need help washing their own hair? It was a luxury, she supposed, one she still wasn't used to.

It was nice to be waited on and not have to worry about cooking meals or cleaning, to always have new clean clothes and bedsheets changed out regularly, but right now she appreciated the work. She didn't think about *him* and what he might be doing or if he was in danger. As the cloth ran over the top of the dark dining wood table, she thought of Aunt Evalyn. "Damn it," Layala cursed and stood straight, resting a fist on her hip.

Footsteps hurried from the corridor and Hel peeked around the corner of the wall. "What happened?"

"Oh nothing. It's just, when I went out the other day and

was bitten by the pale one, I went to get my aunt things from her list. I never got them to her, and I didn't tell her I was leaving so now she's going to worry." Layala dropped the towel into the bucket and blew a stray hair off her forehead. "I assume I can't get her a message through realms."

He looked relieved. "I gave them to her."

Layala's brows shot up. She didn't even know Hel knew about Aunt Evalyn beyond that she was the woman who raised her, let alone about the list or where she was. "You did?"

"Before we left. I wanted to know why you were out in the woods in the first place and discovered the note she sent in your room, so I found the items and list on your horse."

Layala watched him warily. "Did you go see her?" How else would he have gotten them to her? She didn't want him anywhere near Aunt Evalyn. And if she knew Layala was with *the Black Mage*, she'd lose her mind.

"And if I did?"

"You didn't—do anything to her. Tell me you didn't hurt her."

He stepped further into the room and set the broom against the wall. "I do you a favor and deliver the items on the list and you think I hurt your aunt?"

"It's not as if it would be wayward behavior for you. You've threatened Piper and Thane on multiple accounts, and if you didn't find Vesstan useful you'd have killed him. I know it."

"I did kill him. He's dead. Notice the old mage wasn't around for the last few lessons."

Layala's heart ached and slammed into her ribs. She recalled this threat about drowning Vesstan in the pond. "You didn't."

He chuckled. "No, I didn't kill him. I do things with purpose and reason."

"You killed the guards the day you arrived!"

"And those guards were so important to you?"

"No, but that's not the point."

"You tried to kill me in the tower before ever even speaking to me. You're not Miss Innocent."

"Oh, I wonder why? And you cut open my wrist and drank my blood without permission."

"I'd say it was necessary, but I wanted to know what you tasted like, too." He smirked. "I'm surprised War put up with your attitude for so long. He needs a sweet girl, and you're far from that."

"Ugh, you're—you're—"

"A fucking asshole, yes. I'm the bad guy. Don't forget it either." He snatched up the broom. "And I didn't hurt your aunt. I didn't even go to see her. I sent the items by magic." He left the room and the sound of the straw broom scraping the floor started up again.

After an hour or so the tension melted away. The three of them sat down for a meal and it was as if they never had the argument.

Layala lost track of the days after that.

She cried herself to sleep at night thinking about and missing Thane, woke up and trained with Hel. Usually practicing magic in the yard, turning herself into shadow over and over or creating a shield to protect herself against his attacks. He wasn't as hard on her as in the past. As if being away from Thane and Palenor put him at ease.

They cleaned, patched holes, ate meals together though she complained about the lack of variety. "Something other than fruit from the trees, nuts, and dried meat would be nice."

Presco slaughtered a giant bird and roasted it, but it lacked salt or much flavor. Without a general store nearby, they didn't have luxuries. And outings to the pub for a drink and a meal were few and far between.

As the days went on they chatted like three old friends. She supposed that's what they were.

Her memory was slow to return, more often when Presco and Hel spoke about the past. Flashes of things came here and there on her own or at times in her dreams. Simple things like riding her chariot through the night sky. The pretty colorful lights over her territory, and how she controlled whether or not to let the sun in or keep the skies dark. It was strange and yet normal to think she had control and power over an entire realm. She even remembered flashes of a beautiful blonde goddess, with a laugh that was infectious, and a smile that lit up the sky. Katana, she thought her name was. She loved her like she loved Aunt Evalyn. Was this her sister?

Some nights Hel left. He never said anything to her; she'd only hear the front door open and close. Where he went, she didn't ask. With the sounds of beasts growling and throaty calls echoing in the dark, and terrifying screams, she worried he wouldn't come back.

With her hair combed and tied back in a braid, Layala came down the stairs with a bundle of dirty clothes. It was wash day again. She only had four sets and according to Presco the nearest large town was two days away, as the dragon flies, and she hadn't made it there yet. Maybe soon but she needed to start cleaning up the yard. The weeds and foliage were overgrown everywhere and took over the outside of the manor, even climbing up to the roof.

She stopped by the library where Presco usually was in the mornings. The shelves were free of dust, the lamps and vases shined with new life. He sat at the desk with a small open book in front of him. His quill scratched over the parchment inside it.

"Good morning," Layala said.

His head lifted with a grin, and he pushed his glasses up. "Morning, Valeen."

"Any plans today?"

"Nothing too important. Would you be interested in going to the city in the next couple of days? I told my wife I'd be here for a few weeks at least but I want to give her an update." He set the quill down.

"That would be great. I need more clothes too," she raised the pile in her hands marginally higher, "and I want to meet her, and your children." She didn't remember Presco well but enough that she cared for him now. Even if they didn't have a past, she would like him. He was kind and good company over the last several weeks, and she got the feeling that he would die for her if he must. That was how much he cared.

"Excellent." He smiled again. "It's funny seeing you like this."

"Like what?"

"Doing laundry, cleaning floors. Not that you ever shied away from work but you're a queen and a primordial goddess."

"Oh," she said and shrugged. "But I'm also an elf raised by a human as well. What are you working on?"

"It's my journal. I've documented many of my days for most of my life."

"Am I in some of them?"

His brows raised and he scratched his head. "Certainly. However, most of them from that time were destroyed after your... banishment. Nearly everything in this manor was confiscated. Most of what is here now I brought over the years. I managed to save a few items before they came, but not much."

Her shoulders sagged. It would have been nice to read about her life.

"We may not have my journals from then, but your journals are in perfect condition."

She perked up. "Mine? Why didn't you mention this before?"

"Well, it didn't occur to me, and they were confiscated rather than destroyed, but they currently reside at the Drakonan Treasury. One of the most secure places in all the realms. Even many of the gods store items there. At least, they did."

"Drakonan?" she repeated. That was Prince Ronan's last name. "That is the name of the royal dragons in Adalon."

"They are one of the most powerful families here. Although not royalty, I'd say they are just as powerful as the king and clan leaders if not more. They have more treasure and hold everyone else's."

"So, if I tell them who I am, will they let us inside?"

He laughed. "Oh no. Unfortunately, they are bought and paid for by the council, and came to an agreement after your apprehension all those years ago. You're an enemy even if they once worshiped you and War."

"Then my journals may as well not even exist." She let out a heavy sigh.

"Not necessarily. They are in a secure vault along with the rest of your belongings. With yours and Hel's magic, we might be able to get in." He leaned back in the wooden chair, and it creaked under his weight. With his hands folded on his abdomen, he said, "But if we manage to get them without being arrested or killed, they are written in the primordial language. It's not the tongue we speak now."

"My original language?"

"Yes. It is what the gods speak. It has only changed marginally over time, unlike many languages that vary and reconstruct on the whim of the next generation. That's why I prefer it."

"How many languages do you speak?"

He cleared his throat and she thought he might be blushing. "One hundred and thirty-two. With all the realms and different species and dialects, I only know maybe even a quarter of those in existence."

"Wow." Layala smiled. "That's impressive, Presco."

"You speak—spoke as many as I, if not more. We often studied together and quizzed each other. We'd pick months where we only spoke a particular language. It drove people at the castle mad. The servants would want to tear out their hair when we'd ask them to do something in a language they didn't understand. We had a good laugh at their expense."

Layala thought about that. "There were many different people in Villhara, from all over the realms so we needed to be able to change languages all the time."

Presco's face lit up and he nodded enthusiastically. "Yes. Most learned the primordial language once they arrived in Runevale, however."

"So, my territory was known as the night territory, and Hel's was..."

"We often called your land House of Night and Hel's House of Magic, or many simply called it Hel's."

"And Villhara?"

"It's what you named your territories when you married and combined them. Everyone moved between the two as one. It was an adjustment at first because we'd kept to ourselves for so long in House of Night, but Hel's people and yours fit well over time. They didn't like the other territories much either."

She smiled. "Weren't his people more... rebellious? I can't think of a better word. I remember going to one of his parties and felt very out of place."

"In some ways. They were open about public affection and less formal in their speech and interactions, but I think it was good for all of us. They learned to be more conservative, and we adjusted to be less rigid. Holding hands in public could be seen as a scandal in House of Night and Hel's people were always touching and hugging. Their culture was more affectionate."

"That's interesting. He doesn't seem that way now." But then again he did touch her often. She always thought it was because he wanted to antagonize her.

"He's changed quite a bit since then."

Layala pressed her lips together. "What happened between us?" She'd carefully not inquired about Hel and her past until now.

Presco glanced out the window. "Perhaps you should ask him those types of questions. I don't want to get in the middle of it or sway you one way or another. It was...challenging enough for all of us then. You asked me to come here with you when you left Runevale, and I did. But because it was with War, it broke Hel in a way I can't quite describe, and what happened after..." he shook his head remorsefully. "Many of the gods not involved pushed Hel to fight, an excuse for them to go to war and take. The dragons' thirst for battle, it's in our nature. It's one of the reasons War is the god the dragon shifters cherished." He frowned. "There was much senseless death."

"But I didn't leave him for no reason." Layala sounded more defensive than she meant to. She hated to think she was the reason behind the senseless deaths he spoke of.

"No, you had your reasons. And I don't think you imagined the aftermath of your choice."

"All because I loved War?"

"You didn't love War in the same way as Hel. I don't want to say more because your perception of the situation and mine would be quite different, and it's been so long my memory isn't as sharp."

She nodded. It was better she knew for herself what happened. "Alright, so are we serious about trying to sneak into the Drakonan Treasury?"

"That depends on how much you want your belongings back."

"I need the journals. It could be years before I remember my life at this rate." She thought of Thane alone against the demon prince. Each day she stayed in ignorance put him at risk, not to mention Varlett was with him. And she didn't trust the dragon witch. "I'll talk with Hel. Have you seen him this morning? We're supposed to train but I thought we could take a day off and clear some of the weeds off the house."

He shook his head. "I haven't."

"Oh, did he come back last night?"

"I'm not sure."

Layala took the clothes out to the silver wash tub outside and dumped them in. She pumped water, filling it up and then put her hand to her brow, shielding the bright sun. He wasn't out here that she could see. The property within the wall was only about ten acres. She'd be able to spot him even among the fruit trees and tall grass.

Leaving the clothes to soak, she went through the dining room and down the hall then knocked on his door. He'd taken a room on the main floor. When he didn't answer she slowly pushed it open and peeked inside. The bed was made, his weapons weren't on the dresser and the window was left open with the blue curtain blowing in the breeze. He wasn't here.

After the clothes were washed and hung out to dry, she started jerking up weeds along the front path. It was nearly dark by the time she cleared half of it away. She stopped to drink and eat but a nagging worry that started small intensified when the sun set. In the weeks they'd been there, he'd never not come back. He hadn't missed a single day of training.

Presco stood at the window with his arms crossed and Layala stepped to his side. "Do you think something happened to him?"

"I'm sure he's fine," Presco said. "It's Hel. He's always been a bit of a wildcard."

"Did he say anything to you before he left last night?"

Presco adjusted his glasses. "Only that he was going to get fresh air. I think he finds it difficult to be around you all the time since you don't love him anymore." It looked like it pained Presco to say it.

"Oh." A sharp sting in her chest came unbidden.

"I'll go check to see if I can find him so we can put our minds at ease."

"But it's dark." The creatures of this realm had already started in on their frightening calls and growls. Sometimes she looked out the window at night and saw huge, winged things snatch something smaller out of the air. Not dragon shifters, though sometimes she thought the wyverns fought each other in the woods behind the manor. And the screeches and screams... Whatever was beyond the wall some nights was terrifying.

"I'm a dragon, Valeen. I'm the biggest thing in this realm," he said with a smile that didn't reach his eyes. "No need to worry about me."

He never displayed the dragon characteristics, like talons,

scales, or horns and she'd nearly forgotten he was a dragon shifter.

"Be careful," Layala called as he went out the front door. He disappeared through the hole in the outer wall and with the dark clouds blocking the stars and moons this night, she barely saw his great winged form vanish in the distance.

Layala didn't ask to go with him. While she waited, she made tea over the wood-burning stove and sipped on it while she paced back and forth in front of the wide windows that overlooked the front.

Sometime later, a dragon's shadow appeared in the sky and then a man's form walked through the hole in the wall. Presco was alone. Except—he wasn't. The front door creaked open, and a pair of glowing red eyes appeared in the gap in the wall.

CHAPTER 37

LAYALA

Layala's stomach was in knots by the time the front door squealed open and Presco returned. "Did you find Hel?" Layala asked, keeping her sight pinned on the pair of red eyes staring back at her. Her skin crawled and her heart began to thud harder. Whoever it was didn't move forward, didn't try to get in—maybe he *couldn't*.

"No." Presco's heavy footsteps traipsed across the floor, and he stopped beside her.

"I think you were followed."

"I don't see anyone."

Whoever—whatever had been there before was gone now. "What has red eyes other than Hel and—a demon?" Hel's eyes didn't glow in the dark like that and only his irises were red.

"It's a rare trait," Presco said slowly, frowning. It seemed they both suspected the demon prince had found them. "Is that what you saw?"

She nodded, clutching at her dry throat. What if it was the

demon prince? If he was here did that mean Thane was... No, she couldn't bear the thought. She couldn't even let her mind go there.

"I think we should keep looking for him."

"No news is good news. I'm certain he's fine."

"Where would he go?"

Presco shrugged. "I don't know but you're safe inside the wall and not outside it. It's best if we wait until sunrise. From what I've read demons can't be in direct sunlight. It weakens and blinds them."

Layala finished her herbal tea and went to her room. While sitting on the edge of the bed, she tugged the curtain aside. A giant bird with a craned neck perched on top of the wall. They claimed nothing with the intent to hurt her could get past the magical barrier but still, she was on edge. Every creak in the house, every screech outside seemed louder with Hel missing. Things were always scarier in the dark. Ironic that she was the goddess of it.

She lay in bed with the blankets tucked up under her armpits, staring at the cracks and stains on the dirty, off-white ceiling. Paint was another item they'd have to get in the city.

A scraping sound like nails dragging across glass made her go rigid. Her heartbeat shot up. Her mind flipped to the demon clawing to get at her back at the castle, those malicious red eyes glowing. He'd come to take his vengeance, to kill her, and she had no obsidian blade to fight. If she couldn't fight him off, she hoped he'd leave Presco alone once he got to her.

Slowly, turning over, she grabbed her dagger from under her pillow. Her magic tingled through her, flushing her skin with heat. Long spiderweb-like shadows bobbed and moved outside. A gust of wind made the house creak and Layala sighed, her body flooding with relief. Branches from the tree scraped the window. Not demon claws.

With her dagger tight in her grip, she lay her cheek down on the flat pillow. She didn't know how many hours she lay there but eventually she slept.

Her dreams weren't memories from the past or normal chaos of scenes and images that didn't make sense. Nightmares plagued her. Lightning flashed in a dark bedroom lighting up the shadows momentarily. Black boots attached to long legs hovered a few feet off the ground. Her gaze traveled up, to a ghostly pale face, with the neck craned in an unnatural position. It took her a moment to process it. For it to set in. Thane hung with a noose around his neck from the rafters, lifeless.

Dead.

Layala screamed until her throat felt like it was on fire. Screamed and screamed.

Someone shook her body; a deep voice kept saying her name. "Valeen. Valeen. Wake up."

She couldn't stop screaming. Thane's lifeless body stared back at her, accusing.

Condemning.

She left him there alone.

With a gasp, she opened her eyes. Before her was a dark halo of hair, a beautiful face—Hel. He gripped her shoulders, his chest heaved up and down. She was already sitting up, feet hanging over the edge of the bed, touching the floor.

Her throat felt raw and sweat dampened her brow. "Hel?"

His usual smug or bored expression was lined with tension. "Gods, you scared the piss out of me."

The image of Thane hanging dead made her want to throw up. She couldn't shake it. "Thane. What if something happened to him? We have to go back!" It felt too real. She tried to get up and he held her tighter, keeping her in place.

"You were dreaming. He's fine."

Tears burned her eyes even though she tried to rationalize the image of Thane dead wasn't real. She had been dreaming, like he said. But what if it was a prophetic dream? "We have to go back. I have to see him and make sure he's alright."

"Tell me about it."

"He was—" The words felt like dust in her mouth. "Someone hung him in his room."

Hel sighed, and it sounded more like relief than frustration. "You know how I know it wasn't real?"

"How?"

"Because War could never be hung to death. As if he couldn't snap the rope with his strength or magic?"

She breathed deeper. *He's right. It was only a dream.* It didn't make the image any less terrifying. "Where have you been?"

He stood up and the heaviness of his grip on her shoulders lifted. He headed for the door as if he wasn't going to answer. "I'll explain in the morning. Go back to sleep."

"I saw the demon."

He halted and slowly turned. "Where? When?"

"Through the hole in the wall. I only saw red glowing eyes, but it must be him."

"And you fear that if he's here then Thane is dead. That's why you had the nightmare."

"What if—"

"He's not."

"How do you know?"

"I just know. I'd feel it if he was gone, and you probably would too."

Layala's brows tugged down. "Feel it?"

"Despite everything. He's my blood. My brother. That last time he died, in the life before this, I felt him go, like a sharp pain in my chest. And it was the same pain for you. I found your body in the barn. We'd only met days before, but I knew you were special." He swallowed and had a far-off look on his face. "You were barely seventeen. I ran to fight whoever it was, and felt the sting moments before I found War's body still bleeding out. He and I had been friends for a couple years. None of us remembered who we truly were but still, I let the assassin kill me after that. I didn't even fight. I felt I'd lost everything in one moment. I gave up."

"You'd only met me days before?" She thought about that. "I wonder if when the three of us are together it creates a power that they can sense."

"Something like that."

"You remember the other times?"

"They are like vague dreams to me. Short lives and forgettable. I only remember the moments we died."

"Always elves?"

"Yes, I think the elven form is the only body that can hold our immortal souls because of their innate magical nature. I suppose we could have been dragon shifters but that's not what fate dealt."

It made perfect sense given how many elves had been mages at one time.

"It's not going to happen again," Hel promised.

The scraping of the branches on the window made her jump. All this talk of death and seeing Thane like that put her on edge. "How could the council be so ruthless toward us? Killing us over and over—it's extreme. Do we ever get forgiveness?"

"It's not about forgiveness. It never was."

"Then what?"

"It's about power, Valeen. We threaten theirs. You could never be controlled by them. You didn't bend the knee." Then Hel lifted a shoulder and sat on the end of the bed. His weight shifted her toward him slightly. He kept his distance and stared down at his hands. "I don't know about you but I'm not waiting for forgiveness. I will fulfill the vow I made them a long time ago. I will rule there, and they will regret ever punishing us like this."

"That's why you need the pale ones, isn't it? To fight for you."

He nodded. "As much as it's regrettable what they are, they were a gift. An army without morals, without fear, and with a sole purpose of serving me. There is a part of me that feels guilty that somehow I am responsible for the curse. That I am responsible for the loss of so many innocent lives and if I could go back in time, I'd find out where I went wrong and stop it before it happened, but I can't." He was quiet for a moment. "I am selfish. And I will use them to take my revenge. Just as I will use you, and War, and Varlett." He looked over at her, stared into her eyes. "Never forget what I've become, Valeen. Trust only that I will do what I must and not what is good. I am not like War, and I never will be."

A chill ran along her spine. Hel was wicked, horrible, but it wasn't without reason. She finally understood him and everything he'd done. The council murdered them over and over and would keep doing it, so he had to become a monster as evil as they.

She slipped her legs under the blanket and lay back down on her pillow. "I will fight with you, Zaurahel. When I'm ready. I will help you take down the council." And it only hit her after she said it. Mathekis and Varlett had been correct when they told her she'd stand beside him.

His eyes glittered in the moonlight shining in from the window. "You only use my full name when..." He closed his mouth and scooted back on the bed to lean on the wall it was propped against. With a deep breath, he folded his hands over his abdomen. "Go to sleep, Val."

She believed every word he said about not trusting him, but she didn't feel in danger with him near. She didn't fear he would hurt her while she slept. She didn't fear him at all anymore and that probably made her a fool, but her eyelids were heavy and even if she wondered when it was she only used his full name, she couldn't stay awake to ask.

Layala woke to sunshine filtering in through the curtains. Surprisingly, she didn't have another nightmare. Just usual dreams shifting from one odd thing to the next. Her spinning in a field of wildflowers with butterflies lifting off blooms was the one thing she recalled. She was oddly at peace this morning. Tears didn't threaten to overwhelm her like many mornings due to a broken heart.

A light wind made the old manor creak and groan. The tip of her nose was icy, but she was warm and cozy under her blankets and extra warm against her back. There was also something... solid there. And something heavy across the topside of her ribs. She didn't dare move but glanced down to find a rune-tattooed hand resting on her torso. *Holy Maker above.* Gentle breath brushed the back of her neck and her whole body tensed. He was on top of the blanket. She was under. The quilt was a barrier but sleeping beside him created intimacy, a trust that wasn't quite there before.

Part of her wanted to go back to sleep and curl further into him.

But she slowly wiggled toward the edge of the bed, and his arm tightened around her, pulling her back to him. Closer than before. Her belly seemed to jump, and her heart fluttered faster. Turning her head ever so slightly, she saw he was still asleep. With his hair half across his face and curled up on his side, he looked serene. Gentle even. It wasn't a word she'd have ever associated with him before but in his sleep he was not a vengeful god. Not someone filled with hate, bitterness, and regret. With a light touch she pushed the hair off his face and marveled at him.

Stop inspecting him and escape, Layala. Right. If she lifted his arm off he'd wake up and she blushed just thinking of what he might say. If she didn't, she was stuck cuddling with him, and he had to wake up eventually. The last thing she remembered, he sat near her feet.

Trying her best not to disturb him, she scooted again, hoping to slip out unnoticed. He mumbled something that sounded like "I love cows," and she pressed her lips together, trying not to laugh.

Carefully, she pulled the corner of the blanket and lifted it, and his fingers brushed against the small gap of exposed skin on her stomach. Goosebumps rose across every inch of her and then his breathing changed—less deep and rhythmic. She froze. The tension suddenly thickened between them. He was certainly awake. And he knew that she knew.

She couldn't stay any longer and slipped out, setting her feet on the freezing floor. Why was it so cold in here? The wind outside must be bitter and the cracks in the house let in a breeze. Goosebumps rose along her arms and across her skin. She wanted to dive back under the blankets.

Without looking back or saying a word, she padded across the wood floor. The boards squeaked lightly under her weight. She cringed each time, until she stooped to the fireplace and picked up the flint. She tossed a bundle of dry grass on top of the wood and hit the stones together creating sparks. After several tries she cursed under her breath. She'd done this a thousand times and yet the stupid thing wouldn't light.

Suddenly heat flared and the fire roared. The wood burned hot instantly, popping and sizzling. She turned and Hel sat up on the bed, leaning casually back against the headboard. He still looked sleepy, with heavy eyelids and disheveled hair.

"Thanks," Layala said, holding her palms close to warm up her cold fingers. The heavy silence stretched between them.

He finally said, "You were shivering."

She stood and turned to warm her backside. "What?"

"Last night. You were cold."

"Oh." *Why not just start the fire,* she thought.

And as if he heard her, he said, "You always hated a fire at night because the light woke you."

She did get her best sleep in total darkness. *And did he hear that thought?* She was sure she didn't send it to him.

He smiled. "Yes."

Her cheeks warmed. "You lied. You can hear my thoughts all the time, can't you?"

"I didn't lie. There are times when you unconsciously let me in. It's when you feel... comfortable with me that I can pick up on your thoughts. When you want me to connect with you, at least that's how it was before."

Is that true? she wondered. *Do I want to feel connected to him?*

He smiled even wider, bringing out his unbearably attractive dimple. *Unconsciously you must.*

Well, my guard is up now.

He chuckled. *Is it? So you're not thinking about what I'd look like naked in your bed?*

Layala scoffed and turned away. "No, I'm certainly not thinking that." But at his suggestion the thought came unbidden, the image of him stretched out on her bed, nothing but smooth bare skin and muscle.

I have tattoos across the "V" of my hips. Do you remember what they are? he silently asked.

She nibbled on her lower lip. Two halves of a crown and in the center in bold script he'd tattooed in black ink "KING". She knew he was trying to get her to think of his body or other parts of him just south of those particular tattoos. *Bloody god of mischief.*

You do.

So, what if I do?

You used to lightly trace the letters with your fingertips. You knew it turned me on, but I don't think you knew just how much.

Layala imagined lying on the bed now, the two of them bare skinned, while she brushed her fingers across all his tattoos, memorizing every inch of him. She cleared her throat and quickly changed the subject. "Where did you go yesterday? Presco went looking. When you didn't come home, we thought you might have gotten yourself into trouble."

He hopped off the bed and started for the door. "I'll show you."

CHAPTER 38

LAYALA

With a blanket wrapped around her shoulders, Layala followed Hel down the stairs. He turned and stepped into the kitchen. On the woodblock counter sat a sack of flour, a block of butter, a jar of milk, salt, a pot of honey, and even a small bag labeled "sugar".

"Where did you get all this?" She smiled, realizing this was why he'd disappeared.

"In the town over from the general store. You've been complaining that you wanted more variety and I thought I'd make you my famous scones for breakfast."

Layala grinned even wider. "You have famous scones?"

"Oh, yes." He grabbed a bowl out of the cupboard and then started by pulling the strings on the flour sack.

"For some reason, and I can't imagine why," she drawled, "you don't strike me as a baker."

He chuckled. "I'm a fabulous baker. It was a hobby of mine,

but it's been a while so hopefully I still remember. You'll have to be the judge."

"Alright." Layala pulled up a stool and sat at the edge of the counter block. The black wood-burning oven suddenly roared to life. Soon the kitchen would warm up and she wouldn't need to hold the blanket so snuggly. "Why did you go to sleep for four hundred years waiting for me? Wouldn't you have gotten just as strong with the time while awake?"

A scoop of flour went into the bowl. "I made myself unkillable while I slept, and it was the only way. Awake, there was a chance I could be assassinated, and I was determined not to have to go through another life. It was the goddess Ellora's idea. I found a way to contact her with the stone and scepter. So, I slept and waited for you and War." Butter plopped into the bowl next and a puff of white splattered across his navy shirt. He cursed under his breath and swiped his hand down to brush it off, only making it worse.

"Were you lonely?" Four hundred years was a long time to spend in a dream world but then again maybe it went by in a blink.

"I didn't seem to awaken or become aware until I felt your presence, which would have been after your magical bond to War broke, but I also had the sense that I'd been trapped in a dream state for a long time, and I wanted out."

Layala thought back to his voice finding her before she knew him. *Come to me. I need you,* he'd said.

He poured milk in, then sugar, and with a wooden spoon began to mix it all. More spilled over the sides. Apparently he was rusty. She smiled, and he looked up at her through thick dark lashes. "What?"

"Nothing."

"You're laughing at me."

"No," she said and then burst out in laughter. It wasn't even that funny, but he looked so out of place with flour all over his shirt, mixing a bowl of ingredients to make scones. He was the Black Mage, the god of mischief, a killer, and a novice baker.

He dunked his hand in the sack of flour and tossed a handful. It splattered across her chin, over her neck, and down her chest. She gasped and dropped her blanket. "Hel!"

He smirked. "If you're so good at it then help me."

She set the blanket down and stomped over to his side, bumped her hip into his and took over. Once it was all mixed, she pushed the bowl back in front of him. "Your turn." As he took the dough into his hands to knead it, she tossed flour at him. It scattered over his hair making the black a dusty gray and over the left side of his cheek.

"Are you serious?" he drawled.

She grabbed another handful and tossed it then dashed around the other side of the wood block and backed toward the archway leading out of the room. He was covered in splatters of flour, and she couldn't help but laugh. He tugged his shirt overhead and shook it out creating a white cloud. Then he tossed it aside, leaving him standing bare up top, and Maker, he looked good bare.

"Once I get these in the oven, you're in trouble."

She kept backing up, smile getting wider. "What kind of trouble?"

"The kind that's going to make you sweat your ass off during training." He pulled apart the dough piece by piece along a metal tray and she took another step back anticipating more flour to be launched. "Don't run or I might chase you."

He was half smiling, and she wasn't sure if he meant it or not. And the rebel inside wanted to test him. "If you want me to train, you'll have to catch me first." She took off running down the hall and threw open the front door. Giggling to herself, she sprinted for the fruit orchard. He appeared in front of her so suddenly she ran smack right into his chest. His warm hands wrapped around her arms, and he moved forward, pushing her back.

She searched his eyes, heart pounding. There was something about the danger that made him infinitely more attractive in this moment. "You were supposed to chase me, not use magic."

"Says who? You didn't lay out any rules." His eyes fell to her lips.

"I know your secret," Layala blurted out.

His brows raised. "I'm full of them, but now I'm curious."

"You pretend to hate everyone, to be evil and wicked, but that's not the whole truth."

Her back hit the outside wall. The wild look in his eyes was like a cat before it pounced. "You know what I hate? I crave you in every conceivable way and I hate it. I hate the way you poison my thoughts, the way you infect every part of my being. I hate the way you laugh at things that aren't even funny, even more that you've become so vulnerable. It makes me want to protect you, to worry over you and to never stop thinking about you. I can't stop thinking about you, morning sun or darkest night you're there. I hate when you nibble your lip when you're thinking. I despise every dangerous curve along your body, but most especially this curve," his thumb dragged along her lips. "I wish you would hate me more than you do. I wish you loathed me as much as the day I came into the castle throne room because... I don't want to want you. I don't want to trust you again or have anything to do with you. When this is over, and the council is no more, I know you'll leave me and go back to War, either here or in Palenor, and I'll never want to see either of you again because it hurts." He shoved off the wall and headed back toward the manor. "The scones are going to burn."

Layala let out the breath she held and sank down the wall, wrapped her arms around her legs, and rested her chin on her knees. *Shit.*

THE SCONES WERE DELICIOUS. Prize winning, in fact, with a spread of butter and a bit of honey. They rivaled even gnome baking, and she wondered if he'd stolen their recipe or maybe they'd taken his. After she ate three, she found Hel outside tearing off long creeping weeds with his hands from the side of the manor. With the force he threw them and the sweat glistening on his muscular back and chest, she didn't approach. She peered from around the corner and then stepped back nibbling her lower lip. Maybe it was best she stayed away for a while. He was clearly upset. She knew with his magic he could tear those vines without much effort, but he chose the physical labor.

But then that left him to do all the work. She stepped around the corner, and without a word, joined him in tugging down weeds. He paused for only a moment then continued on. At least a half hour passed before she said, "The scones were delicious."

"I'm glad you like them." He didn't pause his work.

"Thank you for going through the trouble to get the ingredients to make them. You didn't have to."

"You're welcome."

"Since the demon is here, shouldn't we find an obsidian weapon?"

"You could get your goddess blade, Zythara—which in the primordial language means—"

"Darkbringer," Layala said and pressed her lips together, finding it strange it came to her so quickly. "I named it that because when I brought it out that meant they'd never see light again."

He broke his scowl and the corner of his mouth threatened to lift. "And the irony of your other sword's name isn't lost on me." He jerked down a thick green vine that snapped halfway from the top and toppled. "But you'd have to remember where it is to do that. I can't pull it for you."

"Pull it from where?"

"The aether. It's a plane where no flesh nor person exists or can see but *things* can go."

Layala fidgeted with the dagger's handle on her hip. She had a feeling it was here, confiscated along with the rest of her belongings. Not stored in the aether.

She watched him continue working, tossing weeds and vines into the giant pile and the mention of god blades struck a chord. "I stole Soulender from you. I killed—" she paused when a flash of her plunging the golden dagger into the chest of a male came across her mind. "I killed a primordial. And Soulender is what you want from me, isn't it? And that's what the council fears. I have the only weapon that can kill one of them."

He didn't even pause. "Yes, you killed Synick, one of the seven originals. Because he murdered your sister with the Sword of Truth, the location of which no one seems to know. I think the knowledge of its resting place died with Synick. And no, you told me where Soulender was. Moments before they executed us, you whispered its location in my mind. But again,

445

I can't pull it; only you can. And you can bet it is the reason the council fears us."

"I'm the reason we were banished. This *is* my fault. Killing a god is banishment if not execution, and I dragged you both down with me."

He stopped and wiped the top of his forearm across his sweaty brow. His chest heaved up and down from the hours of exertion. "It wasn't the sole reason for our banishment, just one among the list but it all began with me. I stole Soulender from my family, from the council."

Layala remembered her dream where they talked about this exact thing. "So you could see me." She couldn't help but slowly smile.

He laughed at himself, bringing out the dimple and his cheeks even colored a light pink. "Yes. I was young and a fool. And you were the most stunning goddess I'd ever seen."

"You were what—five hundred? It's not that young. And even now, though it's been two thousand years, most of that time doesn't count. We weren't even alive through much of it."

"If we're being technical with time spent breathing and in the Void, I'm nine hundred and three. You're an old lady. Even with the two-thousand-year gap, you're at least ten thousand years. There was a time when you primordials didn't even keep time. It's hard to say how old you really are."

"That's—bewildering." She couldn't truly comprehend it.

He chuckled. "A little bit."

Layala jerked up a huge weed that grew nearly as tall as she. She wanted to ask about the wars but that would be a touchy subject considering they'd been on opposing sides. For weeks, both of them avoided talking about anything to do with the time she left him and after.

He waved for her to follow and started for the clearing

they'd battered down. "Come on, let's train before we lose motivation."

The tall golden grass lay flat in nearly a perfect circle, making it easy to move around in. He rolled his neck and cracked his knuckles. The sunlight glistened off his bare chest, illuminating his tattoos and rune marks. Layala stayed a few paces further away than normal. He usually wore more clothes.

"Shadow."

Layala focused on her power and felt her body shifting. Shadows enveloped her entire being and then returned.

"Good. Shield." A blast of red crackling energy careened toward her.

She threw up her hands and the attack crashed into her barrier, fizzling out.

"Excellent." He began to pace slowly back and forth. "You should be able to levitate by now."

"It's hard for me to imagine lifting off the ground with no wings or reason. And after I jumped off the cliff and it didn't work..."

"And it's easy for you to imagine changing entirely into shadow?" He waved a dismissive hand. "You should also be able to persuade. Your speed and strength are as much as they'll be until we get our immortality back."

"Like command someone to do something and they have no choice but to do it?" She thought back to him demanding she take her clothes off and though her cheeks were already warm from the sunshine and work, the heat intensified.

"You should also be able to resist persuasion. We've been at this for over nine weeks now."

"Test me," Layala said, holding her arms out to her sides.

He closed the distance between them, leaving inches. He

gently grasped her chin between his fingers, garnet eyes locking onto hers. "Tell me you hate me."

She felt a sensation, like light invisible fingers gliding through her scalp and said, "But I don't hate you."

He smirked. "Tell me why you're afraid of me."

"I'm not."

"Then tell me what it was like the first time you took me into your bed."

Her cheeks flamed as a flash of him unbuttoning the back of her dress flitted across her mind. She scowled up at him. "Why do you always have to be an ass?"

"Why is my asking being an ass? We were married. It was our wedding night. You asked me to wait. A test of my devotion." She felt his power grow stronger. "So, tell me. Did you enjoy it?"

Layala smacked his hand away. "Stop it. I'm with Thane—" but she wasn't.

His scowl deepened. "No, you're not. Or did you forget your last conversation with him and why you cry every night and every morning?" He may as well have stuck a knife in her chest and twisted it. It was bad enough he'd witnessed their breakup and now he heard her crying about it? "And the only time you haven't cried was this morning—with me there."

When he curled up with her, warm and vulnerable.

With tears burning, she turned her face away.

"You didn't answer. Did you like it when I carried you to the bed and laid you down for the first time?"

She remembered her dress falling around her ankles and he slipped one arm behind her back, one under her knees and swung her up against his chest. The way he looked down at her, she'd never seen someone more in love. It wasn't her first time but with him it felt new, magical, intense.

Turning away, she pushed back his magic she felt wrapping around her like a cloud.

"Of course, you liked it," he said. "You loved it. You wanted me all the time. You wanted me like you wanted air."

With a snarl Layala whirled around. "So did you. You couldn't keep your hands off me. You were in love with me from the moment I kissed you. You would have done anything for me. If I'd have made you wait a hundred years, you would have."

"No, the moment I fell in love with you, Valeen, was when I saw you standing at the top of those stairs in my house. There were a hundred ladies there, but I only saw you. You came to me when you should have let me go. You promised me forever, and I, you." He raked his fingers through his hair. "That's why I can't understand where it all went wrong. Tell me why."

She was shaking her head, baffled at it herself. "I don't know." Because she knew she'd been in love with him, that she'd have done anything for him. She'd have gone to the ends of every realm to be near him, fought any monster, forsaken all others.

But he did something.

Broke her heart.

Crushed her soul.

She felt the ghost pain now, but she couldn't think of a reason.

Why couldn't *he* tell her what went wrong?

Something was missing from both of their memories.

He grabbed her arms, squeezing gently. "Tell me." His magic enveloped her and the pull to spill her every secret was there, but no memories surfaced, no words came.

"I don't know!"

He let go of her and turned, stalking away.

"How long were we married?" she shouted after him.

He stopped and whirled back around. "Nine years. It's nothing in the life of a god. It may as well have never happened." He flicked his fingers out to the side. "Just a blip, the blink of an eye. It doesn't matter."

"It does matter! Nine years ruined the last two thousand years of our lives!"

"Yes, it did," he said with a sneer. "Which is all the more reason for you to remember how to open the way back to Runevale. You're the one who closed it. And the sooner you know how, the sooner we can part ways."

"Me?" Layala stared at him, realization crashing in on her like a brick wall folding. "That's what you want. You need me to open the door for you."

"Yes. So how did you do it? Because not me nor any other god or goddess has been able to lift whatever magic you did to trap them there and keep us out. Not even the goddess of wisdom knows how. She only knows it was *you*."

CHAPTER 39

LAYALA

Later that evening, after Layala packed her bags to leave for the city, she went looking for Hel. Her journals could be the key to unlocking the past fully. The key to knowing how to open the way to Runevale.

They could stay behind the walls for a few more months, hiding away from the demon prince, and she might remember everything but what if it took years? Even the weeks being stuck here made her slightly stir crazy and that's when she had chores and things to do.

She popped her head into Presco's study, where he usually was. He had several beakers lined up on the desk. One bubbled a bright green, two purple, and one like liquid silver. "What are those?"

He jumped, apparently not seeing or hearing her approach. Clearing his throat, he pushed his glasses up further on his nose. "I'm experimenting with potions. It's how I make my livelihood now."

451

"What do they do?"

He smiled and his face lit up. "Many things. Most I make are simply for fun or vanity and it is a lucrative business. If you drink this lighter purple, it turns your skin or scales purple for a few hours. I'm trying to perfect the formula for a longer duration." He held up a finger. "Or I have a recipe to change your hair color if you'd rather that. That change will last until you buy another potion. Hair is less stubborn. Very popular with the ladies." He lifted the silver beaker. "This one is my newest formula and I'm afraid it's finicky." It bubbled and hissed. "I'm attempting to create a formula that when taken will give the user dragon scales for armor. Temporary of course, but if I can make it happen, it would be worth a fortune. Imagine if the elves had it. A bite from a pale one wouldn't penetrate. A sword wouldn't break skin. Unfortunately, my last test subject turned an odd shade of green, vomited for hours, and there were no dragon scales."

"It's fascinating. I'm certain you'll get it right. And maybe I'll turn my hair pink for a day." She wondered if she drank a potion for black if the white streak in her hair would go away.

He chuckled. "I have a bottle on my shelf at my shop in the city. It comes in various shades too. Just say the word and it's yours."

"Alright," she said with a smile. "Did you see where Hel went?"

"He went out the front door about ten minutes ago."

"Thanks." She stepped out into the cool evening air, with the last of the dying light, hoping he hadn't left for the night already. A splash of water caught her attention. *He must be washing clothes. Although, wouldn't he do that with magic?* He always did. She even watched an enchanted broom sweep the floor for him once.

Well, he wasn't washing clothes. Layala stopped, blood running hot and cold at once. He was naked in the metal tub. *I guess I should be thankful he's not naked outside the tub.* Steam rolled out of the water. His head laid back against the rim, strong muscular arms resting on the sides. The tub only reached up to his armpits but was long enough he could stretch his legs. Her sight fell directly to the lily mark on his chest. The one she gave him by trying to stab him with Soulender. She apparently had a habit of trying to stab males she would fall in love with.

He opened one eye and then closed it again. *Well, he saw me. No point in running off now.* "Why didn't you tell me sooner about me being the one to close off Runevale?"

"I couldn't have you open the way unprepared or without me if you remembered."

"And what makes you think I won't now?"

He lifted his head and splashed water over his chest. "You won't. You know you need me." He cupped water in his hands and rinsed his face. Then scrubbed his hands over his hair and lifted his chin. "You just going to stand there and watch? I mean, if it was the other way around, I think you'd try to murder me... but I don't mind. Look all you want, love." *I know you like what you see.*

I never said I didn't. You've always been beautiful.

A little bit or a lot? he teased.

More than you deserve to be.

He laughed. *Why don't you come closer and get a better look?*

She knew he was teasing but folded her arms and shook her head.

Without warning, he stood, water cascaded down his very naked body. Layala didn't let her eyes travel down before she spun on her heel. "Are you serious? Can you put on a towel?"

"It's not anything you haven't seen before."

"Well, I don't want to see it now." She gritted her teeth. "Presco wants to leave for the city in the morning. Are you coming?"

She heard the water splashing and imagined he stepped out of the tub.

"You want to sneak into the most well-guarded institution in all the realms and we have a demon on our tail. As if I'd let you go without me." He walked right by her, flashing his bare back, naked ass, and all.

Layala's jaw dropped, not even registering what he said. Did he have no shame? *But with an ass like that... No, bad, Layala.* What he didn't have was a sense of modesty which rang true for him. From what she remembered the people in his territory weren't bothered by skin showing, yet they didn't walk around fully nude.

With a quick glance over his shoulder, he winked and vanished from sight. This male had split personalities. One moment he was telling her how much he hated everything about her and that he never wanted to see her again, and the next he was flaunting himself like a peacock.

WITH HER BAG slung over her shoulder, she stepped out through the hole in the outer wall to the waiting dragon. Presco had pearl-white scales with baby blue horns, the tallest horns she'd ever seen, and spikes all along his spine. Compared to the others back in Adalon he was colossal, bulky, taller, longer. He lay down with his head resting on his massive paws, but his back spikes still rose higher than the fifty-foot wall surrounding the manor. Even though she knew of his gentle nature it was intimidating to stand beside such a large dragon.

"Hop on," Presco said, lifting his head. "It's a two-day flight."

She stepped forward, and Hel took hold of the strap around her shoulder. "I'll take this for you." The weight of it lifted as it vanished into nothing. She was going to have to learn to do that soon. The convenience alone.

"Thanks."

Hel stood back and crossed his arms. "Let's see you get up there." He held up his finger, "Without your vines."

"You mean, levitate?" She hadn't done that yet and with Presco waiting and watching, it wasn't the ideal time to try.

In answer, he arched a brow and shrugged.

"You know, we don't always have to make everything into a training exercise."

"I'm always testing you, even when you don't know it. Get up there."

She sighed. "Fine."

It can't be that difficult. All I have to do is float. She rolled her eyes at herself and imagined her feet lifting off the ground first. Nothing happened. Her magic tingled along her limbs, and she tried again, leaning into the memory she had of lifting out of the water. *Come on, I'm Valeen, the goddess of night. This is easy.*

The pressure of the ground beneath her feet proved otherwise. With Presco watching hopefully and Hel's smug expression, she desperately wanted it but the more effort she put into lifting off the ground, the more resistance she came up against.

Alright, shadow then. Her solid form dissipated but kept her shape, and she climbed up Presco's leg. When she weighed nothing, the climb was quick. One jump moved her up ten feet.

Straddling a horn, she brought her solid form back and waved down at Hel.

As quick as a thought, he was behind her, leaning back against another spike that towered over his head by three feet, keeping a careful sword's blade distance between them. Although this was a dragon, not a horse, she thought of her rides with Thane and the way he pressed against her backside. Hel seemed as desperate to stay away as Thane had been to be close.

Presco lifted into the air, barely jarring her with his smooth takeoff. Once they were level and soaring, Layala turned around, bringing her knees up to her chest and rested her back against the spike. With her hair secured in a braid, only the stray hairs around her face whipped about in the wind but Hel's shaggy dark hair took the brunt of the blast. The whooshing of Presco's wings and the howl of wind from their speed was loud enough she didn't feel the need to talk to Hel. After everything they said the day before, the energy between them felt heavy. Recalling bits of her life as the goddess of night added tension and settled like a weight in her gut.

Hel flicked his wrist and the wind calmed to nothing, as if a surrounding bubble enveloped them. They sat quietly, staring off in opposite directions. Presco's flying was relatively steady but a sudden gust of wind and a jump up, sent Layala sliding forward. Her fingers clawed at his slick scales but did nothing to stop her momentum and she collided with Hel. He caught her around the waist and to her horror, her thighs were now straddled on top of his. His face was inches away, his garnet eyes stared into hers.

"You need to hold onto something," he said.

If he were Thane he'd add something like "and that something can be me," and she'd remark something back, but Hel didn't say anything. He held onto her waist like he didn't want to let go, and he stared at her like he wished she would stay in his arms. And for a moment she found herself wanting to stay, too. A part of her knew what it was like to be in love with this beautiful male, and how for years he was her gift from the All Mother, an answer to her lonely prayers.

She wanted to fold into him and hold him like he was her Zaurahel and she was his Valeen and the last two thousand years never happened. Like he was the god who brought light into her darkness and she the goddess who broke through his walls and claimed a male who said he'd never fall in love. Even if she couldn't remember it all, she felt it, felt his magic curl around her, felt her own answer to its call. Her lily mark even throbbed like a heartbeat of its own. She wanted to give in to him, just once, a kiss, nothing more. She couldn't remember what his lips tasted like and if they'd move in sync with hers, if her heart would sing.

He leaned forward, and heavy-lidded eyes sought her admission. His fingers lightly dug into her ribs and his lips parted. His breaths came faster, so did hers.

Just once.

But then she remembered before. *Just one kiss, he'd said.* Just one kiss changed everything and that wasn't who they were anymore.

It felt like a betrayal even thinking about kissing Hel and at the same time, being with him felt like where she should have been all along. Before she could even lean away he gently pushed her back. The buzzing connection severed, and she quickly turned her body around and scooted up toward the dragon spike. As her arms wrapped around the spike his voice entered her mind, *It wouldn't stop with one kiss, love.*

She faced forward, unable to look at him. *I know.*

I would want more.

I know. Her throat thickened and tears came unbidden. *All those things you said you hate about me...*

A long pause. *Are what I love about you. And I can't have you. That's why I hate them.*

CHAPTER 40

LAYALA

I n a shaded alleyway Layala peeked around the corner of a white brick building. The street was packed with dragon shifters, and unlike the small Podunk town they'd left behind days before, every one of them was dressed in expensive suits and dresses. Their bodies dripped in gold, silver, and precious jewels. Many ladies strolled with lace umbrellas or wide-brimmed hats to shade the sun. Unlike the dragon kingdom in Adalon, in this part of the city there weren't layers upon layers of houses and bridge-like roads intersecting hundreds of feet in the air. No dragons shifted into their beast forms, and no one wore their wings or horns.

"This is a no-fly zone, or I'd have dropped us in at the other end where my shop is," Presco said.

A black carriage with gold fixtures pulled by hippogryphs creaked by on the cobblestone street. Layala gawked at the half-horse half-bird creature. "Why?"

"The wealthiest of dragons pride themselves on being more

civilized and less beastly. You won't see scales or wings here unless something extreme happens." Presco adjusted the collar of his jacket. The back of the black coat reached his knees, and with his hair combed back and fancy shiny shoes, he could be ready for a ball.

She had chosen to wear her favorite usual fitted brown trousers and a simple linen blouse, but as she stood surrounded by the glittering crowd in their expensive gowns, she suddenly felt underdressed. With a gust of wind, her clothing began to transform into an evening dress. Layala brushed her hands over the empire-waisted champagne dress hugging her curves. The long sleeves were sheer and wide, tightening in silk cuffs at her wrists. Moments before it had been on the mannequin in the window across the street. She narrowed her eyes at Hel who wore a black suit much like Presco's. "That's stealing, you know," Layala said.

"Add it to my list of offenses, love."

Layala lifted the flier for an opera she found pinned to the wall. Hosted by none other than the richest family in the realm, the Drakonans. "Are we going to this tomorrow night?"

Hel raised the crook of his elbow to her. "It's our best opportunity to be introduced to the Drakonans and find a way into their treasury." He turned to Presco. "It's best if you're not seen with us in public. If something goes wrong, you and your family will be ruined as well. There's no need for that."

"Fine. I'll walk a few paces ahead. Follow me."

Rather than take Hel's offered arm, Layala stepped out into the sunlight and the busy street keeping an eye on Presco's back. Even with heeled shoes Layala was the shortest female in the crowd and although her pointed ears were covered by her long hair, dragons' gazes drifted to her. Hel slid up beside her and slipped his arm around hers.

"While we are here, you are my wife. We're wealthy elves from the east, a city called Neptu, in the diamond trade. New money or they'll expect to know who we are. You can go by Layala. They won't know that name and call me Zar. Our surname is Black." With a snap of his fingers, a diamond bracelet, and a gaudy necklace, heavy around her neck, appeared.

"Oh yes, how could I forget Mr. Black. You thought about this on the way here, didn't you?"

"Obviously. And you'll have to pretend you actually like me, dear wife."

"*And* I'll have to pretend I'm actually your wife. Don't expect the benefits."

"You are my wife. There's no need to pretend, benefits or not."

"You keep saying that but even if this wasn't an entirely different life, didn't we get divorced? Or is that not an option in Runevale?"

His brow lifted. "Have I ever called you my 'ex-wife'?"

"No."

"We chose a blood-bonded marriage, and you must go through a ceremony to end it. We never did, and neither of us ever signed the documents to record an official separation."

"Why?"

Hel lifted his shoulder. *Because a part of us didn't want it to be over?* she thought to herself. He gave her a knowing look that made her spine tingle but said nothing.

Layala cleared her throat. "Where did the diamonds come from?"

"That shop right there." He pointed right to a robin-egg-blue building with pink peonies filling the ledge of the inside window surrounded by displays of diamonds and other

461

precious jewels. "We can return them when we leave if it will make you feel less guilty."

"I'd feel less guilty if you paid for them to begin with."

"First she calls our marriage pretend, now she wants me to buy her diamonds," Hel said loud enough for Presco to hear.

Presco glanced over his shoulder. "Give her whatever she wants. Best advice my father ever gave me when it came to my marriage."

Hel laughed, crinkling the corners of his eyes, and Layala couldn't help but smile at how genuine it sounded. Hel picked up her left hand and swiped his palm over top of it. Her left ring finger now held a silver band with a half-an-inch long, pear-shaped black diamond with two crescent moon diamonds on each side facing inward. She brought it closer to her face, and flecks of silver inside the black diamond looked remarkably like the night sky. Even if she remembered being married to Hel it still felt like someone else, and to even play pretend when it wasn't pretend made her insides squirm. "It's huge. Is this from the shop, too?"

"Of course, it's huge. We're diamond dealers. We must play the part. Act like you're better than everyone and I'm sure you'll fit right in."

"You'll have no trouble with that."

"Ha." Hel tugged her closer until their hips met. "When you're a god it's in the core to be a pompous ass."

Layala rolled her eyes. "Need I remind you, you're an elf now. A powerful one but not immortal."

"Best keep talk of gods to a minimum," Presco said quietly. "I don't think anyone will recognize either of you given the length of time passed, but the blood of the gods is very present in your veins. Many will believe you to be descendants. Don't give them any reason to ask further questions."

Layala pressed her lips together. "Why do they hate the gods so much?"

"Us dragons were attacked in a brutal war and then abandoned. Most don't know why the way was shut."

Layala stared at a lady with fuchsia hair in a matching dress strolling past and another with vibrant blue locks, and the closer she inspected under those hats or umbrellas the more she noticed bright hair colors. There were few who didn't look to enhance the color even if it was a shiner brown or a brighter red. "You weren't joking when you said your hair potions were a lucrative business."

Presco nodded to a passing couple who waved at him and said "Hello," after they passed, he peeked back once more. "Well, I don't like to brag but Presco's Potions has become a staple in the lives of many ladies."

"Congratulations on your success, Presco," Hel said.

"Thank you," he said grinning with pride and turned back around.

Hel reached up and twirled the white lock of Layala's hair around his finger. "Perhaps this can be turned back?" He stared at her a moment contemplatively. "On second thought, I think I like it. It's unique, as are you."

Layala lowered her voice to say, "You don't have to start pretending to be a good husband. No one is watching."

He leaned in close, until his lips brushed her ear. "Oh, yes they are. And it's not an act. I meant it."

The line between hate and love was becoming increasingly thin.

Presco turned into his shop "Presco's Potions" and they paused for a moment outside then turned in. The crowded lobby was filled with shelves and shelves of different colored potions with labels she couldn't decipher, and ladies drinking tiny tubes full of bubbly liquid with handheld mirrors, watching their reflection for their hair to instantly change color, or grow longer. One lady's hair went from straight blonde cut at her shoulders to bright red curly hair down to her hips in a matter of seconds.

Layala looked up at the sign on the wall with the prices and nearly gasped. A thousand silver for one bottle, two for one thousand five hundred, and the ladies in here were testing out different colors and styles like they were free.

"Presco, dear, you're back," a female crooned, sliding her gloved hand along his bicep. Her long nose curved slightly to the side as if it had been broken once and never repaired. Her sleek white-blonde hair was pulled back into a low ponytail. With crows' feet around her eyes and smile lines, she appeared older, but Layala could never guess her exact age given how long the dragon shifters lived. "We're running low on stock." She smiled at Layala and Hel. "May I help you two find something? I love the white streak in your hair. It's quite tasteful and modern."

Layala realized she understood every word the lady said but she wasn't speaking the language from Adalon.

"Ayva, this is Layala and Zar, the Blacks. Diamond Dealers from the east. I met them on the way in. They're looking for something particular. Perhaps we can show them the private stock in the back?"

"But we don't—"

"The private stock upstairs," he prodded, eyes flashing.

Her brows tugged in; his introduction seemed to confuse her. She blinked a few times and then recognition flashed across her face. "Oh!" she exclaimed. "Of course... our private stock."

Many of the patrons glanced their way too often not to be

eavesdropping. "This way, please," Presco said and started through the busy room, stepping around crowds of ladies and toward a dark wooden door in the back corner.

Hel gestured ahead of himself. "After you, love."

The burning jealousy in the reptilian eyes of the lady shifters as they passed was unnerving. Many whispered about why they weren't invited to see the private stock of Presco's Potions. "Elves."

"New money."

"What does Presco keep in the back?"

"Blood of the gods," one whispered, watching Hel with narrowed eyes.

Layala pushed through the door, walking in on an apparent argument. "You brought them here to our home." His wife's eyes darted around nervously as if she were hiding something illegal. "Dragons' breath, I wasn't expecting—when you said you needed to check on the manor I never expected them to be there. This is *them*."

"I didn't either, my dear." He patted her back gently. "Say hello, please. She speaks Murelien best."

Once Hel closed the door behind them, shutting out the chatter and noise from the storefront, Ayva began to pace.

"I understand the language you're speaking now," Layala said. "Hello."

Her bright lavender eyes fell on Layala. "I apologize for my rudeness." She dipped into a bow. "It's pleasure to meet you both, Layala and Zar—er, wait," she said the names as if she were unsure of them. She patted her sleek silver hair and brushed her other hand over the front of her light blue silk dress. "That's not your real names. My apologies." She glared at Presco. "If you'd warned me, I might have put on something better to meet *them*."

Layala could see she was having a remarkably difficult time not using the word "gods" as if saying it out loud would sound crazy.

"You look quite nice," Hel said. "Presco has told me much about you, Ayva. You're a remarkable potions' master yourself I hear."

She stared at him awestruck. "Zar... oh my, you're—" she gasped as if just realizing something, "Zaurah—I'm sorry I'm so flustered. You're not supposed to exist anymore, but you're the... god, Zaurahel."

"Unfortunately for some, I'm still existing," Hel said.

She stopped pacing and stared at Layala. "And Valeen, the goddess of night, a primordial." She slowly lowered down to one knee and then the other and bowed her head.

"You don't need to do that," Layala said, flushing with embarrassment. "Please don't, in fact."

Presco took her hand and brought her to her feet. "Valeen never liked people to kneel before her unless they were pledging allegiance or to prove a point."

"Presco told me all about you and how close you two were, well, all of you." She ran her palm over her hair again, nervously smoothing down white-blonde hair that was already sleek. "You two were married and then of course the wars and the exiles. Never mind, let's not talk about all that. How are you now? I feel like I know you both after everything Presco told me. And you're as lovely as he said you were."

Layala and Hel exchanged a glance. "We're fine," Layala said with a shrug. "I suppose. We're here to get my things back from the vault."

Her ivory skin visibly paled. She turned to Presco and communicated with a look, the way two people who have been married a long time do. "How exactly will you do that?"

"Not for you to worry about," Hel said. "We won't involve your husband."

"You won't?" Presco balked. "This was my idea."

"You don't need to risk your life and freedom or hers."

Presco pushed his glasses up the bridge of his nose. "You're forgetting who Valeen is to me. She's my queen, and I am her right hand. I swore an oath to her before you ever *met* her."

Hel growled, and Layala stepped in between them. "Let's not. We'll discuss this later." She met Hel's garnet eyes. *This is not the time or place to fight with Presco,* she said to him silently. Surprisingly, Hel didn't respond, only turned away. "For now, can we be shown to our rooms?"

"Upstairs, there is a guest room, second door on the right," Ayva said.

"Only one room?" Layala asked, and her stomach dropped a little.

Presco gave an apologetic smile. "Our place in the country is bigger. Here we only have a small apartment above the shop."

"We really do apologize. I'm sure you're used to much more luxury and your own chambers as well as a shared room," Ayva said.

Hel slipped his arm around her waist, and briefly kissed her temple. Her skin burned where his lips met. "We'll not complain about sharing a room. You're doing us a favor." He gestured toward the stairs. "Shall we?"

CHAPTER 41

LAYALA

At the top of the stairs Layala was met with a set of loveseats, a small round table centered between them. A gold vase of peonies sat on top, and the floral scent drifted in the air. A kitchenette with pristine copper pots and pans hung along the wall above the sink and white countertop. The entire right side opened up to floor-to-ceiling windows offering a spectacular view of the busy street below.

Hel stepped through the second door on the right as instructed and Layala quietly followed him, until she gently closed it behind her. He was already sprawled out on the massive bed that dominated most of the room. It was at least eight feet long and even wider. A small loveseat sat next to the one window overlooking the street. Layala tugged the forest-green curtain closed. "I take it you're claiming the bed." She plopped down on the matching, green velvet couch.

"This bed is plenty big for the both of us, even if you're a cover stealer and flop around like a fish on land."

With narrowed eyes, she crossed her legs. Rather than argue the point that was a clear exaggeration, she said, "Why are you trying to leave Presco out of this plan?"

Hel sat up and crossed his arms. "Look, it may have been two thousand years ago but much like demons, dragons don't forget. There will be dragons old enough to know Presco was connected with you. If we're parading around with him, it won't be long before they figure it out. And you heard what he said, they don't hold favor for the gods anymore, and I'd rather not spend time in a dragon prison or be executed."

"I could just as easily say that about you and me together."

"Actually, it's the last thing they'd expect given we were enemies locked in a war against each other before." The corner of his mouth tugged up. "So, the more you're hopelessly in love with me the less suspicion they'll have."

Layala chuckled and rubbed her thumb over the top of the massive diamond on her finger. She had a feeling it was hers from before. "I'm a great actress. If either of us is going to expose the truth of our marriage and we're not the happy couple we claim, it's you. You even hate the curve of my lips, remember?"

"Oh, and you're so fond of me?" He rolled his eyes.

Pressing her lips together, she didn't know what to say.

His stare seemed to heat her from within. Several beats passed in silence until he finally said, "Are you?" His brows furrowed and his garnet eyes sparkled in the sunlight filtering in from the window.

Layala kept quiet. The truth was she did care about him. "If I didn't know any better, I'd say you were concerned for Presco's safety and you're getting a little soft. Don't worry, I'll keep your secret."

Hel let out a dark chuckle. "But you do know better. His and his family's safety are more your area of concern, but if it will encourage you to side with me, then yes. Presco going to prison or being killed would devastate his family."

Layala's stomach seemed to knot, thinking of his wife's screams if he didn't make it, and his children... "Anyway, you were going to show me how to push and pull things from the aether, and I need to test my persuasion skills before this opera event."

He scooted off the bed and picked up a potted fern from the stand next to the bed. With a curl of his finger to call her forward, she stood, and he pushed the fern into her hand. "It's easy. All you have to do is think of the aether, imagine this fern vanishing and it's gone, tucked away in your own hiding place. When you want to retrieve it again, you imagine the same object in your grasp. Your powers will do the heavy lifting."

"Alright." Layala rubbed a fern frond between her fingers and thought of a place where no one could exist, but things could go, a place of nowhere, and imagined the weight lifting from her palm and it disappearing. The tingle of her magic warmed her skin, but the fern didn't budge.

"I'll help you the first time." Hel placed his palm flat beneath hers. His warm touch sent a pulse of electricity through her. She couldn't help but stare into his eyes, surprised at the gesture. His methods were usually much more brutal or tricky.

She nodded and kept her gaze pinned to his. The longer they stared the more the temperature in the room seemed to rise. He swallowed hard. "Think of how vast and endless the stars and worlds are and then picture the blackness in between," he said.

Eyes closed, she imagined the moons, shimmering constellations, colorful nebulas, the vast inky blackness surrounding it all and found herself dancing with Hel there, both of them smiling and laughing, carefree in a way Layala had never been. In a heartbeat, the weight of the fern was gone. She opened her eyes to Hel's smile.

He let his hand drop to his side and the electricity flowing between them dissipated. "Good. Now call it back."

Keeping her palm up and open before her, she pictured it there again, the weight of it, the smell of dirt and feel of it, the fuzzy texture between her fingers, and suddenly it was there again. Smiling, she lifted her gaze to his. "I did it."

He chuckled. "Yeah."

She quickly set the fern down, and thought of Darkbringer, her goddess blade and imagined feeling the weight of it, the smooth pommel, but after several beats, it didn't come forth. With a frown she tried again and no luck. It must be locked in the vault, and magical wards would prevent her from being able to retrieve anything that way.

But Soulender.... It too was gold, shorter than Darkbringer, with an inscription along the blade though she couldn't recall exactly what it read. She stowed it in a silver chest with black runes engraved all over it. It wasn't just left floating around the aether for someone else to pull, even if it was a rare talent. In her mind's eye, the lid to the chest popped open, and in reality Soulender flashed into her palm, heavy and yet light. She sucked in a sharp breath, felt the hum of its power, a subtle vibration. The only weapon left in all the realms that could kill a god, the true reason they were hunted.

Hel stared at it, face unreadable. What if he'd lied and it was the thing he'd been after? She had it right here out in the open for him to take. Whoever possessed this dagger was the most powerful being in all the realms, the most feared.

"You should put that away," Hel said. "Someone might sense it."

Breathing a sigh of relief, it vanished back into the chest, sealed in tight.

"Are you ready to mind control some poor fool to do your bidding?"

"Not to do anything bad," Layala said with a scowl.

"You do something bad? Of course not," he said with a smirk. "We'll save the fun for me."

NIGHT FELL and the stars shined above, as did the twin moons. Several streets over from the affluent Pearl Avenue they came upon what appeared to be a party for young adults. Hooting and hollering young males jumped off the roof with wings spread wide. A whirlwind from them speeding past whipped her loose hair. A few roaring bonfires gathered groups. Loud music of drums and tambourines and other thumping instruments came from the mansion with four white pillars holding up the overhanging balcony. Young dragon ladies wearing scant dresses with horns growing out of their brightly-colored hair, some with wings on display, some not, gathered in groups in the front yard with bottles of what must be wine and liquor in their hands. A stark contrast to the upscale wealthy street of establishments they'd been at with Presco.

"Ah perfect," Hel said, coming to a stop outside the white picket fence surrounding the home. "Now, when you're using your persuasion, look them in the face, and it works better if you touch them. A brush of contact is all it takes for most. For more resistant minds, longer touch."

"I remember." She hadn't forgotten how he made her follow his commands.

"Be subtle about it, casual. We don't want anyone figuring out who we are." He flashed his pretty white teeth. "Smile. Use that charm I know you have somewhere in you."

"I got it," Layala drawled. "What are you going to do?"

"I'll be around. Grading your performance."

Layala rolled her eyes and walked through the open front gate. *Alright, this is simple. Look someone in the face and command them with your power. Maker above, taking someone's free will isn't what I should be doing.* But she needed her journals, and if they were going to get into the vault she'd likely have to persuade a few guards to take a break or look the other way.

She walked down the gravel path leading to the house, searching for a target. It was better she chose someone alone or in a small group so no one could see what she was doing. With the amount of alcohol being consumed, she wasn't sure it would matter either way, however. Before she chose some poor unsuspecting fool, as Hel put it, a young male approached her. His dragon's scales were the color of brushed aluminum, and they flexed and moved like rippling fishes underwater in the torchlights. Even without the dragon scales, his broad shoulders and seven-foot stature made him an intimidating figure to stand next to. With a tilt of his head, his scales shifted to tanned skin. "It's been a while since I've seen an elf."

She held out her hand. "My name's Layala."

He smiled and grasped her palm, dwarfing her hand in his massive grip. "Caliban Drakonan."

"Drakonan," Layala murmured and kept holding his hand. They might not even need to go to the opera if she could get him to spill secrets. "Your father must own the treasury."

"My great-grandfather does but it's more of a family business." He looked down at their connected hands, smirked, and kept a gentle hold. At least it wasn't awkward.

She finally pulled her hand away. "I'm new in town and was passing by and saw the party. I thought I'd drop in. I hope I'm not intruding."

"Not at all, Layala..." he fished for her surname.

"Black."

"That's a nice ring you have. Married?"

She looked down at her hand, thankful she hadn't taken it off. They almost planned to go into this party not knowing each other but that would have ruined their story at the opera with Caliban here. She was sure Caliban would be there with his family. "Yes, he's here somewhere." She glanced back but didn't see him among the crowd.

"What brings you to Akliv?"

"We're in the diamond business and looking to open a shop on Pearl Avenue."

"And you know you'll need the backing of my great-grand-father to do that." He chuckled and rubbed the back of his neck. "So your husband sent in the pretty elf in elegant clothes to meet with me first and get your foot in the door?"

Layala smiled, realizing how overdressed she was compared to the others in fine but still more casual attire. "My husband doesn't send me to do anything, dear."

He laughed at that. "My mum's the same way, even if my father would never admit it."

Layala brushed her hand against his and locked in his gaze. "I was hoping for an invitation to the opera tomorrow night. Is that something you can provide?" Her magic tingled, her voice sounded more melodic, sultry.

"Of course," he said, looking dazed. "I can get you onto the balcony with my family."

Alright... it actually worked. "That would be wonderful. Mr. Black will be pleased." Layala took a breath. "I've been so curious about the treasury. We'll of course need to store our money and some diamonds there. How will our goods be protected?"

He blinked and cleared his throat. "That's not something we discuss but you can rest assured anything you keep there will be safe. It's never been breached."

Layala gulped, losing confidence in her ability. If he got suspicious and she couldn't get him to forget, their cover was blown. "That's great," Layala said, gut sinking. *Hel, the treasury has never been breached.*

His voice entered her mind immediately, *I'm aware. How's baby Drakonan?*

Strong willed, but I did get us an invite to the Drakonan balcony for the opera.

Excellent.

Layala searched the loud groups around them but couldn't find him anywhere.

"Caliban!" a group of boys shouted at him, waving wildly from the roof.

"I should let you go. I look forward to meeting the rest of your family tomorrow evening. How will they know to let us in?"

"Just tell them I invited you and show the guards this. It will get you in anywhere in this town." He wrapped his hand around hers and pressed a small round coin in her hand. "See you there." With a wink, he spread his wings and leapt into the air.

The gold coin in her hand had the Drakonan name printed on it with a roaring dragon. If it got her anywhere, did that mean she could walk into the treasury without trouble? She still had to figure out which vault had her things in it and how to get past the wards or anything else that may be guarding it.

She started toward the house again in search of Hel. *Where are you? He gave me a Drakonan coin.*

No answer. She hurried up the steps and inside. The grandeur rivaled that of Castle Dredwich even if it wasn't half the size. Bold chandeliers, floors of pearl marbling with flecks of silver, gold vases, even some of the tables and furniture were made of pure gold. It wasn't her taste but beautiful, nonetheless.

Hel?

Layala spotted a black lily on the ground. Then another and another, leading to a girl sitting alone in a chair. She touched her wrist and locked eyes with her. "Did you see who left the flowers?"

"Yes."

"Where did he go?"

She looked confused. "I don't know."

Layala cursed under her breath. He'd probably persuaded her to forget, damn it. "Forget I asked." Hurrying down a wide hallway lined with navy-blue carpet, she opened doors one by one peeking inside. *Where in the realms did he go? No one got to him did they?* If either of them would be a target, it would be him. He was the one who invaded the dragons all those years ago; Valeen fought with War and the dragons not against them.

She found another trail of blooming lilies to a lone young male leaning up against a doorframe. He hiccupped and smiled at her. Layala gripped his wrist. "Tell me where the elf you encountered is."

"I don't know. I didn't see anyone."

Layala groaned and was about to walk away but stopped

herself. She could persuade just as easily as Hel. "I need you to forget what he told you and remember. You must remember."

"He said he's outside in the gazebo waiting for you," he said, pointing out the window to the dark of night.

Of course, this was training. "Now forget you saw me and go join your friends."

He simply nodded and Layala quickened her steps. When she found him outside, he sat in the gazebo with his arms propped up on the back of the bench. She would be remiss if this didn't remind her of the night the demon attacked but with him here, she felt secure.

He watched her approach with a predatory awareness like a hawk might a mouse. "That was easy. Pretty soon you won't need me. I think I'll miss that."

I might miss that too, she thought.

"Did you know this was the Drakonan's house? I thought this was only to practice my persuasion skills."

"Yes, and yes." He patted his lap, a gesture for her to sit.

"Um, no."

"I was a little jealous of the way you charmed baby Drakonan. You don't smile at me like that." The tiny magical lights floating above their heads reminded her of stars and gave his skin a soft glow. She noticed the darkening circles under his eyes and knew what he would need from her soon. She gave Hel an even closer inspection, glossy eyes, flushed cheeks, and he smelled of alcohol. He must have taken a few shots of strong dragon liquor. She held out her hand. "Come on. I passed your test. It's time to leave now."

He grasped her hand and the rough calluses rubbed against her skin. When he stood, he didn't let go of her hand. "We're not quite done yet. Ask me something. Persuade me if you can."

His wasn't a mind she thought she could crack but there

wasn't harm in trying. "Fine." She met his stare, and the intensity of it made her insides flutter. Clearing her throat, she squeezed his hand. "How did you get the scars on your chin and eyebrow? You should have healed perfectly."

"Well, love," the cadence of his speech slowed, and he blinked lazily, "that's not one I like to talk about. Ask something else."

He was certainly under the influence of alcohol. Their elven bodies couldn't seem to handle dragon spirits as well. "Then it's not persuasion. It's just you being willing. A conversation. So, tell me where the scar came from," she pressed, adding a smile for good measure. Her magic spiraled down her arm and into him. His refusal had her more curious than before. She'd witnessed his healing abilities herself so what could have given him scars?

The corner of his mouth twitched. "You'll have to do better than that."

"Better you say?" She shoved his chest and he fell back onto the gazebo bench with a surprised smirk. She sat sideways on his lap, and his hands quickly curled around her hips. Her fingers brushed over the scar on his chin. "I want to know who hurt you. Tell me."

He licked his lips and leaned in a little further. "You're getting closer."

Despite the cool breeze, her core felt like simmering coals. She traced the rune mark behind his ear, three lines that looked like a star, and felt his body tremble. "When do I call you by your full name?"

He smiled. "When you want me to know what you're saying is a promise. Occasionally, when I better watch what I say next."

"Do you still love Valeen?"

He shifted a little, gripping her hips tighter. "You're entering dangerous territory now."

"It must be hard to look at me and not find her. To search for recognition and find confusion."

"Yes, but what is more difficult is knowing you still care about him but look at me like that." He held her tighter. "Hold on."

CHAPTER 42

LAYALA

The world went dark before Layala's feet hit the floor in Presco's apartment, but everything around her didn't tilt and spin as much as previous times. Hel released her and took a seat on the couch. The tension still lingered from the moment they had, but she plopped down on the huge bed and tugged off her high-heeled shoes. She wasn't used to the style and her toes throbbed from the squeeze and the extra weight pushed to the ball of her foot. It wasn't until the fabric tangled around her legs when she attempted to climb under the blanket that she knew she couldn't sleep in this dress.

"Hel, I need my bag so I can change."

From the time she'd looked down to take off her shoes and lifted her head, he'd already changed into his loose sleeping pants and remained bare up top. *Why does he insist on being shirtless?* It was difficult to keep her gaze averted and not ogle.

Without a word, the bag appeared next to her on the bed, and she rifled through pulling out her blue long-sleeved cotton top and matching pants. They were the only sleepwear she brought, and she suddenly wished she had something more appealing.

"I'm going to change in the bath chamber, don't lock me out."

He leaned back and kicked one leg over the arm of it. He was tall, and the two seats were hardly enough room for him. "Promise," he said with a wink.

In the bath chamber, she stared at her reflection in the mirror above the gold sink. Her heart raced and she felt short of breath, and she couldn't even say why. Running a brush through her hair, she smoothed down the stray pieces and caught a whiff of her body odor, faint but there. She quickly doused a cloth with the rosewater in a bottle off the shelf and wiped her body down.

Using a scented lip balm, she brushed her finger over her lips and scrubbed her teeth. *Why are you worrying about your appearance, Laya?* she berated herself. Because she was. She had her typical nightly routine but tonight she spent extra time making sure her hair looked nice and her breath and body smelled pleasant.

With her palms pressed against the white countertop, she leaned heavily on it and took in a few deep breaths. "You can convince him to sleep on the couch. It's not a big ordeal," she murmured to her reflection. "And even if he doesn't, you've slept in the same bed before. It meant nothing." With her night clothes on, she tugged her long hair through a satin tie, and took one last deep breath.

Buzzing with anxiousness, the floorboards creaked under her feet. Presco waved to her from the couch in the living area and she waved back, cheeks flushing. Would he think they were going to do anything? Because they wouldn't. She didn't know why she felt the sudden urge to go tell Presco that nothing was going on between her and her... husband.

Shaking her head at herself, she stepped back into the guest room and gently shut the door, latching it shut. Staring up at the ceiling, Hel lay on the loveseat with his legs hanging over one end, his arms tucked close, and hands over his abdomen. He looked incredibly cramped and uncomfortable.

"Are you sleeping there then?" she asked, fidgeting with the hem of her top, in the middle of the small room.

"Yes."

"Alright." She climbed under the silk covers and tugged them up to her chest. The soft feather pillows behind her head offered perfect support, and she could stretch out fully and still not touch any end of the bed.

At night the street below was quiet. Only the occasional groan of the house or the hooves clopping on stone with the creak of wheels interrupted the silence.

"You smell nice." She could hear the smile in his voice.

"Thanks," she whispered, wanting to smack herself in the head for bothering with the perfume water. A few beats passed. "The bed is big enough for the both of us, as you said."

The sofa squeaked as he shifted. "It's fine. I don't want it to be awkward."

Layala sat up. "This, right now, is awkward. That couch is much too small for you, you look ridiculous and I'm giving you permission to sleep next to me. Just don't get any ideas that it means anything more than it is."

"If you insist." He chuckled, and the bed shifted as he climbed up and over her. Without getting under the blankets, he laid out on his backside and then turned away to face the wall. They sat in silence for a few moments until he said, "The scars are from one of the three demon princes. His name is

Servante, the oldest and most powerful of the three. Not the one who is chasing us. That's Morv. I went to the underrealm thinking it was possible the reason my mother left me as a newborn was because she was ashamed of who my father is. There has always been something dark about me, and I thought maybe he was one of *them*."

Layala stopped breathing for a moment. Hel—half god, half demon? But it couldn't be, could it? It was difficult to imagine a beautiful goddess and that hideous creature together. It hit her that they'd had this conversation before, a very long time ago. "But he isn't, is he?"

"I don't know. I thought it could only possibly be Servante because he was the only prince allowed to leave the under-realm during the time of my conception. There had been a meeting."

"Did you fight with him?"

"He called me a fool for entering his domain. One of his hounds bit me. As you know, their venom is toxic and it made me hallucinate, made me weak. He took advantage and threw me in a cage for weeks—months, I don't know. Then one day he came into the darkness, grabbed me by the face and cut me across the chin and through my brow so that every time anyone looked at me they'd know someone had gotten the best of me. And every time I looked in the mirror, I would know that the only reason I was alive is because he allowed it. Then he let me go. And through every life, it has remained."

"But you were a god. He couldn't have killed you."

"He could have kept me there with steady poison, trapped with the damned dead in the underrealm. It wouldn't have been living."

She was suddenly angry, furious that he'd been there alone.

"Someone would have come for you eventually, wouldn't they?"

"I don't know."

Layala had the urge to reach over and touch him, brush her fingers over his beautiful, tattooed wings, and comfort him somehow. Old feelings, the goddess who'd loved him, desired to slip her arms around him. "*I* would have," she whispered, clutching the soft blanket. "I would have come for you."

"We hadn't met yet, love."

She couldn't stand the thought of him in a cold dark cage for so long. The image of him sullen and defeated made her shudder. "You get to choose who you want to be. It doesn't matter who your parents are, born with darkness or not. You always have a choice."

He turned partially to look at her. His heavy-lidded darkened garnet eyes settled on her face. "You always believed the best in me, even when I didn't deserve it, and I thank you for that, but it doesn't matter how long you've kept a serpent, he'll always bite."

Layala gently placed her palm against his back and goosebumps peppered his skin. He was warm and soft. "You've forgotten that I was born of the dark. Your serpent's bite doesn't scare me."

"What do you want from me, Val? Because when you touch me like that, and say things..."

"I don't know," she breathed.

"You don't," he said flatly and sat up. His vulnerable eyes narrowed.

Don't look at me like that.

Like I'd die for you a thousand more times? Because I would.

A tear slid down her cheek and she quickly swiped it away.

She grabbed her dagger off the bedside table and sliced open her wrist. "Take it."

He turned away. "I don't want to."

Layala pressed her palm gently to the side of his face and turned him. "You're weakening. I can see it." She raised her bleeding wrist up. He watched the red line slide down her skin until it reached the bend in her elbow.

"You're fine with this? Because last time..."

"I'm offering it to you. I want you to have it."

He nodded then his tongue caressed the underside of her forearm, licking up the blood to her wrist. He gently closed his mouth around the cut and pulled. It didn't hurt. It didn't even sting. It was sensual and she moved closer. His arm wrapped around her back, and he tugged her onto his lap. Her knees bent, and her thighs closed around his hips.

His mouth came away from her wound, and his thumb swiped over it, closing it instantly. And there they were, tangled in each other's bodies.

"We're in dangerous territory again," he murmured.

Her chest heaved up and down rapidly. "I like danger. It makes me feel alive."

He was the first to press his lips to her collarbone, then her throat. She sighed and tilted her head back, giving him access to roam. Feeling him harden beneath her, she dug her nails into his back.

"Fuck," he murmured and dragged his tongue up her throat. "This is not a good idea."

"It's terrible." Layala began to slowly rock her hips against him, and he moaned, and wrapped his hands in her hair.

He ripped her shirt over her head and tore off her bralette. "Gods, I missed seeing these and touching them." Both hands cupped her breasts, and he caressed her nipples. "And seeing you come apart when I do."

Her body was aflame with desire, and he was the match. "Hel," she breathed, moving her hips in slow circles. "We should stop."

"We should," he said and trailed kisses of fire across her chest. *Tell me to and I will.*

No.

We can't take it back once it happens.

I don't care.

Through his soft pants, he hardened even more if that was possible. The thin fabric between them did almost nothing. Layala moved her hips faster. He grabbed hold of the bend between her thighs and hips and rocked her harder against him. "I don't need to be inside to make you come, love."

Just him saying that brought her to the edge of bliss. Her moans grew louder but she bit down on her lip to quiet herself. Presco and his wife were in the other room. He lifted one hand and a shimmering bubble formed around them. "Be as loud as you want. No one but me will hear now."

Layala wrapped her arms around the back of his neck and pulled herself against him. Their lips hadn't met once, and she briefly wondered if that was on purpose, but the pleasure kept building and building, distracting her from that, and she buried her face into his neck. He smelled so good, felt so good.

"Val," Hel growled. "I can feel you getting wet through the pants." He panted like he was even more turned on than she was. "Take as long as you want. Enjoy it."

"Hel." She squeezed him harder. "I want you to feel as much as I do." She reached to tug down her pants, but he gripped her hands, and intertwined their fingers. Then pushed her onto her back where he hovered above her, pinning her to the bed.

"Don't tempt me with that unless you mean it. If you think I'll let you go back to him after I've been inside you, you're fucking wrong." One hand slid to her throat and his gentle touch was almost enough to make her lose it. "Once you give yourself to me, you're fucking mine. There won't be a choice."

Layala closed her eyes and waited for a breath... two... her heart thundered like galloping horses, her body was on the verge of combustion, but she shook her head. Everything he said brought her out of her almost animalistic desire to have him and cleared her blind lust.

"I thought so," he said but slid his hand underneath her pants, between her thighs, and she saw stars.

THE NEXT EVENING, Presco stood in front of the stairs in the apartment with his arms crossed. "I'm coming with you."

Layala tugged up on the white glove at her elbow. With the assistance of Presco's wife, her hair was styled in an elegant half up half down with loops, braids, and waterfall curls down her back. "Presco," Layala started with a sigh. "It's best if we aren't seen together anymore."

"Then Ayva and I will go separately but I will be there to assist if you need it."

"Fine."

Hel's footsteps lightly padded on the wood floor. His arm slipped around Layala's and then he leaned closer to Presco. "Stay out of my way tonight." He fixed the popped front lapel of Presco's suit and patted his chest.

Presco was a full six inches taller than Hel and broader in

every way but at that moment Hel was more intimidating. A moment of silence passed and Presco gave a curt nod. "Of course, Hel."

On their walk down the city block, they were both quiet. Hel had been gone most of the day. She didn't know what he'd been up to. He wasn't in the bed when she woke up that morning.

He slipped his hand into hers and gave it a gentle squeeze. "Last night doesn't need to mean anything."

"Alright," Layala murmured. But it did to her. She didn't do sexual acts with males who didn't *mean* something to her.

"It was a momentary lapse in judgment on my part. I shouldn't have let it get to that point. We shouldn't have shared a bed. We won't tonight."

"We didn't have sex, so like you said, it doesn't mean anything." Her heart felt like it was crumbling with each word.

He kept his eyes forward, deliberately not looking at her. "No, it doesn't."

AFTER SHOWING the gold coin that was given to her by Caliban Drakonan, Layala and Hel were escorted up to the top balcony level of the opera hall in the Drakonans' mansion on Pearl Avenue. "Mr. and Mrs. Black," the bellman said with a dip and quickly left.

The group of six males and five females stopped chatting and scrutinized the intruding couple. Layala felt like slipping away but Hel whispered in her mind, *Raise that chin, love. One day they will kneel to you.*

She thought of the entire dragon court in Adalon dropping to their knees and smiled. It was the only reminder she needed.

Caliban Drakonan grinned and gestured toward them with a lazy hand. He wore a black suit, and his golden hair was combed back and tied at the nape of his neck. He almost looked like a different person than the one Layala met at the wild party the night before. "Grandfather, this is the elven couple I spoke to you about."

The dragon with salt-and-pepper hair, aged but still strong looking, dragged his eyes over Hel. He had distinct eyes; one was brown the other a bright green. "So, it is. I am Rugar Drakonan, and this is my home. Welcome."

"And a lovely home it is," Hel said, and reached out his hand. "The name is Zar, and this is my wife Layala."

The Drakonan Opera House boasted three levels with golden sculptures attached to each balcony personifying harmony, poetry, and music. The stage below was closed off by a velvet navy curtain.

Rugar shook Hel's hand. "And what a lovely wife." He inhaled deeply. "You're mages and descended from the Runevale gods. I smell it in your blood. It's been a long time since I sensed that." Unable to decipher his rough tone, Layala worried he was going to have them thrown out, then he smiled. "My grandson is a good judge of character."

Hel smiled and slid the back of his hand across Layala's cheek. "I think your grandson was dazzled by a pair of pretty blue eyes."

Rugar let out a deep belly laugh, and slapped Caliban on the back and squeezed his shoulder. Caliban's cheeks reddened. "He's a young male, what can you expect?" Rugar went around and introduced the others on the balcony. His wife, son, brother, their spouses, a business partner not related to the Drakonans. Layala would never remember all their names, but his wife had soft pink hair and a cleft in her chin that made her memorable. Then Rugar said, "Caliban said you are looking to open a diamond shop on Pearl Avenue."

"We are, as well as hold our precious belongings in your treasury," Hel said. "We hear it's never been breached so our wealth will be safeguarded well."

"Certainly. You have my personal guarantee."

A steely lady with a soft pink gown, stepped to Rugar's side, and placed her hand on his shoulder. Rugar's wife, Kira, if Layala remembered correctly. "How long have you been married?"

Hel looked down at Layala, "How long have we been married, love?"

"Nine years," Layala said. It was how long they were married in their previous life.

"Are you young?" Kira asked, brushing her light pink hair behind her ear. "You certainly look it, but one never can tell with elves."

Layala did some quick math in her head. If they were married nine years, she had to be at least thirty for it to be plausible. "I'm thirty and Zar is twenty-nine." He was younger than her after all, by thousands of years.

"Babies," the older woman crooned with a laugh. "Dragons don't usually marry until they are at least one hundred. I thought elves were much the same given your long life spans."

"Typically," Hel said, lifting his shoulder. "But when I met her, I knew she was the one," he smiled at Layala, and it reminded her of the night before at the gazebo and that led to other thoughts of him kissing her bare breasts later, "and I simply couldn't lose her to someone else by waiting. She's intelligent, ambitious, and beautiful of course."

"A smart male," Rugar said.

"To be young and so in love again. I can see it in your eyes,"

Kira said with a soft sigh. "But I can always tell by a kiss if the couple will last. The early years are like a hot flame, burning and often flickering, but long marriages are made of those left-over embers, eternal, unquenchable and simmering. Rugar and I have been married for twelve hundred years."

Layala looked up at Hel. Was she implying...

"Well, go on," Kira said while motioning with her hand. "Let's see it."

Everyone watched them with curiosity. Layala gulped and felt heat creeping up her neck. He deliberately hadn't kissed her last night even if they did other things.

She and Hel locked eyes, *Only if you want to,* he said in her mind.

But kissing on the mouth is special to you...

You're special to me, love.

You'll want more.

I will always want more.

His hands slid up the sides of her face, and he leaned down ever so slowly. She could hardly breathe. Her heartbeat thundered in her ears. Something about this was almost as intimate as last night even with people watching them. His sweet breath swept across her lip first, and he waited there for her. He didn't force it, he waited.

Her fingers wrapped around the lapels of his suit, one beat, two, and she pressed up on her toes; their lips met.

Gentle at first.

Uncertain.

And then it was like Kira described: a flame, hot and unquenchable, wanting, *needing* more. Everyone else may as well have disappeared as his arms closed around her, her hands gripped harder at his suit. His lips claimed hers, gentle and yet possessive. His teeth softly clamped on her lower lip, and he

491

gently sucked. A quiet moan escaped her, and he slowly pulled back.

Layala stared up at him. He couldn't seem to pull away either. That was a mistake, a monumental mistake. Just like the night before, and yet...

"Now *that* was a kiss," Kira said, pulling their stares from each other to her. "I think you were meant to be."

They finally pulled apart and Hel cleared his throat. "It might even be written in the stars," Hel teased and gave her a chaste kiss on the cheek.

Rugar brought the back of his wife's gloved hand to his lips. "My wife is never wrong."

Now is the time to go find out where your vault is, Hel whispered in her mind. *The show is about to start. I'll keep them distracted.*

Alright. "I'm going to freshen up my lipstick. Excuse me."

She dipped into a curtsy and turned away. She peeked over her shoulder on the way through the curtain to see the others chuckling, Kira patting Hel's forearm affectionately, and Hel staring after Layala with the kind of look that made her believe that kiss, last night, and the time they shared meant more to him than he would admit. That even if he said it didn't mean anything, it meant everything, and he would forgive all her past and give her the world if she forgave him, too. And for one moment she thought there might not be a line he could cross that she wouldn't forgive.

Layala hurried through the empty corridor and made a quick turn. According to Presco, the opera house was connected to the manor where they lived, and the Drakonans' main offices were on the top floor. Turning to shadow, Layala slipped through the dimly lit halls, passing servants and guards undetected.

Her thoughts kept sliding to Hel and that kiss, but she must focus. Once she reached the top floor Presco stepped out of a darkened inlet. Layala returned to her solid form and frowned. "You're not supposed to be here. I don't want you getting into trouble."

"This way, quickly." He waved and with the shake of her head, she followed him. At the end of the corridor was a door nearly as wide as it was tall. "This is Rugar's office. He'll have the files to tell you which vault number is yours at the Treasury."

Layala pressed her hand against the keyhole and a vine crept its way inside and broke the locking mechanism. She pushed down on the handle and quietly pushed it open.

"I take it you've done that before."

"On occasion."

For someone with as much wealth as Rugar, his office was rather plain. There was an oversized wooden desk, shelves behind it loaded with books, a single fern in the corner, and several file cabinets lining one wall. With sweat sliding down her back, she began rifling through the first drawer. Each file had a name and a folder. "Abbner, Silo, Murdoc, I can't make sense of the order, and there are thousands of files. It could take us hours."

Hel's voice entered her mind, *Baby Drakonan left to use the facilities, but it may have been a cover. Keep a watchful eye.*

"We need to hurry."

Presco's nimble fingers crawled over the tops of tabs. "Fairbanks, Novello, Dramvor... It's grouped by race. Fairbanks, Novello, Dramvor are dragons. Abbner, Silo, Murdoc are feline shifters, and within it, it looks like order of importance maybe or highest wealth. Silas Fairbanks is the wealthiest dragon behind the Drakonan family."

Starting from opposite ends they pulled open drawers looking for gods and goddesses. They'd almost met up in the center when Layala came upon a name she knew... Katana. The folder before Valeen. She jerked the file free and opened the navy folder. Inside was a piece of paper with Katana's vault number but, on the page stamped in red ink it read *"deceased"*. The word struck her more than she thought it would, but there wasn't time to dwell on it, so Layala shoved it back inside and pulled her own file.

"Vault 118." Her file did not read *"deceased" as* her sister's had but did read: *belongings confiscated. Vault only to be opened by Drakonan blood. Access denied to all others.* She slipped the folder back where she found it. "I'm going to need a Drakonan."

Presco glanced toward the door and ran a worried hand over the back of his neck. "Valeen, you can't trust any of them."

"I don't need to trust them. I just need one of them to open the vault. The file says only to be opened by Drakonan blood."

"That doesn't necessarily mean that only a Drakonan can open it. It means that according to his will only someone with Drakonan blood is allowed to lawfully open it. Someone in his family, and not someone married in."

"What if..." Layala nibbled on her lower lip. "What if it means literally by Drakonan blood?" Maker above, where was Ronan when she needed him?

Footsteps and voices outside the door had both of them scrambling for somewhere to hide. "They should be watching the opera," Layala hissed and grabbed Presco to drag him to the curtains pushed to the sides of the windows. There was an inch gap between the curtains and floor. Their feet would still show.

"Turn us into shadow," Presco whispered, tugging the heavy velvet curtains around himself.

She didn't know it was possible, but she grabbed his wrist

and felt her magic tingling, felt herself shifting into shadow. She focused on Presco. The door creaked open, and he urged with his eyes for her to hurry. *Shadow shadow shadow* her shadows crept up his arm, changing his flesh into a dark transparent haze.

The heavy footsteps stepped inside. Layala peeked through the slit in the curtain... it was Caliban Drakonan. What was he doing here? He went straight for the file cabinets and tugged open the one near the center, flipped through the files and pulled one, but not just anyone, Valeen's file.

Holy All Mother, he knows.

He turned the paper over and looked at the backside. Layala didn't do that herself and her heart nearly stopped when she saw a sketch of her.

Layala looked up at Presco. His jaw was clenched, eyes steely. "I need a Drakonan," she whispered. Presco slowly shook his head. Layala thought of Hel and silently said, *Hel, Caliban Drakonan knows. He figured it out. I'm going to stop him.*

That's impossible. He'd be the last one in the family to know it.

He's up here in the office with my file in hand. I'm hiding in the corner watching him now.

Don't move. I'll come up.

Caliban pushed the folder back into the cabinet and started for the exit. They didn't have time to wait for Hel. Layala moved like the wind and was on his back before he had a chance to turn. With her legs locked around his torso, she slipped her elbow under his chin, hooking it tight and squeezed. *Go to sleep.* But his flesh shifted and hardened beneath her. *Shit.* Layala dropped and backed off. Soulender would go through scales, but she didn't want to kill Caliban.

He turned revealing his silver scales across every inch of

him. Very similar to Ronan. It must run in the family even after thousands of years.

"Mrs. Black," he said, surprised but then his eyes narrowed. Presco stepped out from behind the curtain and Caliban's brows shot up. "Presco?" He glanced back and forth between them, and a slow smile pulled at the corners of his mouth. "My grandfather once told me you were the pet of the night goddess." His reptilian eyes shifted to Layala. "And I wasn't entirely sure you were Valeen, but now I know my hunch was correct. I wrote an essay about the great war of the realms last week for a class, and my focus was on the goddess of night. The timing is—interesting. So, I presume if you're Valeen then *Mr. Black* is the god of war."

"Mr. Black is *not* the god of war." Hel's deep voice cut in. The door closed quietly behind him. "Mr. Black is someone much more ruthless and sinister."

Caliban took a step back, scanning him like he'd never seen him before. "What do you three want?"

"My wife needs her belongings back. Bring her to her vault and I won't kill you and your entire family. They're all here in one place. It would be easy."

The evening sunset reflected off Caliban's silver scales creating sparkling light on the wall behind him. He moved another step back, closer to the window. "You're... Zaurahel, aren't you? The god of mischief and magic."

The pressure of Hel's magic enveloped the room with a heavy cloud. It was like a rabid animal locked in a cage too small and fought to break free. "You know, you're too clever for your own good Mr. Drakonan."

"If threats were all it took to be let into the vaults, we wouldn't be the Drakonans."

"I thought you might say that." Hel raised his arm.

Layala rushed forward and grabbed hold of Hel's hand, intertwining their fingers. "Don't kill him. We need someone of Drakonan blood to open the vault."

Hel frowned, and with the snap of his fingers said, "Nighty night."

Caliban crumpled to the floor, his scales turning back to flesh. Layala gritted her teeth, watching for signs of life. His chest moved up and down, and she loosened a breath in relief.

"Since you're here, Presco," he started. "Pick the boy up. I'll set the stage on fire and buy us some time."

CHAPTER 43

LAYALA

Screams drifted up from the lower levels of the Drakonans' home, and then the scent of burning wood. Hel only disappeared for a moment but that was all it took to set the stage on fire and cause a distraction. With the snap of Hel's fingers, Layala's dress changed into black pants, a loose-fitting tunic with her usual black corset overtop, and her boots.

"Thanks. Now I'll be able to move easier."

Presco threw Caliban over his shoulder and nodded.

"And you'll probably need to fight, too." Hel gripped both their arms. "I can get us inside the treasury but the magic there will stop us at the door to the vaults. Ready?" Layala and Presco nodded.

The pressure and darkness of shifting through space surrounded them and was gone as quickly as it came, and they stood at a giant black door with rune markings carved into its wood illuminated only by blazing torches on the walls. Layala peeked over her shoulder. Down the long, stone corridor the walls opened into a room with golden pillars, a large dark wood desk with stacks of papers and piles of gold and precious jewels the workers counted. Luckily everyone in the main room had their backs to them and were none the wiser they had intruders at the vault chamber door.

Presco set Caliban on the gray stone floor and rested his back against the wall. He pulled a glass vial from his suit pocket. Inside a vivid blue liquid bubbled. "What's that?" Layala asked.

"It will stop him from being able to shift into dragon form. But we only have an hour at most. Caliban may seem like a sweet young male, but his dragon is ferocious. He fights in the underground fighting ring and has been champion for the last year even against much older dragons." He pulled the cork, parted Caliban's lips, and poured in the liquid. A little stream trickled out of the side of his mouth, but he swallowed most of it, and then his eyes fluttered.

"He's waking up." Wide eyed, Layala turned to Hel. "Get the door open before he yells for help."

Hel ran his fingers over the runes, and murmured under his breath. "Clever," he said, "I can fly but I have no wings. I can cry but I have no eyes. Do you know what I am?"

Caliban groaned and pressed a hand to the side of his head.

"Now would be good, Hel," Layala urged, peeking down the hall again. The sounds of coins clanking, patron chatter, and paper shuffling came from down the main chamber. Footsteps came next. Someone was coming.

Hel pressed his finger to each runic letter, which glowed faintly after he touched it until he spelled out the word within the riddle, "C-L-O-U-D."

The shiny silver vault door slowly opened inward, not

making a sound. Presco dragged Caliban in, and Hel promptly shut the door.

"I hope we weren't seen or it's over already," Layala said.

They waited quietly for an alarm bell or raised voices, but none came. "I think we're in the clear," Presco said and bobbed his head to continue.

Torches on the walls lit with their presence and led down a long windowless brick passage. The air was stale and a little damp. There was no telling how long the tunnel would go. It went as far as she could see.

"How did you figure out the riddle so quickly?" Layala asked, glancing down at Caliban who rolled over onto his hands and knees.

"I'm the god of mischief, love. I practically invented riddles." He flicked his wrist and Caliban lifted up, body rigid and jaw tense. His toes were several inches off the ground. "Now, Mr. Drakonan, I expect you to be on your best behavior. If you try anything, I'll rip out your heart and use the blood from it to open her vault. Is that clear?"

"Infinitely."

"Good boy."

Presco grabbed Caliban by the shoulders with a blade at his throat and the group started down the brick-lined corridor, until they came to a split off into three different directions. A quiet rustle of wind swept past, making the place sound like an endless hollow cavern. There were no signs on the walls to direct them, just various colors of brick walls and ceilings and torches lighting in all directions. It was strange; although there was no one else here, she felt as if someone was watching. Layala scanned the wall to her left, and for the briefest moment she swore she saw a pair of eyes. But she blinked and it was only stone.

"Which way is vault 118?" Layala asked.

Caliban lifted a shoulder. "Don't know. It's a tunnel of mazes that shift and change all the time. It could be anywhere in here."

Over the tunnel to the left, a wall began to click into place, forming brick by brick, until it was as if the entryway never existed at all. A few feet over another way opened up. "If it's always changing, how do *you* find the vaults?" Presco asked.

A deep rumble came from somewhere below their feet as if the floor groaned and might shift too and give out on them. There was nothing to hold onto, nothing to grab if it did. The brick wall to her right appeared to have a strange outline at its center although she couldn't quite distinguish what it was. It might be the depiction of an animal of some kind. Then it disappeared to reveal plain brick again.

There was something down here with them, but what?

With a pit growing in her stomach, she glanced at Hel. *Are you getting the sense we're being watched?*

Yes. Hel gripped Caliban's face between his fingers, digging the tips into his cheeks, and said, "How do we find the vault?" His voice changed slightly, smoother, and only someone who paid close attention would notice the shift; he was using his gift of persuasion.

Caliban stared at him, mouth twitching but blinked and spat in Hel's face. "Drakonans train all our lives to resist mind compulsion and not even you will get me to talk."

A moment of utter silence passed. Layala knew she'd compelled him over something minor but when it came to the treasury, he didn't break then either. Hel let out a low growl and she winced, knowing something harsh and swift would follow. He reached inside his suit jacket and pulled a knife. The glint of its blade reflected the torchlight, and he shoved it into

Caliban's side. He gasped. Hel ripped the blade out and a splash of blood hit the ground, followed by Caliban's strangled cry.

"You have twenty minutes before you bleed out and die. Presco drugged you with a potion so you can't shift to heal and fight back," Hel said. "Tick-tock, Mr. Drakonan."

Caliban's face scrunched in pain, and with pitiful puppy dog eyes, turned to Layala for mercy. She couldn't be the weak link here. They needed to get to the vault. But Maker above, could she stand by and let an innocent person die so she could get her journals?

Layala paced back and forth as several minutes passed. Caliban was white as a sheet, and sweat beaded on his brow. The air filled with the coppery odor of the blood pooled at his feet. Hel was rigid, staring up at the ceiling and along the cracks in the walls. The tick of Presco clicking his fingernails together was loud in the quiet space. Claustrophobia began to make everything seem darker and the air thinner. The way they'd originally came closed off, leaving her with a feeling of being trapped.

"You don't look so good," Hel said, finally breaking the silence. "Are you willing to die for this?"

"Yes," he groaned. "I'd rather die with honor than be the one who let my family down. I'd always be remembered as the Drakonan who was weak enough to let the treasury be breached."

"You have a long life ahead of you," Hel crooned. "Many maidens to love, adventures to take, a name to make for yourself. None of that will happen if you don't take us to the vault. You'll be in the favor of two of the most powerful gods in all the realms. No one even needs to know we were there."

This was good, a better direction than threats. Layala stepped in front of Caliban and gently touched his forearm.

"Caliban, you know my story. Look, if Hel and I can move on from the past, and trust me, it hasn't been easy then so can the dragons. I fought beside you against the other gods when they invaded. You know I was taken by the council, and they murdered me. What you don't know is that they've done it again and again and again. I am on my fourth life. I don't know how many more I'll get. Please, I need to get inside my vault. I need to fight back against them. I won't even take everything. I just need one thing. That's all."

Blood dribbled out of the corner of his mouth and a single tear slipped from his eye. "If you're lying to me..."

"I speak the truth."

He gave one slow nod, and attempted to push off the wall and fell back, slinking to the floor.

Layala crouched down in front of him, and lifted her chin to Hel. "Heal him."

"Not until he holds up his end of the deal."

"He'll die before we get there."

Hel grabbed him by the arm, jerked him to his feet and slung his arm over his shoulder. "He'll make it. More motivation to get there faster. Now which way is it?"

With his hand pressed firmly over his wound, Caliban leaned heavily into Hel but nodded down the tunnel straight ahead. Dragging him forward, Hel started off. Caliban's toes scraped unsteadily on the ground as he struggled to keep pace.

"Presco," was all she had to say for him to catch up to Caliban's other side, and put the young dragon's arm around his shoulder, bearing most of his weight.

"Stay close," Caliban croaked over his shoulder. "The maze can sense when someone doesn't belong. It will try to separate us." The passageway ahead abruptly closed into a wall, and two pathways on either side opened with torches lining down as far as she could see. Another breeze carried with it the smell of something foul.

"Which way?" Hel snapped.

Caliban inhaled and looked back and forth between the two. After a moment he said, "I'm not sure."

"Get sure." Hel's eyes turned menacing, and he gripped his arm tighter.

"The maze is built on the intention of the one given permission to enter and the maze shows them the way. It... must sense I am under threat. It's not revealing the way to me."

The groaning noise happened again, not of the shifting of bricks but something other... a beast? Was there a dragon down here to guard the treasure? The knots in her gut intensified. They could get trapped here in an endless maze spelled to keep them lost with a beast hunting them.

"How is the way revealed?" Hel demanded, getting in Caliban's face.

Caliban's jaw muscles twitched but he said, "It's a scent that only a Drakonan can detect."

"Heal him, right now," Layala snapped. "Before we get stuck down here forever."

The two paths ahead closed off, the torches died out, and suddenly there was nothing but four walls and darkness. *This is not good.*

A white orb lit up the space, floating above Hel's palm. He sent it up to the eight-foot-high ceiling, revealing they were trapped in a possible ten-foot-by-ten-foot room with no doors, no windows, no means of escape.

Presco backed into a corner, breaths coming faster and faster. "Have I ever mentioned I'm extremely claustrophobic?" Dragon scales moved across his skin, and he began punching at the brick; sparks from the impact rained down at his feet; small chunks of stone came loose but he didn't even make a dent. "I have to get out," the growing panic in his voice increased with each hit.

"Presco, calm down. We will get out," Layala said but she too was finding it harder to draw in breath. "This is magic, Hel, do something."

"I can't break through wards like this without knowing what they are."

The walls began to move inward scraping and groaning with every inch. Presco shoved his palms against the wall and pushed but his shoes only skid backward. Layala rushed to the other side, letting her magic hum, turning her hand and arm to shadow, she tried to push through the wall, but it hit against the solid barrier. Their powers seemed muted here or the wards to escape were stronger. There was no walking through walls to get out. Hel rolled his neck and closed his eyes.

Are you meditating at a time like this?

I'm trying to get the ward to reveal itself to me. With a flick of his fingers, varied blue rays of light slithered along each wall, rolling like ocean waves. Hel's mouth pursed. "This is even more complicated than I thought it would be."

The walls kept moving in.

"Each variety of blue is a layered spell. Each has a code of its own, a different makeup. It would take me weeks to get through them all."

Caliban coughed up a spray of blood.

"Then heal Caliban!"

"Fine." Hel nodded and thrust his palm against Caliban's side and a warm glow emitted from beneath it. In a moment, Caliban breathed easier, his face no longer contorted with pain. But the walls were still moving in, making the space between each other smaller inch by inch. They'd soon be shoulder to shoulder.

Caliban flung himself at the wall, pressing his palms to the stone, and chanted in a language she didn't know. The blue waves Hel revealed began to vibrate and then darkened. The walls halted and began to retract again. Torches appeared and lit and a moment later, a corridor opened ahead. "It's that way." He sounded out of breath.

Turning to Presco, Layala gave him a reassuring nod. "You're alright now. We're going to make it out."

His entire body trembled, and his blond hairline was soaked in sweat. Those gold-rimmed glasses were crooked on his nose. He fixed his spectacles, straightened his suit jacket, and together they trudged on.

Hel leaned closer to Caliban and said quietly, "If you betray us, I will heal you and hurt you over and over again and not let you die."

"I won't."

After several hallway switches and pathways opening and closing, they came upon a monumental door labeled *118*. It must rise at least twelve feet tall and half that wide. It wasn't made out of wood but a silver metal that looked to be ancient with a smattering of rust and dirt. There was no door handle or any visible means of entry.

Caliban swung his head from side to side as if he expected someone or *something* to appear out of the tunnel behind them. That made Hel watch him with suspicion, and she knew he was showing much more restraint than he wanted to. *He won't betray us. He wants out of here too.*

You're too trusting, Hel said back.

What sort of beast do you think is down here with us? A dragon? But it wouldn't fit. These tunnels are eight feet tall at most.

Don't think these walls can't expand the same as they can close in. And it seems likely given this is a treasury owned by dragons. He glanced over his shoulder. *If I tell you to run, you run.*

I won't leave you.

He held up a finger and his eyes flared. *You'll do what you need to do. I'll get out, don't worry about me.* "We're waiting, Caliban," Hel snapped. "Don't make me torture you. I'll do it with a smile."

Caliban sneered at him then pressed his first finger against his canine until blood welled up. Then he smeared a thin line of blood across the metal surface and said, "Caliban Drakonan." The offering absorbed until there wasn't a trace of it and the door lifted upward retracting into the ceiling.

"You first," Hel said, shoving him in the back, forcing Caliban to step across the threshold and the others followed. "Presco, keep hold of him while we search for the journals. We don't need him stepping out and locking us in here."

Presco gripped his arm and held him close to his side. "Got him."

Chests of various sizes looked to be tossed in here without care. Some were open with clothes or diverse decor spilled across the floor. Broken glass from pottery crunched under her shoes. There was also furniture, paintings, and even several containers of gold coins. Hel started on the right, opening lids to the trunks, moving quickly. Layala spotted a chest in the back with a book hanging out of the open corner. Shoving past all the old furniture, hopping over a broken dusty couch, and around crates she got to it and lifted the lid. The books were simple hard covers with various designs and colors. Some had pages hanging loose. They looked in almost new condition which made her believe they were spelled with magic to preserve them. They'd have to be thousands of years old.

"I think I found them." She grabbed the first one on top and opened it to a random page and began reading.

It's been seven hundred and eleven years and thirteen days since I set foot outside my territory. It's more difficult than I thought it would be staying here and not exploring the realms or even other places in Runevale. I'm supposed to be a protector of the realms. It's not in my nature to sit idly by.

SEVEN HUNDRED YEARS... of a thousand. There wasn't time to dwell. She set it down and grabbed another book. There was one specific time that she was desperate to know. She skimmed the pages and picked up another and another. Hel stood at her side, arms crossed. "We'll need to bring them with us."

"I know." The more she pulled out the more appeared beneath it as if I was spelled to keep thousands in a chest that should only hold maybe twenty at most.

The rumbling growl of the beast was louder, closer than before.

"We need to leave," Caliban said urgently.

With her heart beating faster, she gripped the chest on both ends and imagined the aether, imagining sending the chest there. But it didn't move.

"It's the wards. It keeps anything from magically moving in or out." Hel flicked his fingers and the chest lifted off the ground and floated beside her. "It will follow. Let's move."

As she was about to walk out the door, she spotted the glint of a golden blade. "Darkbringer."

The low roar sounded nearby. Much closer now.

"Valeen!" Hel shouted at the threshold. "Move your ass!"

She darted for the blade, snatched it up and sprinted out

the door. The group ran behind Caliban with the chest flying alongside Layala. "What is it?!"

"They are the guardians of this place," Caliban called over his shoulder.

"That's not very specific," Hel snarled.

The hallways shifted and changed as they ran. Caliban never hesitated on which turn to choose. "We're almost there!" and with the last word the corridor in front closed. Caliban ran into it and slammed his fist into it. "Damn it! They know you took something without permission."

"They," Layala shoved a finger into his chest. "*They, they, they.* What are they?"

Panting, Caliban turned and looked around frantically. "Shit," he muttered and pressed his back against the wall sweat glistened on his brow and temples. "They're—"

The sound of grinding stone from behind made Layala whip around. The tunnel began opening, the bricks melting away, shimmering out of existence to reveal a massive dark cavern with a ceiling that could be a hundred feet high. It wasn't one beast but several, coming out of the shadows. Ten-foot-tall creatures with grotesque faces that resembled a misshapen lion, with great wings... and made entirely of gray stone. Each footfall rumbled the ground, like a stampede of horses. There must be twenty of them.

"Gargoyles," Hel murmured. "I should have known."

"What are gargoyles?" Layala whispered.

"Unkillable guardians made of stone."

Hel appeared in front of Layala, and a sword made of blue light formed in hand. "Stay behind me."

"Open the way, Caliban," Layala said.

"I'm not in control anymore."

"What do they want?"

"Whatever you stole."

She backed up slowly, gripping Darkbringer tighter. "No. The chest and contents are mine. The sword is mine. Can't you tell them they're not stolen?" They were fifteen yards away now and closing in slowly. The gargoyles were slow; that was about the only advantage they'd have over them. "And are you saying they can control the tunnels?"

Caliban moved his hands along the black cavern wall. Hel's orb was the only thing giving off light, but it was bright enough to see the monsters and that there was no way out.

"You took it without the permission of my family. And yes, that's what I'm saying."

"But they do obey your family," Hel said, raising a dark brow. "So, tell them to back off and open the way."

"They're intelligent. They'll have recognized you threatened me on the way in."

The eyes she saw, the outline in the bricks... they'd been watching the entire time.

Ten yards away now. The slow stomps of their wide stone feet shook bits of rock and stalagmites loose from the rounded cavern above.

Caliban wiped sweat from his forehead. "But when this happens an alarm is set off. My family will know intruders are here." He swore. "And that I led you down here if we don't get out."

The first gargoyle reached Hel, bringing its massive stone sword up high. Hel swung his own weapon and sliced the creature's arm clean off. It hit the ground with a crack and broke in two. Hel leaned back, brows pulled down in confusion as the stone arm grew back and the sword came next.

"Well, fuck," Hel said backing up a step, then two. The gargoyle towered over him by three feet and was twice his size.

"Maybe I'll go for the head." Hel's white wings materialized, and he lifted off the ground and smashed his sword through its head; it crumbled and a new one appeared moments later.

The other stone monsters were close now. Layala dashed forward and hacked at a gargoyle leg while Hel fought off another.

Presco half shifted, pearl scales covered his body and his clawed hand broke through the stone monster in front of him. "Umm, a weakness. We need to figure out their weakness!"

Hel hit it with a blast of fire, it blackened the gray, but it only took seconds to regenerate. "It's not that."

"What is stone's weakness?" Presco mumbled. "Earth? No. Water?"

Layala swung her sword, cutting gargoyles in half, but they regenerated almost as quickly as she could break them apart. The ten-foot monster in front of her chopped his sword at her with a swiftness that caught her off guard; she ducked, and it whooshed over her head. Another at her back hacked its blade, she dove and rolled, springing to her feet. Her vines tore through the ground, circling the monsters but they broke through them like they were but blades of grass.

Their steps and swings came faster. They seemed to get quicker each time she hit them... and now she was surrounded, leaving her nowhere to go. Four of the gargoyles closed in on her. Her eyes darted back and forth waiting to see who would strike first. The one directly ahead kicked when she'd expected a sword strike, and slammed her straight in the gut, knocking the wind out of her. She stumbled back into the one behind her. Another's sword came up, and she threw up her shield; it smacked with a hard crack, sending her flying to the ground and rolling across the floor.

"Val!" Hel roared and dropped down in front of her. With

one swing he cut down the four gargoyles attacking her. Their stone bodies crumbled and instantly started rolling back together. He pulled her up and held her close. "Are you alright?"

She nodded, brushing the dirt and bits of stone from her clothes. "It's just a bruise."

"Presco! We need a weakness! I've tried wind, water, electric volts. Nothing is working!" The gargoyles swung harder, faster. Layala and Hel fought back-to-back. Sweat dripped down the side of her face, her arms began to tire. She moved side to side, ducking and dodging to miss attacks, like she'd practiced her entire life, but the ground beneath Layala's feet became slick with mud.

"Ice!" Presco blurted out. "Try ice!"

A blast of icy white frost shot out of Hel's palm, covering the gargoyles in moments.

"Hit them now!" Presco shouted.

Hel swung his magic sword, and in one chop, the gargoyle shattered into a thousand pieces. After, Hel went wild, slicing through them all, swinging his sword with precision and grace. She had to admit it was attractive the way he brandished his weapon, his wings carrying him from one to the next, twirling and spinning in almost a dance.

When there were no gargoyles left standing and only crumbles remained, Hel smirked and lowered to the ground. "Well, that wasn't as hard as I thought it would be."

"Now would be a good time to open the way," Presco shouted and Caliban, who hadn't moved once from his spot on the wall to help.

The small frozen shards of the gargoyles began to roll and come together. "That wasn't the end. They're reforming again."

Hel stood on the other side of the cavern, opposite of them, having just cut through every gargoyle in here. She didn't like him so far away. The first gargoyle rolled together in front of her and before its head even came back on, its huge arm back-handed her and crushed her into the wall. The back of her skull hit hard, and darkness flitted across her vision. "That hurt!" she snarled and struggled to stand up. She couldn't stay down. They'd keep coming. Warm wetness trickled down the back of her neck. She touched it and her hand came away bloodied. *I'm bleeding. Shit, I'm bleeding.*

Presco was suddenly swarmed by them, swinging his clawed hands while taking hits. Hel appeared in front of her and scooped her up around the middle and they rose high and hovered above the gargoyles. *It seems they truly cannot be killed,* Hel said in her mind. He touched the back of her head, and the warmth of his magic began to heal her.

If there's no way out... Hel, what can we do? She gripped the collar of his suit and swung her other arm around his neck. *We can't die down here.*

I'll think of something. Still holding her close, his wings beat steadily, his eyes scanned every crevice and every dark corner of this cavern. "There."

"The way opened over there!" Caliban shouted pointing left to a brick tunnel opening once again. "Hurry!"

Hel tucked his wings and dropped into a dive until his feet hit the ground at the tunnel's entrance. He pushed her inside and turned, blocking the attack of a gargoyle. Her chest of journals flew in right after her and hovered at her side.

"Presco!" Layala shouted. He was still under siege by several and looked to be tiring.

"I'll get him, just go." Hel vanished and reappeared beside Presco. He threw another blast of ice, from his palms, freezing the gargoyles, but it was only moments before popping and snapping echoed around the cavern as they broke free. Hel shoved Presco toward the tunnel and ran behind him.

"Come on!" Layala hollered, waving for them to hurry. Presco made it in, but the brick wall appeared in an instant, leaving Hel on the other side.

"Hel!" Layala slammed her fist against it. "Open it!" she shouted at Caliban. "Open it now!"

"It's too dangerous," Caliban said, stepping into the torchlight. "And Hel was the one who started the wars against our realm to begin with. He might do it again."

"You were the one who closed the way, weren't you?" She snarled and brought the tip of Darkbringer's blade at his throat. "Open the fucking wall."

"You won't kill me," he challenged. "You need me to get out."

Panic swelled in her chest to the point it ached. "OPEN IT!"

Hel, are you alright? Tell me you're alright. He couldn't fight those gargoyles forever. They'd just keep regenerating until he eventually ran out of stamina and energy.

Silence.

Layala gripped Caliban by his suit jacket and lowered the blade. "We may need you to get out, but you don't need your pecker to do that."

"He's her mate, Caliban," Presco said, gently. "She won't survive his death. Open the door."

Caliban ground his teeth, swore, and then the bricks in the wall fell apart, creating an doorway. The smell of loose dirt, and damp earth filled the corridor. Layala took a step forward to peer into the cavern, ready to rush inside to help him. He stumbled through with the edges of his clothes torn and parts shredded. "They got much faster once the wall closed."

The bricks shifted again, closing the gargoyles off in the cavern.

Layala sighed with relief and threw her arms around his neck. "Are you alright?" she backed off a step and patted his dusty shoulders. "Why didn't you answer me? I thought... You better answer me next time."

"I'm fine." His mouth twitched as if he held back a smile.

After that, Caliban took them on a straight shot to the main door of the treasury vaults. "Is there really an alarm sent out to your family? Will they be waiting outside?" Layala asked.

"Soon, if not already," Caliban said.

Layala took a deep breath as the big metal door opened with Caliban's touch. All they had to do was get outside and Hel could use his magic to get them out in an instant. The hallway was clear. No one waited to arrest them. *Thank the Maker.*

When the door swung closed, the group seemed to let out a collective sigh. The hallway was lit with torches and a skylight at the end let in plenty of light. Down at the far side, the archway opened up to the main area of the treasury and was still busy with patrons and workers alike counting money. They appeared to have no clue the treasury had intruders or that anything was stolen.

"That was intense," Caliban said, running a hand across his sweaty brow. "Honestly, the most excitement I've had in a long time, minus the stabbing and almost dying part."

"Thank you for getting us out," Layala said. She pushed off the wall, heartbeat steady once again. "How can we repay you for your help? For your silence?"

Hel let out a dark laugh. "I'll tell you how we can repay him." In the blink of an eye, Hel shoved his magical sword straight through Caliban's chest. Layala squealed in shock, and then slapped her hand over her mouth. "You closed us in there on purpose. You tried to have us killed."

"Hel, he got us out," Layala whispered. "He—"

"He knows who we are, Valeen. You think he wouldn't go directly to his family after this? You think they wouldn't hunt us?" He jerked his sword free, and Caliban slid against the wall, and fell to the ground with a thud. "We don't need another enemy right now."

She watched the blood pool around him. He was so young. Honorable. He died to protect his family name. Even if he did trap them with the gargoyles, he changed his mind. He set them free. With tears burning, she looked up at Hel. "He didn't deserve to die."

"I told you once I'd kill who I needed to keep you alive, and I told you I'd do things that would break your heart." Without waiting for her to respond, he grabbed her wrist and then Presco's and they vanished. Leaving the youngest Drakonan dead in the back of his family's treasury. His family, the city, likely the entire realm would be in an uproar, looking for his killer. They could no longer stay at Presco's.

CHAPTER 44

LAYALA

L ayala sat next to a small fire, propped up on a pillow and blanket under the night sky. Rather than being inside the manor, her soul longed to be under the stars even if it was a chilly night. Since Hel knew the exact location of the manor they traveled with his magic. They'd grabbed their belongings from the apartment above the potion shop and told Presco and Ayva to keep the business running as usual. If they closed and left, it would look suspicious, and as it stood, no one should suspect Presco or his wife of anything. Hel was right. The only public interaction they'd had was guests being shown a "special" backroom.

Presco planned to meet up with them in a couple days in case anyone came and questioned him; he didn't dare leave his wife to go through an interrogation alone.

Layala cracked open the first journal. They'd gotten home the day before, but she'd put this off. She knew it would change things between her and Hel and right now, she didn't want that. He lay beside her with his hands behind his head and his eyes closed, humming a familiar tune, one she thought she knew from before.

To read through all these journals would take years so she picked something in the middle.

Entry 29973

Katana believes in true love. She believes there is one perfect match for us. I've been alive a long time and I don't know if it's true...

She looked down at Hel, admiring the curve of his jaw, the way his skin seemed to be luminescent under the moonlight. Her fingers twitched, aching to touch him. His long dark lashes fluttered, and he opened his eyes as if he sensed her gaze on him.

"What is it, love?"

"Nothing."

He turned onto his side and propped up on his elbow. He plucked the book from her fingers. "Katana believes in true love," he read. "She believes there is one perfect match for us." He smiled, the dimple on his cheek deepened. He snapped the book shut and set it aside. "You didn't think so then. Do you now?"

She took her lower lip between her teeth, and traced the outlines of her wedding ring. "Maybe."

He sat up. "I'm going to do something selfish. It's wrong but I'm going to do it anyway."

Her eyes lifted to his face. "What?" She thought he might lean in, kiss her again, but he didn't.

"Ask for your forgiveness. You're going to read horrible things about me in those. Things I did."

"Just tell me what you did." She thought back to the dream she had sitting in at the table with War when he asked her what happened with Hel, and feeling like her entire world imploded and went dark, she never thought she'd see light again.

"Fuck, Valeen. What didn't I do? For one, I joined against you and War with the council when they found out you had Soulender." He looked away. "I was angry... it was more than that. I don't know if there is even a word for what I felt." He abruptly stood. "Just keep reading. I'm going to make us something to eat."

"Alright, Hel." She watched him walk back inside the manor and already wanted to forgive him. So, she read through her journals, sparking memories that made her laugh. Reading about times spent with her sister made her remember how much she loved her and then hours later getting to her sister's murder brought it all back. Standing beside her lifeless body, holding her limp hand. Even in death Katana was the most radiant and beautiful of the goddesses.

She slammed the journal shut and broke down sobbing like it happened all over again. Tears poured down her face and she curled up on the blanket wishing she could go back and see her one more time. She remembered not crying or thinking about Katana for years and then one day something would remind her, and she'd be sobbing, like now. Hel appeared at her side. He didn't ask. He just scooped her into his arms and carried her inside. He laid her on her bed and kissed her forehead.

"I miss her," she whispered.

"I know," he said.

He left a plate of fruit and his delicious scones and her chest of journals. She read about meeting Hel for the first time and the memory of it made her stomach flip. The first time seeing him was like the world stopped for a moment. Then she couldn't figure out why. She'd seen many beautiful males, but there was something different about this one. Something more.

She read most of the night, and with each passage she felt a little more like the goddess inside.

The next three days she spent reading in her room, only stopping to train and eat meals with Hel. Presco showed up alone and said that he'd been questioned as had everyone who attended the opera and then cleared. Hel and Layala's pictures went up all over the city on *Wanted for Questioning* posters. The authorities didn't know if they were involved but the Drakonans found it suspicious they came to town and left as soon as Caliban died.

It wouldn't be too long before word traveled to the small town they resided in. Her heart ached thinking about how comfortable she'd gotten here and that they wouldn't be able to stay much longer.

But neither of them rushed her to read faster, and they didn't ask about what she remembered, even if every time she reemerged from her room Hel looked both hopeful and yet terrified. But all that she'd read only made her grow fonder of him. Made her heart long to be near him. She found herself wishing he was in bed beside her each night, but he stayed in his own room.

Sitting in bed with her back against the headboard and her legs crossed, Layala opened a new journal. Waterdrops smeared some of the ink. Not just water drops, she realized, teardrops. Gulping, she started at the top of the page.

It's with a heavy heart that I write this. I still sometimes think it's a nightmare I'll wake from, and then the morning comes and there's still a hole in my chest, throbbing and yet empty. I haven't eaten in three days. War was kind enough to bring me here to his home in Ryvengaard, and I fear what the consequences may be for him. But I needed time to think.

I found Hel in bed with Varlett. But that wasn't even the worst of it.

WITH A GASP, Layala looked up from the page, and then like she'd been slapped with her journal, the memory flooded in...

VALEEN STEPPED *out of the bathtub. The water cooled enough to tell her she'd spent plenty of time there. After combing through her hair and changing into her nightgown, she started down the hall at House of Magic, toward her bedroom. The torches provided a dim light to lead her way and enough to spot her door was cracked allowing whispers to slip through it. Brows tugging down, she paused outside, peering inside.*

Hel sat on the bed with Varlett standing between his thighs. "It won't be much longer now," Hel said. "And you know this marriage is just for appearances. It was a marriage for power. It's you I truly love." He stroked the side of her face with the back of his hand. "I need her to give me a child, a full-blooded god, you know that."

"It's been nine years and no child," Varlett argued.

Hel chuckled. "Nine years isn't long for us. My Uncle Synick and I had a wager from a long time ago. Who could get the primordial goddess to bear a child. He tried to force her because he was a fucking imbecile. I got her to fall in love. He'd be jealous if he were still alive. You know it was almost fate that she killed him for me."

Varlett slowly went to her knees before him, leaned forward and kissed him on the mouth. "How have you fooled her this long? Or is it me who's the fool believing that one day you'll make me your queen?"

"I'm the god of mischief, love, fooling people is what I do. But you're too clever for that, little dragon." He paused and glanced toward the door. She was nauseous as she sank back a step, and he continued. "Valeen told me last night that she wants to have my baby and that she's finally ready. The only primordial without a child, and after thousands of years, I'm the one who will break her." He smirked and peeked at the door again. "She'll return soon. We'll have to make it quick tonight."

Valeen's legs felt weak, watery. The pounding of her heart drowned out the rest of their conversation. The edges of her vision seemed dark, like the walls were closing in around her. She almost charged in there and let them both feel the pain burning her from the inside out, but she found her feet moving backward, and her body silently carrying her down the hall. Where she was going, she didn't know, but she had to get out. She couldn't breathe—air; she needed fresh night air.

Tears streamed down her face as she bolted along the road down the side of Hel's mountaintop castle. The wind tugged at her hair as she pumped her arms, as bare feet slapped over stone. A scream burned the back of her throat but never released. Trees and boulders whipped passed until time seemed to disappear and she was at the bottom of the mountain. Panting for breath, she shoved her hands into her hair, scraping her nails across her scalp. How could this be real? How could she have been fooled for so long?

"Valeen?"

She whirled around to find War standing there, his features made clear in the light of the moons. Even in the dark she knew he saw tears streaked across her face, her usually pristine hair, disheveled, and barefoot in her short, silk nightgown.

"Valeen," War breathed and stepped toward her; she retreated *in reaction. Was he in on this too? Did he know? "Did something happen? Are you hurt?" His gaze roamed over her to check for injuries no doubt, but her wounds were not seen by the naked eye. "Where is Hel?"*

She buried her face in her hands and her shoulders shook with silent sobs.

"I'll go get Hel," War said, and before he could step back, she gripped his wrist.

"No." She had to get away from Hel. He'd played her for an utter fool, and she'd allowed it. She'd made her vows to not involve herself with the other gods, to not bear children for a reason, and now she was reminded the hard way why. The first time she learned that lesson was the death of her sister. Now it felt like her own ending. "Take me to Ryvengaard, to your house."

War pulled out of her grasp, nearly stumbling to get away from her. "I don't understand."

"I can't stay here anymore. Please," her voice broke on the last word. She didn't like to beg, to plead with anyone.

He shook his head. "I can't do that."

"You're my friend, War," she said. "I won't stay long just...until I figure things out. Until I can control my pain. My fury." Her hands shook from the unrelenting emotions that seemed to set fire to her soul. If she went back, if she stayed, she'd burn through every person in that castle and not everyone deserved her wrath.

"Why?"

She didn't want to say. Varlett was his fiancée. There was more than one person wronged. Valeen had thousands of years on War to learn to control her emotions, her temper. War had a short fuse. She pressed her lips together and stayed silent.

"I won't start a war for you. And if I take you away in the middle of the night to my home, that's exactly what will happen. You know

what Hel will think, what anyone would think. You and I have been close for years."

"It's not like that."

"But it would look like that."

"I must get away from here. I don't know where else to go."

"House of Night."

"No, he'll go there looking for me tonight and I just can't see him. I need a few days, or I'll do something terrible."

House of Night must be protected. She shut her eyes and felt her power rise. It was time to close the wards again, to keep them safe from the outside while she figured out what to do. Using the strength of the moons, she pictured the shimmering wall forming, locking in her territory, separating the land from Hel's, from the rest of Runevale once again. The hairs on her arms rose, her skin prickled as the magic set into place. As long as the moons hung in the sky, the wards would hold. But with their marriage bond, he'd be able to go through. Her blood from the ceremony ran through his veins. It would take time to lock him out.

"I don't understand," War said. "Did he hurt you?"

She swallowed the lump in her throat and tears streamed down her cheeks. Fury and sadness warred inside, and her chest felt like it was splitting open. "More than I could ever say. He ruined me." Those words shattered her composure, and her knees gave way and cracked against the stone road.

War crouched down before her and lifted her chin. "You are the goddess of night. No one ruins you." He didn't ask why, or push her for answers, he just scooped her up off the ground and brought her to his home.

Two days later, Hel barged into War's house. The door crashed against the wall with a crack. From the second-level bedroom Valeen stood in the doorway, trying to calm the rush coursing through her. She knew she'd have to face him at some point. He'd spoken to her through their bond, wondering why he couldn't find her, why the people were in an uproar about the ward blocking the night territory. Some of her people were locked out and some of his locked in.

She wouldn't answer.

He begged her to tell him what was wrong. She shut him out. If seeing him with Varlett, if hearing what he said was agonizing, this bond between them was torture. She couldn't be separated from him even in another realm.

But someone must have seen her, and War leave together, bringing him here.

"Where is she?" Hel's voice was cool, even.

From here she could only see his black boots and legs, as well as War's. "She doesn't want to see you."

"Did you really think you could come into my house and take my fucking wife? Where is she?"

"I didn't take her. She left you."

"Bullshit. What did you tell her? I know you've had feelings for her. I can see the lust in your eyes when you look at her."

"You know why, don't act like you didn't do this to yourself."

"Valeen!" Hel shouted. "Valeen, come talk to me."

Tears trickled down her face.

War groaned. "Remember when you said, 'I don't fall in love, War. I want bragging rights. Didn't you even have a wager at some point?' Well, she finally figured it out."

Silence.

Hel's boots shuffled back a couple steps. She imagined they stared at one another; a truth of another time Valeen hadn't been privy to.

More silence.

Until War said, "You're just like Synick."

"That's not true. Did you tell her that?"

"I didn't have to."

"Valeen," Hel shouted. "I may have said those things, but that

was before I knew you. Before I loved you. I was a fool, alright. You mean more to me than anything in any world. Please come home. At least talk to me."

She wished she could believe him. He sounded so truthful, as if he meant it, but she saw him, heard the truth with her own eyes and ears. And with Varlett of all people, with his brother's betrothed. The thought of her kneeling between his thighs, tugging at his pants made her want to vomit. He confessed that it was the dragon princess he loved, and Valeen was only for power.

The god of mischief, indeed.

"If she wanted to come out, she would."

"You tricked her, didn't you?" Hel snarled. "You dare betray me? Lie to her and get her to fall for you behind my back. You're supposed to be my best friend, my brother."

"That's not what happened. And I thought you'd changed. I thought you were a better person because of her but I was wrong. Everything is just a game to you."

"You're fucking my wife, and you think I'm the wicked person?" The house began to tremble with Hel's magic, the walls creaking, a crack opened in the ceiling above Valeen's head. She'd have to go down there and intervene if a fight broke out.

"I haven't touched her. Get out of my house until you can cool off. If she wants to see you, she'll come to you."

"I guess our brotherly bond means nothing when it comes to a goddess, huh? And you can tell her not to bother coming home. I don't want her if she can be so easily fooled."

Then he was gone. But that wasn't the end of his attempts to speak to her. His voice entered her mind, asking her to talk to him but she wouldn't. He kept telling her how much he loved her, but she never responded. What she saw could not be unseen nor was it something she could ever look past. He promised he wasn't like the others. He promised she was his one and only and he lied. He promised he wouldn't use her for power, and he lied. There was no reason to speak to him, to let him convince her it wasn't true. He'd fooled her for long enough.

Until one day there was nothing but silence and instead of a call to her mind, there was an invasion of an army. For a god who let another steal his wife was weak and so he would have to fight to get her back. He might have the council on his side, but Valeen had the one thing they wanted most.

VALEEN SHOT TO HER FEET, her bedroom darkening with storm clouds of fury. Layala was gone, the girl who would have mercy, the girl who would forgive. The goddess turned to shadow and dropped through the floor into the center of the main room. Presco closed his book and stood from his chair, concern lining his eyes. "Is something wrong?"

"Where is he?" she snapped, voice harsh and full of shadows.

"You remember."

"Everything." Not only did she remember the betrayal with Varlett, his betrayal of their sham of a marriage, and his lies trying to cover it all, but she knew everything that she ever was, the thousands of years old goddess born of darkness in the remnants of a fallen star at the birth of Runevale. The goddess who ruled House of Night, who became the greatest weapon in all the realms to avenge her sister. The goddess who foolishly fell in love and then fought against her powerful husband, and the brutal council of Runevale and nearly won.

"I think he went outside."

She didn't have to take a step before Hel appeared at the end of the room with a table, chairs, and multiple sets of furniture between them. With his hands in his pockets, he stood there, with a line formed between his brows and his careful, garnet eyes watched for any sudden movements.

When you remember you'll hate me even more, he'd once said. *He had the fucking balls to ask for forgiveness for this?* Maybe he felt guilty for what he'd done but in this case time did not heal wounds.

"Let's get this over with, love. Let me have it."

"Don't you *'love'* me!" She picked up a vase and threw it. It crashed into the wall just beside his head. "You selfish, lying, manipulative fucking bastard!" She was shadow and moved faster than light. Her fist crashed into his jaw and knocked him through the wall, opening up a Hel-size hole to the outside.

This was a long time coming. She had two thousand years to process her grief and let the wound fester. She jumped through to the outside and stalked toward him. He was already on his feet, shoulders tense, defensive. "How dare you try to turn this all around on me and War. You act like you're the one who got burned. Then you have the fucking nerve to come into this life and threaten *me*, and try to convince me that I am just a whore who left you for his cousin?" Soulender was in her trembling hand. "If I could kill you with this I would. Who knows, maybe I can." She slashed at him, but he vanished as it sliced through the air.

"That's what you're angry about? That I called you a whore?" He chuckled darkly, shaking his head. "And here I thought it would be because we destroyed everything we loved in a bloody war. That even after you allowed War to wrongfully convince you I only used you for power over a fucking bet, so he could snake his way into your heart, I still came to fight for you. I started a war with my *brother* to get you back."

"Ugh!" she screamed. "It's the hypocrisy," she snarled. "The lies. You made me look like a complete fool. You ruined my life.

You and Varlett are the reason I left, and why our marriage ended, not me and War. He didn't trick me into falling in love with him behind your back. You tried to turn it around on me with your mind games."

His eyes narrowed and he slowly stepped to the side. They began to circle one another, waiting for a strike. "You're going to have to explain that one, Valeen."

"You can't talk your way out of this. I saw it myself. I heard every word of betrayal from your very lips. You are a serpent. More than I ever thought you were as the Black Mage."

His brows furrowed. "What betrayal? My immature stupid ass saying I only wanted you for bragging rights before I ever married you? Varlett had nothing to do with anything."

"Don't act like you conveniently forgot that but remember everything else. And here I was falling for your poor, pitiful, 'no one cares for me' act yet again. The sad orphan who was abandoned by his mother and doesn't even know who his father is. With your deceit, I'm more than certain you're half demon. You are my greatest mistake. I gave you my whole heart and you deceived me." Tears of fury and anguish slid down her cheeks. "I was ashamed I ever trusted you. So much so that I couldn't even face you."

His eyes darkened. "Valeen, tell me right now what you're talking about."

"I saw you with Varlett in our bed. I heard what you said. I heard from your own mouth that you only wanted me for a child, just like Synick, but it's her you love. And it's more than obvious all these years later. You're still fucking that bitch. She's still with you."

His eyes grew wider with every word. "That's impossible."

"I said, I saw it!" she screamed, eyes burning with tears. She swung at him, and the blade sliced across his shoulder, cutting open his flesh, revealing a thin red line. She threw her fist and cracked him in the jaw. His leg swept her feet out from under her, and he took her to the ground. They flipped and rolled fighting for control, until she ended up on top, pinning him down by the shoulders. "Stop with your lies, your manipulation. You got caught, god of mischief."

He bared his teeth. "I'm not lying. I never touched Varlett until I was the Black Mage. I didn't even know her well until she decided to join the war on my side."

"Why would she join your side if you didn't know her?"

"Because you took her place, Valeen! She was supposed to marry War and he was in love with you." His knee knocked her in the side, dropping her to the ground onto her back, and his legs cinched around her thighs, his hands wrapped around her wrists above her head.

"No." She shook her head, breathing heavily under the weight of him. She didn't fight him anymore but stared into his garnet eyes. "No, I saw you together. But the worst part is you only wanted to use me to get a powerful child. Just like Synick wanted. You wanted to be the one to break the goddess of night. Well congratulations, Hel, you did. You utterly destroyed me. Let's all give him a round of applause."

He released her arms and rested his palms flat in the grass on either side of her head, hovering above her. "I don't know what you're talking about. I loved you. You're my wife, and my mate. If we never had a child, it didn't matter to me. I just wanted *you*. That's all I ever wanted. And I may have said some stupid comments to War about bragging rights and I might have even had a wager with Synick, but it was all just bullshit from when I first saw you, but it meant nothing after I knew you, I swear it. I am sorry I ever said those things. I fell in love with you. It was real."

"Stop it," Valeen snapped, but a sob caught in her throat at his words. *It was real...* "Stop lying. Drop the act. It's been long enough. War wasn't the one who told me about what you said or your deal with Synick. It was you that said it to Varlett."

"I'm not lying," his voice lowered, to almost a plea. "I never said those things to her. I didn't sleep with her or even give her more than a single glance. She was just War's fiancé. We weren't even friends."

Her elbow slammed into his left arm, collapsing him then she thrust her hips and dumped him over to regain the top position. "I'm going back to Adalon. Back to War. He needs to know he's with a cheating manipulator, and he doesn't need to feel guilty about betraying his cousin because it was the other way around. I don't know what you two have planned, but it's over." She moved to get up, and he vanished from beneath her, and stood in the way of the manor.

"You're not leaving until this discussion is over."

"Get out of my way," she snarled, low and venomous.

"Hit me." He held out his arms, leaving his body and face open for assault. "Hit me, stab me, do whatever you want until you can speak to me with a clear head. I can take it. I deserve it but not for *that* reason."

Her fist opened and closed at her side, and she ground her teeth, tucking away Soulender. "You make me crazy."

"I'm not letting you leave this time. I don't care how long we have to fight."

"You know, I never even slept with War back then. Not even once. Not until I was reborn as Layala."

"I wouldn't even care if you did at this point. I need to know exactly what you saw and where."

She took a deep breath, attempting to calm her coursing anger. "At your castle in our bedroom. I had just gotten out of the bath and while I stood in the hallway, I heard you talking." Her mind flashed to the scene of Varlett knelt between his thighs and she shook with rage. The sky darkened, not from storm clouds but like the sunlight couldn't penetrate the realm, as if it fell from the sky. Hel glanced up briefly and his jaw muscles twitched. The goddess of night saw him perfectly in the dark, saw everything, from the grass in his disheveled hair to the bead of blood at the corner of his mouth. "After I saw and heard everything, I left. I couldn't stay. You hurt me too much."

Hel lifted his palms in a way one might stave off a threatening animal. "Valeen, I know you're angry but think about it. I don't believe War is capable of magic like this, but Varlett is a master sorceress. Even back then she was gifted. She's unusually talented with magic. I know you think that is what you saw, but it never happened. I swear it."

Light crept back in as if the damper on the sun lifted. "What are you saying? I saw what I saw. I heard you."

"I believe you. I'm sure you did see that, but it wasn't me."

"Are you saying she made me see it? Created some sort of illusion. Only you are capable of something like that. Something good enough to trick *me*. Magic is detectable. I would have felt it." Valeen scanned every inch of Hel's face searching for the lie, but the god of mischief was notoriously hard to read. Any magical oath, or even truth serum Presco could give him couldn't be trusted. Hel was too powerful, and smart enough to outdo them. Zalefora, the goddess of truth would be the only one to definitively see a truth from a lie and even if she was one of the few goddesses she trusted, she couldn't contact her—and it wasn't as if she couldn't lie, too.

Maybe he only regretted his choice after he lost her. Maybe it was only then he realized he loved her, but it was too late now.

"There are few capable of magic that good but she's one of them. There are ways to cloak magic. I've seen her. I know her."

"Supposing Varlett was capable, why would she? And how could she know about Synick?"

"She was engaged to War. He knew all these things. He might have told her, thinking nothing of it. She was going to be his wife, and he must have told." He pressed his lips together. "But why? I don't know. It makes no sense. She was a dragon princess, poised to be the wife of a god."

Valeen narrowed her eyes. She wanted to believe him, and at the same time she didn't because if it were true that meant everything happened over an illusion, over one young dragon sorceress who had no business dealing with gods. And that illusion would have had to have been phenomenal. She even *smelled* the dragon in that room and left no hint of magic. She knew things she shouldn't have like Valeen's insecurities about only being used as a vessel to create powerful heirs. How could she know that?

Valeen shoved her hands into her hair and began to pace. But Hel was deceptive, intelligent, and a master manipulator when he wanted to be. It would be easy for him to come up with a story like this to win her back... "Did you tell the council I had Soulender after I left? Because they knew."

"No. I would have implicated myself by doing so. Someone else knew."

"If Varlett knew I killed Synick, she knew I had Soulender." She stopped pacing and a cold chill ran through her body. "Remember the person who blackmailed me into getting the demon prince's ring? I never saw her face. What if it was Varlett? She could have created an illusion like that with the power of that ring." All things she thought were separate issues, now fell together. She looked up at Hel. "Holy All

Mother, she said I'd remember something that happened between you and her and I could never speak of it. Her stipulation was silence, or I'd break my end of our deal. I think... I just broke it."

Hel looked paler than usual. "Because it wasn't real, and she didn't want you to realize it by talking to me or even War. Do you think I'd have helped you get your journals if I'd had an affair with Varlett and only used you? If I had a secret like that and I even considered you knew, I'd have done everything to prevent you from finding this out. If I did that and was so desperate to get you back now, I would have burned those journals, and I probably would have killed Varlett to keep her mouth shut."

Well, that was certain to be true. "Not if you loved her."

His hands trembled at his sides. "I don't love that bitch. I never have," he growled. "I asked for your forgiveness ahead of time for fighting against you, for what I said about only wanting bragging rights and the wager with Synick, not for this."

Synick. In that room with Varlett, he called him *Uncle* Synick. Hel rarely if ever called him Uncle. "But we'd talked about having a child. How could she have known?"

"You came to me, and you brought that up, not me. I never did. Not one time because I knew how you felt about it, and I told War when you did. I thought he was happy for me but maybe he'd been in on this whole plan with Varlett. He loved you then and loves you now. Maybe he wanted you enough to plan this with her."

She thought back on it. It had been her who asked if he wanted a child. She felt like it was right. He was her mate. With him it felt safe. The All Mother had blessed her, and she trusted him. "I don't believe War would do that."

"Funny how you trust him straight away but not me."

"You are deceptive by nature. He is not."

"Maybe not," he relented. "But love gets in the way of better judgment. And even if he wouldn't deceive you like this, Varlett would. I always knew there was something she hid from me, but never could have guessed it was this."

"Why did you think that I left you for War so quickly? You assumed it without question."

Hel's upper lip curled, and she could see he was about to fire off an answer but then he paused, took a breath. "One of my servants, a trusted one who'd been with me for centuries, told me he saw you kiss War. Weeks before you left. He said you'd been sneaking around talking in the shadows behind my back. So, I watched every interaction with suspicion, but I couldn't fathom it until he said he saw you in War's arms as he carried you away, and I couldn't find you anywhere. He suspected you'd planned to leave for a while. I didn't believe it until I found you at War's house in Ryvengaard."

"Who was the servant?" Valeen snapped.

"O'Ryan."

Valeen sneered. "The *dragon* shifter O'Ryan. Who would take orders from his dragon princess over you." It all started to make sense. "I still don't understand what motive she would have; all this because War loved me and not her?"

"There's probably more to it, but I'm sure that was part of it."

"But Varlett loves *you*. Not War. I saw it on her face in the tower."

Hel was quiet for a moment and then said, "Varlett doesn't love me. She loves what I can give her."

"And that is?"

"Power a dragon could never have on her own even with a

demon prince's ring. Do you know how much stronger she grew just being around me, learning from the god of magic? She told me once she always thought she should have been born a goddess. She asked me to make her immortal. Even if I could, I wouldn't have." He paused. "I thought our fight before I went to sleep was her jealousy of you, and maybe it was in part, but if she did all this, it was more than that. You threaten her power more than anyone, and the only reason she didn't kill you was because she knows you're the key to opening the way back to Runevale."

Valeen thought about what Varlett told her in her cottage in the mountains. *"You know what he cared about more than me? His power. And you know what I cared about more than him? Mine."* This wasn't about love at all, it was all about power.

"Do you believe me?" Hel asked. There was a desperation in his beautiful face she'd rarely seen.

It would be convenient to be able to blame everything on Varlett, and even if they had this discussion all those years before, she wouldn't have believed him. It was too raw, too real, but time had softened her to Hel again. Time had given them the gift of chances, but what convinced her the most was Varlett's stipulation of silence. There were too many coincidences for it not to be true.

At her hesitation, he dropped to his knees.

Broken.

Shattered.

Never had she seen him this desperate, not even last time. Before he'd been angry. Now he was groveling. A tear slipped down his cheek; his fingertips clasped his thighs indenting the fabric. His face was a beautiful mess of anguish. "I will beg. I will do anything you ask. After everything I've done, how I treated you, I know you shouldn't trust me, but I swear

I didn't betray you. I have only ever loved you. I love you still."

"Stop." Her chin quivered.

"I'll drink any serum. I'll let you into my mind to hear my every thought. I will do anything to prove that never happened. Fuck, Valeen, if you won't believe me, then just kill me. End me right now."

I do believe you.

Hel was in front of her, gripping her face between his palms. Longing and fear warred on his striking features. "I don't care about anything that happened anymore. If this life has shown me anything at all, it's that you are the reason I breathe. I live in an eternal midnight, and you are my moon giving me light in darkness. I have no heart unless it's in your hands, Valeen."

"Hel," she breathed.

"Let me finish. I am desperately sorry for everything I did to you in Adalon and before. I was wrong. And the truth is you shouldn't forgive me. You should despise me for the rest of forever, and I would rather burn in the agony of your hatred than feel nothing at all but love me or hate me, I can never let you go. I won't. I will always fight for you. I never told you this, but the one time I prayed to the All Mother for mercy, to help me find warmth in my endless winter, the next day you came to my Uncle Balneir's party. She gave me *you*."

Her chest throbbed, and tears spilled down her cheeks. It was hard—impossible not to give into him right there, to press her lips to his and love him with every part of her body that had been denied her for so long.

She did love him. Once the tormentor of her soul and now the possessor of it.

Maybe through it all, she never stopped loving him. Even if

a dragon sorceress or wars or jealousies wanted to pull them apart, as fate had decided, their souls would always call for the other.

Presco once told her that a soul match could be your best friend, someone you're drawn to, a person you felt you knew for a long time before you ever met, but a soulmate was a love match of two flames that sparked life into the other and burned with the eternal flame. That's what he was to her.

A part of her still loved War, too. He'd been there for her when she believed Hel had broken her all those years before. He had an easy smile and a warm heart. He carried her when she couldn't carry herself. He cared more about her than his own feelings, and he'd been patient, kind and loving. He'd saved Layala from herself. Even if the past few months they'd grown apart... "I—" she took a deep breath. "I need time to think."

"Because you love him," Hel said. "Val, he sent you away with me."

"You know he did that because he loves me. You never would have been so noble." But she thought back on it; he'd let her leave twice, and he didn't fight hard for her to stay. Once, when she left to break their mate bond, and again with Hel.

"You're right. I wouldn't have. Not in a million fucking years would I have sent you away with him if the situation was reversed. I would have found a way to protect you myself, not give you up and risk losing you forever. I would have never stopped touching you and loving you or pushed you away while waiting to see if you still wanted me once you remembered. I would have fought for you. I may not be selfless or noble, but I do love you and I'd do *anything* for you but give you up."

Anything, including starting a war with his cousin to take her back, including creating a curse for an army so he could stop the council from being able to kill her over and over. Even if he hadn't meant for them to be monsters, he created that spell with the intent of having a loyal following. She knew deep down the reason Adalon burned was because Hel loved her even through hating her, and that devotion drove him to become the most feared and hated person in the realms. Passion pushed him almost to the point of madness, and she loved him for it.

His fingers brushed her hair behind her pointed ear and his touch sent goosebumps down her spine. Darkness built in his face, storms of jealousy and anger, and then it faded away to understanding. Valeen closed her eyes, letting a tear slide down her cheek, and his thumb swiped it away. "I don't blame you for falling for him. He's easy to love. So, I will wait for you to find that he was best for Layala Lightbringer, but I am the only one for you, Valeen, goddess of night."

CHAPTER 45

VALEEN

Valeen stood in what had been her bedroom for the past two months, staring at her packed bag. Hours had passed since she fought with Hel. Hours to contemplate her love for two people who'd come into her life at different times when she needed them, and to comprehend the sorrow and loss she and Hel faced because of what Varlett did to them. She cried for the choice she had to make. She cried for the one she would hurt. Because she did love them both, for different reasons and in different ways.

Fear held her in its grip knowing what her choice would do to either of them.

From the dresser she picked up the winged horse statue of Midnight given to her by War. In her first life when she moved to Ryvengaard with War, he never once pushed her for a relationship. He fought beside her against Hel and the council. He gave up everything for her then, just out of true friendship. Because he believed it was the right thing to do.

It was Thane in this life she'd truly fallen in love with, not War. Thane the Elf King. He got her to fall for his charm, his relentless pursuit of her, and he loved her enough to not take advantage of her ignorance, and even selflessly sent her away with Hel because he knew that was what she needed to remember. He had a heart of gold. How could she not love him?

She set the statue of Midnight down, knowing who she was going to hurt and a part of her would die with that choice.

"Presco, we're leaving." Valeen came down the stairs of the manor with her bag of belongings slung over her shoulder.

Presco poked his head from around the corner, pushing his glasses up. "To..."

"Adalon. You're coming. I know you have a wife now, but I need you."

He stepped into the hallway, squared his shoulders, and bowed. His golden hair fell forward, and he brushed it back as he stood. "Absolutely, my queen. Shall we not worry about the hole in the wall then?"

She stopped and inspected the space they'd spent the past two months. The light blue couches they'd gathered around, the dining table they'd spent hours chatting at, and the long months she'd spent here with War. The hole in the far wall she'd knocked Hel through let in a breeze that ruffled the curtains along the front windows.

"It doesn't matter. I don't believe I'm coming back."

"Ever?"

"Ryvengaard is not my home."

Presco's brows raised, and a smile tugged at the corner of his mouth. "You want home to be House of Night again? Hel said you could open the way... Or do you intend to stay in Adalon?" He suddenly appeared worried to hear the answer.

Hel stepped into the doorway of the front entrance and leaned against the frame. His brows pulled tighter, jaw muscles clenching, eager and worried to know the answer to that question. After all, House of Night, Villhara was the home they shared together.

Two thousand years had passed since she'd been the ruler of that territory. There was no telling what had become of her people or who ruled there now. No doubt it belonged to another god or goddess, although it was possible her wards held up all this time, keeping out anyone who didn't belong. The thought made her smile. She liked to think they were happy, thriving and waiting for her to return, not slaves of some asshole.

She searched Hel's face, those garnet eyes so foreign to her memories, with the hope that she might be with him again, the only one who ever held those pieces of him together. Her soulmate.

Despite all his faults, he was the love she couldn't give up. He was the first and should have been the only, and even though it would hurt War, he would have to understand. Hel was right. Thane was the love and mate of Layala's life, but Hel was Valeen's. He was the only one who could match her fire, and she could embrace his darkness because she was part of it. With a deep breath she met Hel's stare. His body froze, terror and anticipation written all over his face, fighting for dominance.

Until she said, "My home is in Villhara."

He looked like the weight of a thousand suns lifted off his

shoulders and strutted forward. He was a king seeking to conquer and she was ready to drop to her knees and submit. "So, we're done with the games? We're done with the uncertainty?"

Her heart pounded with how sexy he looked coming for her, gliding like a predator going for the kill. "Yes."

"You might want to make yourself scarce, Presco."

He was already on his way out.

Valeen set down her bag and fell off the last step into Hel's arms. Her lips crashed into his. His mouth opened allowing her tongue inside, and his grip on her hips tightened, his fingers digging into her skin.

"Mmm, you know what this means."

"That you'll want more?" she said and smiled against his lips. "I love you, Hel. I wish none of this ever happened. It was always supposed to be you. My heart is yours." She pushed a lock of hair off his forehead and kissed the scar on his brow. "I knew it at Presco's apartment. But I was too scared to say it. You asked me what I wanted that night. I want you. Every part of you. The good and the bad."

"It feels like I've waited an eternity to hear you say that." She hadn't seen him genuinely happy in a long time, but he was now. He circled his arms around her waist, lifted her off the step then they were moving through darkness until they stood on the rooftop balcony overlooking the manor's property. The cool night air swept through his hair. The stars and moons were bright enough to see the plains of his face, his body, but it was dark enough to keep secrets. The sounds of chirping crickets and the coos of birds filled the evening around them. A bed waited up here, along with a few books and a gold pot of jasmine.

He tossed her onto the soft feather duvet, and she fell back waiting for her king to take what was his. "Are you absolutely certain?" He climbed over her, straddling her body, pinning her arms down beside her head. His lips crashed into hers, and a soft moan escaped her.

I'm certain.

He let out a low growl and his lips moved down her throat, leaving a trail of heat like molten lava, the kisses intense with passion and need. "You want me to make you mine, love?"

"Yes."

He released his hold on her and sat up. "You know my rule." He slowly unbuttoned his shirt, agonizingly slow. "Once I have you, that's it. There is no one else."

"There is only you."

His smile was pure seduction. "You're not afraid of my darkness anymore?" She gripped the soft blankets beneath her, eagerly awaiting his touch.

"It was never your darkness I feared. It was that I craved it. Give me your serpent's bite. Infect me with your venom. I want it all."

He let out a wicked laugh and pulled off his top, revealing his glorious body. His low-hanging pants revealed his "V" and his KING tattoo, and she remembered achingly clearly how she used to trace those letters over and over and what it did to him. With a snap of his fingers her clothes vanished, and she was in a crimson nightgown as sheer as his want for her.

"Good gods, I knew you'd look delicious in that but damn."

She trembled as he climbed over her, and hooked her legs around his hips. His fingers trailed across her lips, just a brush, a tease. "You're the most wonderful being there's ever been, goddess of night." His light touch trailed down her throat and over to the lily mark on her arm. "I have thought about this night for months now, and how I would do this if you gave in to me."

"Oh?" Valeen arched a brow and ran her fingers over the rune on his chest that resembled the outline of a thick, black teardrop with two arcs through it. It was for healing others, one of his few selfless runes. "Is that why you set up this spot out here?"

"At first, it's where I came to escape when I couldn't stop thinking about you. When I wanted to come into your room and fuck you senseless." His warm lips met the spot below her ear; she gasped at the softness of it. "But sitting out here under the stars alone only made me wish you were with me, and I set out books you'd like, and your favorite color of blanket. Plum purple." He flicked his wrist and lit candles appeared along the edges of the balcony. The smell of the jasmine drifted on the breeze, mixed with his delicious masculine scent.

She pushed her fingers into his hair as his lips pressed on the swell of her breast. "And did you touch yourself thinking of me while out here all alone?" He'd once teased her about that. It was fun to taunt back.

"More than once," he admitted, and his hot breath brushed against her skin, sending tendrils of desire through her.

"And in your mind did you have me on the bed? Or perhaps against the railing over there." She arched into his kiss on her chest. "Tell me."

She felt his smile against her skin, and he lifted his head. His hands closed around her wrists like steel cuffs. "Naughty girl. You're being impatient. I've waited a very long time for this. You'll wait and see."

Valeen dropped her legs from around his waist. "We can do it more than once. If I recall correctly you're good for three, maybe four rounds."

He chuckled and smashed his lips to hers. Restraint be damned. "Because you're a greedy thing. Always demanding more."

On his knees, between her legs, he dragged his fingertips down her body, tearing through the red nightgown like it was soft paper. The cool breeze pebbled her skin and she let out a strangled moan. Those hands of his left a trail like hot coals on her skin.

"You're even more stunning than I remembered. Look at you." She blushed and his magic slithered up her legs, her thighs and over her hips and belly like fingertips. His heavy-lidded eyes drank her in. "You're everything I ever dreamed of and more." He lightly touched the top of her thigh brushing his thumb over the rune mark that saved her from a pale-one bite. A breath later his mouth was on her belly, tongue dragging over salty skin. "You taste like Serenity."

"And you look as sinful as the underrealm."

More kisses explored her body, her shoulders, her neck, her chest, and she ached for more. Then his tongue slid along her inner thigh, stopping just before the apex, and she whimpered, body trembling. "Hel, don't stop."

He lifted his head with a wicked grin. "Tell me what you want?"

No more teasing, no more waiting. "Show me why you're the god of mischief."

All the playful banter faded for shadows and midnights. A soft pink ribbon snaked around her wrists, pulling her arms overhead, anchoring her to the mattress. He lifted her left leg and kissed the inside of her ankle, where his lips met a glimmering black kiss imprint was left tingling her skin with a pleasant sensation. The heat of the mouth lingered when he moved to the inside of her knee leaving another mark, then the soft skin of her inner thigh like new vibrant tattoos or his runes. Each imprint felt like his lips still remained until it slowly seeped into her skin and vanished.

"That's new," she said, fascinated by it.

"Like I said, I've had a long time to plan this." His hands and mouth roamed over her body, and he left those prints everywhere, marking her as his in that moment. They seemed to be illuminated under the moonlight.

"Oh gods." She arched against his touch. "That feels good."

Across her belly his fingertip slowly caressed her, and she found he wrote: *Mine.*

"You've branded me," she said with a giggle. "I almost wish it would stay."

He smiled deviously and then said, "I could arrange that. But for now, I want to taste you. I want to hear you say my name." His tongue slid against her, and she closed her eyes, getting lost in bliss. That mouth of his was magic of its own. She melted into the sheets, gripping the ribbons. Until he pulled away. "Those noises... I can't hold back anymore," he breathed. "Hold onto those ribbons, love." Her stomach fluttered with excitement and trepidation.

His pants vanished, leaving him completely naked and she bit her lower lip at the sight. He was every bit a god in every way. He lowered himself into her, bare flesh met bare flesh and they both sighed at the connection. At long last. He gave her only a moment to adjust to him and then there was nothing gentle about the way he took her. It was need driving him, exactly what she desired.

"Valeen," he moaned. "I've needed you for so long. Fuck, you feel better than my memory could ever do justice."

Her moans grew louder with each breath; his hands gripped hers, with their fingers intertwined. The bedframe creaked along with the trees in the breeze surrounding the property.

I need to touch you. Let me touch you. She tugged against the silk ribbons holding her arms up. His body was perfection, and every muscle, all his luscious skin needed to be praised by her hands.

Then break free, love. If you can, he taunted.

She jerked on the soft fabric hard. They held fast. Until she turned her hands and wrists to shadow and slipped free of both his grip and the ribbons. Her nails scraped his back, then her teeth nipped his neck, marking him as hers. He hissed lightly but she knew he loved it.

"I love it when you get feisty." *And I love every curve, every freckle, every sound you make.*

The breeze moved across damp skin. The full moons shining down from the heavens made her feel stronger. The dim light illuminated his face and created shadows at once. Revealing the two sides of him; the one she knew and the other he gave the world.

Then he slowed his rhythm, deepening it. *You're mine,* he whispered in her mind. *Never forget again that you're mine.*

I'm yours.

My wife.

Your wife.

He kept his intense, deeper rhythm until she wanted to beg him to go faster, but reveled in every touch, every kiss, every brush of his fingers across her skin that left his magic on her, and every sound he made.

Say you're my wife again.

She smiled, wrapping her arms around the back of his neck and kissed his lips softly. "I'm your wife, Hel." *You're my husband.*

He shuddered and goosebumps rose along his skin. Then he hooked his arm around her back and rolled her on top. She licked the salt from his skin off her lips. Magic slithered along her like his hands everywhere. It was enough to drive her to the edge.

"I love you, Hel," she said, gazing down into his eyes. Shadows began to roll off her, and he moved quicker with her. "Gods, I love you. I love you inside of me. I love you touching me, and the way you say my name."

Valeen. "You're close," he murmured. "Come for me, love." He already knew what those shadows meant. "Don't hold back."

Her breathing came faster. She rocked harder, and he moved himself rapidly against her. She gripped the top of his hands resting on her thighs, and let the pleasure overwhelm her. She didn't look away from his piercing gaze as she lost herself in him. Her moans grew louder; anyone nearby would hear. "Hel," she crooned. A glittering shimmer, like a thousand falling stars rippled across her skin from her core down to her toes and up her chest.

"You're so beautiful like that. If you could only see what I do." And with a deep groan, he gripped her thighs, holding on like he might disappear if he didn't, and gave in too. Every one of his runes lit up with a glowing amber outline that lasted a few seconds before they faded to flat black once again.

She rolled into bed beside him, breathing heavily. Being next to him was like locking in a lost piece of a puzzle. One that had fallen and been lost for so long and to find it was like coming home. He curled one arm beneath her and pulled her flush against him. "I want to see you do that again. But I need a minute."

She laughed and folded into him, nuzzling her nose into his neck. "Mmmmhmm."

WHILE SHE LAY her head on his stomach, she lightly trailed her fingers over every tattoo, and every rune on his torso. "The one good thing about all this is I got to fall in love with you all over again."

He smiled. "And this time around was much harder of a fight."

"Was the payoff everything you desired?"

"Do you even have to ask? You sent me to Serenity and back."

She smiled and pressed her lips to the letter "K".

"Baby, don't do that unless you want round four."

"Maybe I do."

His laugh vibrated her body. "I'm going to need a rune for stamina and a hard cock."

She burst out laughing and pulled herself up to his chest so she could look him in the face and tugged the soft blanket up with her. "I'm more than satisfied."

His hand slowly rubbed up her bare back. There was something she needed to tell him, but she didn't know how it would make him feel. And to lose this peace under the stars, wrapped in a warm blanket...

"What is it?" he asked. "I know there's something you want to say. I can sense it."

She gulped and let out a slow breath. "We'll need War to open the way back to Runevale."

"That's fine," he said without hesitation. "I always planned to go back. We're not leaving him there."

Her rapid heart slowed. That reaction was different than she anticipated. There wasn't even a spark of jealousy in his face. "No, of course not. But I didn't want you to be surprised. It will require all three of us to be at peace with each other, to be on the same side. After what happened, I didn't want us to go back until we were happy again."

"You have such a good heart. If it had been me it would have required vengeance, the heads of all my enemies, and maybe their offspring too. Not love and peace."

Valeen rolled her eyes, but he wasn't joking. "I never would have guessed. You wanting vengeance and heads rolling? Never."

He smiled revealing his dimpled cheek and wrapped a lock of her white streak of hair around his finger. At some point she decided she'd keep that streak as a reminder to never hesitate. If she hadn't hesitated in that fight, she'd have never been bitten.

"Do you think if he knows you chose me, there will be a problem with opening the way? If so, don't tell him until after."

"I don't know how he'll react. I hope he'll be alright. I don't want to hurt him."

His body tensed and he stopped playing with her hair. His garnet eyes locked onto hers. "Remember when I said, if I had you, you're fucking mine." He gripped her inner thigh. "I think I'll tattoo 'property of Hel' right here just as a reminder you only spread those pretty thighs for me."

Valeen yanked on a lock of his hair, then kissed the hollow of his neck. "Stop it. I made my choice, and proved it to you over and over tonight. But he's still my friend and yours. He's your family... It's War. He was a victim of Varlett and her scheme, too."

And he was Thane. The part of her that was Layala still

loved that part of him. Some of her would always be the elf Layala Lightbringer, raised by Aunt Evalyn in the human lands of Svenarum, the young mage who fell in love with a king. Even if she got her immortality back, she'd have this body with elven ears and features.

But even as Layala she fell in love with Hel too.

"Don't even say her name. Once that bitch is dead, I don't ever want to hear it again."

Then he sighed, rolling her off his chest onto her side next to him, and worked his thigh between her legs. Propped up on his elbow, he brushed her hair behind her ear. "This will be hard on him." Hel's voice was softer now, almost remorseful. "He truly loves you, and I know what it feels like to watch from the other side."

"I know."

"It's up to you to decide if you tell him before you open the portal to Runevale. I trust you," he said.

She nodded.

"I was thinking of something a few hours ago. If Varlett has the demon prince's ring, the last thing she'd do is summon its master. So either the council made promises to him they couldn't keep and sent him to assassinate us, or she's working with them and likely has been for a long time, and someone will get double crossed."

"Well, when the demon and Varlett are dead, it won't matter." *And that bitch is on her last day.* "We need to take the advantage of surprise. The best thing we can do is pretend I'm still naive Layala and I don't remember her deception. The only issue with that is if the price of me breaking my silence is something she'd notice right away. So far nothing has happened to me, but she promised it wouldn't cost someone's life or soul."

"It could be any number of things, but it will likely be

something to benefit her. And what will our reasoning be as to why we came back before you remembered who you are?"

"I'll say I had a dream that Thane was going to die, and we were worried."

Hel lifted a shoulder. "We'll see if she falls for it. And the demon?"

"If he followed us here then he'll follow us back. If he's still there then we'll take care of him. I have Darkbringer and Soulender now. Without his ring, he's nothing."

"I wouldn't say *nothing*, love. You're not an immortal at the moment. He can kill you and we'd be doing this all over again."

"He could kill Layala. He won't touch me."

Hel laughed. It warmed her heart to see him genuinely laugh again. It made her think of their early years together. "Alright. But you will not try to take Varlett on by yourself, understand?"

With a smile, Valeen tilted her head. No longer was she simply a twenty-five-year-old elf. She was an ancient goddess too. She slid her finger along his jawline and then her thumb across his lips. "I will forgive you for things in the past, given what you thought happened between me and War, and how you felt betrayed. I understand it. But, remember who you are talking to now, Hel. I am not a young naive elf anymore. You will not speak to me like I am."

He peered down at her; she'd seen that look before. It was one of admiration and longing, desire. "Allow me to rephrase, goddess. *Please*, don't take her on yourself. She betrayed me and used me as much as you. I could argue I've been slighted the most."

"That's better. We'll do it together."

CHAPTER 46

VALEEN

Valeen and Hel stood at the base of Castle Dredwhich's front steps. Guards patrolled along well-manicured paths. Bathed in the golden light of the sunset, the grounds were bright and green and smelled of lush foliage and summer blossoms on the trees. Butterflies and buzzing bees flitted from bright colorful bloom to bloom. Everything looked the same as it did the last time she'd been here.

They left Presco on the other side of the ravine to keep an eye out for the demon prince.

With her stomach in knots, she started up the deep gray stone steps. Before she could talk to War about anything, they had to take care of Varlett. She couldn't guess what transpired between them over the past couple of months. They'd once been engaged so she didn't know if that was something he would have rekindled while she was gone or not. She hoped that wasn't so because she was going to cut that wench's head off.

The guards dipped into bows as they approached and then pulled the double entrance doors open. "Lady Lightbringer," they said in surprise.

She paused before entering. "Where is King Thane?"

"Behind you, Lady."

Hel had already turned to find him at the bottom of the stairs dismounting Phantom. War's long dark hair blew in the breeze. It had grown even more, down to his waist now. His bright green eyes took her in, and he smiled warmly. Her stomach fluttered and she started down the stairs, slowly at first. Then moved quicker until she was in front of him and wrapped her arms around his hard torso. He was safe.

"You're still here," she breathed.

He put his arms around her, hugging her back. He smelled like the woods. "Did you think I was going somewhere?"

"I was worried." She pulled back and let out a long slow breath before she glanced over her shoulder at Hel. There was no sign that he was bothered, although she knew her affection for War wouldn't please him. The smooth planes of his face were neutral as he sat on the steps, with a civar, watching them through the haze of the smoke. She realized then he hadn't smoked at the manor and their time together there but now he was back at it. A habit that he kept when he was unsettled.

"She was convinced you were going to die and insisted we come to check on you," Hel said. "Prophetic dreams or some such nonsense."

War's brows furrowed. "I'm sure I'll be fine. I thought you two weren't coming back until..."

She hated lying to him, but she'd have to keep up the facade until they found where Varlett was. They couldn't risk her overhearing and figuring out they knew the dragon's secret. They wanted surprise on their side so she wouldn't run. "I remember some things, not everything." She tucked her arms behind her back.

"Where's Varlett?" Hel asked.

"I haven't seen her today." He pulled off his black riding gloves. "We've been hunting the demon. We took down one of the hounds three days ago and he vanished after that. Varlett didn't come back with us."

"You found the obsidian," Valeen mused.

"Yes, up north in dragon territory. The Drakonans had a stash."

Valeen turned to Hel. *That means the demon Morv was never in Ryvengaard. Who could I have seen then?*

Hel lifted a shoulder.

If Varlett didn't come back, do you think she knows?

That's what I'm thinking.

War cleared his throat and looked back and forth between them. "You're talking to each other silently, aren't you?"

"Should we call you Thane or are you War?" Hel asked, pushing up to his feet. He tossed his civar and stepped on the burning end. "War would know that. Thane wouldn't."

"I remember everything now but among the elves, I'll always be called Thane. So, what is it you don't want me to know?"

It was still too risky to tell him. Varlett could be anywhere, hiding. War's eyes flicked back and forth between them, and his throat bobbed. "You came to tell me it's him, didn't you? That you choose him."

Hel's eyes flicked to her. *Be convincing.*

"No, that's not why," Valeen said softly. Shit, this was going to be a disaster.

"You know the reason you left him was because he was using you for an heir and he was cheating on you. You never did tell me who it was with." He glared at Hel, fists clenching at his sides. "You deserve better, Layala."

"Thane..."

You're not doing a very good job convincing him you haven't made your choice, Hel chided. *We don't have time for this conversation with him.*

War's lips pressed firmly together. "You don't look surprised."

"That's because she isn't," Hel said. "And if you don't shut up, you're going to ruin our upper hand. Dragon in the sky." He pointed up. High above, soaring in the clouds was a sleek black dragon. The dying light glinted off her scales, glittering like a vast lake. "Guess who."

"Zaurahel," Valeen warned. "Don't do anything rash."

"What's going on?" War asked.

Hel's white wings materialized and without so much as a look her way, he shot into the sky.

"HEL!" Valeen shouted. Her heart slammed into her chest so hard and fast it ached. "Damn it! That bastard tried to get on my ass about not going after her myself and he turns around and does that exact thing."

She searched everywhere for another dragon, someone to get her up there fast. Her shadow form could rise up there, but she lacked the speed and maneuverability she had on the ground. Too bad she hadn't taken Hel up on those wings he offered her. "Where is Presco?" she said more to herself than War.

War looked utterly confused. "Layala, tell—"

"It's me, it's Valeen. There's no time to explain but Varlett betrayed Hel, you, and me, all those years ago. She tricked us."

She peered across the ravine where they'd left Presco but couldn't spot him. She took off running, simultaneously checking the sky. Hel's wings beat swiftly, carrying him rapidly upward. The sunset shined off them like silver armor. He was seconds from reaching Varlett.

Hel, you wait for me!

Sorry, love.

"Demons!" someone shouted.

"Shit," War cursed, and grabbed her arm, dragging her to a stop. "We need to get you inside. He must have spies or—"

Valeen pulled free of his grasp. "I am the goddess of night. He will fear me."

War broke into a smile and shook his head. "I told you one day you'd realize you were the queen, the most powerful chess piece on the board, and they would fear you. I'm glad you finally have."

Her fingers ached to touch his beautiful face one last time, but she only nodded at his encouragement. "Varlett played us all against each other."

"I don't understand. We were engaged but then once you came to live with me, she left to join with Hel, but how does that mean she played us?"

At the bridge, a demon hound tore into the guards and body parts flew in the air. The gate dropped with a slam, but the demon hound crashed through it, spraying bits of metal everywhere. Screams echoed against the castle as the guards ran toward the danger and servants and other guests ran away from it. Valeen watched in horror as the horses bolted through the pasture, trying to escape one of them. She spotted Midnight and Phantom among them.

"Oh, you better not touch my horse!" She took off running

at a full sprint. The wind tore through her midnight hair, her boots flew over the emerald-green grass.

War caught up to her side, running along with her. "Is that Presco?"

"Yes." A searing hot pain ripped into the back of her thigh, nearly dropping her to the ground. "Ahh!" she screeched through gritted teeth and stumbled forward, gripping her hands around her leg. War caught her around the waist before she fell and held her up.

"Holy Maker, you're bleeding." He tore the sleeve off his left arm. Down the back of her thigh a huge gash opened, spilling blood down her leg onto the grass. No one had snuck up on her. No arrows flew by. *How in the realms did that happen?*

She looked across the grounds as the horses broke through the fence, their hooves thundering in a stampede, and the hound turned its attention to the guards running at it. Servants ran past Valeen and War to escape into the castle. One young lady's dress was torn at the bottom and blood splattered across her face.

As War stooped down to tie the sleeve around her thigh, another burning sting slashed across her abdomen and she doubled over, slapping her hand over a tear in her top through her vest. Blood oozed out from beneath her palms. "Ahhh," she groaned. "War, what's happening?" It felt like icy fire burned through her midsection and the pain made her woozy.

His eyes widened in horror as he took in the blood spilling into the fabric of her top. "I don't know, but it's alright, I'll heal you. It will be alright." He sounded like he was trying to be calm for her sake and that scared her even more. He pulled his shirt off and pressed it to her belly. "I need you to lay back. You won't heal fast enough on your own."

"We have to get up there and help him." She pushed against his shoulders and tried to step back.

War gripped her waist, holding her from escaping and pressed his bundled-up shirt harder against her. "Valeen, sit down. Hel can handle Varlett on his own."

Up high among the clouds, Hel slashed at Varlett with his illuminated blue magic sword. Her fierce claws swiped at him, cutting through the air but missing his agile movements. On her underbelly was a gash...

Varlett's fire breath blasted in an arc of orange flame. Hel tucked his wings and rolled, disappearing entirely, and reappeared then stuck his sword through her left wing and jerked the blade up, tearing through it like it was paper. Another pain stung Valeen's back, as if he'd slid his sword across it. Valeen cried out in sync with a roar from the dragon shifter.

No. Valeen shook her head in disbelief. *No, no.* Her head swam as realization struck her, their bargain. The price. Her good leg wobbled, and she gripped War's shoulders for balance.

"How do I stop this?" He put more pressure on her wound and it knocked the wind out of her. Her mortal elven body was inferior to her goddess form in almost every way. "How is this happening?"

Hel, stop hurting her, she called to his mind.

Another gash split on her arm, and War cursed. "Tell me how to stop this!"

"It's Varlett!" she bellowed. *Every time you hurt her, you hurt me,* she shouted in Hel's mind. *STOP!*

His wings whooshed, driving him backward, creating distance between him and Varlett. *How is that possible?* The horror in his voice was evident even in her mind.

Varlett's dragon suddenly shifted to human form, and she

was free-falling from the clouds, every second bringing her closer to impending death. Her golden hair rippled upward like waves of amber wheat dancing in a storm.

All Mother, give me strength. With a surge of energy, the pain dulled, and she shoved away from War and ran as fast as her injuries would allow. *Get to her, get to her before she hits the ground,* she chanted, keeping her sights fixed on Varlett dropping faster and faster like a stone. Her body was curled inward, and her arms and legs were still like she'd gone unconscious.

"Presco!" Valeen hollered but he was high up and she didn't know if he could hear over the chaos of demon snarls, swords clashing, and the screams.

A hulking black form caught the corner of her eye. Her focus shifted, and a demon hound barreled toward her, teeth gleaming red with blood dripping from its mouth. She clenched her jaw and altered into shadow, calling Darkbringer to her palm. The hound charged head-on, and she dropped onto her knees, leaned back and as the hound ran over top of her, she slid her goddess blade through the underbelly of the beast. No howls came, no cries. It stumbled through its last steps and collapsed behind her.

Varlett's life is tied to mine, Hel! Get her!

Varlett was seconds from hitting the ground and Valeen wasn't close enough to make it. But her vines could. They ripped upward ready to catch and wrap around her, and then a blast like an ocean wave slammed into her, knocking her to the ground. She lost control of the magic, but Hel swooped in and grabbed Varlett, cradling her in his arms.

"Hello again goddess," came the gravelly voice of the demon prince Morv, pulling her attention.

Pushing up to her feet, she turned to face him, this time with courage, not fear. But black spots flitted across her vision.

The wounds on her body weren't healing fast enough and the expenditure of power and energy weakened her. The rush of the fight had kept the pain at bay momentarily, but it all caught up to her. Waves of unbearable agony rocked her core and her legs buckled. She dropped to her hands and knees, barely able to draw in a breath. Blood plopped onto the grass, below her, *drip, drip, drip.*

Where is War? she wondered. *Where is Hel?*

A deep laugh made her skin crawl. "What a sight to see the goddess of night as such a feeble thing. It almost takes the pleasure out of killing you. Almost." The demon prince's horns protruded out of messy white hair, and those bright red eyes pinned on her with disdain. He was immortal and her goddess blade wouldn't kill him, but it would send him back to the underrealm... if she was strong enough to wield it against him. The black spots in her vision grew darker and spread more. *I cannot pass out. Stay awake. Stay awake.*

All seven feet and powerful muscle of him strutted toward her with his magical staff in hand, and another hound at his side. There had been three, and she only killed one. That meant another one was around somewhere.

Shit. She gripped Darkbringer and debated on calling forth Soulender, that would end him for good, but he could easily turn it against her, and then not only would she be dead forever, but he'd also be the most feared being in the realms. She couldn't allow him the chance to get it.

Boots hit the ground with a heavy thud beside her, and Hel tucked his wings away. "Your first mistake was coming for *my fucking* wife. The second was believing you ever had a chance."

She smiled. *Hel.* His name was all she needed him to hear to know the relief in her voice.

"You wanted a fight. Now you've got one." War stood at the

demon prince's back with a black-bladed sword in hand. "I like our odds better than yours, Morv."

The corner of her mouth tugged up; Hel and War were back fighting again and this time, not in opposition. The black spots in her vision thickened. She could barely see the dying sunlight now, as it dipped behind the high mountains. Her arms gave out and she collapsed onto her side. The pain was too much. She was so tired; sleep beckoned her.

Not sleep. She wouldn't wake up, but her eyes closed anyway. There were screams nearby—she needed to help. The sound of swords clanking, and soldiers shouting orders. Someone was crying. Her core felt cold now, where the blood had once been warm.

Suddenly she was lifted off the ground and brought against a strong, firm chest.

"Hel," she murmured, opening her eyes again to find his face. She let her head fall against his shoulder; his huge white wings spread.

"Fuck him up," Hel said to War, and then lifted off the ground, gripping her tighter to him.

A burst of panic shot through her and she clutched at Hel's battle leather top. "He can't fight them both alone!"

They rose higher, the wind whistling in her ears, ruffling her hair.

War charged, driving his boots into the grass, and let out a warrior's cry. Morv whirled around on him, and the hound barreled ahead of his master. Its terrible snarling cry made her shudder.

"He's not alone, and my priority is you." Over Hel's shoulder, she spotted Leif, Fennan, and Piper charging in. Presco dropped in from the sky shaking the ground with his heavy weight.

Suddenly everything went dark. Space seemed to pull and crush her body at once until they appeared inside the stone circle where Varlett lay unconscious. It was quiet over here. The ribbits of the toads in the pond were louder than the battle in the distance.

Gently, Hel set Valeen down on the stone, careful to cradle her head as he did. "I'm so sorry I did this. I didn't mean to." His voice cracked. "I didn't know."

He placed a light hand over her abdomen. The warmth of his magic soothed the pain away in a moment. "You couldn't have known." She laid her palm on his forearm to reassure him.

The warmth in her core began to return, her pumping heart beat stronger, and the blackness sprinkled across her vision lifted like a fog on a sunny morning. It was remarkable how quickly the god of magic's healing powers worked. Her husband's power. Almost as good as having her impenetrable immortal body. Then he moved to the wound on her back, her thigh, and arm.

Valeen stared up at the sky, stained red with the setting sun. Red like it was painted with the blood of all the people dying that night. Her throat thickened and anger revved up in her chest. She would end Morv for good.

"I needed to bring you here to make sure she's healing, too."

"If it doesn't, I'm in trouble." Turning her head, she found Varlett curled on her side with her back toward them. Parts of her golden waves of hair were stained deep reddish-black with blood. Her clothes were torn in places exposing her injured flesh that closed as she watched.

Energy returned to her limbs, and her thoughts became less muddled.

"Talk to me. How are you feeling?"

She pushed herself up to her elbows then Hel took her arm and pulled her to her feet. He looked her over, searching for anything he may have missed, but she turned her attention to War and the others. "Can you stand on your own?"

"I think I'm better now." She moved her upper body side to side, shifting her torso to make sure, and rolled her shoulders. No pain. "It's time to end this, Hel."

He took her hand and grinned, wild eyed and ready to kill. "Let's see the night goddess take her vengeance."

They appeared at the edge of the fight. Fennan, Leif, and Piper took turns swiping at the remaining hound, narrowly missing his snapping jaws until Presco roared in and snatched the hound around the belly, ragdolling it in his giant mouth until the creature went limp and he tossed it; it arced through the air until its hulking black body fell into the ravine. Another hound's body lay nearby with its head torn off. That meant all three were dead.

War and Morv fought sword on sword, weapons clashing, wooshing, clanging. They moved like a dance with eloquent footwork striking here, dodging there.

But something was wrong. Morv was good but flawed so why hadn't War ended this yet? No one was as good with a blade as he was. He picked anyone else apart easily. Then she saw the torn flesh from a bite on his left forearm... the hound... Its poison.

None of the others survived a bite from the demon's hound, and War was not immortal this time.

CHAPTER 47

VALEEN

Valeen tossed Darkbringer to Hel and summoned Soulender right to her palm and sprinted for Morv, rage fueling each step to move faster and faster.

"Valeen, wait," Hel called after her, but she didn't look back.

Piper, Leif, and Fennan backed up several steps as she trudged by them. Whether they were surprised or afraid, she didn't care at the moment. War's feet faltered. His swings and blocks slowed as the poison worked its way through him.

"It's me you came for, Morv," Valeen shouted, with shadows rolling off her body. Thrusting out her palm she sent a blast of silver energy, fueled more by the crescent moon shining in the sky now. It slammed into Morv, sending him flying several feet back and crushing him into the base of a tree. The pink blossoms fell like rain from the impact. Half shadow she moved like a phantom in the night and hacked her sword down at him. The blade crashed into his staff and snapped it in two.

He roared, jabbing the broken end of what was left as nothing more than a stick at her belly. She dodged, and he flew back up as if boosted by a gust of powerful wind and leveled the top half of his staff at her. A red sizzling line of destruction careened at her. Her shield came on instinct and the impact of the two magics was like a thunderclap. The crackling energy colliding with her shield did nothing but make noise. She'd withstood much more powerful forces.

With a smirk, she pushed her own shielding power forward, driving Morv's back until his power collapsed. He dove to the side, avoiding the blowback.

"You're not so formidable without your ring, Morv." Valeen strutted toward him, white knuckling Soulender. "I wonder, what happens to a demon when he dies? Does your soul disappear into eternal darkness? Do you become one of those sickly creatures in your underrealm, weak and powerless?"

Hel appeared at her side, brushing his shoulder against hers. "Personally, I hope it's eternal darkness."

Half crouched, his upper lip curled back in a snarl. "It doesn't matter what happens to demons when they die. But we all know what happens to you two. You'll be cursed to be born again and again and again, always forgetting each other. Now that is eternal punishment. What life is this now? Three, four? Let's make it five!"

With his head lowered like he meant to hit her like a bull with his horns, he huffed out steam from his wide nostrils and charged. She readied herself to move at the perfect time and bring Soulender down on his backside, but he brought out a sword at the last moment. Their weapons hit with a ringing that sent a shockwave down her arms. His strength overpowered hers and she turned to shadow and whirled away. He fell forward with the sudden loss of force against him.

A bright ball of light lit above Hel's palm, rivaling the sun. Morv threw up his arms to shield his eyes and hissed. "Ah, what's the matter? I thought demons loved sunlight. It's so bright and sunny in the underrealm."

Morv backpedaled, nearly stumbling to get away from it. "I know what you are," he said, shielding his eyes. "I know who your father is, Zaurahel. And I know where your mother is too."

Valeen stilled next to Hel. Her palm went sweaty, and she had to adjust her grip on Soulender. She imagined his mind whirling at the possibilities. *He's lying,* she said to his mind.

Hel's fingers closed around the ball of light and darkness blanketed the landscape once again. "Who? And where?"

"That's not how this works, god of mischief." He cackled and tapped his sword against his side. Bright red eyes glowed in the dark and his horns gleamed in the pale light. "I need my ring first."

"Why would I believe anything you say?"

He's buying time. Take him down.

"You don't have to but if you kill me, you'll never know." Morv gripped the edge of his cloak. Smoke started around his feet, building up toward his knees, ready to make his escape again. "Don't worry, I'll be back. I don't care how long it takes. I'll take your pretty wife's head and make it a trophy for my wall. Wouldn't that be a sight? The goddess of night's mouth can take my cock even in death."

In a single heartbeat, Hel appeared behind him, yanked on his horn to drag him down and shoved Darkbringer through the back of his neck.

Kill this bastard for good.

Valeen dashed forward, half shadow, and drove Soulender

straight into the demon's chest until it sunk to the hilt. With wide terror-filled eyes, Morv stared at her, and then his solid body began to crack and splinter, changing into blackened ash and bits of him floated away on the breeze, until he crumbled into a pile of soot.

Now there were only two demon princes of the underrealm, and Valeen just made them her enemies.

Hel's garnet eyes shined bright against dark lashes and pale skin as he held her gaze. His chest heaved up and down and he was suddenly before her, inspecting her. "Are you hurt? Let me see you." He tilted her chin, grabbed her shoulders.

"I'm fine." She gripped his arm with her free hand. "I'm alright."

"Layala!" Piper shouted. "Thane stopped breathing!"

Blood running cold, she turned and several yards away Fennan, Leif, and Piper were gathered around him as he lay unmoving on his back. Presco paced nearby muttering possible solutions. *This can't be happening.* Valeen's heart skipped a beat.

With torches in hand, guards and Raven soldiers ran toward them. "The High King! The High King is down!"

"No," she heard herself say and dashed toward him. "Thane!"

Hel was already there, cradling his bitten arm. A warm glow emitted from his palm. "You stay with me. You can't leave me. We have plans, and I need you here. I lied before; you're still my brother. Nothing you could ever do will change that."

Tears blurred her vision as she fell beside him. She gripped his lovely face, lifting his head and leaned down to hear breath. None came. "No, no, no." Helplessly she lifted her head, the Ravens on the grounds gathered in close. The bright orange torchlight lit up the area to see his skin looked paler than usual. "You can't die!" She shook him, and slammed her fist hard into his chest, hoping to shock his heart. "Wake up."

"Layala," Piper cried, dropping beside her. "Save him." Her voice came out strangled; pain struck Valeen right through the heart. Gods, she was going to break his heart tonight. She was going to tell him it was over forever, that she didn't choose him, and now she would give anything to keep him here.

"Thane, you must come back to us. Please. Please." She shook his shoulders again, his head lolled back and forth.

"Hel, do something!" If anyone could save him, it was him, but she saw the worry etched on his face. The growing panic.

"It's not working," his voice wavered. "I think the poison has reached his heart."

Presco stopped. "If you can draw the poison out it might work."

"I'm trying," he snapped. "But this isn't natural, it's from demons."

"Create a rune like you did for me. Stop it."

Hel's chin trembled. "I can't stop it if it's already too late."

"We're not giving up on him. He never gave up on me." Valeen hit his chest again and again. With tears pouring down her cheeks, she took his face in between her palms once more. "You have to stay here. Do you hear me? You can't make us wait to find you again." He didn't stir; his heart didn't beat. "*Thane*, please," her voice broke, and she felt her insides crumbling, felt the hope slipping away like a bottle going out to sea.

The sound of Piper's sobs filled the silence. Fennan kept saying, "No, no, no."

She fell back onto her behind and wrapped her arms around her knees and let out a scream that burned her throat.

Then Varlett appeared and shoved Piper aside. "Move, all of you."

Was there hope in the person who nearly destroyed them all? They all gave Varlett plenty of room. Hel began to pace. "Varlett, I swear on everything that is holy; if you don't save him, I will find a way to kill you."

Varlett pushed a thick silver and black ring on her finger and placed her palm flat on his chest. Words in a foreign tongue slipped out of her lips.

Why the dragon shifter helped them was beyond her, but it didn't matter. Valeen's body trembled as she watched War for signs of life. *Please, please, wake up.*

A green liquid—the poison—drew out of his mouth until it hovered in a wavering ball above, and Varlett flicked it aside with a wave of her hand.

One beat.

Two.

"Come on," Varlett said and pushed down on his chest in fast, steady motions. "You're the god of war. You don't get to die again. Get up!"

His lips drew in air, his chest rose, and his eyelids fluttered. Relief flooded Valeen and she let out a choked sob.

With a long exhale, Varlett fell back onto her hindquarters, and dropped her head into her hands. "He's alive." She let out a sharp breath. "He's alive," she repeated.

Everyone around started to cheer, clapping hands with the Raven beside them or throwing a fist into the air. Leif kissed the inside of his fingers and held his palm up to the sky in a gesture to the Maker.

War coughed and rolled onto his side, breathing heavily like he'd been sprinting for miles. He blinked rapidly and slowly pushed himself up. The confusion on his face at everyone gathered around him, said plainly enough he didn't realize how close to death he'd come. "Are they gone?" he blurted out before anyone else could get a word in. "Did we kill them all?"

Valeen threw her arms around him, squeezing him hard, like if she didn't he would leave them forever. "You're alright." Happy tears came now. "Thank the All Mother, you're alright."

He nuzzled his face against her neck and breathed in deeply. "I'm not going anywhere. I couldn't leave you."

She pulled away and forced a smile at him. "Do you feel fine? Can we get you a drink? Do you need Hel to heal you anywhere?"

They both rose up and he patted down his body like he was making sure it was all there. "I'm good, I think. You killed Morv?"

She glanced back at Hel. He watched them with a guarded expression, even a little bitterness. "He's gone," Hel answered. "For good. Valeen has Soulender."

He nodded and then turned to his Ravens. "There are people who need help. Bring all the injured to the infirmary."

There were murmurs and nods of agreement as the gathered crowd began to disperse. Some of the soldiers came by and clapped him on the back. Many smiled and acknowledged him as High King before they left.

When all that remained was the usual group, Valeen turned to cut a glare at Varlett.

Saving War didn't absolve her of anything. "Bind her."

Presco was the first to move but Varlett jumped to her feet, holding up her palm, with the demon ring, and he halted. "Look, it was a long time ago."

"Your betrayal is fresh in my mind." Valeen's fists clenched at her sides. "You must have forgotten who you're dealing with."

"I knew exactly who I was dealing with, goddess of night,

whom my life is now bound to. I knew you wouldn't be able to keep that secret, that you'd never stay silent after what you witnessed."

"A lie. It was all a lie."

Varlett let out a dark cackle. "Hel was so devoted to you it was pathetic. I'm surprised you believed it, although I am good. That illusion worked better than I ever hoped. All it took was a dash of truth, a play on both of your insecurities, a few whispered lies to all three of you, and it was over. The mighty always crumble from within."

In a flash, she had her hand wrapped around Varlett's throat, not tight enough to hurt but she was barely able to restrain herself from choking her. "Why?"

"Careful." Hel was right beside her; his hand wrapped around her shoulder easing her off Varlett, but she didn't let go entirely. "You could hurt yourself."

Varlett licked her bottom lip. "Why? Because you had everything I wanted. Immortality, might, love, devotion, the god of magic who I knew could give me power like I'd never dreamed." Her reptilian eyes flicked to Hel. "I learned how to create illusions from your personal spell book that you stupidly left unguarded in your castle." She turned back to Valeen. "You even had the heart of *my* betrothed, and now because you were foolish enough to make a deal with me, everything that happens to me, happens to you. If I die, so will you. If I get a scratch, so will you. I bet my life on you, the possessor of Soulender, and the fact that Hel and War would do anything to protect you, and when you become immortal again. So. Will. I."

Valeen clenched her jaw, restraining herself from attacking the dragon shifter. The person who'd ruined her life and countless others was now bound to her. Clever witch. She would get her wish of becoming an immortal after all. "This isn't over."

"Oh, no," she said. "It's just begun."

Hel's hand wrapped around Valeen's upper arm and turned her toward him and away from Varlett. She reluctantly released the dragon shifter, and they took several steps away.

I will find a way to undo this. But it won't be easy even for me. Something like this can't be undone with a simple spell. It will take time. "And Varlett is going to help us get our immortality back." He looked at her. "Aren't you? Because it benefits you, and you care more about yourself than anyone or anything."

She smiled, reptilian eyes flashing. "I am at your service."

As much as Valeen wanted to punish her, what could be done?

War stepped forward, standing between the three of them. He shook his head in disbelief and raked a hand through his hair. "If I'm putting the pieces together correctly, you're saying that the only reason you left Hel was because of her? She was the one you thought he had an affair with? But..."

"But I didn't," Hel finished.

For assurance, he turned to Varlett. "It's true. He was never unfaithful back then, at least not with me. Although in this life, we did have many hot and heavy nights, mornings, afternoons..."

"Shut the fuck up," Hel said, ready to charge her. "I may not be able to kill you yet, but don't think I won't find the darkest, dirtiest prison cell imaginable and put you there."

War looked like he was going to be sick as his emerald eyes went back and forth between Hel and Valeen. "We would have never been together or even lived here in Adalon at all. You never would have fallen in love with me. This wasn't supposed to happen." He looked off into the distance and ran his hands down his face. A smear of dirt and blood spread over his cheek.

She wanted to comfort him, to say it wasn't true but that

would be a lie. The truth was it was always supposed to be Hel. He was always the one she was supposed to be with and that was destroyed, stolen from them. So, she stood in silence staring at him, unable to find words. Unable to go to him because she wouldn't break Hel to do it.

Piper put a hand on his shoulder. "Maybe it wasn't supposed to happen, but it did. And you're here with us now."

Fennan stepped up to his other side and nudged him with his shoulder. "We wouldn't have it any other way, Thane. You're our High King. And my best friend."

In that moment, she realized even on the darkest of nights, when all seemed lost, and no light could shine at the level they had fallen, a glimmer of hope could always be found.

"Don't you all get it? If it wasn't for her, Hel never would have become the Black Mage. There would be no curse and no war with the pale ones. The elves would still have their magic..." His chin shook and his eyes filled with tears as he met Hel's stare. "And I never would have lost my brother."

For the first time ever, Varlett looked guilty. It wasn't an emotion Valeen thought her capable of harboring.

His pain made her even more angry with the dragon.

"And we can't take it back," Hel said, striding forward. "But we can let it go." He jerked him into a hug, and Valeen couldn't hold back tears.

CHAPTER 48

VALEEN

Valeen paced the hallway outside her old room. Everyone had come inside to bathe away the blood and dirt of battle. Varlett was held in one of the rooms with katagas serum in her and handcuffs. With their new connection, the serum affected Valeen too, but she'd take dimmed magic over letting that horrible dragon wench run free. Hel lay on the bed in her room to give her time to talk to War alone. She just hadn't gotten the courage to knock on his door yet.

There was no time like now. With a deep breath she rapped her knuckles on the door and stood back to wait.

Footsteps lightly hit the floor and the door swung inward. "Valeen," he said in surprise.

The smells of sage and cedarwood lifted off his clean skin and hair. "Can we talk?" she asked.

"Of course." He stepped aside and gestured for her to step

in. He closed the door and made his way over to the huge four-poster bed. She wandered around the edges of his room. Taking in the furniture she'd come to know. The candlestick she once threw at him. The bed where she tried to kill him and made love to him. It felt different now, like she didn't belong.

"How have you been?"

He smiled and shifted back on his bed to lean against the headboard. "You came to ask me how I've been?"

"I haven't seen you in months. It's a proper question."

"Um, well." He sighed and rubbed his chin. "I was worried and miserable. I was scared I made the wrong decision and also terrified it was the right one. I found your ring on the pillow in your room." His gaze fell to her hand. "I see you have a new one, well, old one."

She'd never taken off her wedding ring. She lifted her hand and inspected it like she didn't have every curve and sparkle memorized. He already knew. "I want you to know I loved you. And if I was only ever Layala Lightbringer, you would have been it for me. You would have been my life, and my mate." Tears filled her eyes. "But I'm Valeen, too. And like you said, remembering the past changed everything."

He nodded, his chest rising. "We would have been happy."

"Yeah," she breathed. Her heart felt like it was breaking all over again, just like when he told her it was over months before. "We would have."

"I wish loving you was enough. But he's your soulmate. Before you left, deep down, I knew it would be him once you remembered."

She swiped at her cheeks. "Why do you have to be such a good person? It would almost be easier if you were mad at me. You'll always be important to me but it's him."

He chuckled. "I could never stay mad at you, and I know."

She smiled through the heartbreak. "Despite every horrible flaw, every terrible thing he's done. I love him. He was always supposed to be mine. And maybe now he won't be so wicked."

"I wouldn't count on that. I think we've only gotten a taste of what he will do to destroy the council and protect you."

"You're probably right." There was no depth he wouldn't go to take vengeance for this punishment, to live up to the vow he promised the council all those years ago.

He nodded, his green eyes sparkling in the candlelight. "All I want is for you to be happy, Valeen. Him too."

"But what about you?"

A single tear fell down his cheek but then he broke into a grin. "Well, it certainly won't be with Varlett."

They both laughed, and she said, "You'll find her one day. Your wife. But she better be damn near perfect."

"It will be hard for her to top you."

She smiled. War had loved her for a long time, Thane too. "You're coming with us to Runevale, aren't you?"

He took in a deep breath and looked toward the window. The long sheer curtains blew in a gentle breeze. Crickets chirped and an owl cooed right outside on the balcony. "I don't think I have a choice. You'll need me to take on the council or we'll all be right back to where we started," he said. "And I can't do this shit all over again. I can't love you and lose you again."

The bed creaked as he got up, his light steps padded on the stone floor as he sauntered over. She swallowed hard as he leaned down and kissed her forehead. "I let you go the day you went away with him. Becoming War changed me, too." He lowered his voice and whispered, "But a part of me will always love you."

SHE FOUND Hel still in her old bedroom, sitting in the corner chair. The soft candlelight on the nightstand flickered and danced. Fingers drummed lightly on the armrest, like the steady beat of her heart. He looked dark and delicious watching her with an expression she couldn't quite read. Something crossed between hunger and need.

Hel sat with his legs wide and patted his lap. With a methodical sway, she closed the distance slowly and dropped onto him. His fingers curled around a lock of her hair, brushed over her throat. With a flick of his wrist a shimmering bubble appeared around them, a veil of silence.

"I don't want him to hear. I could hear your conversation like I was in the same room. These walls are thin."

She knew he would. "Although a part of me is sad, it's you I can't live without. Even when I thought you used me, that it was Varlett you loved in secret, I was still so in love with you. It's why I couldn't face you back then. I feared I would give in even after what I thought I saw."

He groaned and nuzzled his nose in the nape of her neck. "I really wish I could put her head on a pike."

"You and me both."

"But knowing her, she'll fight and scheme and do everything in her power to make sure you get your immortality back, for herself. And I think she proved she's even better at scheming than me."

His button-up shirt was left open to his chest, revealing his runes and the lily mark. She drew little circles on his bare skin. "If she so much as looks at you."

"I'll put her in her place. Don't worry, these eyes are only for you." He turned her face and kissed her lips softly. "I want to marry you again. Or at least renew our vows. It's been too long; too much has happened. I want to be married to Miss Lightbringer, too."

He nipped at her neck, and she giggled. "A closet romantic."

"I'll get you a new ring to represent both the elf and the goddess. Your Aunt and your friends will always see you as Layala," Hel said.

She couldn't help but smile. "Be careful. Your heart is showing. And I'll get you a new ring, too."

"You'll have to because I destroyed my last one."

"Of course, you did," she said and rolled her eyes.

He laughed and it sounded joyous and wonderful. "And this is the part where you say 'Yes, Hel, the most wise and powerful god, I will."

She chuckled, thinking back on their training sessions where he told her to call him that, and gave him a brief kiss. "Yes, Hel, the most wise and powerful god, I will marry you again."

THE ROUND STONE portal in the middle of the unnamed forest looked as beautiful and ancient as it ever had. Bits of moss grew at the edges of the weathered gray stone. The red thorny roses at its base were in full bloom. The sun shined down through the thick trees above creating streaks of golden light.

Leif stood at attention, his bright blue eyes keenly searching the area around them. This forest was notorious for dangerous creatures, after all. "When you open it, will they know?"

"Not unless they try to travel outside the realm," Valeen

answered with her moon and stars crown glittering on her head.

"They probably have someone test it every day," Piper murmured, toying with one of her red braids. Looking at her made her think of Fennan back at the castle, left in charge as regent until High King Thane's return. He said he would keep that name among the elves, but they could call him War if they wanted.

"For two thousand years?" Tif said, creeping out from behind Valeen's boot. "Seems like a bit of a stretch. Exhausting too."

"They'll test it often enough. We won't have much time before they know," Presco said, adjusting his glasses.

With crossed arms and a smug chagrin, Varlett nodded in agreement. "The spies will tell if not."

War scratched at his smooth cheek, brushed a hand over his Raven-armored chest with the emblem of Palenor on it. Valeen wore her Raven armor too, a tribute to Layala Fight-bringer.

"This is going to take strategy, finesse. We can't waltz in there to demand our immortality back," Hel said in black battle leathers. A much lighter armor than the rest of them wore.

"Clearly," War said all but rolling his eyes.

"If my wards still stand, we'll have a stronghold in House of Night. They'll fight for me."

"Home." Presco smiled at that.

"And if the wards don't stand?" Hel asked.

"It won't matter. We'll find a way. We'll face whatever it is head-on. We are warriors. Warriors like the sword are beaten, burned, and battered but through it are made stronger." Valeen thought about her last moments before the blade came down across her neck. How she'd gazed at the two people she loved most and how she'd drawn on their power to close the way, paid for with their lives. The goddess of wisdom once said the key to ending the curse in Adalon was Hel's heart. She had that now. He wasn't bitter and angry anymore.

The key to opening the portal was the three of them being one again, fighting on the same side. The curse would no longer exist in Adalon. Hel kept the pale ones confined to the Void until they would call on them in Runevale to fight.

"Give me your hands."

Hel and Thane both held out their palms and she took them, squeezing them both, drawing on their power. She felt their magic mingle with hers, Hel's, dark and cool, War's, warm and bright. There was no pressure on one or the other to be stronger or to fight. They were at peace, finally. The three magics seemed to have missed each other as they warmed her body and made her almost giddy.

"What death closed, let love open." A ripple of power blew her hair back and shook the ground. The portal sprang to life, a swirling pool of gray-blue until it cleared, revealing the other side; wavering colorful lights painted the dark glittering sky. A vast landscape of lush green hills and black rock mountains. House of Night was still there waiting for her return, waiting for fate to call the elf, the queen, and the goddess home.

The three of them stepped through first and the others followed behind. "You told Aunt Evalyn, right?" Tif said sweetly.

"Of course," Valeen answered. "When this is all settled, I'll be able to bring her to House of Night."

The colorful lights streaked across the night sky above their heads. The aroma of rain on dry grass filled her nostrils and she took a deep inhale. Home. It smelled like home.

A loud *pop* then a sizzle and crackle jerked her attention to the left. Another portal opened... two more. One bright like the sun, the other dark and menacing. Hel took a step closer to her, brushed his hand against hers. "Did you open another doorway?"

"I only meant to open this one but..."

A female appeared in the swirling bright circle, stepping into the dark realm of House of Night. Valeen's heart dropped into her stomach. Bright white-blonde hair, golden skin, and the most beautiful of all the goddesses stood there. It was impossible but it was her sister. "Katana?" The bright circle of light snapped in on itself and was gone. She looked around, appearing confused and disoriented.

Valeen took a step toward her then froze. The other circle next to the portal they'd opened from Adalon sizzled and swirled like a black pool of tar. It groaned like the hull of a large ship, until another figure came through.

Hel took a half step in front of her, a protective move, and gripped her arm. *It's going to be alright, love. I won't let him touch you or Katana.*

It took her a moment to realize who the male was and why Hel reacted that way.

"Synick," Hel said. "You're supposed to be dead."

To be continued in book 4: Night Meets the Elf Queen

Acknowledgments

I have to give a special thank you to Jessica Boaden, my story consultant, meme sharing friend, Aussie friend I've never met in person but chat with all the time. You talked me through so many amazing aspects of this story. You cheered on the characters and talked me through the dumpster fire first draft and reread it again once it was polished! This book would not be what it is if you didn't spend your time with me working through problems while cheering me on and getting excited with me about this book! You've been with me for years and I love working with you on each and every book, and I appreciate how invested you get in the story and each character! Your comments make me laugh, give me a confidence boost, and also give great constructive criticism. Thank you!

Another special thanks to Brittany O'Barr, my sister! You've been with me since day one of writing books all those years ago and spend hours with every book I write, but especially this one. You spent so much time talking with me and helping me work through plot issues, and brainstorming ideas. You give phenomenal feedback and I appreciate it. You're an amazing beta reader, and helped me make this book the best it could be! Thank you so much for being invested and helpful!

Thank you Tiffany Boland! Your excitement for this book and good eye for details was so helpful! I've loved working with you on the Elf Queen series. It's been such a joy, and you've been a great help in making this story what it is. It means a lot to me to have you read the books and love them like me! I do believe you called this book a "masterpiece" and I want to thank you for that too because that is a serious confidence boost on a book I spent nearly a year writing!

Thank you very much Charity Chimni, my amazing proof-reader and assistant! I couldn't do this without you. You find errors that always surprise me and are a great help with all my book launches! I appreciate all the work you do with me and thank you so much for sticking with me all these years!

Thank you to my family for believing in me all these years. Thank you to my husband for being so supportive and taking care of our kiddos for hours each day so I am able to write and do what I love.

Thank you to all the readers who love my books, my characters, and help spread the word about this series. You've helped make my dreams come true!

About the Author

J.M. Kearl is a fantasy romance author. She writes feisty heroines to love and hunky heroes to fall in love with. She's also a mother of two and happily married to the love of her life. She lives in Idaho but is usually dreaming of somewhere tropical.

Sign up for J.M. Kearl's Newsletter: http://jmkearl.com/newsletter